William Hayward

The black angel

A tale of the American Civil War

William Hayward

The black angel
A tale of the American Civil War

ISBN/EAN: 9783337224684

Printed in Europe, USA, Canada, Australia, Japan

Cover: Foto ©Andreas Hilbeck / pixelio.de

More available books at **www.hansebooks.com**

THE

BLACK ANGEL:

A TALE OF

THE AMERICAN CIVIL WAR.

BY THE AUTHOR OF "HUNTED TO DEATH" ETC.

THE

BLACK ANGEL:

A Tale

OF

THE AMERICAN CIVIL WAR.

BY THE AUTHOR OF

"THE STAR OF THE SOUTH," "THE FIERY CROSS," ETC., ETC.

LONDON:

CHARLES H. CLARKE,

PATERNOSTER ROW.

CONTENTS.

iv CONTENTS.

PAGE

BLACK ANGEL.

A ROMANCE OF THE AMERICAN CIVIL WAR.

CHAPTER I.

LIEUTENANT DARCY LEIGH.

AT last the long threatened storm had burst—the thunder-cloud so long visible in the horizon had reached the zenith, and had belched forth an instalment of its contents. "Cry havoc, and let slip the dogs of war." Rebellion—stern, bitter, savage—had raised its head; a war of brother against brother, father against son, friend against friend; a disastrous, desolating civil war is about to commence with our story. South Carolina has, in a daring, defiant tone, declared itself independent of the Union—of that glorious Union made sacred by the names of Washington, of Franklin, of Jefferson. State after State hastens to follow the example of South Carolina; angry meetings—defiances—the evacuation of

B

Fort Moultrie; then the culminating act which precipitated into a fratricidal war eight million Southerners against twenty million of their fellow-countrymen is consummated — we allude to the bombardment of Fort Sumter. As the echoes of the big guns on Charleston batteries boom forth in the distance, thinking men turn sadly away, and we hear in the hoarse thunder the knell of the United States as well.

*   *   *   *   *

*   *   *   *   *   *   *

*   *   *   *   *

THE scene opens in a richly-furnished New York drawing-room. The costly hangings, immense mirrors, velvety carpets, the rich service of plate on the sideboard, the elegant dresses of the inmates, bespeak it as the abode of a wealthy man. It is the town house of Webster Gayle, senator for the State of Pennsylvania. The firm of Gayle, Gayle, and Co., of New York and Philadelphia, was reckoned one of the wealthiest in the States. The senior partner, Webster K. Gayle, was looked upon as endowed with great wealth, great shrewdness, and though a man of rectitude and probity, still one with whom the "almighty dollar" was of paramount importance.

This was the man at whose house was now assembled a large party of friends. The rooms were blazing with a hundred lights; the most costly wines and liqueurs were as plentiful as water; while a band of excellent musicians, stationed in the conservatory, played now martial and inspiring, now soothing, melting airs. But in all that company one event was the absorbing topic of conversation; that event was the terrible rebellion

which already shook the Union to its foundation. The
news of the bombardment of Fort Sumter had arrived
but the day before, and every one was speculating on the
turn which events would take.. Some prognosticated a
speedy and prompt crushing out of the so-called rebellion; others thought it could not be effected without a
long and desperate struggle; while yet another party
shook their heads, and declared it as their belief that
the proud and fiery Southerners could never be brought
back to their allegiance.

See those two fair girls, the centre of a group of
admirers. They are the daughters of the host—Stella
and Angela Gayle. Notice the flashing eyes of Stella
Gayle, the colour mantling on her cheek, the delicate
nostril dilating, and the lip curling, as she speaks contemptuously of this " wicked and paltry rebellion."

Notice, too, the soft blue eyes of Angela Gayle, how
sorrowful they seem, almost brimming over with tears.
She is in earnest conversation with a young man in the
uniform of a lieutenant in the United States' navy.
This young man is Darcy Leigh.

" Good heavens ! Lieutenant Leigh," the fair girl
says, " what will be the end of this dreadful rebellion ?
Your sister, my sweet friend Laura—what will she do ?
Surely your father will hasten to bring her North, and
place her in safety."

" My father, Miss Gayle, will, I know, do what he
considers his duty, as will his sons, myself and brother."

" What he thinks his duty ? Surely there can be no
doubt of that. Surely Washington Leigh can never be
a rebel. Surely Lieutenant Darcy Leigh can never be
a traitor to his country ?"

" A traitor !—no," replied the young man; " should
I consider it inconsistent with my duty, with my order,
with my native State, the ' Old Dominion,' any more to
wear a sword in the service of the United States, I
should at once throw up my commission. There could
be no treachery in that. Freely I entered the service,
faithfully I have done my duty, and therefore I consider
myself free to retire at any moment."

"Who speaks of retiring from the service of his country?" said Stella Gayle, overhearing his last words to her sister; then turning her flashing eyes full on the young officer, "Is it you, Lieutenant Leigh? Shame on you to talk of retiring at such a time—at a time when your country requires the strong arms and brave hearts of all her sons! Retiring, indeed! I pray you give it its right name; desertion—a base, cowardly desertion; for no other name would rightly describe such an act."

Darcy Leigh turned very pale as the young lady spoke these bitter words.

"Am I to understand," he said, "that Miss Stella Gayle insinuates that I—I Darcy Leigh, could ever be a coward?"

"Am I to understand that you, Lieutenant Darcy Leigh, spoke in sober seriousness of retiring from your country's service at the present time?"

"I spoke of the possibility of such a thing, should I consider it essential to my honour or my duty."

"Then if it be possible for Lieutenant Darcy Leigh so to act, it is possible for him to act as a traitor and a coward!"

With these words the young lady rose, and casting a scornful glance on Darcy Leigh, crossed to the other side of the room.

He followed her retreating figure with his eyes as she moved gracefully away. He was as pale as death, and his voice trembled as he said to Angela Gayle, who kept her seat,—

"Your sister uses hard words. A traitor and a coward! —I, Darcy Leigh, a coward!"

"My sister is heart and soul for the Union," said the blue-eyed Angela, "and in her excitement has said more than she should. She will be sorry ere long, and will express her sorrow for the injustice she has done you; for I feel confident that whatever happens, you, Darcy Leigh, can never prove a coward."

"Angela, I thank you," said the young officer, pressing her hand; "whatever may happen, and I confess

that the future is dark and gloomy enough, be assured I
will never disgrace the name I bear. As for your sister,
let her keep her opinion. The day will come when she
will acknowledge that, at least, I am not a coward."

So saying, the young officer wished Angela good night,
bowed coldly to Stella as he passed her, and left the
saloon.

" A coward ! " he muttered to himself, as he walked
down Broadway to the quay, where the gig of his ship—
the United States' sloop-of-war Spitfire—was awaiting
him; "a coward—she said I was a coward! I, Darcy
Leigh, a coward! Ha! ha! the proud beauty! But
she shall yet know that at least I am no coward. A
coward !—I, Darcy Leigh, a Southern gentleman—a
coward ! "

Thus muttering and fuming to himself, he reached the
gig; ordering the crew, who were lounging about, into
the boat, he seated himself in the stern-sheets, and gave
the word.

The boat shot out on the calm waters, and in five
minutes more he was pacing the quarter-deck of the
Spitfire.

Some other young officers joined him. They spoke in
low muttered tones, in tones of doubt and distrust; but
among many there prevailed a feeling that the tie between themselves and the service in which they had been
bred was virtually severed for ever. The word " secession" was more than once uttered, much oftener thought
of; for be it known that a great majority of the officers
both in the army and navy were the sons of Southern
gentlemen and planters, and, of course, with all a
Southerner's sympathies and tendencies.

Lieutenant Darcy Leigh was the second son of Colonel
Washington Leigh, of Virginia. The Colonel himself
had, from the very beginning of the movement, thrown
himself heart and soul in with the Secessionists. His
eldest son, Gerald Leigh, was a captain in the United
States' army; his second son, Darcy Leigh, a lieutenant
in the United States' navy. The sympathies of both
were, of course, with their father and their father's

cause; who then could wonder that the young lieutenant should be gloomy and full of distrust at the assembly of Webster Gayle, the merchant?

For hours after the other officers had turned into their hammocks, Darcy Leigh paced the deck alone. Let us glance at him in his solitary vigil.

Dark, slender, and pale, rather beneath the middle height than otherwise, he seemed even younger than he really was. His age was two-and-twenty, and he looked scarcely eighteen; dark brown hair, piercing grey eyes, a thin Grecian nose, and a beautifully cut mouth; such were the features which first struck a stranger. He had no whiskers, and but a very small moustache, which latter, indeed, was scarcely too strong or rough for a woman. His complexion was naturally dark, and exposure to the sun had so embrowned it that he might well have passed for a creole, were it not that his hair had not that betraying curl, and that his hands and feet were small and delicate.

There was in his manner a quick, nervous restlessness, which bespoke a daring, wild spirit, and in the clear outlines of the mouth and the thin lips, a physiognomist would have predicated a resolution as undaunted as the spirit was daring.

Such was Darcy Leigh. With his brother officers and the men beneath him, his dare-devil spirit made him a favourite; with the ladies his unmistakable good looks, and a certain charm of manner, had a like effect, and until this fatal rebellion broke out he was considered a brave, dashing young fellow, and as promising an officer as any in the United States' navy.

CHAPTER II.

STELLA GAYLE AND LUPUS ROCK.

LET us return to the mansion of Senator Gayle.

Immediately after the abrupt departure of Darcy Leigh, Angela arose, and approaching her sister, who, sooth to say, now felt some remorse for the hard words she had used, said,—

" Oh, Stella, how could you have said what you did to Darcy Leigh—the brother of our dearest friend ? He is deeply offended; did you see how pale he turned when you said coward ? "

"Indeed, Angela, I care nothing for Lieutenant Leigh's turning red or pale. I said what I meant, that this is no time for a true American to desert his colours. What say you, Mr. Rock ? "

" Miss Gayle," said the person addressed, bowing obsequiously and showing his white teeth, "you are in this, as on all other occasions, perfectly in the right; your devotion to the Union does honour to your head and heart, and I am sure all friends of the Union must feel honoured at having an advocate at once so loyal and lovely."

The colour mantled slightly on Stella's beautiful cheek as she listened to this speech, in which the flattery was so direct and fulsome ; but it was not the flush of pleasure.

Slightly bowing acknowledgment of the speech she arose, and taking her sister's arm, crossed over to where her father was standing.

" Angela," said Stella, " how I do detest flattery ; do not you ? "

" Indeed I do, and in the present case I not only detest the flattery, but also the flatterer. I know not why, but, cousin though he is to us, I never did and never can like Lupus Rock. There is something at once sneering and obsequious in his manner, as if he knew all the while he was uttering his soft speeches that they were as hollow and false as I believe he is himself."

" Nonsense ! " cried Stella ; " don't talk so. I know he has a habit of flattering which is detestable, but otherwise I am sure he is most agreeable ; indeed, he has always been most kind and considerate to us. There is nothing he thinks too much. Witness, the other day, the pains he took to get us tickets for Mr. Davis's private theatricals ; witness the manner in which he is always glad to wait on us."

"Yes," interrupted Angela, "and witness how he was proved to have had a half share in the slaver which was captured and brought into New York but a month ago, and condemned with two hundred poor wretches on board, the survivors of three hundred and eighty kidnapped from their homes; he who pretends to be a Northerner, and attends abolition meetings, and goes to church. Shame on him, I say. Darcy Leigh would never act so, although you did call him a coward."

As she spoke, the soft blue eyes of the gentle Angela sparkled, and her voice trembled with excitement.

"Darcy Leigh!" exclaimed her sister passionately; "Darcy Leigh, nothing but Darcy Leigh! Every one is trying to persuade me what a fine, brave, gallant fellow he is, though, for the life of me, I never could discover it. Darcy Leigh! since you are so infatuated with him, for Heaven's sake, take him, for me."

"Nay, I fear that is impossible," said her sister, smiling, "for, by all accounts, this dark young French Creole at Charleston, whom all the Southerners coming North so rave about, reigns paramount at present. I know he has her portrait, for he showed it to me, and a very beautiful girl she appears."

"A French Creole," replied Stella, colouring, evidently not well pleased; "I have heard of her, and doubt not she is no better than she should be, or Darcy Leigh would not have her portrait."

"Nay, sister," said Angela, noticing her vexation, but ill-concealed, "do not be jealous or unjust."

"Jealous!" exclaimed Stella, "jealous of a boy like this young Leigh! really, that is too absurd," and she burst into a peal of laughter, real or forced. "Now, if I ever could possibly care for a traitor to the Union, certainly Gerald Leigh, this boy's brother, would command my preference—there is a nobility and grandeur about him to which this slight, dark Darcy can never pretend."

"I have not one word against Gerald; I believe that he, like his brother, is a brave, noble fellow—both may be mistaken in the side they take of this wretched rebel-

lion, but I value the little finger of either one of them
more than the whole body of Lupus Rock."

" What is that you are saying about your cousin Lupus,
Angela?" said her father, who had approached unseen.

Angela coloured, but answered at once, " Well, papa,
if you must know, I said I did not like him."

" That is wrong of you, Angela, for your cousin is a
most estimable young man—a thorough man of business
—in fact, my right hand. I do not know what I should
do without him. I am sure Stella has no such foolish pre-
judice. Is it not so, daughter?"

But Stella was perverse this evening, and would not
acknowledge, any more than her sister, to liking her
cousin, and while they were yet discussing the point
Lupus Rock himself approached them.

Let us take a survey of this person about whom the
two sisters were almost about to quarrel.

A tall, well-formed young man of about thirty years
of age, aquiline features and beautiful white teeth,
small piercing black eyes, surmounted by rather heavy
eyebrows; curling, dark-brown, almost black hair, and a
well-cut but somewhat large mouth; such was the *tout
ensemble* of Lupus Rock. The most characteristic features in his face were the eyes and mouth; the former
small, piercing, and with an ever changing, restless
glance; the latter somewhat large, slightly drawn down
at the corners, giving the whole face a sneering, sardonic,
cruel expression.

Nevertheless, Lupus Rock was universally acknowledged to be an exceedingly handsome man.

" Fair cousin Stella, may I have the honour of con-
ducting you to supper," he said, when he approached the
two young ladies and their father

" Dark cousin Lupus, you may," said Stella, forcing
herself to seem pleasant, " on one condition."

" Name it."

" That you pester me with no more of your unmean-
ing compliments and flattery."

" Flattery!" said the gentleman; "that is impossible
—the highest terms of praise, when addressed to Miss

Stella Gayle, fall so far short of the truth as to render the homage the words express——"

"Thank you, Mr. Rock, that will do," interrupted Stella, hastily; "I have heard quite enough. You can conduct some other lady to supper."

Then turning to a tall, gaunt-looking Yankee, standing near her she said,—

"Captain Hiram Squails, will you take me down to supper?"

"With all my heart," said the rough sailor, bluntly; "I did think of going aboard my ship now, but I'll take you down anyhow, if I leave before supper's over."

"Thank you," said the young lady; "you at least will not sicken me with flattery."

"Flattery!" said the gallant captain. "Well, I reckon you're a tarnation nice gal, and that's all the flattery you'll get from Captain Hiram Squails, of the United States' sloop Spitfire. Thunder! if you gals want soft sawder and pretty speeches, you must look out one of these dancing jackanapes, with their kid gloves and scented handkerchiefs. Rot 'em, I've got more than one aboard the Spitfire."

"Like Darcy Leigh, for instance?" asked the young lady, probably wishing to hear his opinion; "he's one of your junior officers, isn't he?"

"Second Lieutenant Leigh? Yes,—you're right, and you're wrong—you're right, for he's aboard my ship; and you're wrong when you say he's like these here namby-pamby fellows that can't stand water, let alone fire. No, miss, that ain't Darcy Leigh; he's a good officer, a good sailor, good at anything, as a true, brave American should be—a rough and tumble, or a breeze of wind; but, miss, is he a friend of yours?"

"Well, we are slightly acquainted."

"Then I hope you won't be offended; but as sure as there's snakes in Ole Virginny, he's a rebel in his heart —by thunder! I know it, and there ain't a man in the United States' navy more sorry than Captain Squails of the Spitfire. The lad's been with me for years, and I always liked him; but he's got these here cursed

Southern notions in his head, and I expect the up-
shot will be, that Uncle Sam will lose as gallant an
officer as ever buckled on a sword—I do, by thunder!
miss ; he's a rebel at heart."

" A traitor ? "

" Well, I won't say nothing about that, because I
don't believe he'd do anything shabby or cowardly ; but
this is what he'll do if these rebels down South are in
earnest—he'll just throw up his commission and go and
join 'em. No, miss, the lad's a rank rebel, by thunder!
but he's no traitor and no coward."

As she heard these words of the young officer's own
captain, Stella Gayle remembered her own, and her heart
smote her.

Meanwhile, it may be well imagined that Lupus Rock
smarted considerably under the rebuff his sycophantic
tongue had caused him.

He turned pale with fury, as Stella so coolly turned
her back on him and took the Yankee captain's arm.

" Curse her !" he muttered between his clenched
teeth ; " I'll break her proud spirit yet—to turn and
leave me for that unlicked cub of a Yankee ! No matter.
my day shall come yet, my proud beauty, or my name is
not Lupus Rock."

Then he turned, and, with a smiling face, said to
Angela,—

" Since your sister has sent me to the right-about in
so cavalier a manner, may I be permitted to take you
down to supper, cousin Angela ? "

Angela, who, as the reader knows, liked him even less
than her sister, gave him her arm in silence, and allowed
him to conduct her from the saloon.

Frequently during the repast his eyes would rest on
the beautiful form of Stella, with a cold, vindictive,
basilisk glance, which boded ill to her, should she ever be
in his power. Truly, they were both beautiful girls—
Stella, the elder one, especially ; although many admired
the gentle, blue-eyed Angela more than her splendid,
dashing sister, with her luxuriant hair and flashing grey
eyes. Tall and exquisitely proportioned was Stella.

There was an easy grace in every movement peculiar to herself. Her features were faultless—the nose thin and straight. Some hypercritical people, it is true, objected that the mouth was a shade too large; but the contour of the lips was perfect—they were rich red, and just sufficiently full—tempting, without bordering on the coarse or voluptuous. But it was when this mouth was wreathed in smiles that it was seen to the best advantage. The flashing eyes, the beautiful white teeth, and the faint glow visible on the beautiful face, at these times made up a picture as ravishing as was ever imagined in a poet's or a painter's dream. An abundance of beautiful brown hair clustering about the oval face, and falling over her neck and graceful shoulders—a figure well developed, yet slender, small hands and feet, and a singularly graceful though somewhat proud carriage; such were the attractions of Stella Gayle.

It may well be imagined that so much beauty procured her plenty of admirers. None, however, had, as yet, even succeeded in storming the outworks of the citadel, for Stella Gayle was at once beautiful as Venus and haughty as Juno.

CHAPTER III.

THE FÊTE ON BOARD THE COLUMBIA.

THERE is a fancy dress fête on board the commodore's ship of the Atlantic squadron of the United States' navy. The Columbia is gaily decked with flags, while the white awnings spread fore and aft protect the guests from the glare of the sun. The fête is a Union demonstration against the rebellion; conspicuous alike among the gay decorations of the quarter-deck and the gay and varied dresses of the ladies are the Stars and Stripes.

The capstan is covered by the national ensign, as are, also, the gloomy great guns on the quarter-deck. The Stars and Stripes are displayed as the centre piece of glittering trophies formed of ship's cutlasses and rifles. Each fair lady contrives to display the national emblem in some part of her dress. The Stars and Stripes wave proudly from the deck and masts of the Columbia; while all around—starboard, larboard, a head, and astern—the old flag may be seen flying from the peaks of men-of-war and the crowd of merchantmen in New York harbour.

The fête on board the commodore's ship is a most brilliant one. All the ladies are in fancy or ball dress, while all the gentlemen are in the uniforms of the army or navy, or in a fancy costume of some kind. Fair bosoms pant and heave, and manly breasts beat high, as the grand strains of "Hail Columbia!" or the quick, inspiriting air "Yankee Doodle" is played by the bands in attendance. All is excitement and enthusiasm. Stella Gayle, with her sister and father, is there, as also is Darcy Leigh—for the last time in the uniform of the United States' navy. Stella is in a graceful fancy costume, while Angela is in plain ball dress.

But, be it understood, notwithstanding all this enthusiasm for the Union and the national flag, there was an under-current of discontent and distrust among some of the company. This state of affairs existed, sad to relate, principally among the young naval and military officers.

For be it known that a large majority of those were Southerners by birth and education; and, as a consequence, their sympathies were divided between the service they had been brought up in, and the cause of Secession, which the fathers, brothers, and friends of some had already embraced; in which course it was more than probable they would be followed by the greater portion of Southern gentlemen and planters. No wonder, then, that many of them stood aloof and conversed together in low tones.

Nor was this Southern sentiment entirely wanting among the ladies; for although, carried away by the enthusiasm of the moment, the booming of the guns, the inspiring strains of the patriotic music, and the enchantment of the brilliant scene, few, if any, gave way to serious thought or to those gloomy forebodings which pervaded some of the other sex; still there was among nearly all of them a pitying feeling for the embarrassing position of the naval and military officers of Southern extraction.

Whether deservedly so or not, these had always been highly favoured by the ladies of the Northern cities. In fact, among the fair sex a Southerner was the type of chivalry, of liberality, of gallantry. They assumed to themselves the right to be considered the aristocracy of the Union; nor was this right disputed even by the Northern manufacturers and merchants, who, for that very reason, looked on them with no very favourable eyes.

Not so, however, with their wives and daughters. A girl who had secured to herself a Southern gentleman— planter or officer—looked with pitying contempt on her less fortunate sister, who was obliged to content herself with a Northern merchant or Yankee manufacturer.

Many, then, were the pitying glances bestowed upon such of the young officers who, although nominally present for a Union demonstration, held themselves aloof from the festivities.

Many an attempt was made by fascinating fairies in the most charming of fancy dresses to win these sullen, moody, distrustful men to rejoice and make merry with them.

Commodore Foote, the flag officer of the fleet, was a veteran of sixty-five, enthusiastically devoted to his profession and the Union.

The secession movement was to him the blackest of treasons, the originators and all the participators in which should be doomed to the gallows.

A passionate, headstrong, obstinate, but brave and determined old man, was the Commodore.

The suns of sixty-five summers, so far from impairing his youthful ardour, had left him more anxious than ever to strike a blow for the old Union and the old flag.

Himself true to the backbone to his country and the Union, he could scarcely believe that men could exist wearing the United States' uniform who did not also participate in his sentiments.

True, he had been informed by more than one post-captain that a strong feeling, if not of absolute disaffection, at all events of distrust and dissatisfaction, existed among the officers and even the men of the squadron. But he could not, would not, believe the sad truth. The young officers in question, he argued, mourned for the folly and wickedness of their relations and friends in the South ; they pitied and blamed, but did not sympathize ; besides, did they not wear the United States' uniform? were they not brought up in the service of Uncle Sam ?

So the old Commodore laughed at the idea of disaffection, and only praying for orders from Government to proceed to Charleston, and blow the rebels—town, forts, and all—to blazes, he hugged his delusion, and was happy.

This day, the day of the great Union fête on board his own vessel, he was doomed to learn the truth—doomed to learn the bitter fact, that treason stalked in the very midst of them, that half those who now wore their swords in the United States' service, would ere long draw them in that of the despised and detested rebels.

The young Lieutenant, Darcy Leigh, leaned smoking over one of the guns in the waist of ship. The gun was covered with the ensign, the Stars and Stripes.

As he played with the folds of bunting with his hand, he thought of the many happy years he had spent under that flag, and was sad.

Then came the thought—would it ever float over his head again? He held in his hand that day's paper. News had just arrived of the secession of several other States. The news of yet more was hourly expected.

He read of meetings, enthusiastic and unanimous, in which nothing but defiance and determination to defend themselves to the last were breathed. He recognised again and again the names of dear friends and acquaintances and relatives. No wonder he looked sad and gloomy. A brother officer, also a Southerner, leaned with him over the gun.

" George," said Leigh, to him, " what will be the end of this ? "

" The end ! " said his friend, rising and taking a fold of the ensign in his hand—" this will be the end,"

Darcy looked up.

IIis friend made a motion, as if to tear the flag in two. "So will the Union be torn."

"I fear so," said Darcy Leigh. "There is but little hope; I know too well the stuff such men as my father and hundreds of other Secessionists are made of, ever to hope they will go back to the Union after once committing themselves."

"And what, then, shall we do—what course is open to us? Suppose we are ordered to-morrow to proceed to Charleston and bombard the town; we all the while having friends, relations, sisters, some of us wives there —what in such a case should we do?"

"I can tell you what I would do," said Darcy.

"What?"

"I would throw my sword overboard, and follow it myself, ere I would draw it on my countrymen and kin."

"You are right, Darcy, and so would I."

"Gentlemen, said a nigger, approaching, "Commodore say cold collation ready—send me tell all de officers."

"Compliments to Commodore Foote, Sambo, and I do not require any."

"Same from me," said the other officer.

The messenger received the same answer from many other officers, to whom the jingling of glasses, the laughter of the ladies, and the applause at the Union toasts, were painful in the extreme.

And now the collation is concluded, and the toast of the day is about to be proposed by the brave old Commodore himself. The long extempore table, ranged on the quarter-deck, at which the guests are seated, is cleared.

The attendance of every officer is requested. This they do not refuse, as there were none even among the most disaffected who would not have been glad to see the Union peaceably restored.

The toast is to be "the Glorious Union."

The old Commodore rises, glass in hand, and in a voice which falters from emotion, addresses the company :—

"*Ladies, gentlemen, and brother officers,—I rise to*

propose a toast which **I** *am* **sure** *will be enthusiastically drunk by you all.* **I** *am a man of few words and an old man. Fifty years have* **I** *spent* **under** *our glorious flag; and had* **I** *fifty lives,* **I** *would* **lose them all to** *maintain* **that** *which* **I** *am about to propose—*'OUR GLORIOUS UNION.' "

The toast was drunk with great uproar and enthusiasm by the greater part of those present. But there were some who drank it in silence and sorrow. Among these were Darcy Leigh and many of his brother officers.

However, in the general uproar, it passed unnoticed.

CHAPTER IV.

TREASON IN THE CAMP.

AND now, under the influence of the wine, which flowed in profusion, the assembly commenced a round of speech-making and toast-drinking, in which bounce and bravado prevailed over sense.

Darcy Leigh remained at the table, as did his brother officers.

At last a rabid New England Yankee got on his legs, and commenced a furious tirade against the rebellion, the rebels, and their sympathizers. Had he marked the gloomy, sullen looks of many of his hearers, he might have moderated his language.

Still he roared on, getting more violent every moment.

He wound up his speech by consigning in anticipation every Secessionist to the gallows, and expressed a hope that should they not make immediate submission, the Government would take means to stir up a servile rebellion in their midst.

"Then, with an army and navy pressing on them from without, and a furious horde of slaves murdering, burning, and pillaging in their midst, the traitors will be swept from off the face of the land. Ladies and gentlemen," concluded the speaker, "I propose 'Our Army

C

and Navy, and may every Secessionist swing on the gallows tree.'"

The glasses were filled.

But among many of the officers and even others a dead silence prevailed. Then might be heard dull, gloomy mutterings of discontent.

Darcy Leigh started to his feet.

"Recall the latter part of the toast, sir," he said, "and I will drink it."

"Aye, recall the latter part," cried a dozen other voices.

"What's all this?" exclaimed the bewildered Commodore, rising; "who are those who refuse to drink a loyal toast?"

Captain Hiram Squails, who was seated on his left hand, touched the veteran on the shoulder.

"Commodore," he said, in a low tone, "for God's sake, for the sake of the Union we both love, make the proposer recall the latter part of the toast. Do you not know that many among our officers have fathers and brothers among those men whose disgraceful death they are called on to toast? Can a son drink to his father's death on the scaffold, a brother to a brother's? I am a Union man, Commodore—but had I a brother or a friend South, I wouldn't drink that toast—I wouldn't, so help me Heaven!"

And as he spoke, tears stood in the eyes of the brave rough sailor, the Cape Cod Fisherman, as he was called jocosely by his men, in allusion to the fact that, at one time when rusticating on half-pay, he had commanded a fishing smack.

"Commodore, make him recall the toast," said the rough uncouth Yankee yet more earnestly, as he noticed that the mutterings of discontent grew louder and more marked.

Once again he entreated the obstinate old man.

In vain.

"And so they ought to hang!" cried the veteran, maddened with rage: "and so they shall hang—aye, hang as high as Haman. Who refuses to drink a loyal toast?"

"I do," shouted Darcy Leigh, starting to his feet, pale and determined; "I do; and may I perish body and soul, ere I drink it!"

Thus saying, he raised the full glass on high and dashed it to atoms on the table before him.

A dozen shouts re-echoed his, and the crash of a dozen and more glasses followed.

"Treason!" shouted the Commodore, "treason in our camp, by the living God!"

For a moment, the old man seemed horror-stricken, paralyzed at the fact which at last was forced upon him.

The crew now flocked in crowds to the very verge of the quarter deck. Darcy Leigh addressed them.

"Men," he said, "I and many other Southern gentlemen have served with you, and I trust we have done our duty. I am known to many of you, and trust, though we can no longer serve together under the same flag, that I and those of my brother officers as think fit to follow my example may bear away with us the kindly feelings of your brave sailor hearts."

"Aye, aye, sir, that you do. Hurrah for Lieutenant Leigh!" and other encouraging cries interrupted him; for Darcy was a general favourite.

Ere he could resume his address, the Commodore started to his feet and shouted at the top of his voice, almost blind with fury,—

"Silence, sir—silence!—your name, sir?"

"My name is Darcy Leigh, and till now I have borne a lieutenant's commission on board the Spitfire."

"Then, Lieutenant Leigh, I place you under arrest for insubordinate conduct and mutiny. You shall be tried by a court-martial."

Darcy Leigh left his seat and went round to the Commodore; Captain Hiram Squails was on his left hand; on his right was Stella Gayle, who gazed horror-stricken at the scene.

"Commodore Foote," said Darcy, "I honour and respect you as a brave and good officer, and regret I can no longer serve under you; I hereby tender you my

c 2

resignation.   I no longer bear a commission in the
United States' Navy."

"I refuse to accept it, traitor, rebel!" roared the Commodore.   "I place you under arrest.   Surrender your
sword, and go on board your ship at once."

"Commodore Foote," said the young man, calmly, un-
buckling his sword-belt and looking at Stella Gayle,
"yesterday I was told I was a coward—to-day that I am
a traitor.   I am neither.   The fact that I refuse longer
to bear a commission under a Government I can no
longer serve with honour and honesty proves that at
least I am no traitor.   It is for me to prove hereafter
that I am no coward."

Then drawing his sword from its scabbard while
every one gazed in blank amazement, he deliberately
broke it across his knee, and flinging the broken
pieces on the deck close to the feet of Stella Gayle, he
said,—

"THUS I SURRENDER MY COMMISSION AND MY SWORD
TOGETHER."

  * * * * * * * *

Utter and blank was the consternation as the young
lieutenant left the quarter-deck, followed by fully a
score of other young officers.   Commodore Foote was
thunder-struck.   He could not, would not, believe in
the terrible fact of the wide-spread disaffection among
the officers of his squadron till it was thus forcibly impressed on his notice.   Looking around him he observed
that scarcely a dozen remained around the table, fully
two-thirds having left the quarter-deck with Darcy Leigh,
and, alas! ominous sign! *they had left their swords behind them.*

"Alas! for the poor old Union!" said Captain Hiram
Squails, the tears trickling down his rugged cheeks,
"when the best and bravest of her sons thus desert in
the hour of trial.   Commodore, 'twas a pity we were not
more gentle and easy with these young fellows.   Hot-
headed and hot-blooded, they have committed themselves; and it will be hard indeed to bring them back to
their allegiance."

Stella Gayle, scarcely knowing what she did, picked up the broken sword which lay at her feet.

" Ah, Miss," said Captain Squails, " if ever that young chap buckles on a sword in place of that bit of broken steel, I reckon it won't be in Uncle Sam's service. You may take my word for it, it will be under the cursed Secession flag—the Stars and Bars."

Stella gazed sadly on the broken weapon, and almost fancied it a presage of the disruption of that Union for which she had so great an affection.

" Well, Captain Squails," said the Commodore, who had now recovered from his fit of passion, " what's to be done? I suppose I must bring 'em to a court-martial ?"

" I suppose so—there's no help for it if they stop—but it's tarnation queer to me if they do—strikes me, they'll be kinder off South, right off, them boys will. Anyhow, an empty house is better than a bad tenant, and an honourable foe is better than a false friend."

And with this wise saw the conversation terminated; but all the mirth and gaiety of the fête had fled. The Commodore leaned his grey head on his hand, and seemed buried in his own thoughts. Captain Squails gazed moodily at the groups of sailors forward on the main-mast, while Stella, pale, sad, and silent, sat with the broken blade in her hand, like a marble statue of melan-choly in gala dress.

CHAPTER V.

AN AUDACIOUS REBEL AND A DESPERATE ATTEMPT.

DARCY LEIGH, on leaving the quarter-deck, did not immediately go on board his own vessel, as ordered by the Commodore.

An audacious design took possession of his head.

No sooner had he matured it than he resolved to put it in instant execution.

He started forward among the men; seeing an enormous negro, he approached him.

" Well, Jupiter," he said.

" Golly! massa Darcy, that you? Lor!—what for you break him sword? By golly! they have court-martial, and Massa Darcy get hung up to yardarm!" and Jupiter shook his woolly head ominously at the pleasant prospect.

" Well, Jupiter, it may be so; but when they do so, I'll take care they shall have a better reason. Now sten. I want to speak to you. You're head-stoker, 'n't you, aboard the Spitfire?"

" Yes, massa."

" How many of you niggers are there?"

" Eight, massa, and two white fellows, but dey 're dem d——d Spaniards!"

" Ah, they 're no use! Are all the niggers with you?"

" Wid me? in course dey is, when we's all down de stoke-hole togeder!"

" I mean will they all go with you—will they all do as you do?"

" Well, massa, dat depends; but I reckon dis child can lead 'em a few, and when he can't he thumps 'em into it. I're foreman over dem niggers, anyhow!"

" Well, now, listen! Your fires are banked up, are they not?"

" Yes, massa, dem's de orders from de engineer."

" Oh, confound the engineer! we'll do without him; he's a Yankee."

" Well, where are the firemen?" continued Darcy Leigh.

" Where is dey?—why on board."

" And how many of them?"

" Let's see, massa, dere's Darby Kelly and dem oder two d——d Irishmen; den dere's tree niggers and two Yankees—re'glar down-easters."

" How long would it take to get the steam up?"

" How long?—why de water 's hot an' de fire 's banked up—may be it might take close on an hour."

" Couldn't you get steam enough in half an hour to steam out of the harbour?"

" Maybe we might, massa; but we isn't agoing out dis afternoon."

" Isn't we?—perhaps we is though. Now, pay atten-

tion to what I am going to say. You were born on my
father's plantation, and in return for your faithful services, my father made you a present of your freedom.
I know you always were a true and faithful nigger. You
have often said, that for my father, my brother or myself, you would do anything."

" By golly! an' so I would, too; cut dis here hand off,
so help me neber, Massa Darcy!"

" Well, now, I am going to put you to the proof. Go
on board the Spitfire, get such of the stokers and firemen together as you can depend on, and await my
coming on board. In the meantime, take the ashes off
the fires, and shovel on a little coke—only a little—just
enough to get the water hot without making much
smoke. Then look out for me. When I come on board,
and all is ready, I will look down the stoke-hole. Keep
your eyes open; I will make you a sign with my hand.
The moment I have done so, fire up like blazes; shovel
the coals on like fury, and make a fire fit to split her
boilers, as quick as you can. Work like devils for just
one hour, and then, Jupiter, we'll laugh at the whole
squadron."

" Laff at de squadron?" said the nigger, in utter
amazement. " What you mean, massa? Oh, by golly, I
can't make head nor tail of dis here business!"

Darcy Leigh glanced cautiously around to see there
was no one listening.

Then he said a few words, in a low voice to the nigger,
which produced a marvellous effect. He opened his
great eyes till the whites were visible all round. He
gazed for some time in speechless horror at the young
lieutenant. At last he gasped,—

" Oh, my Lor a God O'mighty, Massa Leigh! nebber
hear such a ting in my life. Why, dey'll hang you,
shoot you, sartin sure. Why, dere'd be a court-martial
and ebery tink. Oh, my Lor a God O'mighty, aint dis
orful?"

" Never you mind, Jupiter, let them do their worst
when they catch me. Now, you just go straight on
board, and do as I told you. Will you?"

"Well, massa, Jupiter never cry a go. As de song say, ' de hole hog or none.' I'll do it, massa; but, Oh my Lor a God O'mighty, ain't it orful?"

" Well, go on board, and tell Darby Kelly and tho other two Irishmen to wait for me. Say it's of importance; I'll be there in half an hour; and mind you, not a word to a soul till all is ready."

Jupiter got into a boat, and went aboard the Spitfire, muttering occasionally, " Oh my Lor a God O'mighty, ain't it orful ? "

Darcy Leigh now hastened up to a group of young officers, and drawing them aside one by one, remained for a short time in earnest conversation with each.

If they did not express their surprise in quite so original a manner as Jupiter, it was quite as great.

" Great Heavens, Darcy! are you serious ?" said one.

" Never more so."

" Is there a chance of success ?"

" A chance ?—success is a certainty. I will succeed— I will succeed—fortune favours the brave."

As he said these words, the young officer's eyes glittered, and a flush came to his cheek. His lips were firmly set, and there was an expression on his face which betokened a desperate determination.

The young officer he was speaking to was silent for some time; he gazed with astonishment on the slight, slender frame and beardless face of the almost boy before him. At last he spoke.

" Darcy Leigh," he said, " you 're a devil—here's my hand—I 'm with you, heart and soul."

With a like result, Darcy Leigh confided his project to other young officers, whom he could depend on.

All were at first aghast at the audacity of the attempt he proposed; but all, influenced by his quiet, determined manner, gave in their adhesion, and cast their lot in with him.

" Now, gentlemen," said Darcy, " go all of you on board, and await me; I will be with you in half an hour. I have business to attend to here first."

One by one the young officers, to the number of

eleven, quietly left the Columbia; and proceeded on board the Spitfire.

Little did the Commodore think, as he still sat moodily leaning his head on his hand, of the desperate treason about to be attempted.

Darcy Leigh disappeared among the crew, and spoke to several.

These men invariably left, and followed the officers who were in the plot on board the Spitfire.

Now Darcy Leigh may be seen sauntering carelessly about the deck, pausing every now and then, and leaning over first one and then another of the great guns.

See how cautiously he looks around him!

For a second he raises the flag which covers each, and passes his hand beneath.

What is he doing?

CHAPTER VI.

THE PLANS OF THE MUTINEERS.

In half an hour the young lieutenant had completed his task, and prepared to leave the Columbia. She carried on the quarter-deck, in addition to the big guns on the main-deck and in the waist, eight brass carronades.

Darcy Leigh gazed wistfully at these, and muttered—

"It won't do—it's too dangerous. Hiram Squails has got an eye like a hawk. However, I'll see."

He then strolled, apparently carelessly, towards the quarter-deck.

Captain Squails and Commodore Foote still remained in deep conversation. Stella Gayle, her father, and some of the visitors were grouped about the quarter-deck, some seated on hen-coops, some leaning over the bulwarks, gazing over the blue waters of New York Harbour.

Darcy Leigh was right in his opinion as to the hawk-eye of the Yankee captain. He had barely passed on to the quarter-deck, and was cautiously looking around him, and watching an opportunity to carry his design into execution, when the harsh, loud voice of Captain Squails was heard,—

"Lieutenant Leigh!"

"Sir," answered Darcy, with habitual promptitude.

"I thought you were under orders to go on board your ship? Commodore Foote has placed you under arrest. What are you doing here? Obey at once, and go on board the Spitfire, and there remain till you have further orders."

"Aye, aye, sir," was the reply, as the lieutenant walked to the gangway, and prepared to obey.

Before leaving, he turned and cast one look around him. Up and down the white flush deck his gaze wandered. For a moment his eyes rested on each of the frowning guns, whose muzzles protruded from the portholes.

"Aye, aye, my beauties," he muttered, "my fierce, black bull-dogs, I reckon I've drawn your teeth for you!"

A mocking smile played for a moment over his face as he descended the ladder, and stepped into a boat alongside.

Hiram Squails had watched the young lieutenant; he had seen his glance around the deck, and the smile as he descended into the boat.

The Yankee captain had known the young man for many years, and duly appreciated his determination and daring.

"I think I had better go on board my ship, commodore," he said.

"Go on board? Nonsense, man!—stay here. I want the company of some one whom I know to be loyal and true. Besides, there's a mail just in from Washington. I expect despatches on board every moment, and you may as well be here to receive my orders in case the Government have decided to send us South to strike a blow. So stay with me, Captain Squails—your ship will not run away."

"I didn't like the look of that lad as he went over

the gangway—didn't, by thunder! He's got something hatching in that head of his as sure as eggs are eggs. I never saw Darcy Leigh look or smile like that but there was something in the wind. Anyhow, I don't suppose he can do any harm in the middle of the squadron. But I don't like it—I don't, and that's the truth."

    *   *   *   *

Meanwhile, we will follow Darcy Leigh on board the Spitfire.

As he stepped on board, he set his lips firmly, and said to himself, "Now then—neck or nothing—death or glory! I'll let them know that I am no coward, at all events."

He was immediately joined by several of the young officers to whom he had spoken on board the Columbia. They spoke in whispers, and at Darcy's suggestion, descended into the gun-room, where the junior officers messed.

Pens, ink, paper, and a chart were produced.

None were present but such as were in the secret, and the door was at once barred.

"Now, gentlemen," said Darcy, with quiet determination, "we are about to engage in a desperate enterprise. If we fail, we shall be shot like dogs without fail; there is no mistake about that—at least, shot or hanged; but, for my part, they shall never take me alive. If any one of you think better of this scheme—that it is too dangerous—let him retire."

There was a silence. Darcy glanced round the mess-table, but he saw there were none but pale, determined faces—not an eye quailed.

"Good," he said, "now to business. We have three distinct operations to carry out simultaneously. We must obtain possession of the engine-room and stoke-hole, and also secure such of the crew as are against us. This last is the more difficult—two-thirds of the seamen are Yankees. No matter; all the more glory to us if we succeed. The engine-room is easily enough managed; I understand the machinery, and will start the engines. The majority of the stokers and firemen I can also depend on; so that the only remaining difficulty we have to apprehend is with the crew. We must get as many as possible down the fore-hold, and then batten down the hatches. Those who remain on deck must be suddenly attacked and overpowered."

"Bloodshed?" asked a young officer.

"Not if it can be avoided," was the reply; "but if the resistance is such as to endanger our success, we must pour out blood like water. All of you have revolvers. Should they not be at once overpowered, shoot them down like dogs—it is no time for child's play. And now to business. Each of you go on deck; sound such of the crew as you think can be brought round to us. If you can trust them, let them into the secret, and give them their instructions and the signal for the attack."

"What shall the signal be?"

"It wants now two hours to sunset. The signal shall be the firing of the sundown-gun on the battery. In half an hour we meet here again and report progress."

The Spitfire was a screw steam-sloop of eighteen guns —four of which were eleven-inch Dahlgren shell guns, equal, if not superior in power, especially at short ranges, to our own Armstrong's.

She was manned by a crew of one hundred and eighty men, and thirty firemen and stokers. She was built, fitted out, and commissioned in Boston, Massachusetts. The great majority of her crew were thorough Yankees, most of them from Massachusetts or one of the New England States.

Of the whole hundred and eighty, not more than fifty, at the outside, could be counted on by the conspirators, to aid in their projected enterprise.

Of these there were some who, though favourably disposed, did not care to run the risk of so desperate an attempt, well knowing that the yard-arm would be their fate in case of failure and capture.

At the expiration of the half-hour the twelve officers met again in the gun-room.

Darcy Leigh assumed the command unquestioned.

All felt and knew that the audacious project was entirely due to him, and none felt inclined to dispute his claim to the command.

"Now, my boys," said Darcy, as soon as they were all assembled, "there is no time to be lost—we have barely an hour and a quarter. Let us arrange our programme, and assign to each man his post. Which of you are the best up in engineering and the management of the machinery?"

"Grey and Wharncliffe," said one of the young men, "know more about it than any of us."

"Grey and Wharncliffe? Well, they, then, shall have the charge of the engine-room. At the gunfire they will hasten down with five men, all armed; if the first or second engineers make the least resistance, they will seize and gag them; if their resistance, or that of any of their men, should seem to threaten the success of the enterprise, they are, without hesitation, to blow their brains out. Lieutenants Grey and Wharncliffe, you understand clearly what is to be done?"

"Yes," replied Grey; "we first overpower the engineers, and then get the machinery ready for a start."

"Right. When I call down into the engine-room, turn the steam full on, tie down the safety-valve, and leave the rest to us on deck."

The young officers signified that they fully understood the part they were to play.

"We now come to the stoke-hole," continued Darcy; "with that we shall have little trouble. Jupiter, the big nigger, is with me, heart and soul, among the stokers; and I believe Darby Kelly, the fireman, would go through fire and water for me, since I saved him from that three dozen the captain ordered him. Burleigh, will you and a couple of men take the stoke-hole and see that all is right in that quarter? Keep the niggers at work at the furnaces as soon as you get the word. I'll send down all that half hundred hams old Squails bought at Boston. I reckon they'll make the fires blaze a bit."

In spite of the desperate nature of the enterprise they were about to embark in, there was a general laugh at the thought of the sacrifice of poor Hiram Squails's hams.

"And now," said Darcy, "we come to the most serious part of the business. The engine-room and stoke-hole will not give us much trouble; but the crew —that's a different affair. They're Yankees, but, by Jove, they'll make a fight of it. I have sent a keg of rum down the fore-hold; that, I hope, will get some half of them in such a state that they shall not know how to fight even if they feel inclined. Then we can reckon on some forty or five-and-forty men. Even these, however, would not care about risking their necks with us, did they not see a good chance of success At least, I gather that the majority of them, although they sympathize with us, and like the audacity of the attempt, still feel inclined to hang back until something decisive is done—in short, till we strike the first decisive and successful blow. This, then, is the state of affairs :— There are twelve of us; two are told off to the engine-room, one to the stoke-hole; that leaves us nine officers. Then, as to the men, five for the engine-room and two for the stoke-hole is seven. We certainly cannot count on more than a score at the most. That would leave us, say twelve men to spare for the deck work. Nine officers and twelve men—that is the material we have to work with. With that few we must clear the decks, batten the hatches down, slip the cable, and, if necessary, man the guns. I suppose we have on board at present about a hundred and fifty men. Then there is the boatswain, the boatswain's mates, four quarter-masters, the first and third lieutenants, and the sailing-master, all Yankees, and all dead against us. The first lieutenant and the sailing-master are the most dangerous; they are brave men, and must be put *hors de combat* at once. I will see to that. Then I propose that each of you take one or two men, and distribute yourselves about the decks among the groups of men. Many of them, although they will not actively assist at first, will look on approvingly. Be very cautious not to attack or offend these neutrals. Others, again, must be secured at once. At the sound of the gun from the battery, four or five of you, who must be already prepared, will at once clap on the fore-hatches, and place the bar across. This will put fully two-thirds of the crew safe. If any attempt is made by the remainder of the Yankees on deck to take off the hatches again, use your revolvers—pistol them right and left. In the meantime, I will train a couple of the carronades to command the fore part of the deck, and will load with grape. Do not stop to secure *all* who resist, but drag such as you can off, and we will put them in irons. Then, if the remainder resist or attempt to take the hatches off, the grape and canister of the carronades will give a good account of them. In the meantime, while some of you are securing the unruly of the crew, two, assisted by the carpenter's mate, who is all ours, will unshackle the cable. The instant that is done, give a shout. I will then give the signal down the engine-room, Grey will turn the steam full on, and I will take the helm; in twenty minutes we shall be clear of the squadron, and in an hour at sea. Then we must place in irons such of the crew who do not choose to join us, and consult as to what is to be done next. Gentlemen, do you approve of my plan?"

" Yes—yes !" is heard on all hands—not a single voice being raised in opposition.

" Now then, gentlemen, to work. Each man to his post. In little more than half an hour we shall hear the boom of the sundown gun. Death or glory ! Let us shake hands all round. Some of us may be sent to our long account ere dark."

Then in silence the conspirators—rebels—traitors— call them what you will—exchanged a friendly grip all round, and separated.

CHAPTER VII.

THE CONSPIRATORS SEIZE THE SHIP.

THE setting sun casts a soft, mellow light over the beautiful waters of New York Harbour. The Atlantic squadron of the United States' Navy is at anchor about a mile above the Narrows, in such a position as effectually to command the channel.

Outside of all is the flag-ship—the stately Columbia— one of the finest frigates in the American navy. Next to her is the steam-corvette Manhattan, and next to her again, the steam-sloop Spitfire. Beyond her are two other corvettes, four sloops, and two gunboats—making up Commodore Foote's squadron.

All is noise and revelry on board the Spitfire. The keg of rum, so thoughtfully provided by the young lieutenant, Darcy Leigh, has had its effect. The sounds of songs, shouting, and fiddling, from the forehatch sufficiently attest the fact.

Some thirty or forty of the crew, however—preferring the cooling breeze on deck to the noise, shouting, and stifling heat of the fore-hold—are lounging about the decks.

Three of the young officers who took a part in the gun-room conference are leaning listlessly against the fore-mast, looking down the fore-hold, apparently amused by the noise and riot going on. Two others are leaning against the bulwarks, at a distance of only a few yards. All five are so placed that they can, at a moment's notice, make a dash at the hatches, which are stacked one above another between the fore-hatch and the mast.

Darcy Leigh is seated on a hencoop on the starboard side of the quarter-deck. His seat commands a view of the companion-way down into the captain's cabin. The first and third lieutenants and sailing-master are down there, sitting at the table and drinking to the glorious Union in tumblers of whisky toddy. No mice were ever watched more closely by a vigilant cat than are these three officers by Darcy Leigh. Opposite him on the larboard side, is Lieutenant George Frewin and two of the most determined fore-mast hands; while Darby Kelly, the big Irish fireman, is leaning against the mizzen-mast in ill-disguised impatience for the fray to begin.

"Masther Darcy," he says, in a gentle whisper, which might be heard half the length of the ship, "when's the foight going to begin? Sure, let's have it over, for, be jabers, I want me tay."

"Silence, you maniac!" is the reply, "or, 'be jabers,' you 'll be having your 'tay' in kingdom come if they hear you."

The sun is on the verge of the low land, on the western horizon. Now the lurid disc of the glowing orb is hidden by the land. In another five minutes it will have set, and the gun from the fort will boom forth the news. The merry sound of the fiddles, and the roaring chorus of the songs ascending from the fore-hatch, are alone audible. All else is quiet. On board the Manhattan all is still. The sentry, pacing slowly up and down at the gangway, and the officer of the watch sauntering lazily up and down the quarter-deck, are almost the only moving objects visible. The crew are all either on shore, in their hammocks, or on board some of the other ships. On board the flag-ship, too, all is equally still. Of the gay party but lately assembled on her decks, there only remained now some five or six ladies, and twice as many gentlemen, exclusive of the officers.

These are assembled on the quarter-deck, admiring the glorious sight which the setting sun presents. Scarcely a word is spoken. The old Commodore is gloomy and morose; Captain Hiram Squails, who is still by his side, snappish and ill-tempered; Stella Gayle is leaning over the starboard bulwarks, gazing sadly up the bay, towards where the Manhattan, the Spitfire, and the rest of the squadron are at anchor.

It is almost a dead calm; there is not sufficient wind to blow out the light folds of bunting composing the ensign, which droops languidly from the mizzen-peak as if sharing the general feeling of depression.

Flash! an interval, and then boom went the big gun,

which announced the fact that another day was ended, another night begun.

Instantly, according to custom, down comes every flag from every war-ship of the squadron. No, not every one, for the Stars and Stripes still float from the mizzen-peak of the Spitfire. Those on board had other things to do than to haul down flags.

Instantly that the flash of the gun was seen, and ere the report had yet reached them, Darcy Leigh bounded to his feet, and hastened down into the cabin, followed closely by Darby Kelly, Lieutenant Frewin, and the two fore-mast hands.

The first and third lieutenants, and the sailing-master, were still seated at the table.

Without a moment's hesitation, Darcy strode up to the first lieutenant, and placing a revolver to his head, said, quietly,—

"Sir, you are my prisoner!"

"What is the meaning of this, Lieutenant Leigh; are you mad or drunk?" said the officer, starting to his feet. "Allow me to pass if you please."

"Silence! or I'll blow your brains out," was the amiable reply.

The lieutenant was a brave man, and seeing the fore-mast hands and Darby Kelly follow Darcy down into the cabin, he at once guessed it was an arranged mutiny.

"Treason—mutiny!" he shouted at the top of his voice, making a dash for the companion-way; "sentry"——

He never finished the sentence, for Darby Kelly hit him a crack over the head at the last word with an iron belaying pin, that effectually quieted him.

With a heavy groan, the brave officer fell back, and lay senseless under the table.

"You great bull-headed beggar!" said Darcy, angrily, to the Irishman; "what did you hit him like that for? Surely you could have secured him without hitting him a blow like the kick of a horse. I hope to G— you have not killed him."

So saying, Darcy stooped down and raised the head of the wounded man, from which the blood flowed copiously.

Taking advantage of this opportunity, the sailing-master leaped over the cabin-table, and rushed up the companion-way before he could be stopped.

"Treason!—treason!" he shouted, at the top of his voice; "beat to quarters—fire an alarm gun"——

The words were hardly out of his mouth, and he had but just reached the deck, when he was felled to the ground by a blow from a handspike.

Then Darcy and Darby Kelly, who had hurried up after him, seized him and dragged him down into the cabin. The third lieutenant was secured without difficulty and bound.

"Shove them down the lazaretto—off with the hatch, quick!" said Darcy.

No sooner said than done. The hatch was taken off, and the insensible form of the first lieutenant bundled down—then the sailing-master, who was only slightly hurt, followed, and the third lieutenant last. Then the hatch was placed on again, and securely fastened.

Scarcely had they finished this part of their work than they were apprised by loud shouts and pistol shots that a fight in earnest was going on on deck.

"Come on, boys—there are five of us, and we five will win the day."

Darby Kelly was first up, and shouting, "Be jabers, I'm into them," dashed forward.

"Come back, you fool—come back," shouted Darcy; "I want you here."

Darby obeyed, and following the lieutenant's directions, he assisted to run back one of the brass carronades. Frewin did the like on the other side, and in five minutes the whole length of the deck was commanded by a gun on each side loaded to the muzzle with grape and canister. Then Darcy snatched up a bugle which was lying near, and blew the retreat.

It was a preconcerted signal.

No sooner was the sound heard than all who were in the secret retreated aft, dragging as many of their opponents with them as they could.

Step by step they retreated till they were **fairly on** the quarter-deck, and behind the carronades.

They had dragged with them about fifteen **of the** crew, most of whom were wounded more or less.

These they hastened to secure.

Meanwhile three officers and two **men**, who had remained to guard the fore-hatch, in order that their opponents might not take it off and liberate their ship-mates below, were sorely assailed.

" Come on, boys, forward," shouted Darcy, revolver in hand, dashing ahead, followed by the others—" down with the Yankees!"

This decided the **fate of the day.** The party defending the fore-hatch were enabled to make good their position, while the remainder of the crew were driven forward right into the bows of the sloop.

" Quick, unshackle the chains !" shouted Darcy.

In less than two minutes this was done.

Then he **hurried to** the engine-room **hatch**, and yelled down, " Go ahead—full steam—all's right above."

His words were hailed with a shout of joy from below, which was followed by the clanking and groaning of the engine. The next instant the screw revolved, and the Spitfire plunged ahead.

The ensign, the Stars and Stripes, still flew at the mizzen-peak.

" Load the larboard **guns** with blank cartridge, Mr. Wharncliffe," said Darcy, who was at the helm, "and the starboard with round shot."

Lieutenant Wharncliffe hastened to obey, and one by one the guns were loaded and run out.

The Spitfire was now dashing down the channel under a full head of steam.

She was abreast of the Manhattan, and had passed her ere the officers of the latter recovered from their asto-nishment at the extraordinary proceedings of the sloop.

Once past her broadside all danger ceased from her, as being at anchor, it would take some time to slip her cable and bring it to bear again.

Now the Spitfire is dashing down the narrow channel,

straight for the flag-ship, about a quarter of a mile ahead of her.

She will be obliged to pass within a hundred yards of her guns.

"Are the larboard guns loaded with blank cartridge?" asked Darcy.

Being answered in the affirmative, he said,—

" Stand by to fire a royal salute when I hoist our flag."

Then Darcy gave the helm to one of the seamen, and casting off the signal-halliards, hauled down the United States' ensign.

He then bent on another flag.

" Now, boys, give her a cheer," he said. " Are you ready with the guns ?"

" All ready, sir."

Then up went the flag.

The Stars—yes—surely it must be the Stars and Stripes!! Yet—no—there are the Stars, surely enough ; but they are too few for the national ensign—and the Stripes—where are they ? Those broad horizontal bands cannot be meant for them ? No—it is not the Stars and Stripes which sways aloft saluted by a deafening cheer and the roar of cannon ; it is the Secession flag—the Stars and Bars !!!

Cheer after cheer rang out in daring defiance. Gun after gun boomed forth its hoarse salute to the full number of twenty-one, and the Spitfire tore ahead through the water with the audacious flag of the rebel South flying from her peak.

CHAPTER VIII.

RUNNING THE GAUNTLET.

RETURN we to the Columbia.

Commodore Foote is still busied in his thoughts, apparently not of a pleasant nature.

Webster Gayle, after an ineffectual attempt to engage in conversation with Captain Squails, rose, and lighting a cigar, strolled away, saying to his daughter,—

" Stella, when you and your sister are ready to return home, let me know. I expected your cousin Lupus would have been on board ere now, but I suppose something has detained him."

Stella Gayle made no answer. Her eyes were fixed on the Spitfire.

" Captain Squails," she said, "look at your ship. Is she going to sea? See the smoke coming from her funnel."

" Going to sea!" said Squails, arousing himself— "thunder! not that I know of."

He looked attentively and with some surprise for a moment at the smoke pouring from the Spitfire's funnel.

" Oh, I suppose it's some of those cursed black stokers and Irish firemen—all drunk together, no doubt. I left orders to keep the fires well banked up with ashes, and I suppose they've been shovelling small coal on as well."

Five minutes more passed.

The sun was now on the point of disappearing.

" Look, Captain Squails," cried Stella again, " look now!"

Captain Squails started to his feet.

" Thunder and furies !" he cried, " what the blazes is the meaning of this ? Why they must be getting the steam up."

" Eh! what?" said the Commodore, waking up; " getting the steam up on board your vessel, Captain Squails ? Who gave orders ?—it must be a mistake. Here, steward, bring me my glass."

While the steward was absent on his errand the sun disappeared—flash, boom, went the sundown gun.

Then all was silent for a time. The flags of all the other vessels were hauled down ; but the ensign at the peak of the Spitfire was still kept flying.

The Commodore placed the glass to his eye.

" Why, who the devil's in command on board, Captain Squails ? Here's gunfire, and they haven't hauled the flag down. What lubber of an officer is in charge of her ? "

"My first lieutenant; but he's no lubber, but a good active officer."

"What on earth's the meaning of this?" cried the old man, starting to his feet; "there's a fight on board of some kind!"

Surely enough the sharp reports of firearms might now be heard. Then a shout, and another, followed by another discharge of pistols.

Every one hastened to the starboard side, and gazed over the bulwarks at the strange scene being enacted on board the Spitfire.

They could just make out that a desperate struggle was going on. The swaying forms of the combatants were distinctly visible, although they could not identify any.

"Another glass, steward, quick!" shouted Captain Squails, trembling with excitement.

The glass was brought.

"By the thunder of heaven, there's Darcy Leigh!" exclaimed Squails; "he's running back one of the carronades, and turning it forward. By G——d, Commodore, they're taking possession of the ship."

"Where's my boat's crew?" he shouted, running to the side; "bring my gig up to the gangway—jump in there, and fire away."

Easier said than done, for Captain Squails's gig was nowhere to be seen. Darcy Leigh had exchanged a few words with the coxswain left in charge of her, and the result was the disappearance of the boat. Not that it would have availed anything, for by this time the Spitfire was adrift, and had swung round with her head pointing right for the Columbia.

"Why your ship's adrift, Captain Squails," said the Commodore, in utter amazement.

"They've slipped her cable!" groaned Squails. "Thunder and fury!" he continued, "they're steaming right down for us."

"Surely they ain't going to run into us?" said the Commodore.

"Run into us, no," replied Captain Squails; "but they're going to run away with her."

" Beat to quarters—man the starboard guns—load with round shot, and sink her if she attempts to pass us."

At the sound of the drums and fifes the men came tumbling up in amazement at the sudden summons. In an inconceivably short time every man is at his station.

The flags are hastily torn from the guns, ammunition handed up, and the battle lanterns are lighted and hung around.

On comes the Spitfire right down towards them.

" See," cried Stella Gayle, who was gazing with fear and surprise at the scene; " see, they have hauled down the flag."

" Yes, and yonder goes another one in its place," said Captain Squails.

She was now barely two hundred yards from the flag ship.

Stella Gayle recognised the figure of the man who was hoisting the flag.

" Darcy Leigh—see, Captain Squails, there is Lieu-tenant Leigh hoisting that flag."

" What flag is it ? " asked the Commodore, whose sight was none of the best. " I can see the stars ; is it the Stars and Stripes ? "

At that moment a cheer rung out from the deck of the Spitfire. This was succeeded by the boom of a gun ; again and again flash succeeded flash, cheer cheer.

" What flag is it, Commodore ? " shouted Hiram Squails, at the top of his voice.

" The Rebel flag—the Stars and Bars, by the living God."

* * * * * *

And now the Spitfire is right abreast of the Columbia, distant about a hundred yards. They can plainly dis-tinguish everything on her decks. The starboard guns of the Spitfire are run out and manned. The men wait but the word to fire.

The shouting and hammering of the imprisoned crew, in their efforts to release themselves, are plainly heard. These efforts, however, are futile, for water-casks, piles of rigging, spars, and lumber of every description, have been piled on top. In addition to this, the carronades have been dragged forward, and their muzzles pointed right down the hatch, so that should the prisoners succeed in their efforts to force a passage, they will be blown to pieces ere they could reach the deck.

Suddenly the spectators observe a gigantic negro run up from the stoke-hole, and seat himself coolly on the capstan.

It is Jupiter. He has in his hand a fiddle. Showing his white teeth, and chuckling audibly, he deliberately commences playing " Yankee Doodle."

" Fire ! " shouted the Commodore, hoarse with rage. " Fire ! blow her out of the water."

" Fire ! " he again shouted, after a moment's pause. " Pour a broadside into her."

Still the great guns were silent. The gunners remained aghast with dismay.

" Fire ! " again roared the Commodore. " Hell and furies, why don't you fire ? "

Still the guns did not send forth their iron storm.

An officer ran aft and said to the commodore,—

" *The guns are all spiked, Commodore !* "

" Darcy Leigh, by thunder ! " groaned Squails. " I knew there was something up when he went over the gangway. I knew he did not stop on board for nothing."

" The carronades ! " cried the Commodore, running up to one, and examining the breech; " they are not spiked ! "

It was true, and in half a minute the four brass guns poured their contents of grape and canister into the Spitfire.

There was a terrible crashing of woodwork; the splinters flew in all directions, showing that the discharge had taken effect. A shot struck the tiller, not, however, carrying it away, but causing the wheel to spin round violently. This had the effect of throwing Darcy Leigh over, who was steering, and dashing him violently against the bulwarks.

Instantly the Spitfire yawed from her course, and

came close under the stern of the Columbia. Had the rebels chosen to take advantage of it, this was a most favourable position, as not a single gun could be brought to bear upon them; they could rake the Columbia from stem to stern.

"Stand by your guns, men!" shouted Lieutenant Wharncliffe, who was wounded by the discharge of grape from the Columbia; "stand to your guns, and fire one by one as you come abreast of the cabin windows."

It was a moment of terrible suspense on board the Columbia. If the Spitfire raked her, her big guns loaded with grape, the slaughter must be fearful.

Stella Gayle clung to her father's arm, and waited in breathless suspense for the expected terrible discharge from the rebel's guns.

"Commence with the bow gun," shouted Lieutenant Wharncliffe, who was exasperated by the pain of his wound, "and fire in rotation. Ready with the bow gun —FIRE!"

The gunners were in the very act of obeying, when Darcy Leigh, running forward, shouted, "No—no! Let not a man dare to fire a gun. There are ladies on board. Wharncliffe, you ought to be ashamed of yourself!"

Darcy Leigh had seen Stella Gayle and her sister He then ran back to the wheel, and commenced heaving it to starboard, in order to pay her off on to her course again.

The Spitfire glided by the stern of the Columbia without firing a shot. One would have thought such forbearance deserved a return.

Commodore Foote shouted, "Lay aft here, marines and small arms men. Fire at the man at the helm—it is that accursed rebel, Lieutenant Leigh!"

The last gun on the starboard quarter of the Spitfire was now just clear of the Columbia. The two vessels were stern to stern at right angles to each other; scarcely twenty yards separated them.

The marines and small arms men hurried aft, and ranged themselves on the starboard quarter of the Columbia.

Now may be heard the rattling of the steel ramrods as the Minnie bullets are driven home.

Every moment increases the distance between the two ships. Still, however, the Spitfire is well in the range of the marines' rifles—certainly not more than sixty or seventy yards off.

"Fire!" shouted Commodore Foote.

They heard on board the Spitfire the voice of Darcy Leigh.

"Lie down, every one of you," he shouted; "let not a man show his head above the bulwarks."

Instantly every man disappeared as if by magic, except the man at the helm. Darcy Leigh himself, who still kept his post, gazed in calm defiance at the levelled barrels of the Columbia's marines.

Jupiter had disappeared from the capstan, but not to be beaten, his fiddle still kept squeaking out "Yankee Doodle" in insolent mockery.

Stella Gayle gazes towards the Spitfire with clasped hands and pale face.

The form of Darcy Leigh can still be plainly distinguished at the helm. He waves his cap in defiance.

CRASH—RATTLE!

The marines poured in their volley. The leaden shower tore up and splintered the planking of the Spitfire.

Stella Gayle gazes earnestly through the smoke.

Darcy Leigh is seen no more at the helm.

He is lying on the deck weltering in his blood.

They can still see everything that passes. Several men run aft, and while one takes the helm the others raise the motionless form before them.

They can see on board the Columbia the pale face of Darcy Leigh, marked by streams of blood, which pour from a bullet wound in the temple.

Hiram Squails, who is looking through his glass, suddenly shuts it up with a bang.

"Shot right through the head, by heavens!" he says.

Stella Gayle gives a little scream, and sinks half fainting into a seat.

"The pestilent rebel!" exclaims the old Commodore.

A tear streams down the rugged face of Captain Hiram Squails.

"A pestilent rebel, as you say, Commodore, but a brave and gallant man. There's not another officer in the fleet could have done this thing. I loved the boy like my own son. He has run away with my ship—I forgive him. He has gone to his last account, and I say God rest his soul."

*   *   *   *   *   *

The black hull of the Spitfire faded gradually away in the gloom of the evening, and in the course of twenty minutes she could barely be distinguished, as she shot through the Narrows and out to sea.

Of course some of the squadron gave chase, but in vain, for the runaway was one of the fastest vessels of the United States' navy, and having the advantage of half an-hour's start, and in the darkness of the night, she made good her escape for the time at least.

The Columbia remained at her moorings, Commodore Foote not considering her fast enough to have any chance of overhauling the sloop.

"What will they do with her?" asked the latter of Captain Squails, who was now without a ship.

"What will they do with her? why, I fancy they'll try to run her into Charleston."

"How much coal has she on board?"

"Less than three days."

"That won't take her there. She'll have to depend on her sails for part of the distance. I will telegraph to Washington to-night. Now—for instructions."

Accordingly Commodore Foote, calling for paper and ink, wrote the following :—

"To the SECRETARY AT WAR, Washington, from Commodore Foote, North Atlantic Squadron.

"A mutiny on board the United States' sloop of war Spitfire. Crew and some Southern officers have run away with her. Ringleader, Lieutenant Darcy Leigh. Probably made for Charleston. Spitfire has only two days' coal on board. Shall I follow and endeavour to intercept?"

"Captain Squails, you will take this up to the telegraph office, have it verified, and wait for a telegram in reply."

Captain Squails took the missive and went on shore.

In two hours he returned, bearing a telegraphic despatch addressed to Commodore Foote.

It ran as follows :—

" From the SECRETARY AT WAR to COMMODORE FOOTE, &c.

" Commodore Foote will immediately weigh anchor and steam to a point off Charleston Harbour, where it is likely the Spitfire may be intercepted. If captured, hang the ringleader, Lieutenant Leigh, without trial, bring the other officers to drum-head court-martial, and shoot immediately."

" Poor Darcy Leigh !" muttered Squails, whose indignation could not overpower his affection for his *protegé*. " He has gone before another tribunal than earthly court-martial. Bullets and halters have now no terrors for him. He has to answer for his treason to his country at the judgment seat of God. May he find mercy."

In a couple of hours' time the Columbia, the Manhattan, and the sloop Miranda steamed out of the harbour for Charleston.

Captain Squails having now no ship remained on board with Commodore Foote.

CHAPTER IX.

PLAN OF THE MUTINEERS.

THE daring attempt of the mutineers had been rewarded with perfect success. The discharge of grape from the carronades had wounded some four or five only, while the fire of the Columbia's marines had hurt no one with the exception of Darcy Leigh.

Immediately that he was seen to fall, several of his brother officers ran to him, and raising his lifeless form bore it below.

All thought he was dead—the blood streamed from a wound in the left temple.

"Dead!" said Wharncliffe sadly, who was himself wounded, "right through the head."

There was a surgeon on board. He approached, and proceeded to examine the wound.

"This is no bullet wound," he said at once; "it is too ragged and uneven."

A closer examination proved that he was right. What at first sight appeared to be the orifice where a bullet had crashed through the skull, turned out to be only the jagged incised wound caused by a splinter of the wheel which had struck and glanced off.

The shock had stunned him without doing any serious injury. In the course of a few minutes he returned to consciousness, and his head having been dressed was enabled to return to the deck.

A deep gloom had fallen on the mutineers when it became known that their young commander had fallen. His re-appearance was hailed with a loud shout of joy.

Although his cut head was still painful, he nevertheless at once proceeded to give the necessary orders for working the ship.

"East-south-east is her course for the present," he said to Wharncliffe; "we must make a good offing, and then lay her to till we decide on what is best to be done."

"What is best to be done?" said Wharncliffe, "surely we are going to run right for Charleston?"

"No," said Darcy, "you forget—we have not sufficient coal on board. Here, Jupiter, lay down that fiddle, and come here."

The nigger, who, when it was discovered that Darcy Leigh was not dead, had again started furious tunes on the fiddle, obeyed, and approached the group of officers.

"How much coal and coke have you below?"

"'Bout 'nuff for tree days, massa."

"Three days," said Darcy thoughtfully, "three days—in that time we can't do half the distance to Charleston. If we attempt to run there direct, we shall be overhauled before we get off Cape Hatteras. We shall be pursued at once; they will guess we shall run straight for Charleston, and some of the squadron with plenty of coal will run down before us, and lay off the harbour in waiting."

"True," said Wharncliffe gravely, "I had not thought of that. What do you propose, Darcy?"

The young officer was silent for some time. He remained buried in thought nearly a minute before he spoke.

"Run right out to sea; keep a full head of steam up all night to get well clear of pursuit. Then let the fires down, and bank them up. Then when we have made some five or six hundred miles under sail, heave to and wait for a week, keeping meanwhile a bright look out. Thus we shall have two days' coal in reserve. We can then take our time, run down to a point off Charleston Harbour, and watch for a chance of eluding the squadron and getting in."

This plan was so obviously feasible and prudent, that not a voice was raised against it.

"We now come to our internal arrangements," continued Darcy. "We will commence with the officers—there are fourteen of us altogether. It is necessary that each has his appointed rank and place. How shall we arrange it? shall we ballot for the command, or shall we let it go by seniority?"

"Neither," said Wharncliffe; "at least as to the command. You, Darcy Leigh, were the originator of the attempt. It is to your foresight in spiking the guns of the Columbia that its success is due. It is but right that on you should devolve the command. Gentlemen, am I right? do you not agree with me?"

"Yes, yes!" cried several,—"Darcy Leigh for captain."

Darcy signified his willingness to accept the command, and they proceeded to elect the officers.

"Now shall we choose by seniority or by ballot?" said Wharncliffe. .

The ballot was ultimately determined on. The post of first lieutenant fell on a young officer named Edward Wilton, while Wharncliffe was second. Third, fourth, and fifth were also disposed of, and the remaining officers ranking nominally as midshipmen.

" And now for the crew," said Darcy. " Muster them all on the quarter-deck, Mr. Wharncliffe; at least, all except a sufficient guard over the fore hatch."

The crew were mustered accordingly; exclusive of stokers and firemen, Darcy found that he had only twenty-five men on whom he could rely—meanwhile there were a hundred and fifty confined down the fore-hold. Darcy feared justly that they could not long remain quiet without an attempt to break forth; and, although ere they could succeed there would be great slaughter, he feared that the force of numbers would prevail.

Fourteen officers and twenty-five men to keep in subjection a hundred and fifty. It seemed a task fraught with difficulty and danger.

" Wharncliffe," said the captain to the second lieutenant, " don't you think a score of those fellows might be brought over to our side? It would be worth trying, for we have not enough to work the ship as it is."

" Dangerous, very dangerous," was the reply, " still, if you think the attempt should be made, by all means let it be done."

" Drag two more of the carronades forward," Darcy shouted.

In obedience to this order the brass guns were run back and hauled forward to the fore hatch.

Loaded to the very muzzle with grape, the breeches were cleared, and they were pointed right at the aftermost hatch. It was now commanded by four guns, all loaded with grape. If, on taking the hatch off, the prisoners attempted to make a rush, the slaughter caused by the discharge of the four carronades into their dense masses must be fearful. In addition, Darcy Leigh stationed his forces on each side of the hatch with drawn cutlasses.

" Now stand by, two of you, to unbar the hatch and take it off. Gunners, ready with the guns, and if I give the word, fire."

These latter were stationed with the string for discharging the cannon in their hands.

" Now, men, ready."

" All ready."

" Off with the hatch."

The hatch was immediately unbarred and removed.

Instantly a slight rush was made by the prisoners for the ladder.

" Back, every one of you, back!" shouted Darcy, " or I'll blow you into eternity. Another step and I give the word to fire. Are you mad? Do you see the carronades?"

The prisoners fell back at these words, and on observing the muzzles of the cannon ominously frowning down on them.

" Let not a man move," continued Darcy, " for if he do, it is at his peril."

The men remained massed together like sheep; low mutterings of discontent were heard, but not a man attempted to advance.

" Now come up the hatch one by one," said Darcy. " Here, you sir in front, come up first."

These words were addressed to a big sailor, named Bob Flinders. The man came up.

" Now, my lad," said Darcy, " and men, all listen to me. You know that we have seized the ship, and are running her out to sea. We have men enough to manage her, and to spare; but still we do not wish to keep you imprisoned if we can help it. You know me, some of you; we have served Uncle Sam together, and there is no reason why we should not still serve together, although the Stars and Stripes do not float over us. Who will serve the Confederate States? You, Bob Flinders," he said to the big sailor, " are you willing to serve with me in an honourable cause?"

The man hesitated; a conflict was going on in his mind between his duty and inclination. For twenty years he had served in the United States' navy, and he could not at once overcome old associations and old

E

feelings; on the other hand, he saw around him many of his shipmates and many of the most popular officers in the fleet, and at their head Darcy Leigh, sometimes called by the crew the " sailor's friend."

" Come, Bob—say yes, and pass on aft for your grog."

" Well, sir, here goes," said Bob; " shiver my timbers if I don't go in along with you, though you might have paid a fellow the compliment of asking him instead of bundling him below, and battening the hatches down on him. Here's my hand, Captain, and there's my heart with it. I suppose it's treason and mutiny; but if it's murder, I'm into it now."

So saying, Bob Flinders passed on aft.

His example went a great way; others of the men with whom Darcy was popular followed his example, and in half an hour they had secured forty more men.

This brought their whole crew up to sixty-five men and thirteen officers, making seventy-eight; then there were fifteen or sixteen stokers and firemen, which brought up their total to nearly a hundred; and the disaffected who still refused to join them did not number more than a hundred and ten; so that in case of an attempted re-capture they would fight with nearly equal numbers, and with all the advantages of arms, position, and discipline.

Nevertheless, Darcy determined to make assurance doubly sure. He had noticed among the men imprisoned in the fore-hold several who, though they did not show in front, yet were endeavouring to incite the others to make a rush on deck.

Darcy determined to secure these men. He accordingly ordered all who were below to ascend the ladder one by one, and come on deck. He had arranged his men in a double line, forming a kind of avenue round the foremast. Thus each man ascended, passed between the double row of men with drawn cutlasses, and then round the foremast back to the hatch, and again descending.

As they passed in procession before him, Darcy closely scrutinised each man.

Now and then, when he thought he had discovered one who seemed as if he might be dangerous by acting as ringleader and inciting the rest, he stopped him, and in an instant the man was handcuffed, and sent off under a guard.

He had secured some ten or a dozen in this way, thus further reducing their strength.

" Now, my lads," he said, when they had all passed in review before him, " I have no wish to be harsh or severe with you; nevertheless we have undertaken an enterprise, and it must —it shall be carried out. I should be sorry to have recourse to violence—sorry to injure any of you; nevertheless, if the slightest attempt is made at resistance or re-capture, the decks shall swim in blood—you shall be mown down ruthlessly by grape and canister! So now you know what you have to expect. I do not wish to confine you more than is necessary, but must provide for our own safety. There are somewhere about a hundred of you below there; five of you can be constantly on deck to cook, fetch provisions, water, &c., for the others."

The prisoners seemed pleased at the clemency and consideration of the mutineer captain; one stepped forward as spokesman : " Lieutenant Leigh," he said, " for my shipmates and myself down here, I thank you. You know your own business best. You've got up a mutiny and run away with the smartest steam sloop in the United States' Navy. If you 're captured you will swing at the yardarm for it, as you know well enough. Well, in my idea, no man is to be blamed for what he does when his neck's in danger. You 've put your foot in it. and to get out of the mess you must go the whole hog. I don't like your treatment to the old flag. I don't like your cause—but I like your pluck, and thank you tor your kindness. If you 're a rebel you're a gentleman, and have always behaved as such. As for us (I speak for myself, and think I can answer for two others) we shall not make any attempt without a fair chance. We know you're a man of your word, and don't believe that with those guns staring down at us, and us mostly unarmed, tha'

E 2

we should have any chance. We know that you'd have no mercy on us, because you and all with you would be fighting with halters round your necks, and I know how desperate men can fight, but I speak for myself. If we are overhauled by one of Uncle Sam's cruisers, and there's a fight for it, then I tell you honestly, I for one will go in and strike a blow for the old flag."

Murmurs of assent greeted this speech.

" Very well, my lads, I'll take care that as long as you behave yourselves you shall be well treated; and as for any attempt you make it shall be my fault if you succeed. As for what you say to our being captured by one of Uncle Sam's cruisers, that will never happen, for I'll put a match to the magazine myself and blow ship and all to eternity ere I'll be captured. Now, Mr. Wharncliffe, set the watch, and make all snug for the night. See that there are not less than forty men and five officers on deck at the same time. Let them be armed with cutlasses and pistols; place a guard over the fore-hatch under a trustworthy officer, and at the least disturbance or attempt, shoot them down like dogs. Meanwhile I will go and take some rest, for my head pains me much. E.S.E. is our course. Keep a full head of steam up till morning, then let the fires down a little, for we must economize our coal."

With these words Darcy went below, leaving the deck in charge of Wharncliffe.

CHAPTER X.

A TERRIBLE PREDICAMENT.

ALL through the night the Spitfire dashed along through the water at full speed. The firemen had built a tremendous fire. The safety valve was loaded, and she could not have been going less than sixteen knots.

The night was dark and foggy, so they could not see whether or not they were pursued. Nevertheless Darcy Leigh felt no alarm, as he knew they had at least three quarters of an hour's start in the first place. This would place them ten miles ahead of pursuit. In the second place, there was not a vessel in the squadron could sail within two knots as fast as the Spitfire, so that at the pace at which they were going every hour increased their distance.

There was yet another reason why he should feel no immediate alarm. He felt sure that the Commodore would imagine they would make straight for Charleston —the head quarters of the rebellion. This they had not done, but were steaming right out into the Atlantic.

At three o'clock in the morning the Spitfire had made by the log, a hundred and fifty miles on an E.S.E. course.

Lieutenant Wharncliffe accordingly gave orders that the fires should be allowed to go down. The effect of this was now apparent, for the sloop no longer tore through the water at such a tremendous pace, but glided easily on at some nine knots.

This was a very necessary arrangement, as the firemen through the night had been making great inroads into their scanty stock of coal, and the engines were straining and working a good deal, the bearings having become too hot to be safe.

A drizzling rain had been falling nearly all night, and so thick and dirty was the weather that nothing was visible beyond fifty or sixty yards.

Lanterns were arranged around the decks, and the watch were kept constantly on the alert by the officers, who constantly went round among them. Down the fore hatch all was quiet. Doubtless the sight of the four carronades with the gunners standing ready by the side, and the guard of a dozen men and two officers armed with cutlasses and pistols, had its effect.

The morning broke dirtily, gloomily.

Darcy Leigh, who had thrown himself on a couch in the cabin, slept a feverish and uneasy sleep. Several times at the slightest noise he leaped to his feet, and snatching up his pistols, which were beside him on the table, prepared to rush on deck. Each time, however, there was no occasion for alarm, and he again com-

posed himself to rest. The wound on his head was now
very painful, and he was altogether hot and feverish.

As the morning advanced, the mist got thicker and
more gloomy. Lieutenant Wharncliffe had stationed
a man at the mast-head on the look-out. This, however,
was almost useless, as he could hardly see further than
the end of the bow-sprit.

Accordingly he also ordered that the fog-bell should
be constantly rung, lest they should in the general
gloom, come into sudden collision with some vessel.

Towards five o'clock the wind, which had been light
and baffling all night, began to rise.

It was well on the starboard-beam, so Lieutenant
Wharncliffe gave orders to set the courses, topsails, jib
and spanker.

The topsails had been sheeted home, the jib set, and
the watch were boarding the main tack, when the man
on the look-out shouted " Sail ho ! "

" Where away ? "

" Starboard bow."

" What is she ?   Can you make her out ? "

" No, only her top-gallant sails—her hull is hid in the
mist; but by the squareness of their cut she's a large
ship, and an American."

Darcy Leigh now came hurrying on deck, and taking
a telescope, ran aloft to the mast-head. The look-out
was on the topsail-yard, but Darcy ascended, and did
not stop till he was seated on the royal-yard.

Then steadying himself by the halyards, he gazed in
the direction indicated.

He could distinguish a large ship looming through
the fog.

She appeared to be making right for them.

" Fire up," he shouted to Wharncliffe, " get the steam
up, fat on the fires; bear a hand," he shouted—" the
strange sail sees us, and is bearing right down."

By degrees the rising wind dispersed the mist, and he
could make out the rig of the stranger.

A large square-rigged steam vessel coming right down
on them.

By the smoke which poured from her funnel, it was plain she had her steam well up.

And now, from his elevation he can see her hull, and even her guns; for he saw at once that she was a ship of war.

Eighteen guns he counted on each side.

It was evidently a large first-class frigate, and a Yankee.

Yes! there could be no doubt of it, for although no flag was flying to denote her nation, Darcy's practised eye recognised at once one of the United States' cruisers.

He cursed his folly for having ordered the fires to be let down.

There was no help for it now, however, and they must make the best of it.

Slinging the telescope round his neck, he came down a back-stay, hand over hand.

Reaching the deck, he ran to the stoke-hole and shouted down,—

"Jupiter, Darby Kelly, fire up there like thunder—get the steam up, for here's Uncle Sam coming right down on us."

The men worked with a will, and dense volumes of smoke poured forth from the Spitfire's funnel.

"Oh, for twenty minutes," said Darcy, "or even a quarter of an hour, and we would show her our heels; but she'll be down on us before we can get a full head of steam up."

"What is she, Darcy?" asked Wharncliffe, approaching. "Can you make her out?"

"Make her out, yes, confound her; I make her out plainly enough. She's a United States' frigate, and will overhaul us in five minutes more."

"Where is she from?"

"I can't say—either from Baltimore or Charleston. If she's from Charleston, we can deceive her, as she must have started some days ago; but if she's from Baltimore, she may have heard by telegraph from New York last night, and run out to cut us off. Beat to quarters; we. must be prepared for the worst and fight like tigers."

The crew came tumbling up in wild excitement at the inspiring sound of the drums.

" Place a double guard over the prisoners, Mr. Wharn-cliffe—don't hesitate a moment to fire into them if they raise any disturbance."

All was excitement and confusion down the fore-hold. It almost seemed that the captives were about to make a rush and endeavour to retake the ship. Had they done so, whatever might have been the ultimate result, the attempt would have been most disastrous to themselves, for the four carronades would have made fearful havoc among their crowded ranks.

" Place the fore-hatch on," shouted Darcy Leigh, as he saw the frigate looming out of the mist, which had not yet quite dispersed.

It was done amid loud cries of dissatisfaction and rage from below. Still, however, no open resistance was made, although the noise, shouting, and confusion were great.

The stranger was now barely a quarter of a mile distant, and in five or six minutes would be alongside.

" Load with round shot and run out the guns," said Darcy.

CHAPTER XI.

A FEARFUL STRUGGLE.

It was done, and the starboard battery manned.

" Now, my lads," said Darcy, addressing them, " we will get away, if we can—if we can't we must fight like tigers, for, if taken, every man of us will go to the yard-arm. Oh! for ten minutes more," added he, " and we should be safe."

By this time the Spitfire began to tear ahead through the water at increased speed. Darcy knew, however, that to attempt flight before the steam was fully up would be sheer folly. They were going now about eleven knots, while the frigate, with full steam, was making thirteen or fourteen.

"How long before the steam's well up?" again shouted Darcy, down into the engine-room.

"Ten or fifteen minutes more will do it."

"How many pounds to the inch now?"

"Twenty-eight."

"Thirty-five will do it—the valve opens at thirty-eight —but with thirty-five or six we can show any ship in the navy our heels."

"Wharncliffe," he said to the second lieutenant, "if they know us, and what we are, we must fight; if they do not, we must gain time till the steam is up. It would be madness to attempt to escape at present."

"Ease her," shouted Darcy to the officer who had charge of the engines.

The stranger was now only a few hundred yards distant.

The frigate fired a blank gun, and hoisted the Stars and Stripes.

"Stop her," shouted Darcy, at the same time running to the signal halyards and hoisting the United States' flag in reply.

"What ship is that?" roared the captain of the frigate through a speaking trumpet.

"The United States' sloop-of-war Spitfire, Captain Hiram Squails. What ship is that?"

"The United States' steam-frigate Wabash, Captain Seth Peabody."

"Where are you from?"

"From Charleston to New York, with sealed despatches for Commodore Foote, of the North Atlantic squadron. Where are you from and bound to?"

"From New York, bound South, on a secret service."

The captain of the frigate made no reply for a minute, but consulted with one of his officers.

"Send a boat on board," shouted the captain of the frigate, again, through the trumpet; "I have despatches for Captain Hiram Squails."

"Ay, ay, sir," replied Darcy, as he leaped down from the mizzen-rigging.

" What will you do, Darcy ?" asked one of the officers.

" Clear away the long boat—bear a hand."

"The long boat," said Wharncliffe, in surprise, " are you going to send a boat, then ?"

" Yes—the long boat—bear a hand, and we will play them a trick, and make them a present of our prisoners. They are a desperate danger and encumbrance to us ; while, I dare say, Captain Seth, of the Wabash, will be glad of them."

The long boat was quickly got out, and brought round to the starboard quarter.

Meanwhile the stokers and firemen had laboured assiduously at their work, and the result was a roaring fire and a full head of steam.

Steam was already wasting by the safety valve, and orders were given by the officer in charge of the engineroom, to weight it down.

The Wabash was now lying to, broadside to broadside with the Spitfire, her head, however, being turned in an opposite direction.

While the boat was being got out, Darcy Leigh called some of the officers around him, and explained to them his plan. It was very simple, and if successfully carried out would at once rid them of a considerable embarrassment, and enable the Spitfire to escape. He proposed that the prisoners down the fore-hold should be offered the opportunity of embarking in the long boat. Then, when the last was in, the boat should be cast adrift, and the Spitfire should steam away at full speed.

Darcy calculated that it would be some minutes before the boat with her load could reach the Wabash to explain the true state of the case, while the captain and officers of the latter would be utterly confounded by the extraordinary and unaccountable manœuvre of the Spitfire. Ere they could recover from their astonishment, and learn the true state of the case, he calculated, with reason, that the sloop would be nearly a mile distant, and as under full steam she was faster than the Wabash by at least two knots an hour, they might laugh at all attempts to overtake them.

All agreed that this plan was both feasible and expedient. Now there remained but its execution.

No time was to be lost, as the Wabash was lying to, in expectation of a boat being sent on board. Darcy Leigh, having given all the necessary orders and stationed every man at his post, hurried forward to the fore hatch.

To the astonishment of the officers on guard, he, without a moment's hesitation, jumped on the ladder and was descending.

"Darcy, are you mad?" cried Wharncliffe, calling to him; "surely you are not going down among those fellows. You will be murdered, to a certainty."

"Lieutenant Wharncliffe," said Darcy, coolly, "I believe I am the captain of this ship; at all events, for the time. I know what I am doing. You attend to your duty on deck; rest assured I shall risk nothing without a sufficient motive."

So saying, the young officer coolly descended the ladder, and fearlessly walked right into the midst of the turbulent assembly of prisoners. The excitement among them was intense, as they knew that the United States' frigate was alongside, and they were waiting in expectation of hearing every moment the thunder of her guns.

"It is certain," thought Darcy, "that if an action once commenced, they would burst loose and endeavour to re-take the sloop."

A momentary lull ensued, when Darcy so boldly came in their midst.

They were struck with astonishment; they could not understand it. That the leader of the mutiny, who had seized the command of the sloop, and now kept the loyal part of the crew in subjection only by means of the carronades pointed down on them, that he, Lieutenant Leigh, should thus venture into the midst of them alone and almost unarmed, seemed so wonderful that they were lost in wonder.

A bold deed always finds sympathy, and even the oldest and most staunch Union tars could not but feel admiration at the cool effrontery with which the young officer stepped in their midst. Darcy gazed around him deliberately before he addressed them.

A murmur of discontent and anger succeeded the first lull.

"Give up the sloop," cried several. "Surrender her to the frigate; yes, yes, surrender her," shouted a dozen voices.

"Hurrah for the Union, and down with all traitors," said another.

This was succeeded by a suppressed shout.

Darcy raised his hand. "Silence, men," he cried, "and hear me." Instantly there was a dead silence; the most ardent among them were willing to hear what he had to say.

"Men," he commenced, "you know doubtless as well as I do what has happened. The United States' frigate Wabash is alongside of us, at scarcely fifty yards' distance."

"Yes, yes, we know it; surrender, and let us come on deck quietly," cried several.

A contemptuous smile played on the young officer's pale features.

"Surrender," he cried scornfully; "I swear to you men by all my hopes of Heaven, that sooner than surrender, the Spitfire shall be blown into a thousand fragments, for I will fire the magazine. Do not imagine, however, that I should do this except in the last extremity, for I value my life as highly as any man, although I value my honour higher."

"Pretty honour, to turn traitor to the flag you were bred and born under."

"Traitor—no—never. I never was, never could be a traitor," cried Darcy, passionately; "rebel I may be, I am, and I will be, until the Confederate States have achieved their independence, but not a traitor. That, however, men, is not the point in question. What I wish you to understand is this. We intend to fight the sloop to the very last gasp, and the very last man if we must. But I would willingly spare the carnage which must ensue. Consider the havoc that will be made among you down here, penned up like sheep for slaughter, for you must remember that the round shot and grape of the Wabash will do as fearful execution and more among you than among us, for we are not so closely crowded together. I wish to avoid this, and now offer you a fair chance. The long boat has been got out, and is now round at the port-gangway. It will take you all. We will allow you to go in peace; once in the boat all of you, we will cast off the painter and take our chance; you can then go on board the Wabash and report, if you please, that the Spitfire has been seized by the rebels, and is now a rebel steamer. Then the Wabash can give chase if her captain chooses. He, no doubt, in these stormy times, will be only too glad of having some hundred good seamen on his books, and you will exchange a prison under the Stars and Bars for comfort under the Stars and Stripes. Now, my men, what say you? there is no time to be lost, but bear these, my last words, in mind—when I leave here I go to lay a train to the powder magazine, and if we fight and are worsted, I will blow the sloop, you, and ourselves all to eternity together."

With these words Darcy turned, and made his way back to the fore-hatch. He had his foot on the ladder and was about ascending, when a tall Yankee behind, who had heard his last words, shouted,—

"Then you shall never leave here till you go on board the Wabash as a prisoner."

At the same moment he dashed away the ladder, and made a blow at Darcy with a handspike. The blow took effect on the young officer's shoulder, and felled him to the ground.

Not much hurt, however, he was up in an instant.

"Quick, Darcy, quick," shouted his friends above, who had gathered around the hatch in fear for his safety, and had heard and seen all, "jump for the combings of the hatch." At the same time a dozen pair of hands were extended down the fore-hold to assist him, could he but jump high enough to reach them.

Darcy, collecting all his strength, gave a leap, which fortunately enabled him to get a hold on the combings of the hatch.

The man who had knocked him down with the hand-spike now raised it to repeat the blow; had he done so it must have proved fatal, as, at the very least, if it did not descend on his head and kill him outright, it would cause him to relinquish his hold and fall back. Before, however, the blow could be delivered, one of Darcy's friends, levelling a pistol, fired, and the ball, striking the Yankee full in the chest, passed right through his body, wounding the man behind him. A dozen pair of hands grasped the young captain, and the next instant he was safe on deck.

This first pistol shot, however, was the signal for a general rising among the captives down the fore-hold.

On seeing the big Yankee sailor fall weltering in his blood, a general rush was made for the hatch. The ladder was raised and replaced, and arming themselves with whatever came to hand, they began pouring up with loud and threatening shouts. The first half-dozen or so were knocked on the head, and sent tumbling down by the defenders of the hatch; but regardless of this, others, urged on from behind, kept filling their places.

"Stand to the guns!" shouted the captain; "ready with the carronades, and fire when I give the word."

A desperate resistance was made by Darcy and his friends to the passage of the Yankees on deck. Laying about right and left with their cutlasses, many a brave fellow was tumbled down the hatch almost as soon as he reached the deck. Still, pressed on by those behind, and encouraged by their wild shouts, a constant succession kept mounting the ladder, till at last a footing was gained on the deck. Some eight or ten had made good their passage, and stood together defending themselves as best they could against Darcy and his friends, who used all their efforts again to force them down the hold.

This would have been accomplished easily enough, had it not been for the numbers who still kept forcing their way up, and blocking the way.

These latter kept our friends' hands full; nor could they, with all their efforts, prevent a part of them from gaining the deck, and joining their friends.

The situation had now become critical. Hitherto, by Darcy's orders, neither the carronades nor, indeed, with the one exception, pistols were used. Now each moment added to the strength of the Yankees who had gained the deck. Some of them had found arms below, while others had snatched cutlasses from their opponents. Already they were in possession of the fore-part of the hatch, and, still keeping their communication open with the ladder, so that their friends below might join them, they began to range themselves in a body about the foremast.

There were now quite twenty on deck, and every moment added to their number. As the Yankees swarmed up from below, cutlasses and handspikes descended on their heads and bodies, in some instances causing them to fall back. But in the great majority of cases, even when wounded, they were forced onwards by the pressure from below, and gained the deck wounded and bleeding, but burning with rage.

The critical moment had come.

Darcy Leigh had hitherto forbore to use the carronades. Now, however, it must be done, or they would inevitably fall into the enemy's hands, who had made good their footing on the deck. Some of them, too, jumped on the bulwarks and in the rigging, and commenced shouting and signalling to the Wabash.

We have already stated that the carronades were placed on each side of the hatch, with their muzzles pointing down. But the Yankees had already possession of all the fore part of the hatch, and encouraged by success, now attacked the men in charge of the guns with cutlasses, of which they had found a plentiful supply in the fore part of the ship.

No time was to be lost. Nearly forty men had now gained the deck; the other sixty would soon follow, if they were not decisively checked. The carronades were in danger, several of their defenders having been wounded.

Darcy jumped on a gun and surveyed the scene.

Pale, stern, and determined, he shouted, "Ready with the carronades?"

"All ready, sir," answered one of the gunners, warding off a cutlass cut from one of the Yankees.

For one moment the young captain paused; he thought of the horrid carnage that must ensue, and hated to give the order. He remembered that the men who, if he said the words, would the next moment have the horrid grapeshot tearing through their crowded ranks, were his countrymen, his shipmates; they had served under the same flag for years, and many of them were personally known to him.

He thought of this, and hesitated.

But then, he thought again of the brave men who had cast in their lot with him. He remembered that were they captured, they as well as he would be certainly shot or hanged.

The next moment he saw a dear friend and brother officer, Lieutenant Hamblin, struck down by a blow from a cutlass.

He lay where he fell, so Darcy knew that he was either dead or desperately wounded.

"On their heads be it," muttered Darcy, pale as death, with the perspiration breaking forth on his forehead. "Ready with the carronades!"

"All ready, sir."

One more second he hesitated.

"Why don't you send your boat on board?" shouted a voice from the Wabash impatiently; "what's the matter on board you?"

"Fire!" shouted Darcy, without replying.

Bang! rush! crash! Bang! rush! crash! The carronades were fired in rapid succession.

First came the roar of the discharge, then the hurtling

rush of the iron hail, and the crashing and splintering of timber.

Then succeeded the most dreadful sound of all—the shrieks and cries of the dying and wounded wretches below.

Once again was heard the loud report, followed by the rush of the grape, the splintering of timber, and the terrible groans and cries of the wounded.

The carnage below was fearful—some fifty or sixty men were massed together right under the muzzles of the pieces. At the first discharge a great number were mown down, for the most part horribly mutilated by the grapeshot. At the second, as many more shared the fate of their comrades; and of all the sixty men who a few seconds before were alive and well in the forehold, there remained scarcely twenty—the rest were killed or wounded by the murderous discharge of grape.

"Lay aft, every man of you," shouted Darcy; "lay aft there—leave the guns—never mind them."

He himself set the example, and hastened aft behind a barricade of water-barrels, hen-coops, &c., which he had caused to be erected across the deck abreast of the mainmast. The men at the word of command hastily left the forehold and the now useless carronades, and hastened to place themselves behind the barricade.

Then they armed themselves with ship's rifles, and commenced firing into the Yankees forward; for their blood was now up, and they thought no more regretfully of old days, or of their shipmates, whom they were now slaughtering.

Meanwhile, immediately after the terrible discharges of grape among them, the survivors down the forehold rushed on deck, horrified at the dreadful scene below and most of them spattered with the blood and brains of their companions.

It was indeed a horrible sight.

Below, in the forehold, lay some forty dead, wounded, and mangled men. Their cries and groans filled the place, and issued with horrid distinctness up the fore-ld. The deck below was slippery with blood—the

F

very beams and bulkheads were spattered with gore; torn and splintered in every direction by the rushing grapeshot.

Horribly grotesque, too, were the survivors of that slaughter; their white "jumpers," or jackets, and trousers were all smeared with the blood which had spattered around, while in many cases their features were utterly unrecognisable, by reason of the crimson splashes which covered them.

There were still between sixty and seventy—the survivors of those below when the carronades were fired and those who had previously gained the upper deck. Although they had no firearms, and but for the presence of the frigate could easily have been overpowered, yet, as circumstances were, they were extremely dangerous, for it would be impossible to fight the guns with some sixty or seventy enemies at large on the deck.

Some of the Yankees now jumped into the rigging, and commenced signalling and shouting to the Wabash. "Fire into her aft!" shouted one who seemed to take the lead, "the sloop's been seized by rebels—fire into her!"

But the Wabash was just at such a distance that the unaided voice could not be heard.

Darcy Leigh smiled scornfully, and seizing a speaking-trumpet, he jumped on a gun and hailed the Wabash.

"Wabash, ahoy!"

"Hillo."

"My men are in a state of mutiny. Fire into the fore part of the sloop with grape or musketry!"

No answer.

Darcy was in doubt for some moments whether his move was successful, and the officers of the Wabash still in ignorance of their real character, or whether they were discovered.

Soon, however, his doubts were dispelled, for a party of marines appeared on the forecastle of the Wabash, and commenced a rapid irregular fire on the Yankees who were grouped forward on board the Spitfire. At the same time a brisk fire was kept up from behind the barricade, so that between the two, the Yankees were being helplessly slaughtered.

The bullets whistled among them, and they kept falling one by one as man after man was hit.

"Surrender!" shouted Darcy, "every man of you, or I'll fire into you again with grape."

So saying, he pointed to two more carronades, whose muzzles protruded from the barricades, completely commanding all the fore-part of the deck.

The Yankees who had jumped in the rigging in the vain hope of giving the alarm to the frigate, had now all got down, and were crouching under the bulwarks or behind anything they could discover for shelter from the bullets of both friends and foes.

The Wabash and the Spitfire had now drifted by the force of wind or current, so as to be at a considerable distance apart.

The captain of the Wabash shouted through his speaking-trumpet.

"Steam up alongside of us, and I'll send a boarding party on board."

"Aye, aye, sir," answered Darcy readily; then turning to his first lieutenant, he said, "They have not the least suspicion yet; if we could only get the rest of these fellows in the longboat. Cease firing," he said to the men behind the barricade, who still kept blazing away wherever they saw an enemy's head or body. "Cease firing; we will give them another chance. If they refuse it, their blood be on their own heads."

"Stand by the carronades again; fire when I give the word, and then all of you charge forward and drive them overboard with cutlass and pistol."

Darcy leaped on top of the barricade.

"Forward there," he shouted.

The firing had now ceased, and one of the Yankees came out on the deck as spokesman.

"You see, my lads, what you have brought on yourselves, by refusing the offer I made you. One half of your number are weltering in their blood—they have perished miserably and uselessly—I now renew the offer

F 2

I made you before.   The longboat is at the port gangway—all who choose can get in it, and go on board the
frigate, or wherever you please.   Or, if you don't choose
to do that, you can go down the forehold again, leaving all
your arms on deck.   If you do not accept either of these
alternatives, I shall fire into you again, and kill or drive
you all overboard with sword, pistol, and cutlass."

The man who had come forward retired to consult his
comrades.

Meanwhile, Darcy gave the order down the engine-
room.

" Easy ahead," for he feared they might suspect something on board the Wabash, did he take no notice of
her captain's order to come alongside.

The screw slowly revolved, and the Spitfire forged
ahead.   Several of the Yankees now came forward, and
declared their willingness to go in the longboat.   Darcy
at once gave them permission to do so, and cast her off
whenever they chose.   The men took the message to
the rest, who were still hiding from the bullets which
they expected every moment to hear whistling about
their ears.   Sullenly and gloomily they came forth, and
passing round to the port side got into the longboat.

Resistance, or any attempt at treachery, was hopeless,
for the whole length of the deck on each side was commanded by the carronades aft, and at least twenty rifles
protruded from the barricade, in case of an attempt.

As soon as the last man was in the boat, Darcy gave
the word,—

" Cast off the painter."

This done, the longboat was adrift, and they were
freed from their dangerous prisoners.

" Go ahead, full speed," was the next order.

The great engines groaned and crashed.   The screw
tore through the water, making the water boil and foam
furiously at her stern, and the Spitfire dashed ahead.

The moment that the longboat was clear of the ship
they got the oars out and pulled for the Wabash, giving
a loud shout, and pointing to the Spitfire in order to call
the attention of the officers of the former.

CHAPTER XII.

WHAT THEY THOUGHT OF THE FIGHT ON BOARD THE
WABASH.

On first hailing the Spitfire, and receiving the reply neither the captain nor officers had the least suspicion that there was anything wrong.

They waited, accordingly, until a boat should be sent on board.

"They're rather slow about it, Mr. Tomlins," said Captain Peabody to his lieutenant; "I heard, too, that the Spitfire had the smartest men and the smartest officers of any sloop in the service."

"Yes," replied the lieutenant, "I sailed with Captain Squails some five years ago, and certainly then there was nothing to find fault with in smartness on board of his ship. We were on the Cuba station then, and I remember when in Havannah that we used to send top-gallant and top-sail yards down in some five or six minutes' less time than either the English or French men of war in the harbour."

"She's a fast boat, the Spitfire, ain't she?" asked the captain.

"Fast! they say she steams a knot an hour more than any other in the navy."

"By Jove!" said the captain, laughing, "she'd be just the thing for the rebels. If they only had her or any like her, couldn't they play the deuce with our commerce?"

"Well, there's not much likelihood, that's one consolation; for they have only about half-a-dozen vessels afloat, and those very old tubs, and not at all likely to overhaul yon clipper-sloop."

"Why what's going on on board her?" said the captain, taking up his telescope, and looking through it at the sloop. "There seems a great deal of confusion and bother, and her upper deck is quite crowded."

He handed the glass to the lieutenant.

The latter took a long look.

" Why, as I live," he said, " they've got two of the car-ronades forward, and an armed party guarding the fore-hatch. There's been a mutiny, a drunken row, or some-thing, I suppose, and Captain Squails thought it better to make all safe."

" Yes," said the captain, taking another look at the glass, " there's been something unusual going on, that's certain. The officers seem to have formed a sort of barricade across the deck, so I suppose it was for the time something rather serious. By Jove! too, there's two of the carronades pointed forward from the barri-cade, and arms and ammunition lying all about the quarter-deck. There must have been a serious mutiny, but I suppose Captain Squails's prompt measures have put it down."

" Yes, if it had not been so," replied the lieutenant, " they would have asked for aid when we hailed them. Doubtless the mutineers are prisoners down the forehold, and the carronades and guard are to keep them in awe."

" Do you think I had better send a score or so of marines, and some blue-jackets on board, and offer them to Captain Squails in case he needs assistance ? "

" No, I think not; Captain Squails is a good officer; he knows what he is doing, and would not like to be in-terfered with. Depend upon it, if he wanted assistance he'd ask for it."

" I think you are right . . . . We shall have their boat on board directly, and learn all about it."

" Hallo, what's that ? " suddenly cried the captain. " It's a pistol shot, by jingo ! "

This was the shot which killed the big sailor, who was about again to strike Darcy with the handspike.

Both the captain and lieutenant of the Wabash leaped to their feet, and gazed anxiously at the Spitfire.

They saw the rush of the supposed mutineers up the fore-hatch—the efforts of the other party to keep them down—they could distinctly hear the shouts of the com-batants, and the clash of the cutlasses.

The captain of the Wabash was in a great state of excitement.

" Get the marines under arms on the main-deck," he
said, "and load and run out the big guns."

" We can't fire, sir," said the lieutenant, "we should
knock the sloop to pieces, and kill friends as well as the
mutineers. We had better wait a few minutes and see
the result. I feel sure that Captain Squails has taken
sufficient precautions to discomfit them, otherwise he
would have asked for aid."

" Well, perhaps you are right," said the captain. "At
all events, get the marines under arms, and boarding
parties in readiness. If the worst comes to the worst,
we can run the frigate alongside, and rescue her from
the mutineers by boarding her."

The lieutenant left to execute the orders, and Captain
Peabody remained, anxiously watching the result of the
fierce conflict going on.

" By Jove !" he cried to the lieutenant, who had
now returned, "the mutineers seem to be getting the
best of it. They are forcing their way up in numbers. The officers and the loyal crew seem to be driven
back."

Snatching up the speaking trumpet, he hailed the Spitfire.

" Why don't you send your boat on board? What's
the matter on board you ?"

Scarcely were the words out of his mouth than he
heard the report of the carronades in quick succession.
There was a moment's silence, and then there swelled
upon the air the fearful shrieks and groans of the
wounded and dying.

" Good God !" exclaimed the captain, " there must be
an awful slaughter going on. That discharge must have
taken terrible effect, to judge by the cries of the wounded
men."

" I thought I was right," said the lieutenant, somewhat exultingly. " I thought Captain Squails had made
his preparations, and that he had a pill in store for
these mutineers. He's spared them as long as he could;
but he's a man who once roused will show no mercy."

Then the crew of the Wabash saw the officers and

those of the men whom they supposed to be loyal run aft, and intrench themselves behind the barricade. Next they saw the survivors rush up from the fore-hatch covered with blood, and join their comrades.

"It must have been quite a serious mutiny," said the captain. "Why there must be fifty or sixty mutineers forward, and God knows how many perished from the fire of the guns just now."

Then they saw some of the mutineers leap in the rigging, and heard voices shouting something, the sense of which they could not catch.

Next moment they heard Darcy Leigh through the speaking trumpet, requesting them to fire into the fore part of the Spitfire.

The marines were all under arms. The captain gave orders for them to station themselves on the fore-castle and open fire. Their fire was followed by a spattering discharge from behind the barricade on board the sloop, and soon not a man was to be seen forward.

The supposed mutineers had fled for shelter from the bullets of friends and foes. Next, the firing on the sloop having ceased, they saw an officer leap up on the barricade, and knew by his gestures, although they could not hear him, that he was addressing the men forward. They saw one of the number come forward as spokesman, listen to what the officer said, and then return, as if to consult his companions.

A few moments later a strange commotion was observed on board the sloop, and the mutineers seemed to be crowding round to the larboard side, where they disappeared one by one.

"I wonder what's up now," said the captain.

The next moment they see the sloop move slowly ahead, and the longboat appears under her stern. In a very short space of time the Spitfire is dashing through the waves under a full head of steam. The group of officers on her quarter deck watch for the moment when the longboat should reach the Wabash, and the true nature of the vessel become known.

"I say, Darcy," said one to the young captain, "won't

they be taken aback, when they hear on board the Wabash what a prize they have let slip?"

Darcy Leigh smiled triumphantly.

"Stand by the signal halyards, one of you, and be ready to haul down the Yankee flag and hoist the Stars and Bars." A seaman hastened to obey, and all again turned their attention to the Wabash. They saw the boat pass under her stern and disappear.

They knew that she was alongside, and next moment they heard a shout on board the frigate and saw a hurrying to and fro on her decks, which told them that the real character of the Spitfire was now known.

"Down with the Stars and Stripes," cried Darcy Leigh, "and up with the other."

Next moment the Union flag came down, and the audacious ensign of treason and rebellion floated in its place. A shout of rage from the crew of the baffled Wabash, was answered by a shout of defiance from the Spitfire, Darcy himself waving his cap and leading the cheer.

The Wabash was at this time with her stern towards them, so that, until she was brought round, she could neither fire at them nor give chase. But they perceived that she was now under full steam, and was hastening to wear round. This, however, was an operation which took several minutes, and by the time she had her broadside to bear they were more than a mile apart.

No sooner was the Wabash fairly broadside than she delivered her fire at the flying sloop. The roar of the guns was succeeded by the rush and howl of the shot as it tore through the rigging overhead, doing sore damage.

"Too high," cried Darcy Leigh, joyfully, "and we shall be pretty well out of range before she can bring her other broadside to bear on us."

However, the Wabash did not attempt it, but as soon as her head was brought to bear on the Spitfire, she gave chase under full steam, firing at the same time her bow gun. This latter was a large Dahlgren gun, throwing a hollow shell of great weight.

The first shot from this roared through the air high over head. Then after a minute or so came another. This last struck the sea about a quarter of a mile astern of the Spitfire, and after splashing and ricochetting several times, it plunged into the water, about twenty yards on the starboard quarter.

This was getting serious. It was evident that they would soon get the correct range, and if not by that time at a safe distance, the big Dahlgren shells would create fearful havoc.

"Fire up, down the stoke hole," shouted one of the rebel officers; "fat on the fire, and fasten the valve down if she wastes steam." This was done, and the Spitfire tore ahead at increased speed.

The next shot from the Wabash plunged into the water only a few feet from her stern, sending the spray over the group of officers on the quarter deck. It was evident that they had got the range, and although in another quarter of an hour they would be in comparative safety, still in that time a chance shot might cripple them.

Again the big bow gun sounded forth from the pursuing frigate; this time, however, the shell fell further astern.

"Bravo!" cried Darcy, joyfully, "we are getting out of range."

The next moment, however, another shell came howling through the air, and plunged into the fore part of the vessel, killing several men, and bursting close to the foremast.

The terrible explosion of this big shell was followed by dense volumes of smoke, and sheets of flame. "Fire!" was now the cry. The sloop was on fire.

Fortunately the hose was attached in readiness to the auxiliary engine, and steam being turned on, a torrent of water was poured down the fore-hatch to the seat of the fire.

Meantime, while the crew are combating with this dreadful enemy, shot after shot came roaring through the air, now plunging into the water astern, now tearing through the rigging overhead.

Darcy Leigh looked anxious. Another successful shot would certainly be most disastrous—might be fatal. With all their exertions it was with the greatest difficulty they could keep the fire under. In spite of the torrents of water thrown by the hose, the flames still roared and crackled, and the smoke ascended in dense volumes.

Ten minutes' hard work, however, produced some effect, and the flames decreased. One more shot struck the fugitive ship, but fortunately, instead of bursting on deck, it passed right through the bows, exploding harmlessly in the sea.

Minute by minute the distance between the two vessels increased, and the firing from the Wabash became less and less accurate, the shots sometimes falling nearly a quarter of a mile astern, and others plunging harmlessly into the sea, on the starboard or larboard side. In five minutes more they ceased to fear the shells from the frigate, as every one fired fell further and further astern.

The fire, too, thanks to the unflagging exertions of the officers and crew, was finally got under, and the Spitfire dashed ahead in a fair way to make good her escape.

The Wabash was now more than two miles astern, and was rapidly losing ground. Still, "a stern chase is a long chase," and it would be many hours before they could distance their pursuer.

Unfortunately, too, the bottom of the Spitfire was very foul; had it been clean, she would have steamed at least a knot an hour faster. It was now nearly nine o'clock in the forenoon, and they could not hope to get out of sight of their pursuer before four or five in the evening.

But now that they were fairly out of range, Darcy Leigh called a council of war to decide on their course of action.

Orders were given to attend to the wounded and dying, of whom many were still in the forehold, and to wash down the decks, which were horribly slippery with blood, also to sew up the dead in sailcloth and commit them to the deep.

The Spitfire was now steering S.E., a course which would take her clear out into the Atlantic. The wind, which at first blew a moderate breeze from the NN.E., was rapidly freshening; the sea, too, was rising, while the fall of the mercury in the barometer, and the heavy threatening banks of clouds to windward, betokened an approaching gale.

In anticipation of the approaching storm, the royal and top-gallant yards were sent down on deck, the big guns were securely lashed, the ballast examined to see there was no danger of its shifting, and all was made snug.

One of the younger officers remained on deck for this purpose, while Darcy Leigh, Wharncliffe, and the others descended into the cabin to hold a council.

A chart was spread out on the table before them, and her present position was pricked off according to the dead reckoning. Darcy Leigh was at the head of the table, on his right was Lieut. Wharncliffe, and the others stood or sat about as they pleased.

After consulting the chart for some time, and calculating by the aid of the entries in the log-book the course and distance made, Darcy Leigh spoke—

" It now becomes a question, gentlemen, as to our immediate course of action. At present we are steaming S.E., which will take us clear out to sea. We are, I calculate, in lat. 39 deg. N., long. about 71 deg. 10 min. W By continuing our present course we shall run right out into the Atlantic, crossing the gulf-stream."

" The question is, whether that course is advisable ?"

" Why not run right for Charleston harbour and make a dash in ?" suggested Wharncliffe.

" Yes," said another; " we have been so far successful, why should we not make a dash for it ?"

" Why ?" said Darcy, " because they will be on the look out for us ; the offing will swarm with cruisers, and we should, to a certainty, be captured did we attempt it now. No, gentlemen, I am as willing as any of you for

a bold stroke when it is necessary, and there is a fair
chance of success; but in this case I see only certain
failure, and I strongly protest against it."

"What then do you propose?" asked one; "let us
hear your plan; we must all acknowledge that hitherto
your arrangements have been admirable."

Darcy mused for a minute in silence before he answered.

"We are now, as I said before, steering S.E. I propose that we keep on that course till evening, and then
alter it to S. by E. We are short of coal, and must reserve some to run in; therefore I propose that, as by the
evening we shall, if all goes well, have run out of sight
of the frigate, we let the fires down, hoist up the screw
and set sail, steering S. to E., or SS.E. for five, six, or
seven days. If the wind holds in its present quarter, by
the fourth day from this we shall be in about lat. 33 deg.
N., nearly the latitude of Charleston, and in long. 70
deg. W., or thereabouts. Charleston is in west long. 80
deg. This would give us a course and distance a little
over 500 miles due west.

"All being in readiness, we might run down these 500
miles of longitude in two days and a half. By that time
it is probable that the vigilance of the United States'
cruisers will have somewhat relaxed, as it will be imagined,
from our non-appearance, that we have made for some
other port. We must so arrange as to make the light
during the night, and watch an opportunity to run in.
If we pass through the blockading squadron unseen, well
and good. If, however, we are discovered, and cannot
succeed in again deceiving them, we must make a running fight of it, and get in as best we can. The Spitfire
is very fast, and as we shall have a full head of steam,
we shall probably succeed, although we may be roughly
handled in running the gauntlet. That is my plan, gentlemen, unless the chapter of accidents supplies us with
a better."

Darcy Leigh then resumed his seat, and waited for the
opinions of the other officers. After some discussion
and deliberation, his plan was unanimously adopted.

Then definite appointments were made of lieutenants, mates, and subordinate officers.

Darcy Leigh was unanimously confirmed as captain, Wharncliffe was first lieutenant, George and Saxon Gainford, brothers, respectively second and third lieutenants, Julien de Brissa, a New Orleans French Creole, sailing master, and Edward Carew, captain of marines ; this last post was somewhat of a sinecure, for there was not a marine on board. It was not conferred without a reason, however; for Darcy Leigh at once decided on training some of the sailors to act in concert and with discipline till such time as they could obtain substitutes. Carew had been educated at West Point Academy, and had also been in command of marines, so that he was well fitted for the post. The other officers were all ranked as supernumerary lieutenants with equal rank.

The captain and officers then went on deck. The order was given to beat to quarters, and the men were summoned aft on the quarter-deck.

A list of their names was taken, and then the muster roll was called over. It showed a crew of eighty seamen, all of whom could be depended on. Besides these, there were about twenty firemen and stokers, and about twenty others whose good faith in the rebel cause could not be depended upon.

As each man's name was called, he was asked if he were willing to take the oath of allegiance to the Government of the Confederate States. With few exceptions all assented to this without hesitation.

" And now, my lads," said the captain, addressing them, " I have to inform you of the terms on which you will serve, subject to the approval of the Confederate Government, of which I think there can be no doubt. All prize money, or the money proceeding from the sale of prizes, will be distributed in the following proportions :—one-third will go to the officers, the other two-thirds will be divided among the crew in equal portions. The articles of war will be the same as those of the United States' navy, with which you are all familiar. In case of mutiny, insubordination, or refusal to obey orders, the penalty will be strictly, unmercifully enforced—that penalty will be death. Should any man leave the vessel for the purpose of deserting, he will, on re-capture, be condemned to death, which sentence will be immediately carried into execution. There will be few if any minor punishments, except such as disrating, pay stopping, &c. Flogging shall be unknown; if a man commits an offence worthy of the lash, he is worthy of death : and under no circumstances shall flogging be resorted to while I am in command. Although this code may seem somewhat severe, it is necessary, for the safety of all, that the slightest attempt at mutiny or treachery be at once crushed. As you are aware, we are fighting with ropes round our necks ; therefore it is the more necessary that we, at the first attempt of the kind, purge ourselves at once and for ever of traitors."

As the young captain spoke these last words, he fixed his eyes on those among the men whom he suspected of discontent and lukewarmness. All of these quailed before that calm, cold glance, and saw that, should they be tempted to rebel, they might expect no mercy.

" Then," said he, " as to petty officers, boatswain, boatswain's mates, quarter-masters, gunners, captains of the top, &c., I leave to yourselves the election, subject to the approval of myself and officers. And now, my lads, I have no more to say, so let us give three cheers for our new flag and our new country."

A loud cheer broke from the sturdy sailors. " One cheer more for Captain Darcy Leigh," shouted one of them. And a hearty cheer rang out on board the Spitfire.

Then all dispersed, the watches were set, and the watch below retired to their hammocks, while the watch on deck were employed in various ways about the hull and rigging. It was now past noon, and the Spitfire had so far distanced her pursuer that the latter was almost hull down.

The wind now hauled a little more aft, so the top-sails, courses, jib, and spanker, were bent and set, and the vessel healed over to the breeze, and dashed through the foaming waves with increased speed.

A full head of steam was still kept on, and with the assistance of the sails, she was going a good fourteen knots. At this pace a very few hours would suffice to place her beyond danger of capture, and officers and crew congratulated themselves on the successful issue of the enterprise.

CHAPTER XIII.

"ALL IS LOST!"

DARCY LEIGH is seated with his first lieutenant on a hencoop near the binnacle. He has a glass in his hand, with which he occasionally takes a look at the Wabash, whose white topsails and top-gallant sails are now discernible astern.

Occasionally he looked anxiously to windward, where heavy banks of clouds are still gathering. The scud flies rapidly overhead, and the mercury keeps still falling. It is evident there is to be a severe gale; minute by minute the wind increases in violence; gust after gust breaks on the vessel, causing her masts and yards to crack and groan, and heeling her over till her bulwarks are almost under water.

The sky overhead gets blacker and more gloomy every minute, and the rising waves are tipped with foam, which give them, in the distance, the appearance of a cast sheet of snow.

"How are the sails, Mr. Wharncliffe? It's the best suit that we have bent, is it not?"

"Yes, the sails will stand the hardest blow we are likely to have; but the maintopmast is not to be depended on. It would be awkward for it to go by the board; some of the rigging might foul the screw, and then, with the Wabash behind us, we should be in a pretty fix."

Darcy Leigh, who was attentively watching the frigate astern, suddenly exclaimed,—"There goes her foretopgallantmast, by Jove! I thought she was carrying on sail pretty stiffly for this breeze."

He handed the glass to Wharncliffe.

"No," said the latter, "the mast is safe enough; it's the yards that have gone in the stays."

"Take a reef in the topsails, Mr. Wharncliffe," said the captain, decisively; "let them carry on sail, if they like. We can't afford to strain the sloop, and risk losing our masts."

Before giving the order, Wharncliffe took another look at the frigate. "Why, may we never see Charleston," he said, "if they haven't sent another top-gallant yard aloft, and are setting the sail."

"They are determined to crack on canvas, it seems. No matter; let them take the sticks out of her if they choose, we'll have a reef in, and make all snug. Wharncliffe, send forward, and give the order."

This being done, the ship's head was brought round more to windward. In the gloom of twilight the Wabash could just be distinguished astern. In half an hour's time darkness hid her from their sight, and the Spitfire laboured ahead in her new course.

As night wore on, the wind rose, blowing sometimes in sudden and furious gusts, so as almost to lay her on her beam-ends. The barometer was steadily falling, and the sky gave every appearance of a hard and prolonged gale. The wind howled, moaned, and shrieked among the cordage; the waves rushed and roared, as driven by the wind, they rose in vast mounds, and rolling on with great white crests, swept by in ceaseless array.

At the first dawn of day Darcy came on deck, and surveyed the scene. It was, indeed, one of grandeur and awe—one which the sailor often sees, but which never loses ought of its grandeur from familiarity.

Although the young commander could not but be struck by the wild and terrific beauty of the storm, he did not waste time in idle gazing. He saw in a very few seconds that the worst had not yet come—that a terrible gale was pending.

Accordingly he gave orders for the top gallant-masts to be sent down on deck, and the top-sails close-reefed.

This was soon done, and the Spitfire now plunged on her way under three close-reefed topsails, reefed fore sail, and fore topmast staysail.

The wind howled and roared with increasing fury, and the great seas, which were rapidly rising, began to dash themselves over her and flood her decks.

Darcy Leigh gave orders that everything on deck should be well secured—water casks, boats, and all other objects which might, by the violent pitching and rolling of the ship get adrift. The great guns, too, were secured by double lashings, and the state of the ballast in the hold inspected.

Darcy gazed with some misgiving on the big guns on the main deck. The Spitfire was hardly sufficiently ballasted, and showed a slight tendency to be top-heavy.

" Shouldn't wonder if we are obliged to throw some of the guns overboard before another day breaks," he muttered to himself; " the vessel strains and rolls fearfully even now."

And so in truth she did, her masts groaning and cracking, and the lee-bulwarks being quite submerged as she rolled over after the passage of each big sea. Still the gale kept increasing in fury.

Presently, with a loud report, the foresail splits right across. For a minute there is heard the thrashing and flogging of the torn canvas, and then there remains nothing of the sail but the bolt-rope.

The foretopmast-staysail quickly follows suit, and now the Spitfire is under her three close-reefed topsails only. The sailors gaze over the weather bulwarks in face of the blinding spray, with serious and gloomy countenances.

There is nothing encouraging in what they see ; the sky—the sea—all looks dark and threatening. The vessel, too, is labouring and rolling so fearfully, that it is with difficulty they can keep their feet.

Darcy Leigh and Wharncliffe are standing together, holding on by the mizzen-rigging.

Darcy gazes anxiously at the canvas aloft, now strained to the utmost pitch.

"Something must go presently," he says to his lieutenant, "rope, canvas, or mast."

"The rope and canvas are both new, and the masts are good. They'll stand a deal before they go yet."

"Well, they must stand it," replied Darcy, "for it would be ridiculous to attempt taking in sail while it blows such a hurricane. The men could not get aloft, let alone handle the sails."

As Darcy expected, the gale increased in fury hour by hour, till it blew so tremendously hard as almost to lay the ship on her beam ends. With her heavy top weight of guns this was most perilous; a sudden gust might at any moment heel her right over beyond the power of recovery. The noise of the wind and waves was such that it was now impossible to hear one another's voices unless shouted in the ear.

Suddenly a furious gust struck the vessel; with a terrible groaning and creaking she lurched over—over—over still she went, as if she were going to capsize. A cry of horror arose from the crew.

Over she heeled under the tremendous pressure of the wind, till her lee bulwarks were right under water; for a moment the wind lulled, and she righted slightly. Darcy hoped that the fury of the squall had passed; he was mistaken, for once again it burst on the unhappy bark with increased rage, and again she heeled over, her timbers and masts groaning and creaking fearfully.

This time she went over till her lee yard-arms were in the water, and she lay right on her beam ends.

To Darcy's dismay, too, he discovered that the ballast, which was of gravel, had shifted. Their situation was now most critical; if she did not right, all would soon be over with them, for the water was pouring into her from a dozen different places.

Presently the fury of the squall passed, and everybody looked anxiously for the ship to right herself. But no, she still lay helplessly on her beam ends. Each moment made her position worse, for the water was pouring in fast. Darcy gazed first at the mizen-mast, with all its belongings of yards, rigging, and sails, and then at the lee yard-arm buried in the water.

"Stand by to cut away the mizzen-mast!" And two men with axes jumped into the weather main chains.

Darcy hesitated to give the word which would send the beautiful tapering spar crashing into the sea; but, glancing to windward, he there saw that another squall had gathered, and was coming down upon them. There was no time to be lost.

"Cut away the mizzen-mast."

Crash! The two axes descended simultaneously, each on one of the strained lanyards of the shrouds.

No sooner was the first lanyard severed, than the others were carried away one after another of their own accord; and the mast itself, without requiring a blow, broke short off to the deck, and fell, with all its yards, sails, and rigging, into the sea to leeward.

It took a few minutes to clear the ship of the wreck, by cutting away all the ropes which connected it.

Then all watched anxiously for the ship to right herself. But, alas! she did not. And now another squall burst on her with even greater fury than the last, bringing her still deeper in the water.

Alarmed at the dangerous and critical position of the ship, Darcy Leigh gives the word to cut away the mainmast also.

He himself seized an axe, and jumped into the main chains. A very few blows succeeded in sending the mainmast over the side to keep company with the mizzenmast already gone. When the squall passed over, the Spitfire, with only her foremast standing, slowly began to right herself.

Scarcely, however, had she begun to do so, when another and still more furious gust burst on the devoted ship, and once again she is on her beam-ends, this time heeling over far more than before.

"The foremast—We must cut away the foremast," shouted Wharncliffe, in Darcy's ear.

"No, no; we must keep the foremast at all hazards. it would be ruin to lose it—we should be a helpless wreck. Let some of the guns be thrown overboard instead."

Eight of the lee guns were soon thrown overboard. This produced the required effect, and when the squall passed over, the Spitfire slowly righted herself.

They found on sounding the well, however, that she had four feet of water in her hold. This spoke sufficiently as to their danger, and convinced all that nothing but Darcy's prompt measures had saved the ship, at all events, for the time. And now all hands are put to the pumps, in order to free her from water.

The storm had not yet reached its climax, and as evening approached the gusts increased both in frequency and fury, so that it was impossible for the men to stand at the pumps, and thus the water gained on them. Each time that the well was sounded there was found to be a rise of two or three inches.

Grog was freely served out. Darcy, himself, and his officers, took their turns at the pumps, exciting the men by their example. The men worked furiously, as desperate men only can work.

They knew that if once they let the water get the upper hand that all was lost, for as the water rose in the hold, of course the vessel sank and fresh leaks were exposed. Night closed in upon them, still pumping for dear life.

Darcy determined to set an example, and resolutely took his spell at the pumps, working till he was ready to drop with fatigue. Then and then only he would give up, and fall completely exhausted to the deck. He would lie for a few minutes, then, taking a copious draught of rum, he would again take to the pumps.

The men could not but admire the determination and pluck with which the young officer—so slight, so delicate-looking—took his share, aye, and more than his share of the work.

"By thunder! he's a plucky one, and no mistake," was the often muttered remark, as he would spring to his feet, and with encouraging shouts, join them in their dreary work.

If Darcy had before a hold on their feelings, he had now a hold on their hearts, for each hardy rugged seaman saw what he did and loved him for it.

Still the gale howled and roared in its fury, and still, in spite of all their efforts, the water gained on them, and the Spitfire sank deeper and deeper.

The strength of the men was fast failing, a few hours more of such work and nature must give in.

Suddenly Darcy gave the word, "Cease pumping."

The men stopped in surprise.

"Throw the guns overboard, every one," said Darcy; "it is our last chance."

In a very few minutes this was done, and the vessel greatly lightened. The top-weight being removed she strained and laboured far less, and consequently leaked less.

Then priming the men well with grog, Darcy set them the example, and for an hour they continued at the pumps with tremendous energy. At the expiration of that time the well was sounded; all waited in breathless anxiety for the result.

A shout of joy rang forth from the nearly exhausted men when they heard the carpenter's report. In that last hour they had gained six inches.

"Hurrah! my lads," said Darcy, "thanks to your strong arms and stout hearts, we have beaten the enemy; we have gained on the water, and the storm has spent its fury."

"No, no," shouted several, "thanks to you, captain; but for you we should have been at the bottom before now." Then one of the sailors gave the word, "Three cheers for Darcy Leigh."

A fresh allowance of grog was served out, and then, with renewed spirits and hopes, the pumps were once again manned.

By dark the water in the hold was so far reduced as to place the vessel beyond immediate danger. The pumps were kept going, but it was no longer necessary for all hands to work at them; the watch was sufficient to keep order and gain on the water.

The gale blew very hard all day, but towards evening it became evident that its force was spent. The barometer, too, began to rise slowly, and the sky did not look so threatening as on the previous day.

Altogether the officers were warranted in thinking that the worst of the danger was over. About midnight sail was made on the only remaining mast—the foremast—but with the close-reefed topsail only, she made but little headway.

The night was very dark, and the wind still blew violently in fitful gusts.

Darcy Leigh, who had been on deck for nearly forty hours, retired to his berth at midnight to snatch a little repose, for he was completely worn out by fatigue. During the night the watch were engaged in rigging a jury-mainmast at such times as they could be spared from the pumps.

Towards morning the wind again freshened up, and Lieutenant Wharncliffe, the officer in command, feared that the gale was about to recommence.

Fortunately, however, it was but the last gust of the expiring storm, and by four o'clock in the morning it blew only a moderate gale.

The sea still ran high, and the sky was dark and overcast. The weather was very thick and muggy, and nothing could be seen beyond a distance of a few yards.

And now another day begins to break, slowly revealing the cold grey sky, the heavy mist, and the broad expanse of sea tumbling and rolling unceasingly.

Wharncliffe, who has the watch, leaves the poop for a few minutes, and goes forward to the galley, in order to obtain a cup of coffee. He returns leisurely, and again ascends the poop. With a lazy yawn he is about to seat himself on a hen-coop, when his attention is suddenly attracted by a slight noise—the creaking of a spar.

He casts his eyes to windward, and a sight meets them which makes his heart stand still.

In the grey light of the morning he sees to windward —quite close—just emerging from the gloom of the mist, a large ship.

One glance is sufficient. She is so close that he can
see the muzzles of her guns—*it is the Wabash!*

Wharncliffe remained for a moment or two paralysed
—aghast with dismay.

He rushed down the companion ladder and hurried
to the cabin of Darcy Leigh.

The young officer slept a sweet calm sleep, after the
exertions of the last few days.

Lieutenant Wharncliffe laid his hand on his shoulder.

Instantly, Darcy, always a light sleeper, started to
his feet.

"What is it?" he asked. "Is anything the matter?"

"*All is lost! the Wabash is alongside!*"

CHAPTER XIV.

DEEP DESIGNS.

IN order that our story may be properly developed
and understood, it is now necessary that we return to
New York.

Lupus Rock and Webster K. Gayle are in earnest
conversation at the mansion of the latter.

"It must be so, Lupus—I see no other way for it.
I shall run a great risk of losing the plantations by confiscation if this rebellion is not crushed at once, and
certainly every day seems to give less hope of that.
Each day some new State joins the cause of Secession,
and the rebels get bolder and more defiant. Yes, certainly, that is the best, the only plan. You must get to
the South some way or another, and nominally, at least,
join their cause. I will give you documents assigning
the estates and plantations to you absolutely. Let me
see, though, to make it legal there must be some con-
siderations."

Webster Gayle paused for some time, and then
said—

"I tell you how I will arrange it, Lupus. I shall
have a deed of sale prepared, in which you are the buyer
for the sum of seven hundred and fifty thousand dollars,

We shall both sign it, and I will give you a receipt for the money. Of course, you know, it is merely a matter of form; for I do not believe you have seven hundred and fifty dollars, to say nothing of seven hundred and fifty thousand. Then you, having espoused the Southern cause, not necessarily actively, you know, the estates will be safe, and, at the same time, I shall not be compromised. Then, when the war is over, you can hand me back the deed, and things will be as before."

"And my reward for the risk, the imminent risk I run in this affair?" asked Lupus, fixing his cold grey eyes on his uncle's face.

"Ah, well—well—we'll talk about that another time."

"No," said Lupus, decidedly; "let us come to some definite arrangement now. What about my suit to my cousin Stella?"

Webster Gayle moved uneasily in his chair.

"Don't you think we had better leave that in abeyance for some time? Stella is proud and haughty, and were I to endeavour to force any one on her she would take an immediate aversion."

"I don't agree with you, sir; girls don't know their own minds. The girl likes me well enough; and you know when I consented to be the scapegoat in that slaver affair you promised her to me. I claim the fulfilment of that promise."

"But I cannot do impossibilities. If my daughter refuses to give you her hand I cannot force her."

"Force her—no; but means can be used to bring her to her senses—pressure can be put on in many ways. The girl is free; I never heard of her being entangled with any one else."

"No. I fancied at one time that she had a liking for that young rebel, Darcy Leigh; but he had a bullet through his head the other day, during that audacious affair of the Spitfire. Do you know, Lupus—I don't know whether you have noticed it—but I certainly fancy she has not been herself since. She never mentions his name, it is true, but there is something in her manner, a restlessness in her eye, which I never observed before."

"Well, it matters not now--the whelp's dead and overboard. Dead men tell no tales, and certainly dead men can't spoil sport by proving successful rivals to the living, more especially when, as in this case, the person in question has the father's sanction, is related by blood, and is, at least, passably good-looking."

There was something. inexpressibly self-sufficient, almost amounting to insolence, in the young man's tone to his uncle. It almost seemed as if Lupus Rock thought that Webster Gayle was either partially or wholly in his power.

The New York merchant noticed it, and, colouring, said—

"Lupus, you will oblige me by not speaking with such levity of my daughter."

"Indeed, I beg the fair lady's pardon," said Lupus, with a half sneer; "I am sure I had no intention of so doing—but here the lady comes."

Stella Gayle and her sister Angela entered the room.

"Good morning, fair cousins," said Lupus, rising and bowing obsequiously. "I trust, fair Stella, that you have not passed a bad night, though, by your pale face, I almost fear so. Surely the beautiful, proud, and fascinating Stella has no secret grief preying on her mind."

"If I had, Mr. Rock," said Stella, colouring angrily, "I should not select you as my confidant."

Lupus bowed in mock humility, and Webster Gayle, addressing his daughters, said—

"Stella, Angela, it is necessary that we remove at once to Washington. I shall be detained here for some days. You will proceed there at once under the escort of your cousin Lupus, and I will follow you in the course of a week at the latest."

"But cannot we wait until you go, papa?" asked Angela. "Is it necessary that we should go on first?"

"If it were not I should not desire you so to do. I have weighty reasons for sending you before me, into which I need not enter at present. Lupus," he said, to his nephew, "I will now go and have the necessary documents prepared at the lawyer's. I will leave you with your cousins. I suppose you are quite prepared to start to-morrow?"

"To-day, if you like," was the ready reply.

Webster Gayle then went out, leaving Lupus alone with the young ladies. There was a silence of some minutes.

Stella had seated herself on a couch, and was playing nervously with the tassels of the cushions, evidently ill at ease.

Angela was seated at the table, bending over a book of drawings, in which she was, or appeared to be, profoundly interested. Neither took the slightest notice of the presence of their cousin.

Lupus glanced frowningly from one to the other. Of late—especially since the affair of the Spitfire—this silent system of warfare, this continued but quiet system of slights, had vexed and annoyed him at times almost beyond bearing.

On the present occasion the desire to please his cousin struggled long with the desire to annoy and show his power. At last the latter won the day.

"And what may be the subject of Miss Stella Gayle's deep reverie?" he said, with a slight smile. "Is her mind busy with affairs of state—is it our glorious Union which engrosses my fair cousin's thoughts—or is it the colour of the ribbon for her next new bonnet? I need scarcely ask. At such a time the thoughts of so zealous a patriot are with her country. Is it not so, Stella?"

"It were well, Mr. Rock, if all daughters, and sons also, of our country were as devoted to her interests as myself, or "——

"Or as me, you would say."

"I have yet to learn," said Stella, in affected surprise, "that Mr. Lupus Rock is devoted to any interests but his own, or indeed to anybody or anything, with the exception of the 'almighty dollar.' "

"And Miss Stella Gayle," interrupted Lupus, bowing.

Stella was about to make a scornful reply, but at this moment her father again entered the room, and drawing Lupus Rock on one side, was soon in earnest conversation.

"The sooner the better," said Webster Gayle; "every hour's delay only increases the difficulty."

"And the papers—the double set of papers? Have you them ready?"

Webster Gayle glanced cautiously round to see that none overheard, and then producing a packet of papers, handed them to Lupus.

"These are the papers," he said. "One set accredits you to the rebel Government and generals as a staunch Secessionist; the other does the same to the Federal Government and officers. You must use the greatest caution, for should these double sets of papers fall into either Federal or Confederate hands they would involve both of us in disgrace and ruin."

"I have thought of that," replied Lupus Rock, producing from his pocket two small cabinets not unlike snuff-boxes in appearance.

"What have you there?" asked Webster Gayle, regarding the small boxes curiously.

Each of these small boxes was fitted with a false bottom, which Lupus Rock removed, and inserted one set of papers in each.

The interior of the boxes were fitted with wheels and springs, in appearance not unlike those of a musical-box.

Lupus, taking a small key from his pocket, proceeded to wind up these works. This done, he inserted a small iron tube, closed at each end, and placing it in a small groove, connected it with the machinery.

"There," he said, "now I think I have made all safe."

"How made all safe?" said Webster Gayle, in surprise. "I do not see what extra safety this manœuvre has given you. Surely, if you were seized as a suspected person, you do not imagine that the false bottom which conceals the papers would escape detection? No, it

would be at once discovered, and then your very life
would be in danger."

"Trust me," replied Lupus Rock, smiling confidently,
" I do not intend to be taken, and if I am, only one set
of papers will be found upon me, and those which are
favourable to the party in whose hands I may be ; for
observe the mechanism these tubes contain—the wheels
and springs ? "

" Yes, assuredly ; they seem to me to be musical
boxes, either out of repair, or purposely left imperfect."

" They are something far more dangerous and deadly.
You see these little tubes ? " he continued, placing his
finger on one ; " well, each of these contains about an
ounce of fulminating mercury, an explosive compound of
great power. Should I be arrested, I merely produce
one of these boxes—the one I wish to get rid of—and
touching a spring, throw it from me as far as possible.
The spring will set the clock-work in motion, and
after the space of about half a minute, a small hammer
will be liberated, which will explode the fulminating
mercury in the tubes, and blow the whole affair to
pieces. The explosion will be sufficient to destroy
every vestige of the papers ; and if any person, seeing
me throw the box from me, is foolish enough to pick
it up, it will, in exploding, inflict desperate if not fatal
injuries."

Webster Gayle recoiled in terror from the little
engines his nephew held.

" For Heaven's sake, be careful ! " he cried, in alarm.
" Don't play with them—they may explode, and blow us
all up."

" Oh, there is no fear. I have so arranged them that
they cannot explode unless I first touch the spring.
And now I am ready to start when you choose."

It was finally decided that Lupus should start with
his two cousins by the first train of cars in the morning.
They would arrive at Baltimore late that night, where
they would remain, and proceed on their journey to
Washington early on the following morning.

As soon as he had made all necessary arrangements,

and received the final instructions of his uncle, Lupus Rock left the house, and proceeded to the St. Nicholas Hotel, in Broadway.

Finding his way to the smoking-room, he seated himself by the side of a man who appeared to be expecting him.

"Well, sir," said this latter, "how is it—all right?"

"Yes—right—everything goes well—could not be better. We start for Baltimore and Washington to-morrow morning. You had better start at once, as it will not do for you to be seen with me."

"Well, I'm ready at a moment's notice. To-night or to-morrow is all alike to Malpas Thong; only look you here, Master Rock, I don't want no nonsense this time, for you know I've never been paid for that last affair of the slaver; and if it had not been for my hard swearing, it would have cost you pretty dear, as you well know."

"Well, well," said Lupus Rock, impatiently, "you know that you have not yet done all the work, and you cannot expect to be paid beforehand."

"That's all right enough, I daresay, but let's have a clear understanding, How much am I to have if we get this affair settled satisfactorily?"

"How much? Ten thousand dollars."

"Ten thousand dollars for an estate worth half-a-million. No, no, Master Rock, you must behave a little more liberally."

"Why how much, in Heaven's name, does the man want?" asked Lupus, angrily.

"How much? Well, I'll tell you," said the other; "I want twenty thousand dollars the day you get the estate; I want ten thousand more the day I put proofs in your hands that a certain lady is a slave."

"Look here, Thong," interrupted Lupus, "I have heard so much talk of this proof of yours, and seen you do so little, that I begin to doubt your power to prove what you say. Now let us have no more nonsense. Can you, or can you not, prove that by the law of the United States the girl I mean is a slave?"

"Certainly; her grandmother, though nearly white,

was a slave; and I can prove it. That is simple enough
—is it not?"

"Yes, simple enough if it is true; but you are
such an incorrigible ruffian and villain that there's no
believing what you say."

"I think, then, we're well met," replied the man, with
a sneer. "I may be bad enough, or may be good
enough, but, at all events, I ain't going to make my
fortune by betraying and ruining my relations. Webster
Gayle is nothing to me, though he is your uncle. An
affectionate nephew he's got, on my word, and yet you
talk about my being a villain and a ruffian; you, who
are going to have your mother's brother thrown into
prison, and take his property. Ah! bah! don't talk
to me in that way any more; we know each other too
well."

"I know," replied Lupus, passionately, "that I could
hang you if I chose."

The man turned white with passion at these words.

"Hang me, could you? and what of your own neck?
Don't you think you'd keep me company, because if you
don't I do; and I well know that on the day that
Malpas Thong swings, Lupus Rock will swing with him."

"I know nothing of the sort. You have no proof,
nothing but your word, and it is not likely that that
would be taken before mine."

"No proof, haven't I?" said the other; "just stoop
your head a little till I whisper a word or two in your
ear."

Lupus did so, and his companion muttered a few
words in a low tone.

Then he looked him in the face, and, with a smile of
triumph, watched the expression of rage and fear which
came over his handsome features.

"No proof, eh! what say you now, Master Rock?
You did not think that I had that little bit of information in the background, did you?"

Lupus Rock, calling for a glass of brandy, affected
to laugh it off, but it was apparent that he was ill at
ease.

" Come, come, Malpas, we don't want to quarrel.
We can both do each other too much injury to be
enemies."

" Well, I don't know but what you're right," replied
the other. "I don't want to quarrel, but I thought I
would show you that I know too much for you to try
any of your tricks on me."

" Well, well, you go on to Baltimore ; I will meet you
at the George Hotel on Thursday morning ; this is
Tuesday evening, and you can be there some time to-
morrow."

" All right ; and now what about money ? "

" Money ! why I gave you two hundred dollars but
yesterday."

After some further conversation, Lupus Rock arose,
and said to his companion,—

" You fully understand how you are to proceed,
Thong, in case any of the eventualities I spoke of were
to happen. It is not probable, but nevertheless we will
be prepared for all eventualities. Now, you will start
at once for Baltimore—you know when and where to
meet me."

So saying he left the room, followed by his worthy
associate.

CHAPTER XV.

A PAIR OF VILLAINS.—THE PLOT THICKENS.

THEY passed down the steps of the hotel together,
when Lupus giving a slight nod hurried away, casting
at the same time a glance around to make sure that he
had not been observed in such questionable company as
that of Malpas Thong.

But it so happened that, at the very moment he was
descending the steps of the hotel, a carriage passed, in
which was a fair lady, who, by the sudden start she
gave, appeared to recognise one or both of the two men.

" Could that have been that villain Malpas Thong, the
slave agent, slave driver, slave hunter ? " she asked her-

self. "I could almost swear to his figure and deport-
ment, although I was unable to see his face. And if so,
what business could Lupus Rock have with him?"

These questions which the young lady asked herself,
could not apparently be answered to her satisfaction, for
she looked troubled and anxious.

The young lady was Stella Gayle, who had taken advantage of the fine afternoon to go out for a drive.

In the evening, when, according to his wont, Lupus
Rock ascended to the drawing-room, and commenced de-
voting himself to the ladies, Stella suddenly said to her
cousin—

Mr. Rock, did I not see you in Broadway this afternoon, near the St. Nicholas Hotel?"

"Very probably," said Lupus carelessly.

Stella was silent for a moment, and then fixing her
eyes on his face, she said,—

"I wonder what has become of that man, that slave
agent, or whatever he was, who was formerly in papa's
service in some capacity or other?"

"What man?" replied Lupus.

"Thong, I think his name was."

Lupus Rock had great command of countenance, and
his glance never quailed for an instant before the searching eyes of his cousin.

"Really, Stella," he said, with a mocking laugh, "do
you suppose that it is part of my business to know the
whereabouts and the history, past and present, of all my
uncle's discharged servants?"

Stella knew her cousin well, and could read even his
well-dissembled thoughts better than he imagined. Nevertheless, he had some suspicion that the question was not
put to him without a purpose.

"Ah," he said, "I wonder whether my fair cousin
saw me speaking to him on the steps of the St. Nicholas?"

He shot an inquiring glance at her from his keen eyes,
but could discover nothing from the calm, beautiful features of the young lady.

Stella Gayle turned carelessly away.

"Ah," she said to herself, "it was then this man Thong with whom I saw him talking. Some villany or other is afloat, doubtless. I wonder whether he was discharged from my father's service in reality, or whether it was merely a blind. If he were really dismissed in disgrace, what should Lupus Rock, in whom my father reposes complete confidence, be doing with him? And if he were not, why should the pretence have been made? It is a tangled skein, and I have a foreboding of evil from this man."

Leaving the young lady to her reflections, let us return for a brief space to the subject of them.

On leaving the hotel, he passed up Broadway and turned down one of the bye-streets.

"So, so, Mr. Rock," he muttered to himself, "it seems you thought to have it all your own way, but I reckon you've got your match this time. Malpas Thong is not the man to be made a cat's paw of, standing all the racket, and reaping but little of the reward. For every dollar you make by this business, my gentleman, I'll have another, or it shall go hard with you."

Then he entered a small drinking-saloon, the bar of which was presided over by a dirty-looking man in his shirt sleeves.

"Anybody in?" he asked.

"Yes—Gargrave and Leroux, in the little room at the back."

"Ah! I expected one of them; just let me through, will you, and send in some drink."

The proprietor, coming round from behind the bar, opened a small side door, and Thong passed in.

Two men were seated at a table, shuffling and dealing with a dirty pack of cards. Apparently they were playing at no game in particular, but seemed to be practising sleight-of-hand tricks.

One of these men on the entrance of Thong immediately laid down the cards, and rising, took a seat at the far end of the table. Thong seated himself opposite him, and producing a pocket-book, they were soon buried in a whispered conversation.

While they are thus engaged, we will take a brief glance at them. One of them at, least, has the stamp of an unmistakeable villain.

The low forehead, hard, cruel-looking mouth, small grey eyes, shadowed by thick eyebrows, and the shape of the head, sufficiently indicated his disposition. But if there were any doubt on the subject, the brutal, ferocious expression of the man's features would at once remove it. Bold, unscrupulous ruffian was written in ineffaceable characters. He wore neither moustache nor beard, with the exception of a small tuft on the chin. He appeared about forty years of age, and his frame was built more for strength than grace.

This was Malpas Thong.

He had passed many years of his life in the Southern States, and was originally one of the class known as "poor whites." He had been by turns overseer on a plantation, slave dealer, and slave hunter. Then for years he was prowling about the city of New Orleans—now runner to a sailors' boarding-house, and crimp, gambling, cheating, and robbing as occasion offered. In fact, the comprehensive word "rowdy" would best describe this part of his life.

Afterwards he got a situation as overseer on a plantation in Virginia, owned by Webster K. Gayle. Lupus Rock managed everything, and finding in Thong a man utterly unscrupulous, who, if it suited him, would stand at no crime, would shirk no danger—thought he would serve his purpose, and got him removed to a situation of trust at New York, where he could at any moment put his hand on him.

For some reason or other Malpas Thong was dismissed from this berth and disappeared. Why he was so dismissed, and what had become of him, few knew.

Lupus Rock gave out that he suspected him of dishonesty; but there were those who whispered that Thong had, for a consideration, consented to become the scapegoat, and bear the odium of a very questionable transaction, in which Lupus and Webster Gayle were engaged in the pursuit of the "almighty dollar."

The other man seated at the small table was not so coarse-looking, nor so utterly brutal. A glossy dark beard concealed the lower part of his face; his features were good, almost handsome; he was carefully, even elegantly attired; his linen was of the finest, and his hands white and delicate.

As to who or what he wa, no one knew.

He called himself sometimes the Chevelier Leroux, sometimes Baron Leroux, asserting that he was a member of a French family in the State of Louisiana, and that he had a right to either of the above appellations.

Be that as it may, no one either saw or heard anything of his family, nor was it known how he lived.

Let us listen to the muttered conversation which the two men are currying on.

CHAPTER XVI.

A NICE PLOT.

"You are sure you have got incontestable proof of both these facts?" he said.

"Perfectly sure."

"Well, no half confidences. Tell me what are your proofs of the first fact, that this bill for ten thousand dollars, drawn by the firm of Gayle and Co. on a Paris house, and which was supposed to be lost, passed through the hands of Lupus Rock?"

The other hesitated, filled his glass, deliberately drank it off, and then setting it down, leaned both elbows on the table, and staring fixedly in the other's face, said,—

"Look here, chevalier: I wouldn't trust you any more than I would him, only for one reason."

"What reason?"

"Why you dare not play me false. Now just you keep your ears open. I'm going to let you into a secret —into two secrets—by which we can both make our fortunes. If you act on the square, as a pal should, it will be all right; if you attempt, with your accursed cunning, to throw me over, by Heaven, I'll have your life!"

Then Thong clinched this fearful threat by thumping his hand on the table till the glasses clattered and jingled again.

" There," said the other, " don't make such a cursed row; you needn't swear so, nobody is going to throw you over; and I am not afraid of your threats."

" Oh, but you are, though; if I thought you wasn't, you should never hear anything from my lips!"

" Well, no matter—go on."

Thong filled another glass, and drained it off.

" No, baron," he said, " I wouldn't, so help me G—d, if I didn't know you were afraid of me. I know you're a coward, though you will fight sometimes when you're forced to it."

" A coward!—who says I'm a coward?"

" I do."

" It's a lie!"

" It ain't—it's true, and I'll prove it. There's a man —and he's in New York at this moment, though you little think it—who'd like to see you, I know. Now I'll tell you the name of his hotel, and I'll wager my life you won't go in the same street."

Thong paused, and gazed mockingly in his face.

" He's stopping at the New York Hotel. Are you game, if you ain't a coward, to go there?"

" Why not?—who is he?" asked Leroux, uneasily.

" Who is he? Well, you ain't seen him for pretty near two years, and I don't exactly know his name, but I'll make you understand. Do you remember, pretty nigh two years ago, you had a muss with an English chap at the St. Charles Hotel, in New Orleans; you tried to draw a revolver on him, and got all the worst of it. I daresay now, if you try, you can call to mind what happened afterwards; how you shot at him, and killed some one else—eh?"

Leroux grew ghastly pale, and glanced around as if he expected some one to touch him on the shoulder.

" It's a lie," he said, in a husky voice; " the fellow's in Spain!"

" Is he?" sneered the other; " I'll bet you a dollar or

two on that. If you don't believe me, just walk up to
the bar of the New York Hotel, and ask for the gentleman in room number forty-nine. I was standing at the
bar when he came to the hotel, and saw his luggage
taken up."

In spite of all his efforts at unconcern, Leroux could
not conceal his terror.

" Pooh—nonsense !" he said; "I'm not afraid of the
fellow; but why should I bother to go up to the New
York Hotel ? If he wants me he can find me."

" He'd like to," said the other, who seemed to take
delight in playing on his fears, " and so he will some day,
as sure as fate. He's not the sort of chap, from what
I've seen and heard of him, to give up a thing. He'll be
down on you some of these days when you least expect
it. Fact is, I don't know, if ever we fell out, that I
shouldn't save myself all trouble, and put some dollars
in my pocket, by just walking up to him, and saying—
' I say, bos, what'll you stand if I'll jest lead you slick off
to where the Chevalier Leroux is ?' I'll be bound he'd
come down handsome."

Leroux's face became livid at these words. He filled
a glass with brandy, and drained it off.

" Come, come," he said, " no more of this nonsense.
I've got no time to spare. Let's come to business. First,
about this bill for ten thousand dollars."

" Well, the bill was lost just sixteen days before it fell
due; on the day it was lost a steamer sailed for England.
The bill went in that steamer, and a letter to Paris, stopping the payment, should have gone too, but it didn't.
The bill passed through the hands of Lupus Rock; *he*
wrote the letter, and gave it to me to take on board the
mail-boat, and give specially to the captain, with a note,
asking him to forward it to Paris immediately on his
arrival. By this means it would reach Paris two days
earlier than if sent in the regular mail-bag. Lupus Rock
gave me the cue, and I *lost the letter !* Before another
one could be written the boat had sailed.* Of course, as
Master Lupus gave me secret directions to lose the letter,
I knew there was something up. But he didn't think I

knew so much as I did. The bill was presented in Paris,
and paid. By the next mail a letter went out stopping
it; but it was too late. The money had been paid, and
the man to whom it was paid was on his way back to
America. Lupus Rock gave the bill to that man, and
received the ten thousand dollars when he returned. The
man had two thousand for his trouble. I know him, and
can produce him at any moment."

" And would he say that Lupus gave him the bill, and
sent him to Paris ?"

" He would; he is a pal of mine, and if he was unwilling even, we could make him. It could be easily proved
that he presented the bill; he would then have to ac
count for possessing it, and would have to state that
Lupus Rock gave it to him, and that he was ignorant
that it was stolen from Webster Gayle, the merchant."

" Then Lupus Rock is in our power ?" cried Leroux.

" Entirely—utterly, although he himself does not yet
know how completely he is at my mercy."

" And what do you propose to do ?"

" Listen. I know all the gentleman's little schemes.
He is as cunning as the serpent, but hitherto I have
managed to keep pace with him. But I don't like him;
he is an ugly customer, and will kick desperately before
we land him. By myself he might be too much for me;
with that accursed quiet manner of his, you never know
what he is about. Now if there are two of us in the
secret, we can laugh at him—defy him. So I ought to
be able to do now, but I know he's got something in hand
working against me. What that is I can't tell for the
life of me. I know he is afraid to break with me openly,
but that makes him all the more dangerous. Supposing
he could get me put out of the way quietly, don't you
think he'd be a deal easier in his mind ?"

The other nodded assent.

" Well, but don't you see if there's two of us, and we
let him know it, he will see that it is useless. We might
easily prove to him that both of us know it, and that, in
the event of our being got out of the way, we might let
him think there were still others in the secret."

" I see," replied Leroux, musingly, " you think, then, that if he thought it would purchase his safety, he would murder us or have us murdered."

" Think! I don't think about it ; I am sure of it."

" He's a dangerous man, then. Has he any particular animosity against you?"

" No, I think not more than he has to anything else which threatens his safety."

" All the more dangerous for that. A man who acts not from temper, but from judgment, is indeed dangerous."

Both men were silent for a few moments. Leroux appeared to be turning over in his mind what he had just heard. He did not appear half to like the situation. Both Thong and Rock were such desperately dangerous characters, each in their own way, that he felt a false step on either side would be fatal.

" Well, what do you think?" asked Thong.

" Why, I think that if it is worth our while, we could, with caution, keep this Mr. Rock in our power, and use him as we like. But is it worth our while to run the risk, for with such a man there is great danger?"

" Is it worth our while! Is half a million dollars worth our while?"

" Half-a-million! and is half-a-million to be made?"

" Certain. He'll clear a million by the plantation alone."

" What plantation?"

" Why, Webster Gayle's plantation in Virginia—you know the merchant is, or ought to be, a Union man. He must, at all events, appear to be so, or he would have his property in New York and Philadelphia confiscated. But don't you see that the rebels, if they are successful, will, on their side, confiscate his plantation in Virginia, with all the slaves, worth a million of dollars. So you see, which ever way he turns he must lose, unless he can get rid of it. Now, the scheme of Lupus Rock is cunning enough. Webster Gayle is to pretend to make over —to sell the estate in Virginia to Lupus, and give him

a receipt for the price. Then Lupus is to go South,
declare for the rebels. and take possession until the war
is over ; then he is to hand back the deed to his uncle.
But he does not intend to do anything of the kind. Once
in possession, he means to stick to it in spite of everything. Do you see ?"

" Yes—a nice little plot, certainly. This is decidedly
worth our attention. And now for the other piece of
information : about that girl ?"

" Ha ! ha ! Chevalier !—that makes your mouth water.
The French or Spanish Creole girl—the richest and the
handsomest girl in all the South."   .

" Well, you say you can prove she is a slave ?"

" I can !"

Leroux's eyes gleamed with a strange fire.

" Well, go on—tell me how ?"

" Ah !" replied the other, " that requires consideration.
We must have a bargain first. If, with your assistance,
I contrive that Lupus Rock gets possession of this girl,
what share of the money do you expect ? You must remember that the information is exclusively mine ?"

" Lupus Rock get possession of her ! H——l and fury
—never if I can prevent it !" cried Leroux, leaping to
his feet, his cheek flushing, and his eye glaring.

Thong gazed on him with astonishment.

" Phew !" he said, giving a long whistle, " that's the
game, is it ? What, do you want her for yourself ? Do
you expect ever to get her ? Are you spoony on her ?"

" Spoony !" cried Leroux, passionately ; " I would sell
my soul to possess her, and possess her I will."

" Easier said than done. Do you think that she—rich,
beautiful—will throw herself away on you ?—who are—
well, no matter what you are."

Leroux, now somewhat calmed down, continued,

" And you say that Lupus Rock wants her ?"

" Yes, certainly, and swears he'll have her too, by fair
means or foul."

" Well, but I thought he was after Webster Gayle's
eldest daughter—his cousin ; he can't have both."

" Can't he ? but he can, though ; don't you see, if he

can prove that the girl is a slave, he would keep her for his mistress, and marry his cousin."

"D—n!" cried Leroux; "and this is what he means, then?"

"Certainly, and a good judge, too. Now, women are not much in my line—one's as good as another to me; but, by thunder, that Creole girl is enough to make any man's mouth water."

"You say you can prove that she's a slave?"

"Yes, again I tell you."

"Can you prove whose property she is?"

"Yes."

"And the estates—to whom do they belong?"

"A slave can own nothing; they belong to her master."

"And that master—he has not the most remote idea that she is legally his slave?"

"Not the least; nor would he take advantage of the knowledge did he know it. He is a relation, and a great friend of the girl's."

And whoever bought her from him would become the possessor of all her property."

"Certainly."

"But if you say the man whose slave she is would not take advantage of the fact, how would he be induced to sell her?"

"Why, Leroux," said Thong, "ain't you got no sense? I thought you knew a thing or two. Why, what reason is there he should know he sold her at all? He ain't particularly well off, and would sell all his slaves for a good price. Five or six thousand dollars would buy the lot. Then, don't you see, that if he gave you a receipt for the purchase money of all his slaves, not mentioning any number, you could claim her too, if you could prove she was his lawful property."

"Of course, of course. Well, then, Thong, will this satisfy you?—I'm content to go shares with you in this affair with Lupus Rock. And about the girl, if you'll manage it so that we can prove she is a slave, and purchase her, I'm willing to give you up all the profit—all the estates—that is, if you can get them, which I rather doubt."

" But I don't doubt it. I know what I am talking about," interrupted Thong.

" Well, well, if you can do this, I'm content to take the girl for my share, and let you have all the rest : I think that's a fair offer."

" Agreed," said the other, holding forth his hand ; "it's a bargain. D——n the girl! I don't want her ; take her, and welcome. The hard dollars are more in my line."

Then the two men shook hands, and drank a glass together to bind the bargain.

Thus was unceremoniously disposed of, in an obscure New York drinking-booth, the liberty and honour of the handsomest girl in all South Carolina, by a pair of as great ruffians as ever felt the hangman's noose.

CHAPTER XVII.

LEROUX AND HIS ENEMY.

AFTER Malpas Thong had left the room, his late companion remained for some time buried in deep thought. He was aroused from his abstraction by the man with whom he was engaged when the slave agent entered.

" Well, Chevalier," said this man, " are you going to finish teaching me that eye-opener with the cards— reckon it's an out and out dodge ; wants some practice, though."

" Oh, hang the cards!" said the chevalier; " I have other things to attend to now. Look here—do you want to earn a dollar ?"

" Not the least objection in the world, if it ain't by hard work."

" Never fear ; it's neither by hard work nor honest work, else I wouldn't offer you the job," sneered Leroux ; " I want you just to go round to the New York Hotel, and inquire about the visitor in room No. ——."

" Do you want me to see him ?"

" Yes, if you can, and bring me word how long he has been there, and how long he is likely to stop. If you can't see him, get hold of some of the hotel porters, and find out what he is like and all about him."

" Right you are, boss," said the man, going out on his errand. " I'll be back for my dollar in half an hour."

Leroux made no reply, but when he was left alone he called for a stiff glass of brandy, and seating himself in a corner, was soon buried in his thoughts, which, from the expression of his face, were far from agreeable.

" It's a difficult game," he thought to himself; " here's Lupus Rock and Thong, both as dangerous men as I know, and to gain my ends I must outwit them both. Lupus, cool, deliberate, and crafty, is perhaps the most dangerous in the long run; but there is the other, with his wild-beast, savage ferocity—positively it is not safe to be in his company. I believe he'd cut my throat without a moment's hesitation, if he thought I was playing him false. I don't know but what it would be better to keep in with him—act on the square—and both of us put out all our strength against this Lupus Rock. Then there's that other—that cursed young bloodhound that has been following me about this many a month—shall I never be clear of him? I thought this time I had given him the slip, and here he turns up again in New York."

At this latter thought Leroux grew very pale, and his fingers mechanically grasped a revolver he wore in his girdle.

" Curse him!" he hissed between his teeth; " I shall have no rest till I put a bullet through his head. He or I must die."

Then he called for another glass of spirits and drained it off.

It was evident that the thought of the man who Thong told him was staying at the New York Hotel caused him great uneasiness.

Shortly the messenger whom he had despatched to reconnoitre returned.

" Well ?" asked the Chevalier, anxiously.

" Gone!"

" Gone—where ?"

" Don't know. I got hold of one of the negro porters; he told me that the gentleman in the room you spoke of left this morning. He put his luggage on a fly, and when he asked him where to tell the driver to take him, told him to mind his own business. He thought that he'd sailed for England, as the mail-boat went out this afternoon, and he drove in that direction."

" Gone!—to England, too!" exclaimed Leroux; " what sort of a man was he—did you inquire ?"

" I did so; tall, rather dark, about seven-and-twenty years old, and an Englishman; very good looking, and well built, with a small scar on the left cheek."

" Ah!" muttered Leroux, " that's my man, and he's gone—you're quite sure he's gone ?"

" Sure," said the other; " leastways if all the porters I spoke to and the hotel clerk didn't tell lies."

" Well, here's your dollar." So saying, he chucked the coin to the man, who at once proceeded to lay it out in fiery compounds at the bar.

" I say, boss," said Leroux to the landlord, " when do the cars start for Baltimore ?"

" For Baltimore ! why yer ain't going to leave us, Chevalier ?"

" Ain't I ? I am, though, and to-night."

" To-night! you'll have to look sharp, then, for the cars start at eight o'clock, and it's past seven now."

" Past seven, is it ? and is the eight o'clock the last train ?"

" It is so."

" Then I reckon I'll wait till morning. Get me something to eat, and keep my bed for me; I'm going out about the town for half an hour; have dinner ready by the time I return."

So saying, the Chevalier strolled out, and walked carelessly towards the Broadway.

As he turned into this great thoroughfare from the by-street he suddenly stopped as if shot—he turned pale as death. His eyes were riveted on a hack fly which was pulled up close to the pavement.

The driver was repairing some mishap to the harness.

The fare had his head out at window, and Leroux heard him say,—

" Confound you, driver, make haste and tie that trace up. There's no time to lose. I'll give you an extra dollar if I'm in time, and break your head if you get me late."

" All right, your honour," replied the driver, jumping on the box. " We 'll be in time for the cars, never fear."

Then the fly drove hastily off. Leroux remained standing as if spell-bound.

" Did he see me ?" he muttered. " No—I think, I am sure he did not, or he would not have driven off. Going by rail somewhere. I heard the driver say something about being in time for the cars. I wonder where ?"

Leroux remained standing at the street corner for a few moments longer, and then retraced his steps, muttering as he did so—" Curse him ! am I never to be rid of him ? Is he like a phantom, to be constantly appearing before me when least expected ? There must be an end of this some day."

CHAPTER XVIII.

BALTIMORE—THE STREET RIOT.

EARLY on the following morning Stella and Angela Gayle left their father's mansion, and, under the escort of Lupus Rock, started for Baltimore *en route* to Washington. It is necessary, in order to develop our story, that we follow these two fair girls.

Arrived at the railway station, Lupus left them for a few moments to see to the luggage. Two companies of a New York regiment were going to Baltimore by the same train, and thence to Washington, which was thought in danger of attack from the Confederates.

All was enthusiasm and excitement. Bands were

playing, banners waving, and the cheers of a large and noisy crowd assembled round the station bade the departing soldiers God speed.

Stella Gayle stood gazing around, a flush on her fair cheek, and her large dark eyes glittering as the troops marched past and took their places in the train.

"Thus ends the rebellion," said Stella to her sister. "A few mad-headed rebels will risk and lose their lives, and then it will be crushed out and utterly extinguished by the strong arms and brave hearts of our gallant soldiers."

"Is it not a pity that it cannot be put down without bloodshed? Is it not a pity that even one misguided man should pay the price of his folly by his life?"

"A pity, no! no pity! death to all traitors, I say"— She suddenly checked herself.

"So say I, Stella," said Lupus, who now approached, "death to all traitors. You witnessed the just fate of the first, may you see the last rebel also meet his doom."

Stella Gayle turned first crimson, and then very—very pale; her hand which rested on her sister's arm trembled, and a tear in spite of herself glittered in her eye; for, spite of her patriotic mania and violent language concerning rebels, Stella Gayle was really as kind-hearted a girl as her sister.

The words of Lupus Rock recalled to her a terrible scene. She saw Darcy Leigh again at the helm of the Spitfire. She heard the command of Commodore Foote to the marines to fire. Then she saw him again with terrible distinctness stretched on the deck—lifeless, and heard the words of Captain Hiram Squails,—"Shot through the head."

Laura Leigh, his sister, had been the schoolfellow and intimate friend of the sisters, and until this rebellion Darcy and his brother Gerald had been great favourites with the two girls.

Stella thought of all this—of her own hard words in her father's drawing-room; she thought of old times—

of the many happy hours she had passed in the society of Laura and her brothers—of visits to Colonel Leigh's plantation in Virginia—of many little acts of kindness which Darcy had done for her—she thought of all this, and remembering the terrible fate of the young lieutenant, the tear which glistened in her eye trickled slowly down her cheek.

"What!" exclaimed Lupus, in real or affected astonishment, "the enthusiastic, the dashing Stella in tears? Is it the past or prospective fate of all rebels which I heard her but now so devoutly wish for that causes her emotion?"

Stella made no reply, but angrily brushing the tear from her cheek, she turned away indignantly, and taking her sister's arm, hurried to their seat in the cars.

She said little during the long, tedious journey; and when Lupus strove to draw her into conversation she so unmistakeably snubbed him that he gave up the attempt, and leaving the sisters together, went out on the platform of the cars and lighted a cigar.

"Curse her!" he muttered, "there is no managing her—no understanding her—one moment all fire and spirit, the next melting into tears. Ah! those tears! what could have been the meaning of them?"

"Angela," said Stella, when Lupus had left them, "do you know I bitterly regret that we ever left New York. I have a presentiment of coming evil. I believe that if ever there was a fiend in human shape it is our cousin Lupus Rock."

Angela looked astonished; for her sister generally took his part. She had never before heard such strong language from her.

"Why, what on earth makes you think so, Stella? You know that I never liked Lupus Rock, but I do not think he is quite so bad as that; and as to a presentiment of coming evil, what evil can happen?"

"I know not," answered Stella abstractedly; "and yet—and yet——" She paused. "Angela," she continued suddenly, "do you remember yesterday I told you I saw that man Thong?"

" Yes."

" He was talking with Lupus Rock on the steps of one of the hotels in Broadway. Well, he is with us in this very train; I saw him get into the cars. Lupus Rock pretends to know nothing about him, but I am convinced he is going with his knowledge. I am sure they have some plot, some scheme afoot."

"Do you think so?" answered Angela anxiously. " Let us write to papa when we arrive at Baltimore."

" Of what use?" said Stella bitterly; "he is so wrapped up, so infatuated with our worthy cousin, that he would listen to nothing against him, and would only laugh at us for our pains. I really believe sometimes that Lupus has some mysterious influence—some hold on our father—that he holds him in a measure in his power."

" Heaven forbid!" said Angela.

" Heaven forbid indeed! but still I cannot help fancying I am right. In no other way can I account for many little things I have observed."

Lupus Rock now returned, and the conversation dropped. They arrived safely at Baltimore, and went into the ladies' waiting-room, while Lupus attended to their luggage.

Far different was their reception at Baltimore to their departure from New York. At the New York railway station the Federal troops were cheered, and every demonstration made of good-will.

At Baltimore, on the contrary, no sooner had the two companies emerged from the cars than they were assailed with groans and hisses on all sides. An angry, infuriated mob surrounded the railway station.

Stella learned from the attendants in the waiting-room that the city was almost in a state of riot—that several Federal regiments passing through Baltimore had been attacked; there had been blood shed, and it was feared there would be more.

On all hands loud and defiant shouts rang forth. " Down with the Yankees!" was the cry.

Looking through the window Stella and her sister

I

could see the mob assembled in the street awaiting the appearance of the United States' troops, to assail them with groans, hisses—perhaps even violence.

Flags were flying among the crowd, and on many of the houses and liquor stores in the vicinity.

But Stella looked in vain for the Stars and Stripes.

It was the Stars and Bars which was hoisted on sticks and defiantly waved by the mob, and which fluttered in the breeze from flagstaffs, housetops, and balconies.

It was evident that Baltimore was rebel to the very core. Lupus now hurried to the two sisters. He looked pale and uneasy.

" Come," he said, "let us make haste and get out of this before the troops attempt to move. They will most likely be attacked in the streets."

" Is it so bad as that ? " said Stella; "is all Baltimore gone mad ? are there no loyal citizens ? "

" It seems very much like the fact," said Lupus. " Meanwhile this is no time for talking. I have a fly at the door, and have placed your luggage on it. Come, let us make our way to it, and get to our hotel as soon as possible."

This was easier said than done. All was noise, shouting, and confusion. With difficulty they made their way across the platform to the gates.

The fly was so surrounded and hemmed in by the mob that it was with the greatest difficulty they reached it. Even when they did so they found it impossible to move, for the crowd caused a complete block.

Several times the driver urged the horse forward, but each time the horse's head was rudely seized by one of the mob; and with oaths and threats the driver was obliged to relinquish the attempt.

They were thus kept in waiting, surrounded on all sides by the rowdies of Baltimore, powerless to move either one way or the other.

In vain Lupus shouted to the man to drive on. Shouts of derision arose from the crowd each time he put his head from the window.

The Union troops were meanwhile being formed in

line. The word was given, " Four deep! " followed by
" right face !—quick march ! "

Then was heard the regular tramp of the troops as
they marched along the platform and out at the gate.

The head of the advancing column had no sooner
appeared than it was greeted by yells and groans. Still,
regardless of this, the men obeyed orders, and pressed
steadily on. But now more serious demonstrations succeeded. Stones were thrown, and even halves of bricks,
while the fury of the mob increased every moment.
Many of the soldiers were cut by these missiles, and
blood flowed freely.

CHAPTER XIX.

CAPTAIN GERALD LEIGH.

WHILE this scene is being enacted in the streets of
Baltimore, we will for a short time leave the mob and
soldiers contending, and take a glance at the inmates of
a small inn in the suburbs.

Ten or a dozen young men are assembled at the bar—
laughing, talking, and jesting. Most of them are smoking,
and several are imbibing wonderful American drinks,
concocted by the skilful barman.

Some are in the undress uniform of the United States'
cavalry, while all have a more or less military appearance. They seem to be waiting for some one, for every
now and then one of them walks to the door and looks
out.

Presently a horseman, coming from the direction of
the city, gallops up, and dismounts at the door. Several
of the young men hasten out to meet the new-comer.

" Here you are at last, Gerald," said one; " we began
to think you had forgotten us. What news ? "

" If you will just wait a moment or so till I wash the
dust out of my throat, I will tell you all about it. Here,
barman, mix me a julep."

While the drink was being compounded the speaker

went out to see to his horse. Let us glance at him.
He is a tall, fair, and very good-looking young man, of
some six or seven and twenty years. Six feet in height,
and straight as a dart, the symmetry of his limbs and
the breadth of his shoulders cause him to look far shorter
than is the fact.

His features are finely cut and unexceptionably good.
A plentiful supply of slightly waving fair hair clusters
around his face; and whether from foppishness or fancy,
is suffered to grow somewhat long, so as to fall over the
neck. His complexion is clear and somewhat pale; eyes
blue and bright—ever changing in expression, and never
remaining for even a moment fixed on one object.

He wears a slight, fair moustache, but has not a vestige of beard or whisker. Altogether, in form and
feature, he may fairly claim to be ranked as an extremely
handsome young man.

This is Gerald Leigh—the brother of Darcy, with
whom the reader is already acquainted.

Darcy is middle-sized, dark, and slight; Gerald is tall,
fair, with limbs like oak saplings, and blue eyes. Nevertheless, the most casual observer cannot fail to notice a
striking family resemblance.

In both brothers the mouth is the same; and there is
one very noticeable peculiarity also common to both—
that is, the incessant restless movement of the eye. In
Darcy Leigh this is more conspicuous than in Gerald,
but even in the latter it is a feature which never fails
to attract attention.

Having seen to his horse, he re-entered the bar, took
his julep, and seating himself, lighted a cigar.

"Now then, you fellows, I'll satisfy your curiosity.
As I told you, I this morning tendered the resignation
of my commission."

" Well ?"

" Well, the fact was notified to the Secretary-at-War,
who refused absolutely to accept it, and ordered that
should any other officer tender his resignation he should
be immediately brought to a court-martial on a charge
of treason."

Loud murmurs arose at this.

" Well," said one, "treason or no treason, I mean to send mine in to-day."

" Do nothing of the kind, Murdock," said Gerald . Leigh; "wait till all is ready. Then, when we make our stampede South, you can send in your resignation on the same day, and be beyond their reach should they refuse to accept it. For my part, I intend to remain perfectly quiet for a week or two, and watch the course of events. I have written to my father, and also to my brother Darcy. He is even a hotter Southerner than I am; so I do not for a moment doubt that he will at once throw up his commission, leave his ship, and join us at Washington."

" How many can we count on to be with us when we start for Washington?" asked Lieutenant Trent, one of Gerald Leigh's brother officers in the cavalry regiment to which he belonged.

" Well, I have written to every one on whom I thought I could depend, and whose heart is with us. Including ourselves, we can make sure of at least forty, nearly all cavalry men."

" Ah, we shall be well up for officers; but what about men and horses ?"

" As for horses, I think there will be no difficulty; I myself will find twenty ; each of you can, at the very least, supply two. Then, as to men, both Baltimore and Washington swarm with fellows who will suit our purpose ; hunters from the West, men who have served in the army, and rowdies. So that I think we can depend on crossing over into Virginia with at least a hundred mounted men."

" And all upon whom you depend are to meet in Washington ?"

" Yes—in about a fortnight's time. Meanwhile we had best remain quiet and watch events."

A general conversation then commenced—each of the young men in turn making a suggestion or asking a question. It was evident that all looked up to Gerald as the head of the undertaking, and he appeared to take the lead, precisely as Darcy had done in the affair of the Spitfire.

Suddenly the conversation came to a dead stop. A stranger entered the bar, and as their talk was treason, it was, of course, instantly hushed. The new-comer was a young man, apparently about the same age as Gerald Leigh. He did not appear to be an American at all; in fact, he bore unmistakable traces of English blood. His attire was a strange mixture.

It would be difficult to say by his appearance what he was—to what class he belonged. He might have been a Californian gold-digger, a merchant officer, a prairie ranger, or even a rowdy adventurer. He might have been any of these, but he was neither.

At the present time he is attired in a manner which, if picturesque, is decidedly bravo-ish. A blue shirt with worked breasts and pockets, black trousers tucked—American fashion—inside the boots, a Kossuth hat with small feather, and a loose cloak, complete his dress. His waist is bound round by a crimson sash, in which is inserted a silver-mounted revolver.

He was of middle stature, dark, and decidedly good-looking. His manner was cool and self-possessed, and he seemed at all times perfectly at his ease.

Slightly lifting his hat as he entered the room, in accordance with the polite Continental fashion, he advanced to the bar and called for a drink.

"Who is he?" asked some one of Gerald Leigh. "I have seen him at the hotel both to-day and yesterday. He is quite alone, and no one seems to know anything about him."

"I don't know in the least—looks like an Englishman, and seems to know his way about without a nurse."

"He seems a decent sort of a fellow; but we had best be on our guard. In these times it is hard to tell friends from foes, or thieves from honest men."

The conversation was proceeding in a low tone, when distant shouts were heard, followed by the sound of a volley. This was succeeded by cries and fresh shouts; and then followed the rapid crack, crack, of the spiteful little revolvers. Every one was at once on the *qui vive.*

The stranger who stood at the bar hastily swallowed his glass and went outside. He remained for a minute looking towards the town, and then, after examining his revolver, walked briskly away towards the scene of the fight.

"Our friend, the stranger, seems determined to see the fun," said Gerald. "See, he is gone off quite at a pace. I wonder what it's all about. That first volley was evidently from regular troops."

"Yes, two regiments are expected from New York to-day. Shouldn't wonder if they have been attacked by the mob!"

Gerald now went round to the stable, and getting his horse out, mounted. All the others did the same, and as Gerald rode off they were about to follow him.

Now, many of them were still in the undress uniform of the United States' army, and Gerald did not think it advisable for them to attract attention by going in a large body, for it was quite possible that if there were a serious affray, they would be obliged to take one side or the other. This he wished to avoid, as their tactics were to remain quiet till the opportunity arrived for striking a blow. So Gerald, turning in his saddle, said,—

"Look here, you fellows, don't let us all go together; some of you ride different ways. Trent, Winstone, and I will go together. You all get back to the hotel singly. We will meet you there in an hour or so."

The others, seeing the force of this, did so; Gerald and his two companions trotting on towards the city. Meanwhile the noise of the affray and the shouts of the combatants increased. As they approached they could hear the oaths and shouts of the mob, and even the shrieks and groans of the wounded.

"Why, the row is up by the railway station!" said Gerald, rising in his stirrups, and gazing in that direction. "It is as I thought; a New York regiment just arrived has been attacked."

"We shall have to pass quite close," said Winstone.
"Forward, then; the sooner the better. Let us see what
it is all about."

Then urging their horses they approached the scene
of strife at a rapid trot. Just as they turned the corner
of a street giving them a view of the railway-station, the
United States' troops had made good their retreat, and
had closed the gates behind them.

"Ah!" said Gerald, "it is pretty well all over. The
troops have got into the railway-station again, and are
safe enough from ten times the number of the mob.
There are other regiments in town, and, doubtless, they
will soon come to their assistance. What infernal fools
these fellows the Secessionists are to waste their blood
in street rows. Even if they kill a few soldiers they do
no good. Far better for them to wait and be organized
by competent leaders."

They now took a turning which hid the tumultuous
mob and the station from their sight. On again emerging into the broad street, Gerald Leigh suddenly spurred
on his horse. His quick eye had seen something which
brought a flush of anger and shame to his cheek.

"Come on, you fellows—come on!" he cried, half
drawing his sabre. "By heavens! those cowardly ruffians are attacking an open fly with ladies in it!"

So saying, and followed by his friends, Gerald Leigh
dashed down the street at a quick canter.

CHAPTER XX.

THE LADIES FIND A CHAMPION.

HEMMED in and surrounded on all sides, the unfortunate soldiers were in a bad way. It was evident that
something must be done, as they were rapidly becoming
disorganized. Hitherto their rifles were unloaded. Now
the officer in command gave the word, "Halt."

This was followed by the order to load. The ring of
the steel ramrods was heard above the shouting and

yelling of the mob, who still kept up a fire of stones and bricks.

The officers hoped that the demonstration made by the order to load might in some measure overawe the mob and procure a free passage for their soldiers. In this they were disappointed. It was but the signal for an increased burst of shouts, oaths, and execrations.

Before the troops had finished loading, the sharp crack of revolvers was heard, and several of the soldiers fell wounded in the street.

The order was given to fire, and, infuriated by the fall of their comrades, the troops poured a volley into the crowd.

The shrieks and groans of those wounded by the discharge was succeeded by fresh cries of rage and fresh discharges of revolvers. The mob outnumbered the troops ten to one, and a large majority of them were provided with fire-arms. On all sides the deadly six-shooters cracked and sent forth their whistling bullets, dealing death and dismay among the ranks of the soldiers.

Those deadly weapons, in so close a conflict, were much more effective than the rifles of the soldiers, and it soon became evident that against such numbers even discipline would avail little, and the order was given to charge with the bayonet.

It was bravely carried out, but produced little effect, for the crowd scattered before them; while, from behind, a most destructive fire of revolvers was kept up. The soldiers were rapidly falling into confusion. Many of their number were wounded—some killed—and the mob increased every moment in numbers and audacity.

Then the word was given to retreat again to the station. This was effected in tolerable order, the men loading and firing as fast as they could, while those among the crowd who had revolvers pressed to the front, and discharged barrel after barrel; then retired to reload and make way for others.

By the time the troops regained the platform, they had lost some twenty men wounded, and five or six killed outright. Once safe inside, the gates were closed, and, drawn up in a line behind these, the soldiers were prepared for a desperate resistance.

Baffled by this timely retreat, the mob were unable to effect any more harm. A few revolvers still kept up a sputtering fire, but it was ineffective.

There were several Federal regiments in town, and the officers in command would, doubtless, soon hasten with their men to the assistance of those beleaguered in the railway station.

Stella Gayle and Angela had been spectators of all this terrible conflict. They had seen the effect of the first volley of the soldiers, sending some dozens of the mob to the earth; and also the terrible havoc which the cracking revolvers made among the troops.

The bullets hissed and whistled around them, while some even struck the fly. The driver, terrified, had left them, and they were at the mercy of the mob.

Hitherto the attention of the mob had been too much taken up with the soldiers to bestow any on them. Now, however, they crowded round the fly, and demanded, with oaths and imprecations, whether the passengers were Federals. Maddened by excitement and the death of so many of their number, they were now capable of anything.

Angela Gayle, pale and frightened, clung to her sister Stella, who, though no less alarmed at their situation, exhibited more presence of mind and self-control.

" They 're Yankees," shouted one of the mob, who had been examining the directions on the boxes outside. " It's Webster Gayle, the Senator for ——"

Now, Webster Gayle was very unpopular South. It is doubtful whether even Abraham Lincoln himself was more so among the rowdy portion of the Secessionists.

" Webster Gayle!" shouted several; " where is he? —drag him out!—upset the fly!"

" No, no," cried Lupus, " we 're not Yankees. Webster Gayle is not here; we 're for the South, and are going South. Five dollars to the man that will drive us to the Fremont Hotel; our driver has left us."

Instantly attracted by the offer of five dollars, a rowdy

jumped on the box, and commenced whipping the horse
and shouting to the crowd to make way.

Every moment, however, they were stopped, and rudely
asked whether they were Yankees.

The man who was driving, anxious to earn his five
dollars, handed into the fly a coarse piece of calico, made
up into a Secession flag.

" Here," he said, "just you keep waving that till we
get to the hotel; I reckon they'll let us go quiet when
they see that flag."

Lupus Rock took the flag, and was doing as directed,
when, to his horror and astonishment, Stella Gayle
snatched it from his hand, and tore it passionately to
pieces. Then she commenced hurling the pieces away
from her, with a look of ineffable scorn on her beautiful
features.

" Stella," shouted Lupus, " are you mad?—we shall
be torn to pieces."

" Better that than purchase our safety by carrying
that dastard flag."

Shouts of rage broke from those of the crowd who had
seen the emblem of Secession torn up and thrown contemptuously away. A volley of stones was poured on
the fly. The driver was knocked from his seat, which he
did not again attempt to mount, while several stones
struck the sisters. Angela screamed and crouched in the
bottom of the fly.

Lupus tried to open the door, in order to escape. As
for Stella, she sat unmoved, pale as death, but on her
beautiful features there sat that grand look of scorn for
which she was so celebrated;—scorn for the ruffianism
of the mob who could thus attack women; and scorn for
Lupus, whose alarm and terror were unbounded.

A stone struck the fair girl on the temple. She
screamed faintly, and fell back—a crimson stream following the blow.

At this moment, when the ladies were in the greatest
danger, a champion appeared on the scene, determined
to afford that protection of which their cousin Lupus
was incapable.

"Shame, shame!" cried a voice in the crowd. "Do you call yourselves men, to stone ladies in the street?"

"They're Yankees," cried one, "down with them!"

Then another large stone was aimed at the fly, which narrowly missed striking Stella.

The man who had cried "shame" now dashed to the side of the fly, and placed himself before it.

"Are there any gentlemen among you?" he cried. "If so, come forth and aid me in protecting these ladies."

A stone, aimed at the fly, struck him on the shoulder, and sent him staggering back. Instantly drawing his revolver, he fired at the man who threw it, and he fell without a groan, shot through the head.

A shout of rage from the mob.

A shout of defiance from the defender of the ladies was answered by another shout from the crowd, and two young men dashed forward and ranged themselves by his side.

"I don't know who you are, sir," said one of these; "but whoever you are, I glory in your pluck. I am a Secessionist myself, but I won't stand by and see ladies insulted and outraged, so I'm with you."

"I'm neither a Secessionist nor a Federal," said the one who had first come to the rescue. "I'm an Englishman. In my country we don't make war on women. You can call me Captain George, if you like."

"Hurrah for Old England!" he shouted, "and down with the ruffians who attack ladies."

"Hurrah for Ould Ireland!" shouted a voice from the crowd. "Be jabers, I'm for the ladies, too. Sure the critters ain't done no harm; and be jabers, if they they are Yankees, they can't help it."

So saying, the speaker, an Irish labourer, left the ranks of the crowd, followed by two of his compatriots, who ranged themselves on the side of the defenders. There were now six; three of them had revolvers, which they were fully prepared to use, while the three Irishmen had sticks.

" Jump up, one of you fellows, and take the reins,"
said Captain George ; " we'll clear the road."

One of the Irishmen mounted the box.

" Make way there; make way ; let the fly with these
ladies pass."

" No, no," shouted some one among the crowd ;
" down with them—they're all a cursed lot of Yankees
together—after them, boys—don't let a man of them
pass alive."

This speech was followed by another volley of stones.
The driver was nearly knocked from his seat, while all
the others were more or less hurt.

CHAPTER XXI.

" GERALD LEIGH TO THE RESCUE."

" To the rescue ! " shouted one of the young men who
had followed Captain George in defending the ladies ;
" to the rescue, Gerald Leigh, to the rescue ! "

He had seen, on turning the corner of the street,
three men on horseback ; one of these he had recognised.
At the words " Gerald Leigh," Stella Gayle started and
leaned forward.

The three horsemen trotted quickly towards the beleaguered fly. They were not in uniform, but wore
swords and revolvers in their holsters.

" Make way there, make way ! " shouted their leader,
laying about him right and left with the flat of his
sword ; " make way there. What's all this about ?—who
calls me ? "

The mob scattered before the clattering of the horses'
hoofs. What mob can or will stand cavalry, in however
small force ?

" Here, Gerald Leigh ; it was I, Lieutenant Murdock ! "
cried one of the young men by the fly.

" What, Murdock, is that you ? " said Gerald Leigh.
" Why, what's the matter ?—your head is cut and bleeding,
and your left arm hangs by your side —not broken, I
hope ? "

" I fear so. As to what is the matter, I was in the crowd, and saw these ladies attacked by the mob. This gentleman came to their aid first," pointing to Captain George, "and I followed."

His light blue eyes flashed with anger.

" What!" he said, "this rabble have been stoning ladies, have they? What the blazes do you mean by it, you dastardly curs?" he cried, rising in his stirrups and addressing the crowd. " Is this the way to win your freedom? Is this the way to fight for your independence? Back, you paltry curs; back to your kennels! We don't want such men as you to fight for us. We will achieve our independence without such a cut-throat rowdy rabble as you. Back, I say, all of you, or I'll cut you to mincemeat."

So saying, he drove the spurs into his horse's flanks, and dashed among the crowd, brandishing his sabre.

All fell back before him.

" It's Captain Leigh," cried several, as they retreated.

" All right, Captain," said another, " we thought they were Yankees."

" And what if they were, you hound! I'll let you know that ladies, whether Yankees or not, shall be respected."

So saying, he gave the fellow a bang on the side of the head with the flat of his sword. He then checked his horse, and, riding back to the fly, took up a position in front, and ordering the driver to follow, himself led the way to the hotel.

His two friends, who were also mounted, rode one on each side, while the three who had first come to the rescue, and the two Irishmen, also marched alongside. Thus escorted, they passed through the streets without molestation.

It was evident that Gerald Leigh was well known, for many hats were doffed as he passed. Under his escort no further attack was made on the fly, still it was followed by a considerable crowd of rowdies and others.

These were mostly the friends of the man who had been shot through the head by Captain George. It was against him that their vengeance was particularly directed.

Arrived at the Fremont Hotel, the fly drew up at the door; Gerald Leigh rode to the rear, in order to keep back the crowd, who still pressed on.

The dilapidated appearance of the vehicle sufficiently attested the fact that it had been attacked by the mob. The landlord of the hotel, perceiving this hastened out, followed by some dozen or so of porters and negro waiters; then forming a line on each side, the door of the fly was opened and the ladies hurried into the hotel.

Gerald Leigh and his two companions, who were also mounted, were engaged in keeping back the crowd, so that he did not see the ladies as they alighted.

When he learned that they were in safety he dismounted, and giving his horse in charge of a groom who appeared from the stables, he entered the hotel. His two friends also followed his example, as did the two young men who had first answered the appeal of Captain George.

This latter did not immediately enter the hotel. He had observed something glittering at the bottom of the fly, and on looking closer, perceived a lady's bracelet. It was broken into several fragments, and it took him some little time to collect them. While he was thus engaged the fly moved on, for the driver, who had re-appeared, wished to get his damaged vehicle home.

Having collected all he could find of the bracelet Captain George leaped out, with the intention of making his way back to the hotel. To his annoyance, however, he found his passage barred.

It was not more than fifty yards to the hotel steps, but that space was held by a mob of rowdies and roughs, who seemed determined to dispute his passage.

Shouts and oaths greeted the Englishman as he turned towards the hotel.

"Down with him! Lynch him! he's a d——d Yankee!" shouted one.

"Give him a slung-shot," shouted another; "that's the fellow that shot poor Josh Terry."

Then the crowd closed up to him in a menacing manner. Finding himself beset on all sides, the young

Englishman retreated towards the fly, which had again come to a standstill.

He looked around for his friends. They had disappeared, except the big Irishman and his two mates. Captain George shouted to these to come to his assistance, which they generously hastened to do.

Having gained the fly, he hastened to make it available both as a means of attack and defence.

In the preceding *melée* it had been well-nigh demolished; both shafts had been broken, and were hanging loose only attached by the harness. He hastily possessed himself of parts of both these, and giving one to each of his Irish allies, he reserved another for himself, and prepared for a desperate defence.

Swinging it club-like round his head, he attacked the foremost of the mob, who were pressing on him with bowie knives, slung-shot, and such weapons as they had.

Fortunately the great majority of them had not revolvers, and those who had were without ammunition.

Captain George had five barrels left. These he determined to reserve to the last extremity.

Dashing forward, followed by his Irish allies, he strove to drive the crowd back and make his way to the hotel. But, although two or three went down with bleeding heads before the broken shaft he wielded, others supplied their places, and he found it necessary to beat a retreat once more to the shelter of the fly.

They now found themselves in a critical position. Surrounded on all sides by an infuriated mob, many half drunk, their chances of safety seemed but small.

Stones again whistled through the air, and crashed and rattled against the vehicle.

By repeated and furious onslaughts, the Englishman was enabled to prevent the crowd closing on him, which would have been fatal; but after each of these attacks, although for the moment successful, he was more closely assailed than ever.

At last he sought shelter inside the vehicle, and closing the door he drew his revolver, and cocking it, held it towards the foremost.

" Back, every one of you!" he shouted; " the first that advances is a dead man!"

Two of his three defenders had mounted on the driving box, where they afforded a good aim for the missiles which came from every side. The third Irishman was at the door of the fly, keeping back the mob with the piece of broken shaft.

Each time that they endeavoured to make a rush, big Pat, swinging his weapon around, would bring some of them to earth.

With such odds against them, however, it was impossible to escape without injury; and already Captain George saw blood flowing from various cuts in the head of his generous defender.

Crash! a stone came, striking him on the head, and knocking him backwards. At the same moment one of the Irishmen was knocked off the box, and fell on the other side among the crowd. With a yell of rage, the other also leaped down to the assistance of his fallen comrade.

The case was desperate; so Captain George, suddenly throwing open the door of the fly, leaped forth revolver in one hand, the broken shaft in the other. He had determined to make one last desperate effort to reach the hotel; if that failed, it would be all up with him, he well knew. Setting his teeth firmly, he shouted to the three Irishmen to follow him, and dashed furiously at the very thick of the crowd.

The three men followed him, big Pat giving vent to a wild Irish yell, which, in itself, ought to have cleared a way. So sudden and desperate was this attack by the four men, that the mob fell back on all sides.

The broken shafts, wielded by desperate men, crashed and smashed about their heads, making the blood flow freely, and in less than half a minute some six or seven were sent to the ground, and the little band passed over their bodies, and made their way towards the hotel.

It almost seemed, for a moment, that they would make good their retreat by this sudden dash, for only some twenty yards separated them from the haven of safety.

At this moment one of the Irishmen receives a blow in the back of the head from a slung-shot, and falls to the ground stunned and bleeding. The mob close around him, and the poor fellow's cries are dreadful.

Captain George, scorning to leave one of his generous allies wounded on the field of battle, turns and furiously attacks the group who have closed around the fallen hero. The other two, with wild yells of rage, follow in his wake, and soon they drive back the enemy, and obtain possession of the body of their friend. The two Irishmen support the insensible man between them, and once again they endeavour to make their way to the hotel steps.

" Clear the way, you ruffians!" shouted the Englishman, drawing his revolver, and pointing it at the foremost of his antagonists.

A stone, thrown from behind, struck him full in the chest, and knocked him backwards against the two men with their wounded friend. He is quickly on his feet again, and mad with pain and fury, discharges all five barrels of his pistol, and then throws himself, with the fury of desperation, right in the midst of his assailants.

One man is killed by the discharge, and four others are desperately wounded.

This for a moment clears him a way. Had he but another revolver, he might have made good his retreat; as it was he had no time to reload, and was forced to depend entirely on the broken shaft. The two Irishmen, encumbered with their wounded friend, are unable to follow him, and he is left alone to contend against a mob of some hundreds.

Desperately he fights against the tremendous odds.

Pale, bleeding, his hat knocked off, he is seen the centre of a group of furious enemies. Then suddenly he disappears. Once again he rises to his feet, and again struggles desperately. Again he disappears, sent prone to earth by a treacherous slung-shot.

Now he is on one knee, gasping for breath, fainting from the terrible exertion and loss of blood. His eyes glare furiously around him on his cowardly assailants.

Once again, with the courage of despair he rises, and

with one last effort of strength, for a moment succeeds in
keeping his feet; then fighting desperately to the very
last, he is overwhelmed by numbers, and the pale, bleeding face is seen no more.

At this instant the loud blast of a bugle is heard. It
is a cavalry call—the charge.

For a moment the crowd pause, and listen in astonishment. The next, the clatter of horses' hoofs is heard,
and a troop of cavalry come thundering down the street.

Again the bugle blast sounds forth. It comes from
the balcony of the hotel, and is followed by a voice,—

"Go into them, boys!—Cut the vagabonds up!—
Show them no mercy!"

Then may be heard the clang of sabres as they are
drawn from their steel scabbards.

At the same time a party of young men issue from the
hotel, and charging down the steps, drive the mob before
them. The horsemen on their flank, cutting, slashing,
and shouting, complete their discomfiture, and the rabble
fly in confusion, leaving behind some dozen or so of their
number killed and wounded.

*   *   *   *   *   *

We have already said that, on arriving at the hotel
all the men who had engaged in the defence of the ladies
entered, with the exception of Captain George and the
Irishmen.

Gerald Leigh led the way, saying to his companions,—

"Come along, boys, let's come up into the smoking-
room and have a weed."

Then Gerald Leigh, Lieutenant Murdock, and the
others entered, not noticing that Captain George did not
accompany them.

"How did this affair commence, Murdock?" asked
Gerald.

"Well, really, I can hardly say. I was coming out of
the billiard-rooms with Marley here, when I heard a
disturbance; then the young fellow you saw with us just
now shouted if there were any gentlemen present to
come to the assistance of the ladies. I saw that he was
overmatched, and as also I saw there were ladies in the fly.

1 and Marley went in with them. Then our ranks were reunited by three Irish labourers, and, lastly, just as we were being overpowered, I saw you and your friends at the street corner, and shouted to you for aid."

" It's lucky we came when we did," said Gerald Leigh, lighting a cigar; " for those roughs and rowdies would have given you a hard time of it. Wasn't one of them shot or something ? "

" Yes, the young fellow, the Englishman, shot one through the head."

" The devil ! how did it happen ?"

" Oh, the rowdy threw a large paving-stone, which struck one of the young ladies, and cut her forehead. The Englishman seeing this, makes no more to do, but pulls out his revolver, and, taking a deliberate aim, fires at the fellow. The aim was true, for the ball struck him between the eyes, and went, of course, crash through his brain."

" Serve him right, the ruffian ! I would have done the same myself."

" Well, it seems that this fellow was a leader, and a favourite among the rowdies, and they determined to avenge his death. By the bye, I wonder where the young fellow is. I thought he came in with us."

" Go down, one of you, and see if he's at the bar," said Gerald Leigh, " and ask him if he'll come up and have a brandy smash with us. He seems a gentleman, and I like the fellow's pluck."

Murdock went down to the bar, and returned reporting that the stranger was not to be found.

The smoking-room was on the first floor, and the window opened on to a balcony looking out on the street.

The shouting of the mob, as they attacked the Englishman and his Irish friends, was now plainly heard. Still the party in the smoking-room paid but little attention to it, as within the last week street fights had been of daily and hourly occurrence.

They went on talking and laughing and chaffing, as young men will, when the sound of five pistol shots dis charged in rapid succession aroused their attention. The shots were those fired by Captain George, immediately before his last desperate attempt to fight his way to a place of safety.

Gerald Leigh, who was seated in Yankee fashion with his feet on the table, rose carelessly and sauntered to the window. He passed on to the balcony and looked out on to the street.

Suddenly he gave an exclamation of surprise,—

" Hullo ! Murdock," he said, " come here. Is not that your friend, the Englishman, yonder ?"

All the young men crowded out on the balcony.

" By Heavens, it is ! " cried Murdock, " and fighting like a tiger-cat too. Thunder ! he'll be murdered. Come on, boys, let's go to the rescue ; he's too brave a fellow to be slaughtered by these ruffians."

It was at this moment that Captain George, desperately fighting, was beaten to the earth.

" Come on, Gerald," repeated Murdock ; " surely you won't stand by and see the young fellow killed before our eyes. See how he is fighting, and against such odds too."

Gerald Leigh had gone out on to the balcony, and was leaning over looking out up the street. He made no direct reply to Murdock, but said, addressing one of the others,—

" Marley, just hand me that bugle from the table."

Marley handed him a cavalry bugle.

Gerald Leigh placed it to his lips and blew a loud shrill blast.

" There," he said, " that will bring more effective help than ours."

" What do you mean ? " asked Murdock.

" Only that I can see a troop of my horse at the corner of Union Street. They'll be down fast enough when they hear the call, I warrant. Now then, you fellows, down you go, and lay about you like Trojans : I'll follow directly."

The four young men hurried down stairs ; Gerald's two friends hastily buckling on their cavalry sabres, while the other two looked to their revolvers. The next moment the thunder of horses' hoofs was heard down the street, and a troop of cavalry dashed past at a gallop.

Gerald Leigh gave another blast on the bugle, and shouting to the troopers to charge, himself hastened down to his friends, and drawing his sword, dashed down the steps and attacked the mob. The reader already knows the result of the combat. The rowdies were at once put to flight, leaving many dead and wounded behind them.

Gerald Leigh and his friends hastened to the spot where they had last seen the young Englishman fighting. They found him lying senseless on the ground, with his discharged revolver tightly grasped in his hand. They raised him, and bore him into the hotel and up into the smoking-room.

While one of them ran for a surgeon, Murdock bathed the head of the wounded man with cold water, and poured some brandy down his throat.

Blood flowed freely from several deep gashes in his head, and there were also severe bruises on various parts of his body, caused by the stones thrown by the mob.

Before the surgeon came he showed signs of returning consciousness. Another draught of brandy revived him considerably, and he tried to rise. This, however, Murdock prevented by holding him down, and proceeded to examine the cuts on his head.

" By Jove!" said Gerald Leigh, stooping over him, " he's fearfully cut about. He must be a tough bit of stuff to have stood it as long as he did."

Murdock, who had some surgical skill, was engaged in cutting the hair off his head with a pair of scissors, so as to be able to get at the cuts. This was no easy matter, as his head was saturated with blood, which had commenced to coagulate. Probably the operation caused the wounded man some pain, for he suddenly started to his feet, in spite of all Murdock's efforts to keep him down.

Giddy, confused, and not in full possession of his

faculties, he thought himself still in the hands of enemies, and with blind fury proceeded to act on the idea. Seizing a chair which was near him, he swung it around his head, shouting—

"Ah! you cowards—you cut-throats—you thieves—would you murder me? Come on, you ruffians, I'm not half licked yet!"

Then suiting the action to the word, he furiously attacked his friends. Murdock received a swinging blow from the heavy chair, which sent him staggering against the wall.

Next he attacked Gerald's two friends, who wisely retreated behind the table. Blundering over this, however, he blindly and furiously attacked them, shouting forth defiance. Gerald Leigh, who could not restrain his laughter, now, however, suddenly threw himself on him from behind, and pinioned his arms.

The Englishman struggled desperately, shouting forth all the time words of defiance and hatred.

"Ah! you cowards, you are ten to one—give me fair play!"

But despite his struggles, he could do nothing in Gerald's powerful grasp. Weakened by loss of blood, his strength was as that of a child in comparison with that of the stalwart and athletic Gerald.

In half a minute he was thrown on his back, and Gerald Leigh and Murdock were again kneeling beside him, this time fully prepared and determined he should not rise again.

"Be quiet, can't you?" said Gerald; "we're your friends."

"Friends!" muttered the wounded man, dreamily closing his eyes from exhaustion, "friends—friends!"

Then he again turned ashy pale, and lay quite still.

"Bathe his face with cold water," said Gerald, "he has fainted again. By Jove, he is a rare plucked one," he continued, laughing; "what a crack he fetched you with the chair, Murdock. I should think your head ached still."

"Certainly," replied the other, feeling his head, "he

has raised a lump as big as a hen's egg; I suppose he calls that gratitude."

"Poor devil! he didn't know what he was doing—thought he was in the hands of the mob still, I suppose. However, I glory in his pluck; I have heard of English bulldog courage, and certainly here was as good an instance of it as one would wish to see—wounded, bleeding, fainting, he yet fought to the last gasp, and showed no signs of giving in even when I had his arms pinioned."

Gerald Leigh gazed admiringly on the face of the prostrate hero, with his pale, bloodstained face. Had he been an enemy, even, instead of a stranger, Gerald Leigh could not have helped admiring his gallantry and determination.

The surgeon now arrived, and after administering a powerful cordial, proceeded to dress his wounds.

Fortunately, none of these were dangerous, and the flow of blood being stopped, he now began to come round. In half an hour's time he was quite sensible, and was enabled to sit up in an easy chair.

Placing his hand to his wounded head, he withdrew it covered with blood, which had not yet quite ceased to flow.

"I have been wounded," he said, faintly, looking at his hand; "how did it happen—and who are you gentlemen?"

"How did it happen," said Gerald Leigh, smiling; "well, that's too long a tale, and as to who we are—we are your friends—let that be sufficient for the present."

At this moment a negro waiter entered the smoking-room, and said that the two ladies wished to see Captain Leigh.

Now on entering the hotel Gerald Leigh had not noticed Stella and Angela Gayle, being otherwise occupied; therefore he was considerably surprised to hear that they knew his name.

"What!" he said to the man, "do the ladies know me?"

"Oh yes, sir, quite well. Ladies been talking about you—call you Captain Gerald Leigh."

" By Jove, I wonder who they can be ? No matter—
lead me to their room."

So saying he followed the waiter, leaving the wounded
man in charge of Murdock and the surgeon.

CHAPTER XXII.

GERALD LEIGH IS INFORMED OF HIS BROTHER'S FATE.

GERALD LEIGH was conducted to a private drawing-
room on the same floor as the smoking-room, but in a
different part of the house. The negro waiter threw
open the door and announced,—

" Captain Gerald Leigh."

As he advanced into the room two ladies hastened to
meet him. He gazed as if in doubt for a moment, and
then exclaimed—

" What! Stella and Angela—is it indeed you ? This
is a surprise."

A flush of pleasure came on his handsome face as he
took a hand of each of the young ladies.

" Why, how stupid I must have been not to have recognised you before. How fortunate, too, that I happened to be in the street as you came by. I hope you
are not hurt ? " he asked, anxiously noticing the cut on
Stella's fair brow.

" No, only a very little hurt, but a good deal
frightened."

" And you, Angela," said Gerald Leigh, looking into
her soft blue eyes—" were not you terribly frightened
at the row ? "

" Oh, dear! pray do not talk about it ; I thought I
should have died from fright. But what has become of
that gentleman who first came to our aid ? He said he
was an Englishman, I think ; but be he what he may,
he is a brave noble fellow. We must thank him."

" He is rather badly hurt," was the reply, " so you
must defer your thanks for the present. But tell me,
Angela, how on earth did it happen that you were alone
and unprotected in Baltimore at such a time ? What

could your father be thinking of to trust his daughters alone?"

"We were not alone," Stella answered, her beautiful eyes flashing angrily, scornfully, "and we ought not to have been unprotected."

"Not alone? Who, then, was with you?'

"Our cousin, Lupus Rock."

"Lupus Rock!—and where, then, was he? What was he doing when you were attacked, for I certainly did not see him?"

"What was he doing?—why looking after his own safety, I imagine. He made his escape at the very commencement of the affray."

"A pretty protector, certainly, this Mr. Rock! Do you know, Stella, I never liked him, this cousin of yours, nor did my brother Darcy. You know, I suppose, that Darcy threatened to horsewhip him once."

Stella turned ashy pale at these words. Gerald Leigh spoke of his brother in a light, careless tone.

It was evident that he knew nothing.

She remembered the terrible scene she had witnessed on board the Columbia, and remained before him with downcast eyes as pale as death. She could not meet his glance. She knew that he was gazing wonderingly and inquiringly at her, and yet she dared not raise her eyes and meet his.

"Stella, what is the matter?" he asked.

No answer. Then turning to Angela—

"Angela, can you tell me the meaning of this? What ails Stella—what ails you?"

But Angela Gayle was in tears, and remained silent like her sister.

Suddenly a light seemed to break on Gerald Leigh.

"Stella," he said, seizing her hand, "answer me—is anything wrong with my brother Darcy?"

His voice faltered as he asked this question.

Stella slowly raised her beautiful eyes to his face. They were suffused with tears.

"Gerald, Gerald," she said, in a sad voice, "do not ask me."

Tears coursed rapidly down her cheeks, and she again lowered her eyes before the gaze of Gerald Leigh.

"Stella," said the latter, with forced calmness, "tell me all—I insist upon it! My brother—what of him? Is he ill—is he hurt—or is he imprisoned or disgraced?"

"No," murmured Stella, weeping bitterly.

"No—and yet you weep. Is it then worse, Stella? Answer me—is my brother dead?"

No reply.

"Stella Gayle, once again I implore you, do not keep me longer in suspense. What of my brother—what of Darcy Leigh?"

At this moment the door opened, and Lupus Rock entered.

He gave a black look upon the man who was there. He had heard the last words of Gerald Leigh.

"What of my brother—what of Darcy Leigh?" repeated Gerald.

Stella Gayle, unable longer to restrain her feelings, burst into a passionate flood of tears.

She could not find it in her heart to tell Gerald, so brave, so noble, so kind, that his brother had perished miserably.

Gerald Leigh gazed in silent consternation from Stella to Angela.

Both were in tears.

"Stella," said Gerald, "let me know the worst. My brother is dead—is it so?"

She bowed her head silently in reply.

"Speak! tell me how it happened, and when."

Neither of the girls replied to this, but Lupus Rock said, in a hard, indifferent voice—

"Lieutenant Leigh was shot by the United States' marines. He turned traitor to his flag, and endeavoured to seize the ship. He was shot through the head at the first discharge."

Gerald Leigh strode up to Lupus Rock, and placing his hand on his shoulder, he held him in a firm grasp.

"Look here, Mr. Rock," he said, "you just now made use of an expression which, if you value your skin, you

will not repeat. **You said that Darcy** Leigh turned
traitor. I tell you you are a liar **to your** teeth! Do
you understand ? "

And Gerald, exerting his great strength, shook and
twisted Lupus like a child.

"Now if I ever hear you say a disrespectful word of
my brother again, whether he be living or dead, I'll take
you by the **neck** and heels, and just throw you out of
the window. So now you know what to expect. And
now you can clear out of this, for I want to talk to those
ladies alone."

So saying he relinquished **his** grasp, and turned towards the two girls.

Lupus grew pale with passion.

"Those ladies have been placed under my protection
by their father, Captain Leigh," he said, "and I cannot
recognise your right to dictate to me. I am not accustomed to threats, and shall not leave the room."

"Under your protection," said Gerald Leigh; "pretty
protection, truly! What became of their protector when
they were assailed **by** the mob in the streets ? "

Stella smiled scornfully through her tears as she remembered the ignominious flight of her cousin. Lupus
looked furiously towards the two sisters.

"Stella—Angela," he said, angrily, "your father placed
you in my charge. I am the best judge of what is right.
There is no necessity for any more of this foolery.
Please to get yourselves ready ; we will go at once to
the railway station, and proceed on our journey to Washington."

"Not so, cousin," replied Stella, calmly and firmly ;
"my sister and I are fatigued, and wish for some rest.
If our father placed us, as you say, in your charge, he
did not intend that we should be as servants at your
beck and call. Besides, with such a valiant protector
as yourself, I almost doubt whether it would be safe."

"Do not be alarmed, Stella," said Gerald Leigh, " I
will myself accompany you to Washington in the course
of a couple of days."

Lupus again grew white with passion.

"Really, Captain Leigh," he said, sneeringly, "I am sure the ladies ought to be much obliged to you. On their part, however, I beg to decline the honour. It is possible that the presence of Captain Leigh, the brother of the officer who attempted to seize a United States' ship of war for the rebels, might be construed unfavourably to the loyalty of the party."

"Lupus," said Stella hurriedly, "you had better leave us. As you cannot refrain from insulting Captain Leigh, both he and we can dispense with your company."

Lupus was on the point of angrily refusing, but glancing at the stalwart form of the young officer, he saw that in his eye which warned him to trifle no further. Accordingly, with a scowl around, he left the room, muttering between his teeth.

"Curse them!—these Leighs are for ever in my path. First it is the younger one, and no sooner is he out of the way than this great bully must start up. No matter —my time will come: slow and sure; that shall be my motto."

"And now, Stella," said the young officer mournfully, and seating himself beside her, "tell me of this sad affair—tell me of Darcy—how did it happen?"

"Gerald," said Stella earnestly, "your brother was rash, misled, and he paid the penalty. Perhaps it is as well as it is; better, far better, than he should have been captured—as assuredly he and all the other mutineers will be—and executed."

Gerald Leigh grew very pale at the word "executed."

"Executed!—Darcy Leigh, a Southern gentleman, executed!"

Stella and her sister were silent, not wishing to hurt his feelings.

"Come, tell me all about it," he said, raising his head, which he had buried in his hands.

Then Stella commenced a recital of all the events which happened up to the supposed death of the rebel ringleader.

She spoke in low, trembling accents, frequently pausing, overcome by her emotion.

"The accursed cowards — the dastards!" exclaimed Gerald Leigh when she came to that part of her recital where Darcy had forbidden his men to fire into the Columbia, although the latter lay at her mercy.

"Perhaps it was no more than their duty; doubtless in giving the order to fire Commodore Foote did no more than he was bound to do."

"No more than his duty! the accursed murdering old ruffian! It makes my blood boil to think of it. But I swear by Heaven that for this foul murder many a Yankee shall bite the dust, many a New England mother and wife shall be childless and husbandless. Ah!" he hissed between his teeth, and clenching his hands, "but we will have a terrible revenge for this!"

Stella looked up in astonishment. She respected his grief, but did not fully gather the meaning of his words.

"Gerald, what do you mean?" she said. "Surely you too are not—I mean, surely you do not also forget the uniform you wear and the flag you serve under?"

"Forget—no, I don't forget," he replied, laughing scornfully; "I know that I wear the uniform of an accursed lot of murderers and villains—that I serve, or rather have served, under a flag which for the future must be alien to every Southern gentleman. I do not forget—I know I wear a sword which, when it is next drawn, shall be in the service of the Confederate States of America—a sword which ere long shall be red with Yankee blood. Yes, Darcy, you shall be avenged—terribly avenged!"

Stella Gayle listened aghast to these passionate words. She had never dreamed for a moment that Gerald Leigh, the frank, bold, dashing Gerald, whom she had been in the habit of regarding almost as a brother, could ever desert the cause so dear to her heart, and enrol himself under the banner of traitors.

"Gerald," she said, an angry flush mounting to her cheek, "do you know what you are saying? Remember your duty, your allegiance—remember and pause."

"Stella," he said, grasping her hand, "I do remember, and I will not pause. How can I forget, indeed? The

scene you have described to me rises vividly before me.
I see Darcy Leigh, my only brother, at the helm of the
Spitfire as she passes under the stern of the Columbia.
I see the big guns frowning from her port-holes, and
ready to send forth their storm of iron death. I hear
Darcy Leigh nobly forbidding their fire, and the next
moment I see him stretched in death on the deck, as the
reward for his forbearance. I remember, and I will not
pause. From this day forth the Yankees have no more
bitter enemy than Gerald Leigh. And now, Stella—
Angela, I must, for the present, bid you adieu. You
are too tired to proceed on your journey to-day. To-
morrow it will not be safe, as there is to be a great rebel
demonstration. The day after to-morrow I shall be back,
and will see you safely to Washington."

"You too, then, are going to Washington?" asked
Stella.

"I, too, am going to Washington, on my road——"

"On your road whither?"

"On my road to join the armies of the Confederate
States!"

CHAPTER XXIII.

GERALD LEIGH STARTS FOR KENHANA.

GERALD LEIGH hurried from the room, and ordered
his horse to be brought round.

He then hurriedly wrote a note at the hotel bar, and
addressed it to Lieutenant Murdock. It ran thus:—

"DEAR MURDOCK,—I have started for my father's place at
Kenhana. I shall be back the day after to-morrow. I have
had bad news—terrible news of poor Darcy. Keep all the
fellows who are with us together. I shall bring horses, &c.,
with me from the estate, enough to mount fifty men. I will
explain fully when I see you. In haste,—GERALD LEIGH."

Sealing this note, he gave it to the waiter to take to
Lieutenant Murdock, and mounted his horse, which had
been brought round. Stella Gayle and Angela heard

the clattering of horses' hoofs in front of the hotel, and looking forth, saw Gerald Leigh dash off at a gallop.

"The mad boy!" said Stella mournfully; "I fear he has some desperate design in view, and trust to Heaven no harm may happen to him."

Stella spoke sadly and feelingly. Her heart was very sad—it seemed that this dreadful rebellion was fated to separate from her all her old friends—old companions. She no longer even thought with that bitter contempt of the rebellion as before. The supposed tragical fate of poor Darcy Leigh, the desperate gallantry of his attempt, which, although blaming, she could not help admiring, and the stern determination evinced by Gerald Leigh, had forced the conviction on her mind that these rebels were terribly in earnest. Leaning her head on her hand, she gazed sadly out at the open window on to the crowded street.

Again sad memories of the happy past crowded on her, and looking forward with misgiving to the future, she felt half inclined to weep. The reverie was interrupted by the entrance of Lupus Rock.

"Well," he said surlily, "and has that young popinjay taken his departure?"

"He is no popinjay, but a brave and gallant officer, which you will never be, Mr. Rock."

"A brave and gallant officer!" he sneered. "No doubt of it; so was Darcy Leigh in your idea, and a treacherous rebel to boot."

Stella started up, her eyes flashing and her cheek colouring with anger.

"Lupus Rock," she said, impetuously, "let me have no more of your taunts, nor speak disrespectfully of Darcy Leigh. He was my friend."

"Friend!" sneered Lupus, "was that all?"

"Yes, friend," continued Stella, passionately, "and though he is dead, and perished in a bad cause, I will not hear him spoken disrespectfully of; were he alive he would horsewhip you. If you further taunt me, or speak disrespectfully of him, I will request his brother Gerald to horsewhip you when he returns, although you are my cousin. And as to going to Washington with you, I tell you plainly I would not do so alone. I would rather remain here in spite of you, and write or telegraph to my father. I shall certainly not think of leaving here until Gerald Leigh returns. He will accompany us to Washington for your and my protection."

The bitter scorn of these words almost drove Lupus beside himself with fury; he gnashed his teeth in impotent rage.

But he knew Stella too well to venture further. She stood before him with her small hands tightly clenched, her beautiful eyes glittering, and with a light flush on her face, which made her great beauty absolutely dazzling. She looked like an angry empress, and Lupus cowered before her.

"Cousin Stella," he said, with forced composure, "you are too hasty. I have no wish to offend you, but since my presence seems to produce that effect, I will withdraw."

He then left the room.

As he walked down the corridor, an expression of fiendish malignity came over his face.

"Were she only a man, how I could hate her," he muttered; "as it is, I don't know whether I most admire her beautiful person or hate the spirit which animates it. No matter, my day will come, Stella Gayle, and then you shall drink the bitter cup of humiliation."

Meanwhile Gerald Leigh tore across the country at a rapid gallop. His destination was a small estate of his father's, situated at Kenhana, about five and twenty miles from Baltimore; and he never slackened rein till he arrived at the station, having accomplished the distance in little more than two hours.

The house was situated in the midst of the plantation, and having never been used by Colonel Leigh or his family, was very plainly furnished. Dismounting from his horse at the door, he threw the reins to a negro who hastened out, and asked,—

"Where's the superintendent, darkie?"

L

" Out on de plantation, massa."

" Put my horse in the stable, and then go and tell him I'm here."

" Bery good, massa."

While waiting for the arrival of the superintendent, Gerald Leigh passed hurriedly up and down in front of the house. He had not done so more than ten minutes, when the superintendent hurried up and saluted him respectfully.

" Glad to see you, Captain Leigh ; didn't expect you, though."

" No, Gideon, somewhat a sudden visit, but my business is pressing—come inside."

Gideon Geary, the superintendent, was a tall backwoodsman, from Vermont. He was not one of the professional overseers or slave-drivers, but had adopted the life by accident.

Ten years previously he had saved the only daughter of Colonel Leigh from drowning, and the colonel, in gratitude, determined to provide a berth for him. As, however, all the property of the colonel consisted of slaves and plantation, he had nothing other to offer but a situation as overseer. Gideon, at first, with all his Free State prejudices on him, refused to become a "niggerdriver." But when it was explained to him that he would have the means of doing great good among the slaves, and of ameliorating their position, he consented to take the post on trial.

He was a really kind-hearted man, and found it so different from what he had expected, that he finally retained it, and had now been in Colonel Leigh's service for more than ten years.

Gideon was a fine specimen of an American backwoodsman—six feet three without his shoes, with limbs like branches of trees. Large bony hands ; a great ungainly frame, with but little flesh, and rugged features had Gideon Geary. He was endowed with prodigious strength, and could shoulder and walk off with a log which two or three negroes could not even move.

Seating himself at a table, Gerald Leigh invited the superintendent to follow his example.

Glasses, wine, and fruit were placed on the table.

Gerald filled himself a tumbler of wine, and drained it off at a draught.

" Gideon," he said, putting the glass down, and looking in the rugged face of the backwoodsman, " I've heard bad news to-day."

" Bad news, Master Gerald.   Don't say so, now."

" Yes, bad news of Darcy."

" The Lord save us!" ejaculated Gideon, "I hope nothing ain't happened to Master Darcy.   He's true grit, and I'd be tarnation sorry to hear he came to harm."

" Gideon," said Gerald, slowly, "my brother is dead."

" Dead!"

" Dead; and it is for me to avenge his death."

There was a silence of some time.   A tear coursed down the cheek of the rough Vermonter.

" Master Gerald," he said, "this is the worst news I've had since my poor old mother died.   To think that he's dead; why it seems only but yesterday that I used to take him out in the woods, 'possum hunting."

" Gideon," said Gerald, after another pause, "this is no time for vain regrets.   He's gone.   God rest his soul."

" Amen !"

" How many hands have you on the plantation ? "

" Five and twenty."

" And what cattle ? "

" Four bullocks and ten horses."

" We must make a stampede, Gideon:

" Make a stampede, sir ? What, leave the old place ? "

" Yes ; we must make tracks for the old place in Virginia.   I have not yet heard directly from my father— probably he has had no opportunity of writing—but I have heard of him.   He has joined the South.   This State will probably fall into the hands of the Federal troops, and all so-called 'rebel property' will be confiscated. So, you see, we must move the hands and cattle South; at least, the horses, for I want them and a hundred or so more."

"When do you think of making a move, sir?"

"To-morrow. It is useless delaying."

"And the crops?"

"Must be left; we cannot stay for them."

"Very good, sir. What must be, must be. I've served your father for ten years, and a noble gentleman I've always found him; and I'm not going to leave him in the hour of trouble."

It was now evening, and Gideon ordered supper to be prepared for his young master, while he went to make arrangements for an early move in the morning.

The horses and cattle were all got in, and several drays loaded with the effects of the negroes and such portable property from the house as it was thought advisable to take. In the morning all was hurry and confusion.

The negroes thought this sudden stampede capital fun, and laughed, chattered, and shouted with all that utter lightheartedness and carelessness for which the African race is so celebrated.

Gerald Leigh himself superintended the arrangements, and when all were completed, drew Gideon Geary on one side to give him his final directions.

"You will make the best of your way to Harper's Ferry, about ten miles higher up the Potomac than Washington. It will take you at least a week to track the distance. I will join you there at the end of that time, and will cross with you over into Virginia, and make for my father's plantation. On the road pick up and bring all the horses you can—at least, all strong useful horses, suitable for cavalry purposes. I think that is all, and I can make the best of my way back to Baltimore."

At this moment an enormous dog, which had been let loose from the kennel, rushed up to Gerald, and commenced bounding and capering around him, evincing its joy by every means in its power.

"What, Lion, old boy, is that you?" said Gerald, caressing the brute's head with his hand.

" What shall we do with the dog, sir ?—take him with us ?"

Gerald thought for a moment, and then replied,—

" No; he shall come with me. What do you say, Lion ?"

Lion, as if he understood the question, commenced again bounding and leaping about.

Then the cavalcade set out, and Gerald Leigh, mounting his horse, galloped off in the direction of Baltimore, followed by the big dog. It was evening when he again clattered through the streets of the city, and halted at the steps of the hotel. Giving his horse to a negro, who came round from the stables, he entered; and going up to the hotel bar, asked for Lieutenant Murdock and his friends.

The clerk thought they were in the smoking room, but on making his way there he found they had left. One of the negro waiters said he thought that the gentlemen had gone to a liquor store in Union-square, where there was a bowling saloon.

CHAPTER XXIV.

RECRUITING FOR THE REBELS.

GERALD LEIGH hastened out, and proceeded to try the various bowling saloons and liquor bars in the square. As he passed out of one of these, his attention was suddenly taken by two men who stood at the bar in earnest conversation.

He felt certain that he knew one of these men, but could not at once call to mind when or where he had seen him. Suddenly it flashed across his mind he had seen him at New York. It was Thong, whom Webster Gayle had discharged from his service.

Gerald Leigh thought no more of the matter, and passed in. At last he found his friends. They were in the back room of a liquor saloon, and he was directed to them by the sound of their voices, which were heard half across the square, shouting, laughing, and singing.

It appeared that they were enjoying themselves.

Gerald Leigh looked gloomy and annoyed; he felt in no humour for mirth, with his brother's death yet fresh in his mind. Passing through the bar, he entered the room at the back, and advanced up to the head of the table, at which was seated the Englishman whom they had rescued, flanked on each side by Trent and Winstone, two of his brother officers in the United States' army. At the other end of the table were Murdock and Irving, and next them were the three Irishmen who had also been engaged in the fight of the previous day.

Captain George, the Englishman, had his head bandaged up, but otherwise seemed none the worse for the scrimmage he had been in. He appeared quite at home, and was on the best of terms with everybody. A shout of joy greeted the appearance of Gerald Leigh.

" Here you are, Gerald, come over here by us," cried Winstone, on Captain George's right; " plenty of room for you, and devilish good company, by thunder ! "

Gerald Leigh looked around him, and saw evidence of a carouse in the flushed faces and glittering eyes of the company. A bowl of punch was on the table, and sundry bottles of wine and spirits.

" Allow me to offer you some punch, sir," said Captain George, rising and offering him a glass; " I can recommend the brew."

" No, I thank you," replied Gerald, with a mournful smile; " I am in no humour just now to join in your merriment; nevertheless, I do not wish to interfere with you; enjoy yourself to the top of your bent—that is, if you think it wise with that cut head of yours."

" Oh, that is nothing," was the laughing reply. " If I never fare worse in my journey through the world, I shall not complain."

Gerald bowed politely, and turning to the other end of the table, said,—

" Murdock, I want a few words with you."

Murdock arose and came round to him.

" Did you get a note from me ? "

" By Jove, yes; I was very sorry to hear you had bad

news of Darcy, upon my soul I was; but these fellows
have been carrying on such a game that I declare they
drove it clean out of my head."

Gerald seated himself at a little table, and invited
Murdock to follow his example.

"Are you sober enough," he said, "to listen to what
I have to say?"

"Well, I am sober enough, as far as that goes,
although I must own to having had a glass or two of
punch."

"Well, to commence," said Gerald, "I told you I had
bad news of poor Darcy."

"Yes; what of him—has he got into any scrape?"

"He is dead," said Gerald, in a low voice.

Murdock looked deeply grieved and shocked.

"Dead!"

"Yes, dead; he attempted to seize the Spitfire, the
sloop he was on board of, and was successful, for they
ran her out to sea. Unfortunately he paid for the
success with his life, for he was shot just as they were
steaming by the commodore's ship; he would not allow
a gun to be fired, although they could have raked her
fore and aft, and the Yankees showed their gratitude by
killing him. But it is of no use talking of the past, let
us look to the future. You have long since made up
your mind to leave the service."

"Yes."

"And join the Confederate cause."

"Yes, heart and soul."

"The others, too—Irving, Winstone, and Trent—
they will also do the same."

"Yes, undoubtedly, and a dozen more who are now in
Baltimore."

"Well, then, I propose to raise an irregular cavalry
regiment at once; some of you have horses, and I shall
have twenty horses to meet me on the Potomac in a
week's time. We can get twenty others about Baltimore, and with what our friends already have, we shall
be able to muster sixty or seventy sabres in less than a
fortnight. We will then cross over into Virginia, above

Washington, when we can soon get our strength up to five or six hundred. Go and speak to the others about it."

Lieutenant Murdock went over to Winstone and Trent, while Gerald Leigh approached Irving, and was soon engaged in earnest conversation.

"What is the matter, Murdock?" said Winstone, as the young officer approached them; "is Charleston bombarded, or New Orleans captured? You look serious enough for something of the kind."

Murdock made no reply, but seating himself, commenced to unfold the plans which Gerald Leigh proposed.

"Raise a cavalry regiment right off; with all my heart," said one of the young officers; "I'm tired of the Stars and Stripes and the United States' uniform."

"And I," said his friend.

"That, then, is settled; you have horses, so have I, and Gerald Leigh will provide some forty. By Jupiter, the Yankees will find out we're in earnest before we've done with them, I reckon."

"Do you think there will be anything of a war, sir?" asked Captain George.

"That depends," replied Murdock; "if the Northerners let us separate peaceably, there need be no war at all; but if they think to keep us in the Union by force, to conquer us back, they will find that we will fight to the last gasp; aye, fight, and conquer too. The Yankees never could beat us, and never shall."

"And do you think they will refuse you your independence?"

"I do; they are so inflated with arrogance and self-esteem, and have, in addition, such strong pecuniary reasons for keeping us still bound to them, that they will never willingly let us leave the Union."

"And you think that the Southerners are fully determined to have their independence?"

"I am sure they are so determined, and that they will assert it; and why should they not? have we not as much and more right to secede from the United States as they had to rebel a hundred years ago, and throw off the English yoke?"

"I do not deny your right," was the reply; "I simply question your power."

"You shall see, sir; before another twelvemonth has passed over, we will give them a specimen of our pluck and determination, which will convince them that we have both the will and the power to be independent."

The young Englishman, whom they knew as Captain George, rose from his seat and went over to the three Irishmen.

"Give his honour some drink," said one of them to the other, "don't you see his glass is empty? Bad luck to ye, where's your manners?"

"No, I don't want any more just now, thank you, Pat. I wish to have a little talk with you."

"Talk away, yer honour, but my name ain't Pat, at your service, it's Mick—Mickey Callaghan they call me. This one here, sir, this one wid the shock head of red hair, is Pat—Patrick O'Brien's his name; but we call him 'Paddy the Soldier,' because, don't ye see, yer honour, he's been in the army."

"Well, and your other friend?"

"Oh, he's no good at all; his name's Barney Quin; the villain! he's not worth a rap, your honour, barring for a free fight, or the likes of that; he's got no edication, your honour. Now, if yer wanted a smart active lad, as clerk, or mayhap, footman or page, it's Paddy O'Brien's the boy for you."

Captain George smiled at the idea of having Paddy, the soldier, with his red head and great hulking form, in page's livery.

"Paddy," said the Englishman to this worthy, "can you ride—ride a horse, I mean?"

"Well, your honour, it would be strange if I couldn't. Sure I was in the cavalry for five years."

"And you, Mickey?"

"Sure and I can; I was a helper in Lord Waterford's stables on the Curragh, when I was a boy, and many's the bit of blood I've had my legs across.

" And you, Barney Quin ? "

" Is it me, yer honour, can I ride ? in coorse I can."

" Go along wid ye, don't ye believe him, sir; he can ride in the inside of a coach, or on the railway cars, that's all the riding he can do."

" 'Deed, then, ye know jest nothing about it, and it's showing yer ignorance ye are, the both av ye, talking av what ye don't understand. Can't I ride, be jabers ? I'll let ye know I can ride. Sure now, didn't I ride over a man at the last Limerick races before I left the ould country ? "

A burst of laughter from his compatriots greeted this speech.

" Ah, you're a fine horseman, the devil doubt ye ! Ride over a man! and is that the way to ride ? Is that what's wanted for a cavalry soldier? "

" Be jabers it is, then, and nothing else."

" Ah, go on wid ye, showing his honour yer igno-rance."

" Ignorance! by St. Patrick, I call it sinse! I'll lave it to his honour, now, and I'll bet ye a York shilling, the pair av ye, I'm right."

" That it's a token of good horsemanship to ride over a man ? I'll bet ye."

" Av coorse it is; what better would ye want for a cavalry soldier than to *ride over the inimy?* Ah, me boys, I had ye then."

Captain George, on being appealed to, declared that Barney Quin had won his York shilling, which he pocketed with great glee.

Meanwhile, Gerald Leigh, Murdock, Irving, Winstone, and Trent remained together in close conversation.

Gerald Leigh had produced his pocket-book, and was taking down names.

" Murdock, you say you know two officers who will join us, each bringing a horse and man; you, Irving, can bring three friends whom you can count on; and you, Trent, three, or perhaps four; I can get seven or eight, at least by to-morrow. This, with ourselves, will make twenty-two. Once in Virginia, we can get as many men as we can provide horses for, of that there is no fear. We can, then, depend on starting to-morrow for the rendezvous, numbering twenty-two men and horses."

"If you are inclined to accept the services of a few volunteers, you can count on more than that, sir," said a voice behind them.

They looked up; it was Captain George who spoke.

"I will find four men and four horses equipped complete. As for the men, I am one, and these three Irishmen, who are accustomed to the saddle, are the others, and the horses are ready at half-an-hour's notice."

"But I thought you were an Englishman."

"And so I am, but that fact did not prevent me drawing my sword and fighting by the side of the great and glorious Garibaldi, nor do I see why it should prevent me fighting by your sides, gentlemen, so long as you fight for what is but your right—your independence."

"Nobly spoken," said Gerald Leigh; "I don't know your name, sir."

"They call me Captain George."

"Then, Captain George, here's my hand."

The young men now all rose and left the saloon to return to the hotel. Captain George gave the three Irishmen a couple of dollars, and told them to be round the first thing in the morning.

He had arranged with them to accept service with him; he had so won their confidence that they cared little what the service was, and when they learned it was to join a volunteer regiment of cavalry for the Confederates, they at once assented.

"Be jabers!" said Paddy the Soldier, "if it was volunteer cavalry for the divil himself, with all his imps to blow the bugles, I'd be one among them."

Gerald Leigh left them on arriving at the hotel, and sent his name up to the two young ladies.

His friends as usual found their way to the smoking-room, where they commenced to discuss their plans and prospects. When they discovered that their new friend, Captain George, besides having served with the great

Italian liberator, had also held a commission in the English army, he rose greatly in their estimation.

There was a quiet earnestness in all he did or said which did not fail to impress them. Notwithstanding his apparent recklessness, he went so quietly and systematically to work at everything, that they began to discover there was much concealed beneath the dashing, careless exterior. As to who he was or what he was they knew not.

He appeared to have abundance of money, but what he was doing in America, and why he chose to lead the Bohemian life which he had done for the last year or two by his own confession, they could not discover.

No matter, they found him a very good fellow, good company, liberal, and ready for any enterprise, and he was soon as firmly installed in their good opinion as if they had known him for years.

On his way to the ladies' apartment, Gerald Leigh encountered Lupus Rock in one of the corridors. He was just issuing from a private room, which Gerald conjectured was his own, and was in earnest conversation with a man whom at first the young officer did not recognise. He nodded carelessly to Lupus, who bowed coldly in return, and strode on towards the ladies' drawing-room.

As he passed on, it flashed across his mind that the form and general appearance of the man was familiar to him. Then he recalled to mind having before seen Lupus in Baltimore, engaged in conversation with Malpas Thong, and he at once concluded that it was he whom he had just now passed.

Stella and Angela Gayle welcomed him heartily, but sadly.

Angela was at all times too partial to the frank, bold-spirited young officer to act otherwise, and even the haughty spirit of Stella had received a shock which had somewhat tamed its enthusiasm.

With the memory of his brother's tragic end fresh in her memory, she could not find it in her heart to speak or even think the bitter thoughts with which she had met the treason of Darcy. She contented herself, then, with entreaties that he would think better of the matter.

Seconded by Angela, who, with tearful eyes, looked imploringly in his face, she begged that he would not join those mad rebels, but would retain his commission in the United States' army.

" What!" he cried, "and fight by the side of my brother's murderers, against friends, relations, even my father, for I know that he has joined the rebellion? Angela—Stella, can you really counsel me to draw my sword against my own father—perhaps to lead my men to an attack in which he would perish?"

" Then, Gerald, why cannot you remain neutral? Why need you identify yourself with this rebellion, which will be speedily crushed out?"

Gerald Leigh laughed scornfully.

" And so, my gentle little Angela, you think it will be soon crushed out?"

Angela was standing by his side, and in the earnestness of her entreaties, she had laid her hand on his arm. Gerald Leigh drew her gently towards him, and bending down his head till his cheek brushed her soft hair, he said mournfully:—

" Crushed out!—Angela, this rebellion will never be crushed out but at the price of extermination. When my bones, and the bones of every one of the hundreds of thousands of Southern gentlemen who draw the sword shall bleach on the field of battle—when the land is a wilderness, deluged with blood—when the Southern people shall have been crushed out of existence, annihilated—then the rebellion will have been crushed out!—then, and not till then! If you believe in the possibility of eight millions of free people, familiar with arms, and willing, nay, eager to fight desperately in self-defence, being subjugated, you may hope that the rebellion will be crushed out."

Angela Gayle, scarcely conscious of what she did, leaned her head on Gerald's shoulder and wept.

Stella looked on mournfully in silence. There was something so noble, so manly in Gerald Leigh, that rebel though he was, she felt no pang at seeing her only sister clinging to him like the honeysuckle to the oak.

Gerald Leigh had been their friend, their companion from their earliest infancy. The visits of himself and his brother to New York, when they were at school together, were always eagerly looked for by the sisters. And when they left school, and went to the military academy at West Point, twice a year at least the brothers were looked for as a matter of course.

After the obsequious politeness and saturnine manners of their cousin Lupus Rock, the boisterous gaiety and high spirits of Gerald, and the quiet, firm, and earnest manner of Darcy came like the sunshine after a gloomy sky. With strangers Gerald was always at once a special favourite. He seemed to jump right into their affections, and it was no more possible to resist his frank, engaging manner, than it was to feel in time the deep influence which the powerful character and quiet energy of Darcy produced.

Whatever might have been the feelings of Stella towards Darcy Leigh, it is certain that the shock of his sudden death had thrown her into a state of gloom and despondency which she would hardly admit to herself. Probably she felt remorse at the ungenerous words she had addressed to him in her father's drawing-room, the last he ever heard from her lips. Perhaps it was this memory which caused her to deal tenderly and gently with the dashing Gerald. Although in some respects so different, there was a certain striking likeness between the two brothers, a likeness rather in expression than feature. Gerald was tall, broad-shouldered, and fair, while, on the other hand, Darcy was of middle stature, slight, and dark. Gerald looked the *beau ideal* of a soldier, handsome, with an upright, noble carriage, and limbs partaking of the grace of Apollo with the strength of Hercules. Darcy, on the other hand, although well built, seemed even slighter than he really was, and usually walked with head down. This gave him the appearance of a slight stoop.

Darcy's features were finely cut, almost effeminate. The thin nose and clearly chiselled mouth, unshaded by moustache, gave him a singularly girlish cast of countenance. Gerald's features, though good and regular, were cast altogether in a larger, grander mould. Notwithstanding these great differences, there were times when the most casual observer could not fail to discover a great resemblance. When Darcy Leigh would wake up from his usual quiet, listless manner, when excited from any cause—anger, pleasure, or otherwise—then the family likeness might be seen, and this so strikingly, that people would wonder they never noticed it before.

As Gerald Leigh stood by the side of Angela Gayle, Stella, regarding him in rapt attention, saw on his handsome features the self-same look as that with which Darcy Leigh left her father's drawing-room for the last time. There was a silence of some time, during which the gentle Angela did not seek to restrain her tears. So far from the presence of Gerald being an embarrassment, she felt it rather as a relief. After a little time she disengaged herself, and trying to smile through her tears, took a seat, while he placed himself beside her.

"And have you then quite decided on this mad, this hopeless enterprise ?" asked Stella, gazing on the ground.

"Yes, quite," was the reply; "to-morrow I go to Washington. I will see you there safely installed in your new home, and then, at the head of some twenty or thirty brave fellows, I shall cross the Potomac, and join the Confederate army."

"Are you then going to raise a regiment ?"

"Yes, a cavalry regiment—irregular cavalry. I have sent on all the horses from the Kenhana plantation. We shall pick up others on the road, and shall doubtless find men to mount them. Then in about a week from this date I trust to rendezvous at Harper's Ferry with about a hundred sabres."

"But suppose you are discovered ? Harper's Ferry is so near Washington."

"We shall take all necessary precautions ; shall leave Washington late at night, and ford the river early in the morning. Once across we are safe."

"It seems very terrible and very dangerous," said Angela mournfully.

"Terrible — dangerous!" exclaimed Stella; "that does not express it. It is madness—madness—madness!"

"Let the event prove," said Gerald.

"I fear the proof will be a bitter one for you, Gerald," said Stella. "I pray Heaven I may be wrong, but I foresee nothing but disaster to you and yours from this step."

"So be it—disaster, death—I brave them all. Disgrace can never come."

"Gerald, will any of your brother officers accompany you?"

"Yes, several, besides that young Englishman who so gallantly came to your assistance. Then there is——"

Gerald Leigh suddenly interrupted himself, and glanced towards the door. This was concealed by a screen placed there in order to prevent draught. Both Gerald and the two girls heard a slight noise from this direction.

"Some one is behind the screen," said Gerald, advancing rapidly towards it.

However, on inspection, he found no one. The door, however, was ajar, and he felt almost certain that he could hear footsteps hurrying away. He closed the door, and returning, said,—

"Some one entered the room behind the screen, I am almost certain; whether by mistake or for the purpose of eavesdropping, I cannot say. I trust not the latter, or, at all events, that our conversation was not heard."

Stella and Angela gazed in alarm in each other's faces, and the former proceeded to urge Gerald to abandon the enterprise, lest he should have been overheard, in which case he might be betrayed. Gerald, however, stoutly refused.

Then Stella and Angela both pressed him to alter his plans—at least to fix on a different rendezvous. He mused for some time in silence.

"I fear it is impossible," he said; "Harper's Ferry is the only practicable one for many miles, and the superintendent from the Maryland plantation is to meet us there with the horses. He is now on the road, and I do not know how to communicate with him."

Shortly after this Gerald Leigh left the two sisters, promising to return in the morning.

"You will accompany us to Washington, will you not, Gerald?" asked Stella, anxiously. "Do you know, I feel so much safer when you are with us."

Had Stella Gayle striven to analyse her feelings, she would have found it difficult to do so. Gerald Leigh was, in her opinion, a rebel, a traitor to the Union for which she had so romantic a regard, and yet she acknowledged that she felt safer when with him. So true it is that the heart of woman clings instinctively to the brave and noble, no matter under what flag they fight, or how antagonistic their aims and desires.

CHAPTER XXV.

THE STOLEN PAPERS.

IT was, indeed, Malpas Thong whom Gerald Leigh met with Lupus. They had been closeted together for nearly two hours in the private room of the latter. The conversation had evidently been important, for the table was strown with letters and papers; and Malpas also carried out with him a roll of notes, which he had not when he entered. The two men passed out together, and strolled leisurely down the street.

"Now I think we thoroughly understand each other," said Lupus to his tool; "you know the part you are to play, and are prepared to carry it out at all hazards?"

"Right you are," replied the man, gruffly.

"By the way, who was that fellow I saw you talking with this morning?"

"That," said Thong, carelessly—"oh, he calls himself the Chevalier Leroux."

"What and who is he?"

"As to who he is I don't know, and much question if he himself could give a clear account of his parentage. As to what he is, he is much the same as you, I, and a few thousand more in this go-ahead country."

"And what is that?"

" A thundering rogue ! "

Lupus coloured with passion.

" How dare you address me so, fellow ? " he exclaimed, with a savage look.

" How dare I ? Now just you look here, Mister Rock," replied Thong, coolly picking his teeth; "as to how dare I, I dare do a deal more than that, as you may find if you play any of yer tricks. If you 're in the boat, by thunder! so am I; and it 'll take a better man than you to trick me out. No, sirree, this child means sticking to you till the last. We began it together, and by G—d, we 'll finish! So now, old hoss, you know yer man. You just stick to yer bargain, and never mind about flying into tantrums, for this child don't care a cuss for all you can do."

So saying, the slave-driver produced a plug of tobacco, and biting off a piece, commenced chewing it indifferently.

Lupus Rock glared angrily at his worthy companion; for a moment his hand sought the bosom of his shirt.

Malpas saw the motion.

" No you don't," he said, keeping his eye fixed on him.

Lupus, with a muttered oath, thinking it useless and dangerous to defy his ruffian associate, answered,—

" Well, well, there is no necessity for us to quarrel; you perform your part, and I will not be wanting in mine."

" Ah, that's something like talk; and now, since you 're civil, I'll tell you all I know of this Leroux. Ever since I 've known him he 's been living by his wits. He 's a gambler and a blackleg, and a d—d clever one; he's game for any villany, but he is in his heart a rank coward. Now, he and I have got a little business together, and if he dared, he would throw me over; but in that respect he 's like you, Mr. Lupus—he 's got all the will, but he daren't do it."

Again an expression of strong hate came over Rock's features. Malpas Thong seemed to take a morbid delight in playing with his fears, as he had before done with those of Leroux,

The two associates now separated, having appointed to meet again two days afterwards at Washington.

We have been speaking of the worthy Chevalier Leroux; let us, for a short space, return to him. Scarcely ten minutes had elapsed after Thong and Lupus had gone out together, than Leroux passed the open door of the latter's room. He was himself staying at the hotel, and his room being on a higher floor, it so happened that it was necessary for him to pass the door of the other's on his way down.

The door was just ajar; Leroux pushed it open and glanced in. It almost seemed the work of instinct. He saw before him a table strewn with papers, law documents, &c.

"Who knows?" he muttered to himself, "there may be a roll of notes among that lot."

Then, cautiously glancing around him, he passed into the room. Advancing to the table, he commenced turning over the papers, &c.

After some minutes of this work, he gave vent to an exclamation of disappointment, and seemed almost inclined to return. There stood before him a small escritoire, open. It contained several drawers, which he proceeded to examine one by one. In each of these drawers were bundles of papers and letters.

Suddenly his eye was caught by the endorsement on one of these bundles, and he took it from the drawer. After a rapid glance at its nature, he turned to leave the room, muttering to himself in a tone of exultation,—

"By Heavens! this may prove of more service to me than dollars."

He then passed out as silently as he entered, with the packet still in his hand. He was walking down the corridor when he perceived the figure of a man coming towards him. He himself was in comparative shadow, so as not to be plainly visible, but the other figure was right in the glare of lamps at the commencement of the corridor.

Leroux gazed for one moment as if half in doubt. Then he staggered back as if shot. He grew white as death, his knees knocked together from terror. The figure advanced carelessly towards him, humming an air.

It was the form of a good-looking young man of about seven or eight and twenty. There was nothing in the appearance of this figure to cause such terrible alarm in the breast of the gallant Chevalier.

He was decidedly prepossessing in appearance, with a light, well-built, sinewy frame; good features, a sharp, bright eye, and wearing an expression half of recklessness, half of calm, deliberate determination.

Certainly to a stranger, the Chevalier's alarm would appear most uncalled for. Suddenly the young man cast his eyes on the form of Leroux, as he remained huddled in a doorway.

He gazed through the obscurity for a second or so with careless curiosity.

Then his eyes blazed, and with a terrible cry of rage, he dashed towards him. Instantly that Leroux saw he was recognised, he darted away with the energy of despair. He dashed through an open door further up.

It led to a ladies' drawing-room, similar to that occupied by the two sisters. It was on the first floor, and opened on to a balcony. Leroux, without hesitating a moment or pausing to unfasten and open the window, dashed himself through the glass, and all cut and bleeding, leaped from the balcony into the garden below, where he fell heavily. He lay for a moment as if stunned, and then, gathering himself up, he crawled slowly and painfully into some shrubs, and disappeared.

His pursuer arrived on the balcony immediately after him. He appeared, for a moment, as if about to follow him, but thought better of it. Drawing his revolver, he fired a shot at the spot in the shrubs where he had last seen him.

A shriek of pain bore evidence that he had, at all events, wounded his enemy. Then he hastily retraced his steps, and running down stairs, he shouted for some of the hotel porters and waiters to follow him.

"A hundred dollars to the man who captures a villain,

who has just jumped from the first floor window. Follow me, my boys—he is a thief—a murderer!"

He rushed out with a crowd of others into the small garden at the back of the hotel. They searched the shrubs carefully in every direction, but could discover no signs of the fugitive. At last they came across a splash of blood.

From this a succession of spots led to a low part in the wooden palisades. These were smeared with blood; so it was evident that the fugitive had by this means made his escape into the adjoining yard which communicated with a public thoroughfare. At a distance of not more than a hundred yards from this was the main street. That once gained, doubtless Leroux had called a passing fly, and was by this time far away. His wounded appearance would have excited no surprise in those turbulent times, and as they could find or hear nothing of him the pursuit was relinquished.

The young man, the pursuer, was Gerald Leigh's new friend the Englishman, whom he knew as Captain George. The sisters Gayle had requested Gerald to send him up to their room, in order to receive their thanks for the gallant way in which he had come to their assistance. It was on his way up the corridor towards their room that he had suddenly encountered Leroux.

Now that it was evident his enemy had escaped, he again ascended the stairs to find his way to the ladies. We have said that when Leroux left the room of Rock, he held in his hand the bundle of purloined papers. In his precipitate flight he dropped them.

Captain George saw them fall from his hand, but did not at the time stop to pick them up. Now, however, as he passed along the corridor again, he remembered to have seen something dropped, and searching as near as he could remember the spot, he succeeded in finding them, and placed them in his breast pocket without examining them, thinking to do so at some future time.

When he entered the presence of the two sisters, he bore on his countenance but little trace of the exciting chase he had just been a party to. He was, perhaps, a shade paler, but that was all. He received the thanks of Stella and Angela in a light, easy manner, declaring that what he had done was quite unworthy of notice. After remaining in conversation with them for some quarter of an hour, he politely took his leave.

He then went to his own room, and proceeded to examine the packet of papers he had picked up. On his way to his room he passed Lupus Rock, who was coming towards the drawing-room of the ladies. One by one, and carefully, he opened each paper and letter, and read their contents.

If he expected that any of them would throw any light or reveal anything concerning the man who had dropped them, he was mistaken. He could make nothing of them. They related to subjects and to persons of which he knew nothing, and of whom he had never heard.

With a look of disappointment he threw them away from him. But, on second thoughts, he carefully gathered them up again, and, unlocking a small desk on his table, placed them within it, and again locked it.

"There is an old saying," he said to himself, "keep a thing for seven years, and you'll find a use for it. Who knows that these papers, senseless and incomprehensible as they now seem to me, may not some day be of good service?"

Lupus Rock, after parting from Thong, returned leisurely to the hotel. Arrived there, he, instead of seeking his own apartments, made his way to that of his cousins. He found the door ajar, and could plainly distinguish the voices of the two girls and of Gerald Leigh in earnest conversation. With a muttered curse, he was about to retire, when a few words uttered by Stella caught his attention.

He pushed open the door and advanced noiselessly behind the screen, where he could hear all without being seen. It is probable he would have waited there until the conclusion of the conversation, but, unfortunately, a slight noise he made called the attention of Gerald, and the eavesdropper beat a hasty retreat.

He again passed out of the hotel, and, walking up and

down in front of the steps, seemed in deep thought. There was an expression of vindictive joy, mixed with a certain amount of uncertainty, on his handsome features.

"Yes, yes," he muttered, "he must be betrayed to Government. But then there comes the question, will it not compromise me with the rebels, with whom it is necessary for me, at present, to keep in?"

All at once an idea seemed to have struck him, for the expression of uncertainty disappeared, and was succeeded by one of perfect gratification.

A smile of triumph played on his lips; the piercing eyes glittered with a vengeful light.

"Of course," he said to himself. "What a fool I must have been. He need not know, no one need know, the source from which the information proceeded. I can manage to get my fine bullying gentleman arrested, condemned, and none be the wiser as to how it happened. It is as plain as day, and simple as possible."

He then returned to the hotel, and hastened to his own room.

During his absence the scene we have described—the flight and escape of Leroux—had taken place.

Lupus, however, knew nothing of this, nor that his room had been entered.

He noticed, however, that the door was open.

"Careless of me, very," he thought, "to leave my room door open, with all my papers lying about."

He advanced to the table, and commenced assorting and arranging them, placing them in the small drawers of the escritoire. Opening one of these drawers, in order to insert a packet of papers, he observed with astonishment that it was empty.

"By Heavens!" he said, "there is something gone from here. I feel almost sure that I did not leave that packet in New York; and yet it is not here."

He then commenced a strict search, but did not succeed in finding the missing packet. He leaned his head on his hand, and tried to think where he could possibly have placed it.

One thing was quite certain, and he was obliged, after

diligent search, to acknowledge the fact — it was not there. It must either then be at New York in his iron safe, or have been lost or stolen. He hoped the former. As to its being lost, he did not see any possibility of that, for if it had been there at all, it would have been in its usual place. But then it might have been stolen.

Who, however, could have stolen it, and for what purpose?

For a moment his thoughts turned to Thong, but he remembered he had been in his company all the time they were in the room together, that he had never left him alone even for an instant. When he left him too, Thong went in quite an opposite direction to that leading to the hotel; so he finally dismissed the thought of Thong being the thief from his mind. Finally he came to the conclusion that he must have left them at New York.

He placed all the papers in the escritoire, and carefully locked it before leaving the room, determined for the future not to be guilty of such folly as leaving his table covered with dangerous documents and the door open.

"After all, even if it were stolen," he said to himself, "it would be quite useless to any one not acquainted with all the particulars. To a stranger the papers would be incomprehensible."

And with this consoling thought he left the room, locking the door behind him, and sought his cousins' apartment.

"I suppose their dear friend, Mr. Gerald Leigh, will have left by this time, unless he intends to take up his quarters with my cousins altogether."

He met the young Englishman just coming from their apartments. He little thought that in the breast pocket of the latter was his lost packet. He recognised the Englishman as the man who had first come to their assistance in the street row.

He bowed coldly, muttering, "More visitors—on my soul, these young ladies seem determined to have their own way and act exactly as they please in every respect."

He did not remain long with Stella and her sister. He asked if they were ready to start for Washington on the following morning.

"To-morrow morning—yes, to-night if you please," said Angela; "for certainly we are most heartily tired of this place, where we have neither friends nor acquaintances."

"Why, I thought you were tolerably fortunate in that respect," said Lupus; "there is your friend Captain Leigh, and I just now met another gentleman leaving your room. Certainly you have no right to complain of the want of male friends."

"That gentleman whom you saw just now leave was he to whom we owe our safety, perhaps our lives; for assuredly it would have fared ill with us had he not so bravely come to our rescue."

"By the way," said Lupus Rock, with affected carelessness, "Gerald Leigh is going to accompany you to Washington, is he not?"

Stella looked up, and cast a scrutinising glance at her cousin. She was not deceived by the affected careless manner.

"Yes," she replied, slowly—"have you any objection?"

"Not the slightest," was the laughing reply; "on the contrary, I shall be very glad of some one to relieve me of a portion of the worry and bother of attending to two young ladies with luggage enough for six."

With these words Lupus rose and left the room.

"Angela," said Stella, earnestly, "Lupus has some design on foot—some treacherous design against Gerald Leigh. Did you mark the change in his manner? Before, he was averse to our seeing him; now, he expresses himself anxious he may accompany us. I am sure there is danger to Gerald in Washington; or, at all events, in the company of Lupus Rock."

"Heaven forbid that he should incur any danger for our sakes!" said Angela, passionately. "Rather, far rather, would I brave any peril or inconvenience than that he, so good, so kind, and noble, should suffer injury through us."

Stella Gayle mused for some time, then she said with a sigh,—

"The whole future seems dark, gloomy, and impenetrable. At each moment fresh terrors, fresh complications, start up. This sudden journey to Washington, so inexplicable, so apparently causeless, but which our father declares absolutely necessary to our interests. Then the fact of our travelling alone with Lupus Rock, and his manner, at times almost insolent, as if with conscious power, either now or in prospect. All these things perplex and alarm me. I see no solution, no way out of the labyrinth."

"We must put our trust in Heaven, Stella, and in Gerald Leigh. I am sure he will never desert us!"

Stella could not help smiling at the *naive* manner with which Angela spoke of Heaven and Gerald Leigh.

"Which do you mean will never desert you, Angela?" she asked; "Heaven or Gerald Leigh?"

"Neither, I hope. Heaven might, if unworthy; but I feel sure that, right or wrong, whatever we might do, in Gerald Leigh we should find a champion."

"I shall write to papa," said Stella, after a time, "and beg him to follow us to Washington as soon as possible, that we are very miserable, and have already been exposed to insult and outrage. Then, if he is not the most hard-hearted of parents, he will come to the rescue of his disconsolate daughters."

Then Stella, seating herself at her writing-desk, proceeded to indite a long, rambling letter to her father, setting forth how unhappy they were generally, and begging him to follow at once to Washington, or allow them to return to New York.

Lupus Rock was at the same time engaged in writing a long letter to Webster Gayle. In this he went at full length into a number of topics, all relating to certain plans and schemes to make enormous profits out of the rebellion; but the particulars of which it is not at present necessary the reader should know. He spoke of the great difficulty he had in controlling the two young ladies, and requested his uncle to write to his daughters, ordering them to observe greater obedience to himself. "For," said Lupus in his letter, "it is monstrous that the success of plans such as ours should be endangered by the waywardness of two headstrong girls." He mentioned Gerald Leigh ; but added that, "after their arrival at Washington, he should so manage as not to be further troubled by him." He impressed on the mind of Webster Gayle the absolute necessity of his remaining for the present in New York. Lupus declared that as things were at present, the presence of his uncle in Washington, so far from doing good, would be highly imprudent, and would involve very heavy pecuniary losses. Chuckling over this last appeal to Webster Gayle's love of the almighty dollar, Lupus Rock concluded his letter.

"There," he said to himself, as he sealed and addressed it, " I'll warrant that will keep my worthy uncle quiet. The fear of pecuniary losses will effectually bar his coming on to Washington for a few weeks, and by the expiration of that time, I will so contrive as further to delay his arrival, and still further get him in my power. Already I have letters and papers under his hand sufficient to obtain his arrest for treason in a short time ; by skilful management I shall have his life in my hands— and then, proud and beautiful Stella, my marble statue, I'll force you to come down from your pedestal, and prove you are but flesh and blood !"

And this was his uncle, his benefactor, and daughter of whom he thus spoke.

The two letters, that of Stella and that of Lupus Rock, were duly despatched by the same post, the former hoping that her appeal might not be in vain ; the latter confident that his would have the desired effect.

CHAPTER XXVI.

WASHINGTON.

On the following morning they all took their places in the cars for Washington. The streets were now quiet, as large reinforcements of United States' troops had arrived, who succeeded in keeping in awe the secession mob.

Gerald Leigh accompanied them as was arranged, but Stella was somewhat surprised to observe the large number of his friends and acquaintances who were also going by the same train.

There were with him Murdock, Irving, Winstone, Trent, and the Englishman, Captain George.

All these Stella knew by sight, as they were, with the exception of the Englishman, Gerald's brother officers.

But in addition to these, there were many in the party who were strangers to her. Some of these, say six or seven, seemed gentlemen, while the others, to the number of twenty, apparently belonged to a lower class.

Lupus Rock was also surprised at this large muster of men, who were evidently acting in concert. He prudently held his tongue, however, and resolved to be more than usually cautious.

The two sisters saw in this gathering of Gerald's friends sad confirmation of his own words—that he was about to raise a regiment of irregular cavalry, and go over to the enemy. These men were the nucleus of the regiment; and, surveying them, the sisters could not but see that, if they proved as good soldiers as they were fine men, it would, indeed, prove a formidable force.

Lupus Rock, seated by their side, watched Gerald Leigh going from one group to the other, giving directions, or merely passing casual remarks. Stella detected a bitter, mocking smile on the face of her cousin as his eye rested on Gerald Leigh; she was gifted with more penetration than most girls of her age; and coupling this with the singular manner she had observed in him on the previous day, she felt certain that the young officer was in great danger, and that Lupus Rock knew the nature of that danger—perhaps might be himself the cause.

She at once determined to put Gerald on his guard; so catching his eye just as the cars were on the point of starting, she gave a slight sign for him to come into the carriage in which they were. Making room for him between herself and her sister, she resolved, on the first opportunity, to tell him of her suspicion—her conviction that there was danger impending.

"Well, truly, fair ladies," said Gerald, laughingly, as he seated himself between them, "you have made me break my word, for I promised to ride in the next car with all the rest of our fellows."

"You are better here, Gerald," said Stella, in a low voice, and with emphasis.

Gerald looked surprised, not so much at the words, but at the low, mournful tone in which they were spoken.

"How so, Stella?" he said.

Lupus Rock, who, seated on the other side, had heard Stella's words, listened intently for what she would say next, and darted a rapid glance at her.

But Stella was too cautious to let him know that she suspected him.

"Why so, Gerald?" she replied; "because we are so dreadfully dull; and, surely you will not be so ungallant as to dispute the fact, that our company is preferable to that of your gentlemen friends."

"Not for a moment, my dear young lady," replied Gerald, "so for the remainder of the journey I am your humble servant, reserving the privilege of an occasional quarter of an hour on the platform for a cigar."

Then they entered into general conversation; Stella determined not to do or say anything which could excite her cousin's suspicion.

"He is as cunning as Satan," she thought; "and, I fear, as bad. So it must be diamond cut diamond."

"I can't make that girl Stella out," thought Lupus Rock. "Sometimes I almost fancy that she sees through me—suspects me. Now this minute I could almost have sworn, by the expression of her features when she spoke to Gerald Leigh, that she had some inkling of my design, or that I had some design against this dashing bully—but the next moment she appears as innocent as possible, and talks quite unconcernedly."

Shortly afterwards Lupus rose, and went out on the platform of the cars.

He well knew that if Stella wished to speak to Gerald

in private, her woman's wit would devise a means, and he was aware of the folly of appearing suspicious of what he was powerless to prevent.

No sooner was he out of earshot than Stella, laying her hand on Gerald's arm, said earnestly,—

"Gerald Leigh, you are in danger—in immediate, imminent danger!"

He started, and exclaimed in surprise,—

"In danger! and from what quarter?"

"From my cousin, Lupus Rock."

Gerald laughed scornfully.

"Lupus Rock! If he is my most serious enemy, I care but little."

"Do not speak so lightly of Lupus—you do not know him as well as I do. He is a dangerous, a very dangerous man. It is a hard thing to say of one's own cousin, Gerald; but Lupus is, I fear, a bad, unscrupulous man. I know he is dangerous and vindictive; you have offended his vanity; that might be a sufficient reason for you to be on your guard."

Angela Gayle now joined her entreaties to her sister's, begging of Gerald not to risk anything, but for the present, at least, to forego his project.

Gerald knew not what to say, with a fair girl on each side imploring him to pause.

He turned from the flashing eyes of Stella to the mild blue eyes of Angela, which already began to dim with tears.

This latter appeared to produce an effect; for, taking the young girl's hand, which she had laid on his arm to give emphasis to her prayers, he said,—

"Well, my sweet little Angela, I will promise you to be very careful and circumspect. At present, no one knows of my design, except three immediately engaged, and your two selves. I can depend on our fellows; and as for you, Stella—Angela, I know you are heart and soul for the Union; still, I scarcely suppose that you would betray a fellow."

"Betray you!" cried Stella, passionately; "I would rather my tongue were torn forth than it should utter a word which could ever endanger you."

"Betray you!" said Angela; "Oh, Gerald!"

That was all she said, but the look with which she accompanied it was quite as eloquent as the passionate words of her sister.

No incident worthy of notice occurred during the journey, and in the evening they safely arrived at Washington. Gerald Leigh busied himself in seeing to the ladies' luggage, and declared his intention of accompanying them to the house. To this Lupus Rock did not make the slightest opposition. Webster Gayle had a house in Washington, which he used when his senatorial duties required his presence in the capital. It was a large handsome building of white stone, situated on a rising ground in the suburbs of the city, and commanding a splendid prospect.

From the upper windows the whole of the city lay spread, panorama-like, before the spectator. To the north might be seen the fertile plains of Maryland, while to the south the still, beautiful waters of the river Potomac divided them from the plantations of Old Virginia.

CHAPTER XXVII.

CAPTAIN GEORGE.

STELLA and her sister, going out on a balcony from the first-floor, gazed with delight at the scene before them. The rapidly increasing fury of the rebellion had caused the city to put on a warlike appearance. Soldiers, mounted and on foot, might be seen passing up and down the street, while already encampments of white tents began to appear in the suburbs.

Gerald Leigh had accompanied them to the house, and after seeing them in safety, wished them adieu, and was about to take his leave when Stella stopped him, and said,—

"Once again, Gerald, be careful how you act; above all, be on your guard against Lupus Rock, or he will work you an injury."

"Where is the worthy gentleman now?"

"Heaven only knows; he went off with a stranger as soon as we arrived, telling us that we could find our way without difficulty to the house."

"Well, Stella—Angela," said Gerald Leigh, "I do not think you need alarm yourselves on my account. I will take all possible precautions for my safety; so now, for the present, adieu, as I have much to attend to."

Then, shaking each of the girls by the hand, he hurried off.

He passed through the broad streets crowded with passengers, military and civilian, and made his way to a small inn on the outskirts of the town. On his road to this place he had passed Lupus Rock in earnest conversation with a man whose back was towards him. As he passed briskly by, he caught a glimpse of the man's face, and recognised Malpas Thong, whom he had before seen with him in Baltimore.

"Strange!" muttered Gerald; "there must be some infernal deep game or other up. I should like to know what it is."

However, he passed on his way without being seen by the two men, and entered the inn I have spoken of. The landlord appeared to be well known to him, for he shook him heartily by the hand, inquiring whether his friends had yet arrived.

"All right, Master Gerald; there's three or four of them in the room up-stairs. I kept it for you when I got the message."

"Plenty of room in the stables?"

"Room for twenty horses in the stables, and a hundred more in the paddock behind."

"That will do—keep it for us, for we shall want it all in a few days. And, by the way, I reckon we can fill your house for you. Don't take any strangers in."

"All right, sir; there was one came this morning before your party, and ordered a room, and as I had plenty to spare then, I just gave him one; but he'll be the only stranger in the house."

"Who is he?" asked Gerald, suspiciously.

"Don't know him from Adam, but if looks go for anything, they're most damnably against him."

" Humph! I must have a look at this fellow—he may be a spy."

It would have been well if Gerald had remembered so to have done, for the man was no other than Lupus Rock's worthy friend, Malpas Thong.

Gerald Leigh, ascending to a room on the first-floor, found several of his friends seated at a substantial tea. There was Murdock, Trent, Winstone, and the Englishman, whom they knew as Captain George.

This latter was doing justice to the good things on the table, and at the same time talking with great spirits and good humour, keeping all amused by his anecdotes and drollery. Already he had made himself a general favourite; his off-hand, dashing manner—the mystery which enshrouded him, and his evident recklessness and daring, had been sure passports to the hearts of the others.

Gerald Leigh was warmly greeted as he entered, and room was made for him at the table.

After satisfying his hunger, he rose from the table, and, lighting a cigar, went out on the balcony. Several followed his example, and a general conversation began on the prospects of the war, &c. After a little time, Gerald Leigh said — knocking the ashes off his cigar,—

" And now, gentlemen, it is time we came to a little business ; by this day week we ought to be all ready to cross over with our men and horses. By the way, we want a few more men ; I propose that to-morrow be devoted to the purpose of looking a few up."

" Gerald," said Winstone, who overheard him, " I tell you what it is, if you are not more careful, the affair will end in our discovery and disgrace. You talk of recruiting men in Washington, as though it were a city in the heart of the Southern States. Already I fancy that there is some suspicion afloat as to our movements."

" What suspicion ? who can suspect, unless we have traitors among us ?"

" No ; I do not think we have a traitor in our ranks ; but there is one man with whom you, Gerald, and some

N

of us are on terms of intimacy, who, I fear, is an enemy, and a dangerous one."

"Who is he?" asked Gerald; "let us know who our enemies are; then we can be on our guard."

"I mean this Mr. Rock, the cousin of the Misses Gayle, with whom you are so intimate."

"Lupus Rock," said Gerald, contemptuously, "I care nothing for him. I believe that he is my enemy personally, and do not fear him. He may have the will to injure me, but he has not the power."

Captain George here spoke.

"Do not be too sure of that, Gerald. I don't like the man, and think that he is to be both distrusted and feared."

"Have you any special reason for so speaking?" said Gerald.

"Yes, I have," replied the young Englishman. "Come and take a stroll up the town with me; I have several things I wish to mention to you."

Gerald accepted the invitation, and the two young men went out together arm-in-arm. Short as the time was since they had known each other, a close intimacy, almost friendship, had grown up between the two young men. Captain George—as he was called—liked and admired Gerald Leigh's frank, bold manner, his unfailing good temper, and brave nature; while Gerald, on his part, was no less attracted by the quiet self-possession of the young Englishman. Of his unflinching pluck and resolution he had abundant proof; and was irresistibly attracted towards him. There was a quiet, dry humour about him too, which never deserted him, even at times when he had reason for being very serious. Two natures more opposite than those of Gerald and the Englishman it would be difficult to find. One, bold, frank, rash, with a dashing genial manner, which won all hearts. The other reserved, with a quiet, unostentatious manner, which was not calculated to attract remark.

However, when attention was once attracted to Captain George, the observer found plenty to occupy his thoughts and speculations. His quiet, cool manner pro-

duced in time a greater effect than even the dash and
rattle of Gerald. People could not help seeing and
acknowledging a strong mind—a determined will. Even
Gerald, who was not remarkable for penetration, did not
fail to observe this.

One day a young officer, who had joined them at
Washington, and who had heard nothing of the affray
in Baltimore, observing Captain George, asked who he
was.

"Oh, he's an Englishman, and has joined us—he has
been in the English army; so his knowledge of European
drill and discipline will be useful to us."

"I have often remarked him," was the reply, "and
wondered who he was. He seems very slow and quiet.
Do you think there's anything in him—that is, any
good?"

"Do I think he's any good?" said Gerald. "Slow
and quiet, you said. Well, all I can say is this, that for
jest or earnest, a spree or a fight, he should be the man
of my choice. With a hundred such men as him—slow
and quiet as you think him—I would engage to lead a
forlorn hope and take the best armed battery in America.
Yes, sirree, Captain George is 'all there;' he's quiet
enough now, but, by thunder, he's a very devil when his
blood is up."

The young officer looked somewhat surprised at hearing this glowing panegyric on the Englishman, of whom
he had previously thought but little; and, of course,
Captain George rose at once in his estimation.

Gerald Leigh and the young Englishman strolled
leisurely up the broad streets of the capital, and presently, coming to a wine store, they entered and seated
themselves at a small table divided by curtains from the
rest of the room. It was, in fact, one of several boxes,
such as are seen in old-fashioned hotels in England.

Gerald Leigh called for wine and cigars, and then
said,—

"Well, squire, what is this you were going to tell me
about Lupus Rock?"

"Well, it is not much, only suspicion; but I deter-

mined to mention it. Yesterday afternoon I went up
to get my revolver put in order. As I returned, feeling
thirsty, I entered this very place, and seated myself at
the table we now occupy. The room was empty at the
time, and I lighted a cigar, determined to rest myself
and do a julep or two. I had not been here long,
when two men entered, and seating themselves at the
next table but one, called for liquor. I saw them,
although they did not observe me. One of these men
was Lupus Rock, the other was a stranger to me. A
dark, thick-set, villanous-looking fellow."

Gerald interrupted him.

"Had he a cut over the left eye?"

"Yes, a cut, or rather, an indentation, as if from a
hammer, or some weapon of the kind."

"Malpas Thong, by thunder!" exclaimed Gerald, dashing his fist on the table. "I saw him in Baltimore, but
did not know he had come on to Washington."

"You know him, then?"

"I know him to be one of the greatest ruffians unhung.
If he is here with Lupus Rock, there is some villany
afoot—not necessarily against us, but I would wager my
life those two men are not laying their heads together for
nothing."

"Well, listen till I tell you the rest. They were soon
deeply engaged in a low muttered conversation; I continued smoking my cigar and sipping my julep, not taking the slightest notice or attempting to listen. Nor
should I have done so, for I am no eavesdropper, but
suddenly my attention was attracted by your name. This
then made me look up; the next moment I heard
the strange man say 'Stella Gayle.' Lupus indignantly told him to hold his tongue. The man laughed,
as I thought, rather insolently, and said some words
I did not catch, concluding with the name of another
female."

"What was the name?" asked Gerald, now thoroughly
interested.

"I can't think of it this moment, but it was a foreign
name—I think French."

He thought for a moment, and then suddenly, as if a thought had struck him, said,—

"Stay, it was the same name as is often mentioned in the packet of papers I picked up in the hotel at Baltimore."

"What papers?"

"Oh, did I not tell you? You remember that I had a hunt after a fellow in the hotel, who jumped from the drawing-room window and so escaped me."

"I was not present, but I heard of it."

"Well, this fellow, when I first saw him, was coming out of a room in the corridor. He had a packet of papers in his hand, which he dropped when he darted off to escape me. That packet of papers I kept, and have with me. I afterwards ascertained that the room from which I saw him come was that of Lupus Rock. I don't know that the papers are of any use, but as things have turned out, I am glad I have kept them."

Captain George produced the papers, and handed them over to Gerald Leigh. The latter glanced at them in a casual manner, turning them over one by one.

All at once, however, he made an exclamation of surprise as he unfolded one of the documents. It was a sort of genealogical chronicle, and went back some generations, ending with the name of a lady.

This was the name which Captain George had heard pronounced the day before.

Gerald Leigh examined this paper with great care, and was evidently thunderstruck at its contents.

Its purport seemed to be to trace back the descent of this lady to a certain point on the mother's side.

The object seemed attained, when an ancestor, a great grandmother, was reached. Her name was Corra Coil, and she was described as a slave purchased by Colonel ——, in New Orleans.

Gerald Leigh finished perusing the paper, and folding it, replaced it in the packet.

Then he handed it back to Captain George, saying,—

"By Heavens, old fellow, these papers have utterly confounded me. They are of great importance, and re-

late to intimate friends of mine. The lady whose name
is mentioned in them, and who you say Lupus and Malpas
Thong yesterday conversed about, is very well known to
me, and is an intimate friend of my father's. I would not
see harm happen to her for worlds. She is the jewel of
the South. Her pre-eminence, both in beauty of person
and charms of mind, is universally acknowledged. There
is some deep, desperate plot on foot, which at present I
cannot understand, as those papers, though clear enough,
doubtless, to those who wrote them, are very vague and
mysterious. Whatever you do, keep them. I have almost a presentiment that some day they will be turned
to terrible account."

Captain George offered the papers to his friend.

" Take them, Gerald; they concern a friend of yours;
so they will be best in your custody."

" No, no, you keep them at present; they are yours.
Perhaps some day they may be of incalculable value to
you, and I feel sure you would never use them to injure
a friend of mine, more especially as that friend is a young
and beautiful girl."

" I would rather have my right hand cut off," said
Captain George, vehemently.

" I believe you, my boy, thoroughly believe you; now
then, go on with your recital."

" Well, as I was saying, I heard your name, Miss
Gayle's, and that of this lady in the papers.

" That roused my attention, and I listened. I could
only catch a word here and there. Your name was frequently repeated, and you seemed to be the chief subject
of their conversation. Finally, Lupus Rock gave the
other a paper or letter, and I fancy told him to take it
to the office of the Secretary-at-War; at least, I know
the office of the Secretary-at-War was mentioned.

" Then the other man rose, and saying, ' All right,
boss, this will put the stuns on Mr. Leigh, I reckon,'
went out.

" That was all I heard, but coupled with other little
things—the obvious dislike of the man to you—I thought
it right to mention it."

Gerald mused for a minute or two.

"I don't quite like it," he said; "I know Mr. Rock would like to play me a trick if he could. No matter— I don't fear him. If he attempts any treachery, it will be my place to defeat and punish the attempt."

"You have definitely fixed the day for starting to join the others at the rendezvous?"

"Yes, we start in three days from this, three hours after daybreak."

"Does any one know the time at which you leave, and the rendezvous?"

"No one, except ourselves."

"Then all is right," said Captain George; "we have nothing to fear."

Then they both rose, and paying for the wine, passed out into the street. Gerald Leigh was wrong. Some one did know both the time and place.

That person was Lupus Rock.

CHAPTER XXVIII.

GERALD LEIGH'S LAST NIGHT IN WASHINGTON.

THE three days passed, and the eve of the eventful day had come. On the following morning, at an arranged time, some fifty young officers and sixty or seventy men were to start from Washington, and rendezvous at Harper's Ferry, on the Potomac. The most careful arrangements had been made to ensure secrecy and despatch.

The appointed time at Harper's Ferry was three hours after daybreak, and all were ordered to start during the night, so as to avoid observation. In no case, either, were more than two mounted men, or more than four who had not horses, to go in company.

Each was, as far as possible, to keep himself detached from the rest, and act as an independent unit till the arrival at the meeting-place. Thus Gerald Leigh and the other young officers in command of the undertaking hoped to elude observation, and pass quietly out of

Washington, and cross the Potomac. There was no
reason why they should not succeed, for at that time
there was no line of sentries, as no rebel army threatened
the capital, as it did a few months later.

Stella Gayle and her sister, though Unionists in heart,
still hoped that Gerald and his friends might get clear
away from Washington. It was a strange conflict in
their minds between feeling and principle. Gerald
Leigh was a rebel, and as such, were they thoroughly
consistent, they should hope for the defeat of his
enterprise, and his own capture.

But then, again, he was an old and dear friend; they
had always regarded him almost as a brother, and now
that he was about to attempt a desperate treason, they
could not help, in spite of patriotism, wishing him, if not
success, at all events immunity from discovery.

We have already said that the appointed time for
meeting was fixed at three hours after daybreak.
Captain George, however, who almost shared with
Gerald the command, so great an influence had he
gained, earnestly advised that, if possible, all should be
at the rendezvous at an earlier hour. Gerald yielded to
the suggestion of his friend, and the word was passed
among all the initiated to be at the meeting-place at
daybreak, if possible.

This alteration in the time was only made on the very
evening before, so that none could know of it but their
own party. All the afternoon and evening, Gerald and
the Englishman were engaged in making their preparations.

Of course, Gerald's personal friends, brother-officers,
and such as held a good social position, could be safely
trusted. It was not so, however, with all their men;
many of whom, though devoted to the cause and to their
leaders, were of that class most amenable to bad
influences, such, for instance, as drink. The principal
occupation, then, for the afternoon was in looking up
these men, and keeping an eye on them till time to set
out.

Captain George had considerable difficulty with his

three recruits, the Irishmen. They had a great idea of having a jovial spree before they started, and it required all his persuasive powers and authority to wean them from the idea.

The day passed and night came. All had gone well, and already many of their party had started for the rendezvous. Gerald Leigh and Captain George resolved to be the last to leave Washington, in order to see that every man and horse had started. By ten o'clock all the men had left Washington, to the number of about fifty. Some twenty of these were mounted, while the others were on foot, and would have to be subsequently provided with horses. There remained in Washington Gerald Leigh and the other Southern officers and gentlemen, who, being all mounted and to be depended on, did not purpose starting till midnight. They were mostly occupied in taking farewell of their friends—a farewell which might be for ever; for who could foresee the issue of the coming struggle?

Towards ten o'clock, Gerald and Captain George wended their way, arm-in-arm, towards Holkar Hall, as the house of Webster Gayle, the merchant, was called.

They were going to bid farewell to the ladies.

"George," said Gerald, as they mounted the hill, "this time to-morrow night we shall be in Old Virginia—the Old Dominion—the most glorious State of what was once the Union."

"If all goes well, as you say."

Gerald Leigh fancied his friend spoke somewhat doubtfully.

"If all goes well?" he said; "have you then, any doubts or fears? All is quiet; no suspicion is excited, and already most of our party are on their way to the rendezvous."

"Fear I have none; doubts I must own to. Do you know, Gerald, I have never felt quite comfortable since I overheard that conversation in the liquor store, between Lupus and the man who you say was named Thong."

" Lupus does not know, cannot know, either the place or time of our rendezvous."

" It is to be hoped not; but I have observed that in his manner which has given rise to grave suspicions in my mind. I have frequently observed him dart towards you singular glances, when you were not looking— glances of dislike and hate, accompanied by a singular smile, as though he thought he had you in his power."

Gerald heard this with more anger than fear.

" If I thought he had, by any means, got hold of the information, and meant to betray us, I would have his life," he exclaimed, passionately.

" Just so; let us be on our guard, and if we discover any treachery, let us act, and make him feel our vengeance. I, for one, would shoot him down like a dog."

By this time they had arrived at Holkar Hall. It stood by the side of the road, at a distance from it of some twenty yards. As they opened the wicket and passed in, they heard the clattering of horses' hoofs up the hill, and waited to see who it was. The next moment Grey and Winstone dashed by at a hard gallop.

They did not rein in their horses as they approached Gerald and his friend. Winstone, who was nearest to them, took off his cap, and waving in salute, said,—

" We shall see you at the Ferry, Gerald, at daybreak, of course."

Gerald waved his hand in reply, but Captain George, in a tone of annoyance, said,—

" Confound that fellow Winstone! I wish to heaven he would not bawl out our destination in that rich, ringing voice of his; he could be heard a hundred yards off."

" And what of it?—who is there to hear?"

George pointed to the house, and said,—

" Lupus Rock is here."

" Ah!" said Gerald, " I see." Then they passed across the garden, and entered together. They found Stella, Angela, and Lupus, seated at supper together. They accepted the invitation to join, and seated themselves at the table—Gerald by the side of Angela, Captain George near Stella.

"Who were the horsemen who galloped by just now, Gerald?" asked Angela; "we heard them speak to you."

Captain George shot a rapid glance of warning towards Gerald, who replied, carelessly,—

"Oh, Winstone and Trent; I suppose they are going for a ride."

Lupus Rock said quietly, with a singular smile,—

"Your friends choose curious times for their 'rides,' Captain Leigh; it is getting on for midnight."

"I see nothing strange in it; certainly it is more pleasant than during the heat of the day."

"Doubtless," replied Lupus, still smiling; "but the evenings are long, and one would have thought they might have chosen some time earlier than half-past eleven."

"I suppose my friends have a right to choose their own time, without consulting you as to when they should mount their horses?"

"Oh, doubtless—doubtless," said Lupus, rising from the table; "I am sure I do not wish to interfere with their horse exercise. I must now bid you good-night, ladies and gentlemen, as I have some writing to do; so beg to be excused."

So saying, he left the room. As soon as he was gone, Stella said to Captain George, who was by her side,—

"Sir, my cousin heard your friend on horseback say, 'the Ferry, at daybreak.' He is quite clever enough to divine from those few words all he needs. He is your enemy, I know; so be on your guard."

"Ah!" said Captain George, "I knew that, but hoped the words were not heard or understood."

"I know they were heard, as I noticed the expression of his face. I do not know whether he clearly understood what ferry was meant, but I think it quite possible he may guess. He is as cunning as the serpent."

"Gerald," said George, "what do you say?—shall we

bid the ladies adieu, and start at once? The sooner we are clear of Washington the better I shall like it; for I feel uneasy."

But Gerald was engaged in a whispered conversation with the gentle Angela; and her soft words and blue eyes were potent to detain him.

"Nonsense, my dear fellow," he said, "you are an alarmist. All goes well, and it is yet early."

Stella Gayle now proposed that they should go out on the balcony, while the supper was being removed. Accordingly, chairs were placed outside, and the four went forth in the cool summer air.

It was a splendid night—the stars spangled the heavens in every direction; while beneath them, the thousand lights of Washington flashed and sparkled, presenting a beautiful and striking appearance.

Gerald Leigh gazed long and wistfully over the city. Holkar Hall being situated on an eminence, commanded a splendid view of the capital and surrounding country. Addressing no one in particular, he said,—

"To-night we leave Washington—when and how shall we return? Perhaps as enemies—as victorious enemies; for Washington, and even all Maryland, must leave the Union and join the Southern Confederacy; or I may come back a prisoner—who knows?—it is the fortune of war. And then, again, there is yet another contingency —I may never come back again. I may fall in the field of battle, gloriously fighting for our independence. If such is to be my fate, I shall not shun it; for, assuredly, I might die less honourably than fighting sword in hand against the enemy."

"Gerald," said Stella Gayle, earnestly, "there is yet another contingency which you have overlooked. In this mad, wicked, and rebellious contest, you may, as you say, be taken prisoner. As a loyal Unionist, I ought to pray that you might; but, God help me, I cannot—old times, old memories arise, and drive back the wish, loyal though it be. Gerald, I am your friend, though the enemy of your desperate cause. There is yet time— pause, ere it is too late."

For a moment she stopped, for her voice faltered from emotion.

" Gerald, once again, pause—*remember your brother's fate!*"

These words seemed wrung from her by a great effort. They were spoken mournfully, tremblingly, and a tear trickled down her check.

She was silent again for some time. By an effort she recovered her self-control.

" Gerald, take warning by his dreadful fate, and remember that if taken prisoner you may meet a worse—*for you may die on the scaffold.*"

Gerald arose impetuously, upsetting his chair as he did so.

He strode up and down the balcony several times.

" Stella, your words are far from deterring me, but give me fresh resolution. My brother's blood—the blood of Darcy Leigh—murdered—*murdered*, I repeat, by the Yankees—calls aloud for vengeance, and vengeance I will have. No, I turn not from my path—come chains —come death, even on the scaffold—I brave it, and defy the enemy to do their worst. I may fall, but before I do so many an accursed Yankee shall bite the dust."

He paused, and, with folded arms, gazed forth on the city beneath. Stella and Angela looked on in silence, deeply affected by his words, which took away all hope that he would relinquish his purpose. The moon streamed full on his tall form as he stood before them. His cap was off, and the young soldier appeared, under the influence of the excitement, to the best advantage. His blue eyes flashed and glittered; while, even by the light of the moon, they could see the flush on his cheek.

They had been in the habit of seeing him so often, had been on such intimate terms with him, that they never thought of his personal appearance; but now the same thought filled both their minds—they were struck by his great personal beauty.

" Is he not handsome?" each thought to herself.

How long he would have remained wrapt in reverie, it is impossible to say; or how long the sisters would have

gazed in silence at him, as he stood statue-like befor
them.

The Englishman, however, disturbed this state of
affairs, saying,—

"Come, old fellow, don't be standing there like a
statue. What say you—shall we think of starting?"

"Going—so soon?" said Angela, sadly, still gazing
at her hero; for in her eyes, despite his treason, Gerald
Leigh was indeed a hero.

"Yes, my little Angela," said Gerald, coming round
to her and taking her hand, "we must leave you now.
Duty and honour call us away; but never fear, I will
return again—not as a prisoner, but as a conqueror.
This war cannot last for ever. Ere long we shall have
wrung a peace from the Yankees at the sword's point.
Then, Angela, I will come and lay my laurels at your
feet."

Angela could only reply by tears; while a slight pressure of the hand told Gerald Leigh that, go where he
would, the heart of a fair girl would go with him. Sho
never knew till that moment how dear he was to her.

Their horses were down in the town. As for baggage,
they had and required none but what they carried at
their saddle-bow in a small valise. Stella insisted on
sending a servant for their horses from the hotel where
they stayed. While waiting for them, they re-entered
the room, Angela having volunteered to brew them a
glass of punch—a stirrup-cup.

Captain George left the balcony last; as he was about
doing so, he saw the form of a man enter at the little
garden wicket, and enter the house. He had before
observed him, and noticed that he came from the direction of Washington, and was much surprised when, on
his approaching close enough, he recognised Lupus Rock.
He entered the room, and closing the window behind
him, said to Stella,—

"I thought, Miss Gayle, that your cousin said he had
writing to do."

"Yes; he said so, certainly."

"Well, he has just entered the house, and has come from the direction of Washington."

"Washington! what can he have been doing there? It is very unlike him to go out so late."

"What, indeed! and why should he have told a falsehood?"

"Oh, it's a habit of our good cousin," said Angela, sarcastically; "he never tells the truth when a falsehood will do as well."

Captain George, though far from easy on the point, said no more; in fact, he could have said no more, for he knew nothing, although he suspected much.

The punch was brewed, and Angela, with her own fair hands, presented to each of the gentlemen a steaming glass.

"There," she said, half laughing, half crying, as she gave Gerald his, "you desperate rebel, drink that; if I were as loyal as Stella is, I should have poisoned the cup before giving it you—traitor as you are."

"Well, Angela, traitor as I am, I drink health and happiness to yourself and sister; and may you find in all Union men you meet as sincere a friend as Gerald Leigh."

"Ladies, your very good health," said Captain George, "and success to the arms of the Confederate States."

"Sir," said Stella, with dignity, "you pay me a poor compliment in drinking such a toast in my presence; you know my feelings, and should refrain. I wish you well, and pray Heaven no harm may befall either of you. It is, methinks, a poor requital for good wishes to propose a toast which you must know is most repugnant to me.

Captain George acknowledged and apologised for his error, and received pardon.

At that moment the clattering of horses' feet was heard rapidly approaching. They galloped rapidly by the house. Gerald and George could hear the rattling of sabres as they passed.

"By heavens! it is quite a number," said Captain George; "there cannot be less than a dozen by the sound of the hoofs. Can they be our fellows?"

"They must be," said Gerald; "who else would be riding in the direction of Harper's Ferry at this time of night?"

He opened the window and went out on the balcony to look; but the horsemen were at too great a distance for him to recognise them. Captain George followed him.

They could see the retreating body of horsemen ascending a little hill. They were quite a quarter of a mile distant, and could not be distinguished. The bright light of the moon, however, glistened on the bright steel scabbards of their sabres, showing that it was a military party.

"Who can they be?" said Captain George, doubtingly. "Very few of our fellows have steel scabbards. And what on earth do they mean by going in such a body? They must be mad or drunk. It is enough to attract attention, and ruin all."

They heard the sound of the clattering hoofs for some half-minute longer; then it suddenly stopped.

"They have halted," said Gerald.

"Or turned off the hard road on to the softer ground by the side," said Captain George.

And now the time for leaving has arrived—the horses are brought round, and stand, saddled and bridled, impatiently pawing the ground at the gate.

A few tears are shed by the girls, which Gerald tries to laugh away. Even Stella, so cold and haughty usually, was deeply affected.

"Stella, good-bye, and may you be happy. I trust we shall meet again in happier times. What! surely those are not tears I see in your eyes. I thought that Stella Gayle, the stern patriot, would scorn such weakness."

But, in spite of all her efforts, the tears still flowed. Her eye fell on a piece of black crape which Gerald wore on his arm. It was mourning for his brother; and as she looked on it, the image of poor Darcy rose before her.

In fancy, she saw him pale, determined, reproachful, with the dreadful bullet wound in his forehead.

In spite of all her efforts, she with difficulty stopped her tears, and affected a composure she did not feel.

One parting pressure of the hand, and they were gone. Angela was already weeping bitterly, and no sooner had the two young men left the room, than Stella Gayle, throwing herself on her sister's neck, gave way to a passionate flood of tears.

Her thoughts are of Darcy Leigh.

CHAPTER XXX.

DEFEATED, WOUNDED, CAPTURED.

LET us now leave the two weeping girls, and follow the fortunes of Gerald and the Englishman.

As soon as they were in the saddle, they gave rein to the impatient horses, and galloped up the road.

The bright moonlight, the fresh breeze, and the exhilarating motion of the horses as they bounded along, all tended to raise their spirits.

Gerald Leigh, who was mounted on a splendid charger, led the way at a spanking rate.

" Come on, old boy," he shouted, turning in his saddle, " or I shall show you my heels."

Captain George spurred his horse to increased speed, and with some difficulty joined and kept pace with his friend.

The road before them was quite straight for half a mile or rather more, and was up-hill; it then took a sudden bend to the right, passing through a large clump of trees, or rather, a small wood. As they approached this bend, Gerald Leigh again spurred ahead; the Englishman, who was not so well mounted, being quite unable to keep pace. Finding this out, he pulled up and walked his horse.

" What a mad-brained fellow it is—tearing along as if charging an unseen enemy. No matter how rash and impetuous, his heart is in the right place, and a braver fellow than Gerald Leigh never stepped the earth. I

didn't think they reared the sort anywhere out of Old
England."

These were the thoughts of Captain George, as he
walked his horse quietly on behind, knowing well that
when Gerald found he was not following him in his mad
career, he also would pull up. This latter had main-
tained the lead, and he could hear the clattering of his
horse's hoofs on the road beyond.

Suddenly this sound ceased—so suddenly, in fact, that
Captain George felt surprised, and spurred on to ascertain the cause.

"Perhaps his horse has stumbled and thrown him—
shouldn't be a bit surprised, at the break-neck pace he
was going."

Trotting quickly on, he also rounded the bend, and
entered the little wood.

As he did so, he heard the sound of loud and angry
voices.

Peering into the gloom, he could distinguish a group
of horsemen.

Quickening his pace still more, he rapidly approached.

"Surrender your sword, sir; surrender—I arrest you
in the name of the United States' Government."

Then he heard the voice of Gerald Leigh,—

"Out of my path, or I'll cut you down."

Then followed some words of command, apparently addressed to a troop of horse.

This was enough for Captain George. He knew that
his friend had been stopped, and was about to be arrested.
They were betrayed.

He knew, also, that Gerald Leigh would never surrender without a fight.

He was now quite close, and could see all.

Gerald Leigh's horse was stopped by a mounted officer,
who barred the road before him.

"Surrender!" cried the officer in command; "resistance is useless."

Behind the mounted officer there were some twenty
troopers drawn up across the road, apparently rendering
any attempt to pass hopeless.

Not so, however, thought Gerald Leigh.

As soon as he heard the sound of his friend's horse's hoofs behind him, he turned in his saddle, and shouted,—

"George, my boy, forward! let us cut our way through these d——d Yankees."

Then, with a loud shout, he drew his sword, and spurring his horse, dashed right at the mounted officer.

Their two sabres clashed for half a minute, and then the Yankee fell from his saddle, and his horse galloped riderless away.

Gerald Leigh, with another shout, rode right at the troopers, barring the road. There was another officer in command, and, by his orders, they closed up, and awaited what they considered the insane charge of the rebels.

"Onward!" thundered Gerald, undaunted by the twenty gleaming sabres before him.

Captain George drew his sword, and feeling in his belt for his revolver, spurred his horse, and dashed after his friend at full gallop. He passed the officer which Gerald Leigh had dismounted, and was now scarce twenty yards from the enemy. He set his teeth and grasped his sword tightly.

The next moment Gerald Leigh dashed right into the troopers. His horse was a large and powerful one, and at the first shock, the trooper at whom he rode went sprawling in the dust. Horse and man rolled over and over.

The trooper immediately on his right aimed a terrible sabre cut at the young officer. At that moment his attention was drawn to another assailant on his left. This latter aimed a blow at his head, which, however, Gerald parried. Scarcely had he done so, however, than the man on his right delivered his cut. This took effect on Gerald's shoulder, and caused him to reel in his saddle. Another horseman now spurred up, and attacked him on the other side.

The situation was critical.

Gerald fought desperately, but could not parry the cuts of both his antagonists. He spurred his horse

violently, causing him to give a great bound forward;
but, at the same moment, the trooper whom he had dismounted scrambled to his feet, and caught the rein, and
presented a pistol.

"Surrender! or I'll blow your brains out," he
shouted.

"Surrender!" said the horseman on his left.

"Surrender!" said the one on his right.

On all sides he heard shouts to "surrender."

"Take him alive—don't kill him—our orders are to
take him alive," he heard an officer cry out.

Gerald's answer to the demand to surrender was
prompt. Swaying on one side, so as to avoid the levelled
pistol, he once again urged his horse forward, delivering
a desperate cut at the man who held his reins.

The cut wounded the man, who fired his pistol, and
still held on, in spite of all Gerald's spurring.

Two other horsemen now rode up, one on each side,
and endeavoured to grasp the rebel officer. Gerald laid
about him desperately with his sword, causing the blood
to flow from each of them. Still surrounded by numbers,
he was at fearful disadvantage, and in another moment
or two he must have been overpowered.

Sabre cuts rained on him from all sides, and he was
bleeding from half-a-dozen wounds. Fortunately, although his cap had been struck off, he had received no
wounds on his head.

Now, however, one of the dragoons, furious from the
pain of a wound inflicted by Gerald, wheeled his horse
round, and coming behind the young officer, aimed a
blow at his bare head, which must have put an end to
the fight and his life together.

The blow was never delivered.

Gerald heard a shout behind him,—

"Forward! Gerald—to the rescue!"

Inspirited by the words and voice—for Gerald knew
it was Captain George—he once more spurred on his
horse; with a violent plunge, the animal dashed forward, trampling underfoot the man who held the
rein.

Then, with another shout, Captain George dashed at full gallop into the group surrounding his friend.

Two horses and riders went to earth, and Captain George's charger fell on his knees, nearly throwing his rider over his head.

He quickly recovered him, however, again dashed forward, and reached the dragoon behind Gerald just as he was about to cut at his head.

Parrying a cut aimed at himself, he shortened his sabre in his hand, and thrust fiercely at Gerald's treacherous foe. His sword entered his back, and went hissing right through the flesh, passing out on the left side of the chest.

George quickly withdrew his sword, and, with a terrible shriek, the dragoon fell back, and lay writhing on the ground in the agonies of death.

Captain George, whose blood was now up, spurred his horse over the prostrate form of the poor wretch, and ranged himself alongside his friend.

All this, which takes some time to narrate, passed in a very brief space of time. Certainly, not more than half a minute had elapsed from the time when Gerald Leigh first charged the dragoons. During that half-minute the two friends, by the suddenness and fury of their attacks, had cleared a way for themselves.

At least, there was now but one horseman in their path. Gerald, rising in his stirrups, drove in the spurs, and rode at him.

The dragoon stood his ground, and parried the cut aimed at him, but the superior weight and blood of Gerald's horse prevailed when the shock of collision came, and the trooper was sent, like his companions, to earth.

Then, with a shout of triumph, the two friends spurred on their horses, and dashed ahead.

The dragoons were encumbered with heavy cavalry saddles and accoutrements, while Gerald and Captain George were in the very lightest marching order.

Their horses, too, especially Gerald's, were superior to

any in the troop, and once clear of them, he felt no fear of capture.

"Forward—forward!" cried Gerald; "we will show these fellows our heels."

The dragoons were so dismayed by the sudden charge of the two friends, that it was some time before they sufficiently collected their faculties to give chase.

It was not till the wounded officer whom Gerald had first dismounted regained his saddle, that he gave the order to pursue the prey of whom they had made so certain.

"Forward, my men!—follow them!—cut them down! Fifty dollars to the man who captures Captain Leigh, the tall, fair one who unhorsed me;" and, led by their officer, the troop put spurs to their horses, and thundered on in pursuit.

The fugitives were now nearly a quarter of a mile . ahead, and were gaining ground.

"Once clear of the wood," said Gerald, "and we are safe. I know the neighbourhood well; when we get clear, we can leave the road, and take the open country. They can never follow us, and we can take a short cut for the ferry, and reach it in an hour and a half."

Onwards they dashed, Gerald leading by several yards. Suddenly Captain George swerved from the road, giving a loud shout.

Gerald turned in his saddle, and looked round with surprise. He saw that his friend, instead of following him, was riding straight into the wood at right angles to the road.

"This way—this way! Where the devil are you going?" he shouted at the top of his voice.

But Captain George kept on his course, and he saw him draw his sword. Immediately afterwards Gerald made out the forms of two men, mounted and wrapped in large cloaks, standing beneath a tree by the roadside. It was these two men at whom Captain George was riding.

The moon, which had been obscured for a moment,

burst forth from the clouds, and threw a bright light on
the two figures. Gerald was further off than his friend,
but he instantly recognised one of the men as Malpas
Thong; the other he did not know. The troop of dragoons came dashing down the road in hot pursuit; each
moment was precious, and here was Captain George
actually going out of his road to attack two men who
did not dispute their passage.

"The man's mad—stark, staring mad!" muttered
Gerald; "he will ruin all. Great Heavens! here come
the dragoons!"

He reined in his horse, determined to see the result of
what he thought his friend's insanity.

"Confound it!" he said to himself, with bitter feelings of anger at Captain George's rashness; "I can't
desert the fellow; he came to my rescue like a warrior.
It would be cowardly to leave him, and yet we run imminent risk of capture."

The dragoons were now within three hundred yards.
Captain George reached the two horsemen and attacked
them furiously. One of them turned his horse's head,
and took to flight. Captain George fired his revolver,
and was spurring forward in pursuit, but the other man,
whom Gerald recognised as Malpas Thong, barred the
way. He was no craven, and stood unflinching, to face
the furious onslaught of the Englishman. Still he was
not accustomed to the use of the cavalry sabre, and at
the third cut it was dashed from his hand, and he himself hurled from the saddle.

Captain George spurred on his horse in pursuit of the
other man.

"Stop—stop!" shouted Gerald, at the top of his
voice; "the dragoons are upon us! Back for your
life!"

But Captain George's only reply was a shout of rage
as he dashed in pursuit of the other. Scarcely had his
horse bounded forward half-a-dozen paces, than, catching
his fore-foot in the root of a tree, he fell heavily, throwing his rider far over his head. Horse and rider rolled
together in the dust.

'All is lost!' thought Gerald, as he saw his friend go down.

The officer of dragoons saw the fate of the Englishman, and not knowing which of the two it was, he struck from the road, and led his men at a gallop to where horse and rider lay.

Captain George was so shaken by the fall, that it was some moments before he could recover his feet. He had barely done so, and was about again to mount his horse, which had also scrambled up, when the dragoons were upon him.

"Surrender!" shouted the officer at their head.

The Englishman, in reply, drew his revolver, and fired, shooting the horse of the speaker, who, for the second time that day, went sprawling.

The next moment, and almost before he could draw his sword, the whole troop were upon him. He was alone and dismounted, and so, of course, stood a wretched chance against them.

A few sabre cuts he parried, and then Gerald saw with grief and rage a big dragoon rise in his stirrup, and deliberately cut him down.

Gerald could restrain himself no longer.

"He is a madman, but he is my friend, and as brave a fellow as ever trod God's earth. So here goes!"

Then he dug in the spurs, and charged right towards the group of men who surrounded the prostrate body of his friend.

Onwards he dashed, sword in hand, possessed with the demon of fury. He thought not of the odds, nor of the certainty of death or capture which awaited him. He only knew that his friend, who, when he himself was in a like predicament, had come to the rescue, was surrounded and overpowered.

Generous but fatal rashness!

As before, he charged sword in hand, and sent the first man who opposed him flying from his saddle; the second shared a like fate, and he had now made his way to the body of his friend, which two troopers were engaged in lifting.

Hardly had he done so, than he received a terrible cut in the shoulder, which staggered him.

The next moment one of the dismounted dragoons made a cut at his horse's fore-legs, and the poor brute fell helplessly to the ground, precipitating Gerald right amongst his foes. He quickly scrambled to his feet, and, sword in hand, made a gallant resistance.

"Take him alive!—take him alive!" shouted the officer in command.

Gerald bounded towards him, overturning a soldier who stood in the way.

"Never!" he shouted, and, at the same time, furiously slashed the officer across the face, who fell to the ground, the blood streaming from the wound.

Then Gerald placed his back against a tree, and continued desperately to defend himself.

"George, man, where are you? Up and fight! Down with the Yankees!"

But the unfortunate Englishman was in a bad way. He had been wounded in several places, and was almost fainting from loss of blood and pain.

He heard his friend's voice and the words, however. A faint light came to his eyes, which were fast dimming.

Feebly he endeavoured to struggle to his feet; he rose to his knees, and grasping his sword, endeavoured to stagger to his feet, saying faintly, in reply,—

"Here I am, Gerald!—fight on!—fight on!"

He never gained his feet; weak as a child, but with the heart of a lion, he was blundering up, when a dragoon, who saw the attempt, hit him a violent blow with the butt-end of a pistol full in the mouth. The unfortunate Englishman fell back, with a groan, and lay helpless on his back.

"Too weak—too weak!" he murmured faintly; "God help you, Gerald, for I cannot. Fight on!—fight! fight!"

The words died away as the blood came gurgling to his throat; the scene faded from his glazing eyes, the clang of the sabres and shouts of the combatants from his ears, and in another second there lay extended on the ground only a lifeless body.

Gerald heard the last words of his friend and saw the cowardly blow of the dragoon.

With a cry of fury, with tears of mingled rage and sorrow starting to his eyes, he bounded from his tree, and hurling himself at the man who had done the deed, he grasped him by the throat, and shortening his sword, plunged it right through his body.

A cry of agony came from the lips of the dragoon, and he fell heavily to the ground, a dying man. A cry of rage and pain also escaped from Gerald Leigh, for he was struck by a sabre between the shoulder blades. He turned furiously, and as he did so, received another terrific cut full on his bare head. For a moment his sword whirled around his head, and then Gerald Leigh, the brave and gallant, fell lifeless on the body of Captain George.

All was over. They had fought like tigers, and fallen like heroes.

"Take him alive—take him alive!" again cried the officer in command.

The dragoon who had administered the *coup de grace* laughed grimly.

"Too late, Captain—too late! I have sent him to his account. By G—d! if I had not done so, there would soon have been few of us alive!"

The man's words were true enough, for three of the dragoons were killed outright, and five desperately wounded.

Thus ended this desperate affair, unprecedented for the daring gallantry displayed by the two fallen heroes, who fought, tiger-like, against such terrible odds to the very last.

"Take them alive, take them alive!"

What a horrid mockery the words seemed, as four dragoons raised the bodies of the fallen men, and making a litter of the horsemen's cloaks and some branches of trees, lifted them aloft, and bore them at a slow pace back towards Washington.

The dead and wounded troopers were also carried back in the same manner, and those of the troop not required in the melancholy task walked their horses slowly behind, leading those of their comrades who were carrying the ghastly burdens.

Tramp, tramp, tramp, tramp,—the procession moved slowly on back towards the city. The sound of the horses' hoofs fell on the earth slowly and with a muffled sound, as they followed behind.

But for that and the measured tread of the troopers carrying the dead and wounded, there was a silence as of the grave.

One short hour before, Gerald Leigh and Captain George had ridden gaily forth from Washington in high spirits, full of hope, and in all the pride of youth and strength; now they were borne back with white, blood-stained faces, hacked and mutilated forms, and with glazing eyes staring blindly up at the sky.

" Take him alive, take him alive!"

The officer in command, who had undertaken the task, little knew the men he had to deal with.

Gerald Leigh had before said that a Yankee or two should bite the dust ere he would be taken. Well, had he kept his words, as the five wounded and three dead testified.

This was almost the first actual bloodshed, at least by land, in this terrible war.

The affair, news of which spread far and wide, created great excitement in both North and South, steeling the resolution of the Confederates to fight to the last gasp, and adding fresh fuel to the flame of the passions of the Northern mob.

They had advanced about a hundred yards only, when they were joined by a man on horseback.

He was not a dragoon, nor, indeed, a cavalry-man of any sort, but was in plain civilian's dress. He rode up to the officer in command of the troop, and addressing him, said,—

" Have you carried out your orders, sir? Have you taken them alive?"

" I have taken them, but not alive; they resisted to the last, and were both cut down."

"Dead?"

The officer pointed to the litters on which the bodies were borne.

"It seems like it," he said, "and not wonderful, for they received wounds enough to kill a dozen men."

The stranger gazed on the two foremost litters, on which were the senseless forms of Gerald Leigh and the young Englishman. Gerald was borne first. He lay on his back, with a hand drooping over each side of the litter. Down the fingers of the left hand trickled slowly a stream of blood, which flowed from a wound in his shoulder. His head had two desperate cuts; his fair hair was dabbled and matted with gore, and a fearful gash across his forehead showed the sabre's deadly work.

Streams of blood had flowed from this wound all over his face, so that it was difficult even to recognise the features.

Altogether, he presented a dreadful and ghastly sight; the deadly pallor of the face, contrasting with the bright crimson of the blood, enhanced the effect; and yet the stranger gazed calmly and unmoved. An expression of triumph, even, crossed his face, and a saturnine smile played about his mouth.

For nearly a minute he gazed at the dead hero, and then turned away. He saluted the officer in command, who coldly returned it. Then he turned his horse's head, and galloped back towards Washington.

"So perish all who dare to cross my path," he muttered."

At the same moment he felt a sudden and unaccountable thrill or shudder pass through his frame. It was like one of those strange sensations which old women tell children is caused by "some one walking over your grave." In spite of himself, a gloomy foreboding of the future took possession of his soul. Visions of vengeance and disaster loomed before him. He gazed uneasily around, as if expecting to see a phantom in his path.

"Pshaw! what a fool I am," he said, endeavouring to shake off the feeling. "I feared him not when living—assuredly I need not fear him dead."

Then drawing his cloak around him, he galloped on. This man was Lupus Rock.

As his form disappeared round the bend of the road, the officer in command, addressing his lieutenant, who was by his side, said, pointing to the litters on which were Gerald and Captain George.

" You see those two poor devils ? "

" Yes."

" Well, they are desperate rebels, but brave men both. They have met their fate; and they met it as brave men should. You see, also, that horseman who has just galloped away, and who spoke to me ? "

" Yes."

" Well, I would rather be in the place of either of those poor devils than in his."

" How so ?" asked the lieutenant, in surprise.

" Because he is a traitorous, treacherous Judas. It was he who betrayed Captain Leigh and the other, whom I do not know. He ate with them, drank with them, and with a smile on his lips, black treachery in his heart, he betrayed them to this, their fate. His name is Lupus Rock, and he is a Unionist; but G—d help the Union if it depend on such men as he !"

CHAPTER XXXI.

FOREBODINGS AND TERRORS.

AFTER the departure of Gerald and Captain George, Stella Gayle and Angela, as soon as they had dried their tears, again went out on the balcony. Stella was restless and feverish. She declared she could not sleep and should not retire to rest. The fair girls had not been on the balcony gazing, in mournful silence, out on the broad expanse of country for more than a few minutes, when there was borne on the air the sound of shouting in the distance.

It came from the direction of the road in which Gerald and his friend had gone. Both listened intently, with vague, undefined alarm.

There was the sound of a pistol-shot and shouting; afterwards the clash of steel could be plainly heard.

"Good Heavens!" said Angela, "what can be the matter? Gerald has gone that road. Can it be that he has been waylaid by robbers?"

Then again the shouts and clashing of steel was heard louder than before.

"It is not robbers, I fear," replied Stella.

"What then?"

"Treachery—I fear that he may have been betrayed, and fallen into an ambuscade."

"Oh Heavens, dont say so!" cried Angela, with pale face—"an ambuscade—and of whom?"

"Of United States' troops, charged to arrest him," replied Stella, slowly and deliberately. "I fear lest his design—even the time and place—should have been revealed to the Government, and a party sent to waylay and arrest him"

"But who could, who would, betray him?"

"I know nothing, but I suspect and fear much. Where is our worthy cousin Lupus? He has again gone out, and, the servant tells me, on horseback. What is the meaning of this?"

Angela could not answer, and they both again listened. But now the sounds had ceased. It was at this time that Gerald and the young Englishman had burst through their foes and galloped off.

The two girls heard some shots in rapid succession, and then again all was silent. These shots were from the carbines of the dragoons, who fired after the fugitives.

After the lapse of a couple of minutes, however, the again heard the sound of shouts. This time the cries although more distant, were more clearly defined an unmistakeable.

Angela clung in terror to her sister.

Although the combatants were quite half-a-mile off, the clang of the sabres, the pistol-shots, and the cries of rage and defiance were plainly heard. The night was calm and still, and favoured the transmission of sound.

The sounds continued for some minutes, and then again all was quiet.

Gerald and Captain George had gone down beneath the terrible sabres of the dragoons. Once again a silence as of the grave reigned around. Breathlessly Stella and Angela listened, but in vain. The fight, if fight it was, was evidently over.

Angela tried to reassure herself and her sister.

" Oh, perhaps it is only some of Gerald's friends, whom they caught up on the road, and they have been firing and shouting for fun, as I have seen them do before. Don't you remember that a body of horsemen passed about half-an-hour before Gerald started, and he was quite angry at their going in such numbers. They were friends of course, and I daresay he and Captain George caught them up; for they went at a terrible pace."

" Perhaps they were friends," said Stella, seriously; " but then, again, perhaps they were enemies."

" Oh, Heavens! if it should be so! Surely Gerald and his friend would not be mad enough to resist."

" Yes," said Stella, " he would to the death."

" Oh, dreadful! who knows but that he may share the fate of poor Darcy."

Stella merely bowed her head, and a tear trickling down her fair cheek, fell on her sister's hand.

Then there was a long silence, each of the sisters gazing out on the moonlit scene.

The table was cleared of its glasses and bottles, from which Gerald and his friend had drank their farewell glass, and when the negro servant came out on the balcony to inquire whether anything more would be wanted, Stella merely shook her head in reply, and once again they were alone with their thoughts.

Below them on their right lay the city of Washington, with the Potomac winding around it. Lights flashed and glimmered from many a wine-shop and bar, for although it was nearly one o'clock these and places of the like description were not closed.

The sound, too, of merriment, shouts, laughter, and

singing, bore evidence to the fact that fear of the
rebels did not prevent the Union soldiers from making
merry.

On the left could be seen the white line of the road
traversed by Gerald and the Englishman; then the
wooded country and the Potomac river again, and
beyond all, the grand old mountains of Virginia.

The moonlight streamed down upon the scene, bathing
the landscape in its soft pale flood.

It was a scene well calculated for contemplation, for
silent thought; and the sisters did not fail to feel the
influence of its deadly calm. Stella, with her chin resting
on her fair hand, gazed dreamily out over the city, with
its flashing lights and white buildings.

Her large lustrous eyes were fixed on vacancy;—she
saw not the scene of the present; but the past, with all
its joys and sorrows, unfolded itself, panorama-like, before
her, while the future arose before her troubled imagina-
tion like a dark and gloomy cloud.

Surely, could an artist or statuary have seen her, as
she sat thus silently pensive, he would have fixed upon
her for a design for Melancholy. Her classic features,
small Grecian head, with the true Venus di Medici low
brow (in woman so great a beauty), conjoined with the
pure white drapery she wore, her perfect motionlessness,
and the calm repose of the scene, might well excuse the
fancy that it was not a lovely girl, but an exquisitely
chiselled statue, which realised nature by its perfection.

Suddenly Angela, who was gazing up the road where
Gerald had last been seen, gave a slight exclamation.
The next moment the sound of horses' hoofs could be
heard approaching. Stella started, and awaking from
her reverie, looked round.

A horseman could be seen rapidly approaching them.
He was muffled in a large cloak, and a hat drawn over
the face concealed his features, so that even when he
drew up at the gate the sisters could not distinguish
him.

"Here, you nigger, Tom—Sandy, come and take my
horse," he shouted impatiently.

" Lupus Rock ! " said Stella, turning in astonishment to her sister.

" Lupus Rock ! where can he have been at this time of night ? Not to Washington, certainly, for he came from the other direction."

" Heaven only knows; perhaps he knows something of the affray we heard or fancied we heard up the road."

The next moment Lupus strode into the room and out on the balcony.

" Here, Sandy," he said to the negro attendant, who had followed him in anticipation of orders, " bring out a small table, cigars, wine, and glasses."

" Well, fair cousins," he added, turning to the ladies, " not retired to rest yet ? Stella, you will spoil the flashing beauty of your eyes if you thus keep midnight vigils; and you, too, Angela, those blue eyes of yours will tell a tale in the morning."

He spoke in a singular manner, a manner which, well as Stella knew him, was strange to her. She looked up and gazed calmly into his face with that searching, quiet glance for which she was so celebrated.

A smile of triumph played on the lips of her amiable cousin.

' He has been successful in something,' thought Stella ; ' he is pleased.'

She did not remove her eyes from his face, determined to read there all she could. Lupus bowed in mockery before her steadfast gaze, as if to say, ' Well, how do you like me ? ' His white teeth glistened for a moment, and he gave a little laugh, at which Stella almost shuddered.

' He has succeeded in injuring some one whom he hates, and whom he fancies dear to us.—It is Gerald Leigh,' thought Stella again.

Still she kept her gaze on her cousin's saturnine countenance. Quickly glancing from the mouth, with its mocking triumphant smile, to the eyes and brow, she still looked full and unfalteringly at him.

Lupus Rock quailed before that glance, and turned his head away to address Angela.

P

Stella saw enough in that scrutiny to satisfy her

'He has betrayed Gerald Leigh,' she said to herself, and turned pale at the thought; 'cunning as he is, I can read him like a book; and if ever fiendish triumph and gratified malignity sat on a man's countenance, they did just now on his.'

The negro appeared with the small table ordered by Lupus, the wine, and a box of cigars. Taking a cigar, he struck a light, and lit it; then pouring out a full tumbler of wine, he held it aloft.

"Stella—Angela, will you drink a toast with me?"

Silence.

"It is a loyal toast."

Still the girls did not reply.

"Here is confusion to all traitors to our glorious Union, and may they all swing on the gallows-tree."

He raised the glass to his lips and drank the toast alone. Then he set it down, somewhat violently, on the table.

"What?" he said, "Angela, and you too, Stella, not drink a loyal toast? I thought you especially, fair cousin"—this was to Stella—"were red-hot for the Union."

"I do not see any necessity to prove my loyalty by drinking toasts at your bidding, sir," replied Stella, colouring with indignation.

"What," continued Lupus, for success and abundant draughts of wine—an unusual thing with him—had combined to take away all prudence, "what, have you, too, turned rebel? Doubtless the effect of bad company, infected by that coxcomb Gerald Leigh, who set out about an hour or so ago to join the rebel army. I wonder will he ever reach them! ha! ha! ha!" and Lupus laughed a loud discordant laugh, which brought the hot blood tingling to the fair cheek of Stella.

How she hated him at that moment!

"How do you know that Gerald Leigh set out to join the rebels?" she asked, with difficulty smothering her indignation, "are you, too, in their secrets?"

"How do I know?" Lupus faltered for a moment at this home question. He was going South himself, ostensibly to join the rebels, and he well knew that if he were ever suspected of betraying a man so influential and so well liked as Gerald Leigh, a fearful vengeance would be taken.

He saw that he had gone too far.

"How do I know?" he replied; "why everybody knew; it was common talk—notorious."

"If then, it were so notorious, I wonder steps were not taken to prevent it by the authorities."

"Perhaps those steps have been taken," Lupus said.

Stella made no answer for a moment or so, but remained with cast-down eyes buried in thought. Suddenly raising her head, she turned sharply towards Lupus, and looking him full in the face with her proud, flashing, dark eyes, she said sharply and decisively,—

"Cousin Lupus, where have you been? whence have you just now come, and what was the object of your night ride?"

Lupus was completely taken aback by the suddenness and vehemence of his cousin's questions. He faltered, and trying to pass it off with a laugh, turned away, and was about to address Angela. But Stella was not thus to be baffled.

"Answer me, sir, if you can or dare!"

So saying, she touched him on the shoulder sharply with her hand.

"Can!—dare!" he replied, in affected astonishment; "I do not understand you."

"You understood my question, I presume?"

Lupus had now recovered his self-possession. He saw that Stella was not to be trifled with.

"Fool, dolt, that I am to show my cards," he muttered; "this girl is a match for me—a perfect tigress—I must beware." Then aloud—"Where was I going?" he said, laughing; "well, certainly, cousin, you seem inclined to cross-examine me pretty closely. No matter—"I heard a body of horsemen come by before your *friends* left." He could not help putting a sneering emphasis on the words. "I was not sleepy, so, ordering my horse to be saddled, I just rode on after them to see who they were."

" And did you ascertain ? "

" Yes; it was a troop of United States' cavalry, under the command of a lieutenant and subaltern. They had some information, the lieutenant told me, and expected to capture some prisoners before morning."

Stella Gayle heard and understood the full import of the words. She turned deadly pale, and compressed her lips firmly.

' Gerald is lost,' she thought. ' Oh, treacherous fiend that you are. But, Lupus, a day of retribution will come for this.'

At this moment Angela, who had been keeping aloof, exclaimed,—

" See, here come a body of men, some mounted and some on foot."

Lupus and Stella both turned and looked in the direction indicated. They saw approaching at a distance of about a quarter of a mile a body of men, some mounted and some on foot.

Lupus Rock clenched his hands and breathed hard.

Well he knew who they were, and the ghastly burdens borne by the dismounted dragoons.

All three watched them approach in silence.

Slowly they wended their way along the white road.

As they did so, the thoughts of the sisters flew back an hour or so, and in fancy they saw Gerald and Captain George galloping away in high spirits and health.

" How slowly they come," said Angela, innocently.

Lupus Rock could not trust himself to speak ; he felt his voice would betray him.

" I wonder who they are," continued Angela, still not thinking of evil.

" The mounted men are United States' cavalry, I am sure," said Stella, " I know the uniform."

" I wonder what the men are walking in front for ? " continued Angela ; " I can see some horses with no riders behind. What silly men to walk when they might ride."

At a distance of about two hundred yards from Holkar Hall the road was sheltered on each side by trees. The cavalcade would have to pass through these and would not emerge from their shade till quite close to the house.

As the foremost of them entered the shadow, Angela, who still continued to watch them narrowly, said,—

" Why, I declare, the men in front are carrying something on their shoulders."

" Perhaps it is a foraging party," said Lupus.

" Ah, yes, of course ; I did not think of that. Doubtless they are trusses of hay and straw for the horses which they are carrying."

Poor girl! she forgot that it is only in an enemy's country that foraging parties go forth by night, and that the neighbourhood of Washington was yet free from any foe.

And now horse and foot have disappeared within the shadow of the trees.

CHAPTER XXXII.

THE WOUNDED PRISONERS.

WITH a vague and terrible presentiment of evil, Stella Gayle darts a rapid glance at her cousin, who is standing in the background, and then again towards the opening in the trees, where, in a few minutes, the cavalcade will reappear.

What a subject for a painter! The two girls in the foreground gazing out anxiously, fearful of they know not what, each in her own style the perfection of womanly beauty.

The tall, haughty, and graceful Stella, with her pale face and large melancholy dark eyes, waits and watches in breathless suspense for the appearance of the troops. Naturally more acute and strong-minded than her sister, she has a vague fear that Gerald and his friend have been made prisoners, and are now being conducted as such back to Washington. Her luxuriant dark hair has partially escaped from its confinement, and falling gracefully over her neck presents a striking contrast to her pale face and white dress. The bright moonlight streams full upon her face as she gazes with parted lips towards the gloomy shadow of the trees.

Lupus Rock, standing in the background, looks on with folded arms.

His eye glanced over the form of his beautiful cousin, and an expression of fierce admiration flashed across his face.

From the small slippered foot peeping forth from her robe, his glance rises to the tapering waist, swelling below in graceful lines into the well-developed hips; above to the softly rounded bust, the gently sloping shoulders; and upwards to a neck and head of which the goddess of old—winner of Paris's prize—might well be proud.

Utterly unconscious of his gaze, at once admiring, triumphant, and libertine, she looked silently out on the night.

'What glorious beauty,' thought Lupus, 'and it is to be mine; yes, mine, mine, mine. It is, it shall be— mistress or wife, it depends on yourself, my haughty beauty; but, by Heavens, mine you must and shall be!'

As he thus stood, with folded arms, glittering eyes, and compressed lips, he looked like Satan gazing from Pandemonium on the bright and distant plains of Heaven, ere yet the thunderbolts of the Almighty had crushed all hope and hurled him to his doom.

"Ah!" cried Angela, suddenly, "it is wounded men they are carrying yonder."

Then, with a shudder, she hid her face in her hands.

"Wounded men!" said Lupus, in affected surprise.

"One, two, three, four, five, six," said Stella, slowly and deliberately; "I can count six borne on litters and two or three others, who also appear wounded, are walking with assistance by the side. Oh, it's dreadful! there has evidently been an affray somewhere."

"So it seems," said Lupus, indifferently.

Stella turned away her head as they approached. She knew not why, but she shrank with almost prophetic aversion from gazing on the sad procession, and yet an irresistible impulse urged her to look.

Tramp, tramp, tramp, tramp!

The measured tread of the troopers, as they march beneath their ghastly burdens, falls on her ear.

The clattering of the horses' hoofs is also heard bringing up the rear, and faint groans from one of the wounded increases the horror of the scene.

Suddenly, as the head of the column arrives abreast of the house, the word is given.

"Halt!"

And all is still.

"Mr. Marley," the voice of the lieutenant is heard to say to his subaltern, "Take a couple of men and ask for water at that house. Our wounded are crying for it."

"No," shouted Lupus from the balcony, and turning deadly pale; "do not stop Lieutenant Edwards; make haste and get your prisoners on to Washington; besides, there is another house a little further on."

"Who are you," said the lieutenant, haughtily, "who know my name and wish me to countermand my orders?"

"I will come down, I will come down," said Lupus, hastily.

He then hurried from the balcony and out into the road. He did not wish the troop to stop opposite the house, for he feared that Angela and Stella, whose kind dispositions he well knew, might themselves hasten down to succour the wounded men.

Then he feared that one of the troopers, or perhaps the lieutenant himself, might betray the part he had taken in the business. Now, however sweet his triumph might be to him, he did not wish to endanger the future; and knowing the character of Stella, he felt sure that had she certain proof that it was he who betrayed Gerald Leigh, his life would be surely forfeited if he ventured South, and in imminent danger even in the North.

Thus it was that he hurried down.

"Lieutenant Edwards," he said, approaching that officer, "it were better that you pushed on further. I have strong reasons for not wishing you to remain here."

"Water, water," feebly cried a wounded man behind the officer.

"I don't care a tinker's curse for you or your reasons, sir," cried the lieutenant, angrily, who, by the way, himself a brave and honourable man, detested Lupus and his treachery; "I only know that some of my poor fellows are wounded and dying for water. So see to it at once, and refuse at your peril."

Lupus turned pale with anger at these contemptuous words and turned away.

Such is ever the traitor's fate—hated by one side, scorned by the other.

The other officer and two men had meanwhile gone up to the door and knocked loudly.

Two or three negro house servants hurried to answer the summons in their pants and shirts only.

"What de matter, massa, what de matter?" asked one sable functionary.

Lupus pushed by them and again went upstairs. He turned on the first step.

"Here, Sandy," he said, "go and get a bucket of water and take it out; some of those soldiers are thirsty and kicking up a row for water."

And this was how the cold-blooded villain spoke of countrymen wounded, perhaps dying and fainting for a drop of water!

He again passed through the saloon and out on to the balcony.

At the very moment that he did so the moon, which had been obscured, broke forth in all its brightness from a cloud, and shone full upon the group at the door.

Stella and Angela gazed together on the scene; the mounted dragoons, the riderless horses, and the six bodies on the litters.

Simultaneously a faint cry broke from Stella and a piercing shriek from Angela.

Lupus folded his arms and gazed, with a bitter smile on his mouth.

They had seen and knew all.

On the foremost litter they saw the body of a young

man extended at length; it was the form of a tall, stalwart young man, with light fair hair, and blue eyes.

But the fair hair was dabbled with blood, the blue eyes gazed vacantly upwards, and saw not.

One hand drooped helplessly over each side of the litter, and hung thus; while from the fingers of the left the blood still slowly and sullenly trickled.

Still, calm, pale, and motionless, it lay before them.

For one moment, Angela gazed on the pale, handsome features now dabbled with blood, and then she fell back fainting in her sister's arms.

" Great God ! " cried Stella, " it is Gerald Leigh ! "

Lupus, with the same demoniac smile, continued carelessly looking on the dead, the dying, and the living.

" Thus perish all who dare to cross my path," he said.

Stella gave him a look of hatred, horror, and disgust, and then proceeded to support Angela, who, though not absolutely insensible, was pale as death, and very nearly fainting with terror, to a couch in the saloon.

Leaving her to the care of the female attendants, she herself followed Lupus Rock, who had descended and gone out to the gate, where the dragoons and the officers in command still remained waiting for the water they had asked for.

Stella Gayle now evinced a courage and a self-possession which took Lupus by surprise. In clear, firm accents, she ordered the servants to bring out not only water, but also wine and brandy.

The wounded dragoons were first given a draught of wine and water, and then Stella, who moved about among the litters noiselessly, rapidly, but quietly, turned her attention to those on which Gerald and George were extended, apparently in the last sleep of death.

Addressing the officer in command of the dragoons, she said, quietly, without a tremble in her voice,—

" Your wounded have been attended to, sir, and are welcome to anything which my father's house can afford. You will not, I presume, object to my bestowing the same care on your prisoners; for such, I suppose, these two

unfortunate friends of mine are; if, indeed, they be not
past all human aid."

The lieutenant bowed, and gazing with wonder and
admiration on the calm and courageous behaviour of the
beautiful girl before him, replied,—

"Assuredly, Miss Gayle, and believe me, no one
regrets more than myself that friends of yours should
have been captured, wounded, and, I fear, killed by my
command. I had a duty to perform, and endeavoured
to do so in the most gentle manner possible. My orders
were to take these two gentlemen prisoners, but to take
them alive and unwounded. The desperate resistance
they made rendered this impossible. They were determined not to be taken, and as a proof of the obstinacy
of the resistance which brought their fate upon them,
witness these poor wounded and killed dragoons."

"Sir," said Stella, "I believe what you say, that you
endeavoured to carry out a disagreeable and painful
duty in the most gentle manner. You have but done
your duty, as a brave and honourable officer should;
you, at least, I believe to be true and loyal—not a
black-hearted, treacherous scoundrel as one I can
name."

Stella's flashing eyes here rested on Lupus Rock
with so evident a meaning that he turned away, muttering a curse.

The young officer of dragoons, who also knew of this
gentleman's treachery, regarded him with a scornful
smile.

At that moment a loud and dismal howling broke
forth.

"Curse you, hold your d——d noise, you infernal
cur," said Lupus, at the same time advancing to a large
dog, whip in hand.

It was the hound of Gerald Leigh, which he had
brought with him from the Kenanha estate. Missing
his master, who, in the hurry of departure, had forgotten
the faithful animal, he had broken his chain, and escaping
from the yard of the hotel, had made his way to Holkar
II: ll, where he had often before accompanied him, and

where now he, doubtless, in his faithful canine mind, thought to find him.

Lupus was about to strike the faithful animal, but the latter seeing him advance threateningly, so far from retreating, showed his white teeth, and, with a low growl, prepared to spring upon him ; whereupon, Lupus, thinking better of it, retreated.

Lupus was standing on one side of the litter on which lay the body of Gerald, which the sagacious animal had discovered.

Stella recognised the dog, and called him to her,— " Lion, Lion."

The dog knowing her voice, passed under the litter, and still howling, moaning, and whimpering, commenced licking her hand and fawning upon her.

Stella now proceeded to dash water in the face of Gerald ; while, at her bidding, a negro did the same for Captain George.

The officer in command remained patiently on horseback while these efforts were being made to revive the wounded men, if, indeed, they were not past all aid. Not so Lupus, however. He looked on moodily and angrily. It cut him to the quick to see his beautiful cousin ministering so tenderly to his enemy, for such he considered Gerald Leigh.

" Come, sir," he said, impatiently, to the officer ; "is it not time that you proceeded on to Washington with your prisoners ? "

" I know my duty, sir," was the cold reply, "and do not require any suggestions from you."

" What is the use of remaining here ? " continued Lupus ; " if they are alive, it is your duty to convey them at once to head-quarters ; if they are dead, as seems most likely, it is equally your duty. Dead, of course," continued the ruffian, carelessly, and contemptuously placing his hand on the breast of Gerald.

Hardly had he done so than the latter, who was by no means dead, gave a faint groan. Lupus started back in dismay, as though he heard a noise from the grave—so deep, so hollow was the sound.

At the same moment, the dog, who had been glaring at him from beneath the litter, bounded forward, and with a savage growl, flew at the throat of the man who had laid his hand on his master.

So sudden and furious was the rush of the faithful dog, that **Lupus Rock** was dashed to the earth. The animal then made a dash at his throat, which he barely missed, fastening his white sharp fangs, however, in his shoulder, which he bit through and through. Lupus **cried** out lustily from fear and pain, and some of the troopers, coming to his assistance, endeavoured to force **the** dog to let go his hold. Their efforts, however, were **not** successful, for the savage brute held on with a deadly **grip**, snarling furiously, and shaking his prey as though he would tear him to pieces.

''Twould serve him but right to let him be killed by the dog of the man he has betrayed,' she thought; nevertheless she went round to the other side, and, calling the animal by name, placed her hand on his collar. The powerful brute, knowing the voice and touch, suffered her with but slight exertion to remove him, and let her lead him away, growling and showing his white fangs as if he did not half like being robbed of his prey.

Lupus, furious with rage, rose from the ground, and running up to one of the troopers, attempted to take his carbine, intending to shoot the dog. The man, however, refused to give it to him, and the officer in command said, sternly,—

"Not so, Mr. Rock. My soldiers' carbines are for a different purpose, neither shall you shoot the dog. It is the property of my prisoner, Mr. Gerald Leigh, and as such I am bound to deliver it with all his other effects into the hands of the authorities. So be pleased to leave it alone."

Lupus, baffled and scorned on all sides, hastened into the house in order to have his wounded shoulder attended to. The whole incident did not occupy many seconds, and no sooner had Stella Gayle removed the dog, than she once again turned her attention to the wounded rebel, Gerald Leigh. A cry of joy escaped from her as she perceived that he breathed and moved. Deep groans, forced from him by pain, escaped from his lips, which, with the rest of his face, was smeared with clotted gore. Stella, with the aid of a handkerchief and plenty of water, removed this, and, with the quickness and skill of a practised nurse, raised his head and poured down his throat a copious draught of brandy.

"He lives—he breathes!" she cried, joyfully, as she noticed that, under the influence of the powerful stimulant, he each moment showed signs of returning consciousness.

Then leaving the litter side, she approached the young lieutenant of dragoons, and said,—

"Sir, it would be cruelty, murder, to take your prisoners on as they are. Let them be carried into the house, and a surgeon shall be sent for to dress their wounds. See," she exclaimed, pointing first to Gerald and then to the Englishman, "they are both alive, and may recover if they have prompt aid. Your own wounded, too, shall be attended to."

Having said her say, she remained standing before the young officer, looking anxiously in his face for his answer.

His must have been a hard heart indeed to have refused such a request from such lips.

Stella stood before him with clasped hands, and gazing anxiously in his face with those lustrous dark eyes of hers. Her beautiful dark hair had escaped from its fastenings, and flowed in rich luxuriousness down her back. She had on neither shawl nor mantle, and even the rough soldiers could not but feel the influence of so much beauty, gentleness, and spirit combined.

The young man hesitated for a moment as if in doubt.

"Surely you cannot be so cruel, so unfeeling as to refuse so reasonable a request," she said. "Surely I am not mistaken in thinking you to be both a brave and generous officer."

"Enough," replied the young man, hastily; "Miss Gayle, I cannot refuse your request. My orders were to convey my prisoners to Washington at once, but when they were given it was not anticipated that they would resist so desperately and receive such wounds."

Stella thanked him by a look, and quickly gave the word to the litter-bearers to carry all the wounded men into the house.

A messenger was despatched on horseback for a surgeon, who quickly arrived, and proceeded to attend to the wounded.

On his arrival, Stella, leaving them in his hands, hastened up stairs to her sister, whom she had left in a fainting condition.

The first words of Angela, when she had sufficiently recovered from the shock to speak, were of Gerald Leigh.

"Ah!" she exclaimed, wildly, covering her face with her hands, "I remember all now. Dead—killed! Gerald so brave and good—murdered!" Then followed a passionate burst of tears.

"No, no, dear Angela," cried Stella, "not killed, only desperately wounded and a prisoner. But he will recover, I hope—I think he will, both he and his friend."

Angela took her hands from her face.

"Oh, Stella," she cried, "you are not deceiving me? —he is not killed?"

"No, no; only wounded and captured."

"Ah! only wounded and captured," said Angela, to whose heart her sister's words had brought momentary relief; "only wounded and captured—what does that mean? First, that he may die of his wounds; and, secondly—Oh, Stella, what does that word 'captured' mean?"

Here the poor girl shudderingly again hid her face.

Stella could answer nothing; for, in the joy at finding that Gerald and his friend had not been killed outright, she forgot the terrible consequences of his capture.

She knew what his conduct would be called—*rebellion —treason—desertion;* for his resignation not having been accepted, he was legally a deserter, and she knew that for that crime there is but one punishment in the time of war.

She knew it; and when Angela again raised her eyes to her face, she turned very pale. The deep pallor on Angela's fair face, to which the colour had for a moment returned at the first joyful news, now bore witness to the fact that she knew the terrible penalty Gerald Leigh had incurred.

That penalty was Death.

CHAPTER XXXIII.

WIFE OR MISTRESS.

IN the course of half-an-hour the wounds of Gerald Leigh, Captain George, and also those of the dragoons, were dressed and bound up. The surgeon declared, as the result of his examination, that all might recover, although the wounds of Gerald especially were very severe and dangerous.

As soon as all was done which medical skill could do, the young dragoon officer ordered the troopers again to take up the litters, and the cortége resumed its march towards Washington.

Gerald, although faint from loss of blood, and sick with the intense pain he suffered, yet recognised the fair forms of Angela and her sister, as, like ministering angels, they flitted about the couch on which he was laid. Now it was Stella who moistened his parched lips with a cooling drink—now Angela who, with gentle care, placed a cushion under the weary head enveloped in surgical bandages. But he was not permitted long to profit by their delicate attentions, for, as we have before said, the word was given to resume the march, and notwithstanding the agony to which it put the poor fellows, they were lifted off the couches and again placed on the rough litters.

Gerald, too weak to lift his head, followed the form of Angela with his eyes, and catching hers, he contrived to throw so much meaning in his glance that the young lady was quickly by his side. With an effort he extended his right hand towards her, his lips moved, but in the effort to speak a rush of blood came to his throat, nearly choking him. The surgeon imperatively ordered him to be silent; so, with a faint smile, when his lips were again cleared of the blood which had flowed from them, he resigned himself to his fate. Angela had taken his hand, which, after the vain effort to speak, had fallen helplessly by his side, and as he was borne forth from their hospitable roof, he pressed hers with what little remaining strength he had left, and casting a glance upon her full of love and devotion—a glance the memory of which she treasured up in her heart for many a long day—he was borne out into the moonlight; and soon the measured tramp of the troopers told the weeping sisters that Gerald Leigh, their old friend—and to Angela something more—was being carried to what they both feared would be his grave, or a more terrible doom.

Scarcely had the party left the house, than Lupus Rock, who had hitherto held aloof, appeared. His face was black as night, and there was an expression on his handsome though sinister features at which Angela shrunk with fear, Stella with hatred and scorn.

"So, so," he muttered, "it seems that it pleases my fair cousins to turn their father's house into a hospital for wounded rebels."

Stella gazed at him for a moment with a glance of withering scorn.

"Better that my father's house were, as you say, Mr. Rock, a hospital for wounded rebels than a home for a treacherous scoundrel."

Stella's words were passionate, and he could not pretend to misunderstand either them or her manner as she turned away from him. For a moment he seemed about to give way to an outburst of fury. He ground his teeth together, and looked like the very demon of hate and malice. But, on second thoughts, he resolved to restrain his passion. He had sufficient cause to know that Stella did not fear him, and was too good a general to show his teeth when he could not bite.

He was possessed of wonderful self-command, and on

this occasion resolved to use it; so he replied, with a strange smile,—

"I cannot affect to misunderstand your meaning, Stella; some day you will repent your language."

This was said in such a manner as to leave it in doubt whether it was intended as a threat, or that she would some day find that she had done him injustice, and would for that reason repent.

Stella, however, did not stay to inquire as to the meaning of his words; but, with her sister, left the lower part of the house; and carefully drawing aside the skirts of her dress in passing Lupus, as though his very touch were pollution, she ascended the staircase without deigning him a word. Indeed, words were not needed; for no words, no scorn she could express, would have conveyed a more bitter and galling lesson to the proud, vindictive Lupus than her silence and the action.

He saw neither Stella nor her sister the next day; for they kept their own room, studiously and carefully avoiding him. He discovered that they had written to Webster Gayle, and did not doubt that the purport of the letter was to complain of him, and beg their father either to join them, or to permit them to return.

Neither of these two courses suited the purpose of Lupus Rock; so he determined to administer an antidote to the poison which their letter would instil, by himself writing another. His conjecture as to the purport of Stella's letter was perfectly correct, with this exception, that she did not therein condescend to complain of him, or go into particulars, but merely begged her father most earnestly to join them at once, for that they were both alarmed and unhappy. Angela joined in a short postscript in her sister's entreaties, and neither doubted for a moment that the letter would have the desired effect.

Alas! they knew not what a letter their amiable cousin wrote on the following day, nor how urgent, and to the merchant how all-powerful, were the arguments he used.

Lupus Rock dwelt strongly therein on the imprudence

Q

of his coming South at the present crisis, and asserted that a whisper was abroad in Washington circles that Webster Gayle had dealings with the rebels, and had absolutely contracted to supply them with a large quantity of arms some time before the rebellion broke out, well knowing the use to which they were to be put.

The fact that Webster Gayle had so done was true, and Lupus having a knowledge of the fact was the curse of his life; and, with some other awkward secrets, of which this snake in the grass had possessed himself, almost placed Mr. Gayle in his power.

He had lately noticed in the behaviour of the latter symptoms of a certain domineering manner, which he had not noticed before, but still he was in the most profound ignorance of the deep and systematic scheme of villany which Lupus contemplated.

This, as doubtless the reader has already gathered, aimed at no less an object than to get the New York merchant completely in his power, to hold his liberty, his very life, in his hands, and then to demand, as the only condition of safety, the whole of the Virginia estates, which he had planned to be assigned to him (as he said, nominally only). But this was not all he contemplated —Stella Gayle was the one object of his desires, and at any price he determined to possess her.

Thus he not only intended to work on the fears of his uncle, and so force him to comply with his demands, but also, by means of the same treacherous weapons, to bend his proud and haughty cousin to his purpose.

He knew that she was devotedly attached to him; for, with all his faults—avarice and others—he was a kind and indulgent father. At one time he had thought to win his cousin, without working on her fears or affection for her father. He knew that he was good-looking, and believed himself to be agreeable; and as for rivals, he had never cause to suspect that any existed, with the exception of Darcy Leigh, whom he feared instinctively —he knew not why; for Stella's manner was not more warm to him than others, but rather the reverse.

Great was his satisfaction, then, when Darcy was, as

all supposed, killed and for ever removed from his path.
This event, however, so far from operating in his favour,
seemed to have had the very reverse effect ; for whereas
before Stella was always civil to him, and would sometimes even vouchsafe a kind word, now she took but
little pains to conceal the fact that she absolutely disliked him.

Lupus Rock, with all the boasted skill and address of
which he was so proud, and for which he was so celebrated, had not the power to read the heart of woman.
It seemed to him perfectly natural that if ever Stella
had cared for this young Leigh, his death ought to
operate in his favour; yet, strange to say, it had not
done so ; and the more Lupus thought on the subject,
the more he felt, he knew not why, that in the death of
Darcy Leigh he had lost his most dangerous rival. Lupus
Rock knew the world well, and also was gifted in a dangerous degree with the power of reading men's minds ;
but with his cousin Stella he was all abroad. He knew
not—could not understand her pure proud nature. He
never dreamed for an instant that many little civilities
paid to himself while the young officer was present, were
dictated by that pride—a pride which had no arrogance
in it, but was the result of deep and sensitive feelings.

Stella Gayle would rather have died than allow any
man to imagine he had the least hold upon her heart,
unless she were fully satisfied that she possessed his,
and also that he was worthy of such a love as she could
give. Now, in the first place, she hardly knew her own
feelings towards Darcy Leigh ; in the second, she knew
nothing of his feelings towards her ; his manner was
constrained, and, what galled her greatly, he treated her
with such rigid politeness and coolness that she sometimes fancied he had an idea that she cared for him, but
did not reciprocate. This last fancy, unfounded though
it was, caused her bitter mortification. Lastly, she was
by no means certain he was worthy of her ; she was, as
the reader knows, a staunch patriot and Unionist, and
hating the very name of Secession, until very lately, she
had also hated, or tried to hate, every rebel.

The letter which Lupus addressed to his uncle was one of his masterpieces. He contrived at the same time to hint at enormous losses and risks involved in certain modes of action, and also held forth hopes of enormous profits if his advice and his course were strictly acted upon. Lupus also dwelt not angrily, but regretfully, on the difficulty he had in controlling his cousins, and the great danger they caused to both himself and the merchant by receiving as their friends notorious rebels.

" This conduct on their part is the more damaging and disastrous to our cause," he said, " from the fact that, when I carry out a certain part of our programme with regard to your Virginia estates—you, from your daughters' great intimacy with such notorious rebels as Gerald Leigh (who, by the bye, has just been arrested, only an hour after leaving Holkar Hall), might be accused of complicity, and thus everything be lost. If, when you write to your daughters, you would just mention this, and also beg of them to be more discreet and considerate, and to act strictly in all such matters as may seem best to me, who, being on the spot, am enabled to judge, it would perhaps tend to remove not only a great annoyance, but also a great, perhaps imminent, danger ; for remember, sir, the perilous times in which we live. Consider what would be the consequence if, owing to any indiscretion of theirs, I were to be arrested. Notwithstanding the fact that I have taken every imaginable precaution, I yet fear greatly that enough would be discovered to ensure the ruin of us both ; should all be discovered, it is quite certain *that one or both of us would go to the gallows.*

" Do not think I am an alarmist in writing as I do. I wish to provide for our safety, and, at the same time, make sure of the enormous profits we anticipate, and also to retain for you your large possessions in Virginia, whichever way the struggle goes. And now for the contract for the delivery of ———. (Here a blank was left.) *You must send the original contract with your signature attached as agreeing to it. But first cut it in half*

*down the middle. Send me one half only, retaining the
other until you hear from me that I have safely received the
first.* By adopting this plan you will be safe; for supposing it is intercepted on the road, either half will be
unintelligible without the other. Do not fail in this, as
if it is to be done, it must be done at once."

This is merely an extract from the letter of Lupus
Rock to his uncle; but in the last few lines the real
purpose of the long letter he wrote was contained.

The contract of which he spoke was for supplying the
rebels with arms and munitions of war to the value of
five millions of dollars.

Webster Gayle calculated to clear a million by the
transaction.

The cunning device of sending the contract in two
halves would remove all danger of detection by its falling
into improper hands; and as to the payment and delivery
of the goods, Lupus, clever fellow as he was, had arranged
all that.

They were to be delivered within the boundaries of the
loyal States, probably somewhere on the Western Potomac, and the rebels would then take charge of them; so
that if they were captured on the road South, the loss
would fall on them alone. As for the payment, that was
to be made on delivery, partly in cash, partly in bonds;
and Lupus had convinced his uncle that they could not
possibly fail to realise by the transaction an enormous
profit.

Still he did not conceal the fact that the discovery of
so gigantic a treason would certainly lead to the arrest
and condemnation of them both. This latter would be
followed by confiscation of all property, and probably an
execution for treason.

The plans of Lupus Rock were laid with diabolical
cunning. He had determined ultimately to join the
Confederate cause, at least for a time—not because he
sympathized with them, or cared one jot for a brave
people about to do battle for their independence, but
because he saw that his interest lay in that direction.

Webster Gayle was to assign the Virginian plantation

to him—as the merchant thought, merely nominally; but Lupus well knew better.

To hold this he would be obliged to join the Confederates, at least if they held Southern Virginia, and he felt assured that, at least for a time, they would hold it. Then, if they won their independence ultimately, the estate would, of course, be confirmed to him; while, if they failed, he would contrive, at the fall of their fortunes, to furnish information to the Northern generals, and maintain that he was loyal all through, and only went South to act the spy on the rebels.

But his last stroke of policy was the masterpiece of the whole deep-laid scheme. By it he felt assured he should gain, not an estate, not a million dollars, but something which he valued even more—something he now felt convinced he could never attain by other means. He would gain what he was determined to gain, what he would peril his life—aye, sell his soul to obtain.

And that was Stella Gayle.

He knew that he could not gain her heart, but for that he cared little. He would, however, gain her hand, her person; and in his mad passion it was that which he coveted.

Webster Gayle would send the contract duly signed. It would be sent in two halves, but Lupus would join the two halves together, and from that day the liberty and life of the great New York merchant would be in his hands.

He could so dispose of the paper that in an hour's time it should be in the hands of the Secretary of State; and within an hour from that he well knew that the order for the arrest of Webster Gayle, the senator, and his committal to the gloomy dungeons of Fort Lafayette would follow; thence to issue a ruined, penniless outcast, or on his way to the scaffold.

Webster Gayle received in due course the two letters, one from his eldest daughter, the other from his nephew, Lupus Rock. He wrote to his daughters begging them to be patient, and on no account to have any communication with any persons suspected of disaffection to the

United States' Government, and also to pay the greatest
attention to the wishes and advice of their cousin Lupus,
of whose wisdom, acuteness, and fidelity, he spoke in the
highest terms. He more than hinted that it was absolutely essential that they should keep on the most
friendly terms with him, and concluded by saying that
he could not possibly join them for a few weeks, at
least.

Lupus also received his letter, with the half of the
contract; he cared little about the contents, but wrote
by return to acknowledge the safe receipt, and asking for
the other half to be forwarded.

By the next mail he received it, and as he gummed the
severed halves together, he said to himself, while a smile
of triumph lighted up his face,—

" Now, Stella Gayle, my proud, haughty beauty, I will
bring you to my feet. Your heart I will win if I can; if
I cannot, you shall be my wife; and if your proud spirit
rebels at that, I will even humble you yet more, and
make you my mistress! My mistress, but not my only
mistress. You shall feel the humiliation of having a rival
near the throne. There is my Creole beauty—perhaps
handsomer—certainly wealthier—than even the handsome daughter of wealthy Webster Gayle.

" Oh, but that will be a noble revenge for the scorn
with which you have treated me. Your father's life in
my hands shall, if I so choose, be only purchased at the
price of his daughter's honour. Stella Gayle, I hardly
know whether I hate or love you most. I love your
beautiful body, but hate your haughty spirit. Wife or
mistress, it depends on yourself; but as one or the other,
Stella Gayle, you shall be mine !"

CHAPTER XXXIV.

FORTUNE FAVOURS THE BRAVE.

GERALD LEIGH and his unfortunate friend, the young
Englishman, were borne off, and, desperately wounded as
they were, consigned to the custody of the provost-

marshal, for Gerald's offence was a military, not a political one; he was considered as a deserter and mutineer, his resignation not having been accepted.

Captain George shared his imprisonment, and would, in all probability, share his fate—and what that fate would be was already well known in Washington.

They would be brought to a trial as soon as they were sufficiently recovered from their wounds. What the verdict would be no one doubted, and the sentence would as certainly be *death*.

It is true Captain George was an Englishman, and might claim the protection of the British flag, but in all probability the Yankees would shoot him first, and deliberate afterwards as to the legality of the act.

Leaving, then, the two unfortunate young men to their wounds, their misery, and the appalling certainty of an ignominious death staring them in the face, we will return to actors in this our drama, whom we have already too long neglected.

We allude to the audacious rebel, Darcy Leigh and his daring crew of corsairs.

*   *   *   *   *   *

It will be remembered (and if the reader should have forgotten, he has but to refer back) that the Spitfire, commanded by the rebel, Darcy Leigh, had succeeded in escaping first from New York Harbour, and afterwards from the still greater peril of the Wabash.

Nor was this all, for scarcely had this been accomplished, than she was overtaken by the terrible storm which so nearly overwhelmed her. At last, the elements had spent their fury, and the crew, worn out by the unceasing dangers and fatigues of the last twenty-four hours, congratulated themselves on having, for the time, at least, escaped. Darcy Leigh, suffering from the wound on his head, had at last sunk into a sleep, which, though fevered and unquiet, afforded some rest to his exhausted mind and body.

When Lieutenant Wharncliffe, who was the officer in charge of the deck, suddenly turned his eyes to windward, and beheld, looming through the mist, the dark form of the Wabash, he was for the moment utterly confounded.

Hurrying down the companion way, he laid his hand on the shoulder of the sleeping Darcy.

Instantly the latter started to his feet, and in answer to his inquiry received the reply,—

" All is lost! the Wabash is alongside!"

But if Wharncliffe thought all lost, Darcy was not one to agree with him, or give way to despair.

Bare-headed, he rushed up on deck, and running to windward, he held on by the mizzen-shrouds and gazed around.

A moment's glance was enough. There, to windward, at scarcely a cable's length, was their dreaded pursuer, the United States' frigate Wabash.

Her great guns frowned gloomily from the port holes, for they were run out as if ready for action.

As for the Spitfire, all her great guns had been thrown overboard, so that the case of the rebels seemed desperate. What hope was there of successfully resisting such overwhelming force? The rebel crew were wounded—all exhausted and worn out by fatigue; while last and worst, their guns were gone, and they had nothing to rely on but the carronades and small arms.

What hope, indeed!

Darcy Leigh, however, lost no time in gloomy anticipations. He and Wharncliffe were the only men on board who knew of their terrible predicament; even the man at the helm, intent on steering, had not yet observed the Yankee frigate.

" Starboard your helm," said Darcy, walking up to the binnacle, " hard a starboard."

" Starboard it is," said the seaman, heaving the wheel up, but looking somewhat surprised at the sudden order.

" Turn the crew up, Wharncliffe, quietly and gently; for, by Heavens, the Yankees have not yet discovered us."

Wharncliffe hurried forward, and rousing the watch, who were lying about on the deck, ordered them to arm themselves, while he went below and called the rest.

Slowly the Spitfire payed off in obedience to her helm.

Darcy remained on the poop, earnestly watching the enemy.

The Wabash appeared not to have a soul on her decks —at least, Darcy could not discover one.

All her three masts were gone close to the deck, and, looking above, he discovered that, although smoke came from her funnel, she had no headway.

While he was gazing through the mist, which now again thickened, and threatened once again to hide the vessels from each other, he perceived moving persons on her quarter-deck. The next instant he heard the sound of some one crying out in a loud voice. •

" They have seen us at last," he muttered. " Now we shall have to fight with a vengeance."

The crew now began tumbling up on deck, rubbing their eyes, and wondering what on earth was the matter.

" All hands to quarters!" shouted Darcy; "every man to his station—run in the guns—load with round shot." Suddenly he remembered that the guns had been thrown overboard. Dashing down the speaking trumpet he held in his hand, he ran down from the poop, and, mingling among the crew, gave his orders rapidly and deter- minedly,—

" Lay aft, some of you," he said ; "load the carronades up to the muzzle—small-arms men in the waist, and boarding party on the forecastle. Bear a hand ! for, by Heavens, we must fight now !"

" What's the matter, captain ? where's the enemy ?" asked one of the sailors, leaping down from the bulwarks, where he had in vain endeavoured to discern anything ; for the mist had again closed around them.

At the same moment, a gust of wind tore over the surface of the sea, scattering the mist on all sides, which rolled back slowly before it.

" The matter !—that—look for yourselves ; that is the matter ;" and he pointed to the weather quarter, where, at a distance of only a few yards, might be discerned the Wabash, broadside on, and as if preparing to rake them.

A cry of dismay broke from the sailors at the sight of

the Yankee. At the same time, a shout was heard from the Wabash; it was not a shout of many voices, but appeared that of one man speaking through a trumpet. Meanwhile the sailors, who knew that soon they *must* fight, and who were prepared to do so, and sell their lives dearly, hastily armed themselves with muskets, pistols, cutlasses, and pikes.

The carronades on the quarter-deck were quickly loaded; and while they were being trained, Darcy Leigh ran to the signal halyards and hoisted the Confederate flag.

As the bunting blew forth in the breeze, he raised his sword aloft, and shouted to his crew,—

" Three cheers for the Stars and Bars, and death to the Yankees !"

Then a cheer rang forth from stem to stern of the Wabash, and Captain Darcy Leigh hurried to his men who were training the carronades.

" Luff—luff !" he cried to the man at the helm.

" Luff, it is, sir."

Slowly the Spitfire answered her helm, and came up to the wind. Wharncliffe had hurriedly given orders down the stoke-hole to fire up and go ahead full speed.

Darcy intended to cross the bows of the Wabash, deliver the fire of the carronades and small arms, and then make a running fight of it, trusting that the superior speed of the Spitfire might enable them once more to escape.

Every man was now at his station, prepared to do battle to the last. The flag of the United States floated from the stump of the mizzen-mast of the frigate, removing all doubt, if doubt there had been, as to her character. Still, however, very few men could be perceived on her decks, and Darcy concluded that they had been ordered to lie down and conceal themselves. He was at a loss to account for these tactics, for they must know that their characters could not be concealed.

And now the Spitfire is crossing the bows of the Wabash. Darcy gives the order to fire, and the carronades belch forth their contents of grape and canister. Next follows a rattling discharge of musketry.

"Load again, boys; fire them once more, and then we will show them our heels."

Once again the small brass pieces were loaded, run out, and discharged, the rattle of musketry all the time being kept up. To the astonishment of Darcy Leigh not a shot is fired in return. But the Wabash slowly comes up to the wind, so as once again to present her broadside.

Almost at the same moment there is a stoppage in the engines of the Spitfire, and the screw ceases to revolve. After a few minutes' interval the engines once again start, but after one or two revolutions came to a standstill. Darcy is hurrying off the quarter-deck to learn the cause, when he is met by Wharncliffe, who says a few words only to him, which words, however, seem to fill him with the utmost dismay.

The engines have broken down, and the Spitfire is within a few hundred yards only of one of the finest and most heavily-armed frigates in the United States' navy. Their condition is now indeed desperate. What hope can they have of successfully resisting the heavy guns of the Wabash with the few small carronades? But little, indeed; nevertheless the rebel commander, though almost hopeless of success, determines to fight to the last.

Although very pale from loss of blood caused by his wound and the disastrous intelligence just received, not a trace of fear or irresolution can be discerned in his features. Hastening to the engine-room, he demands of the officer in charge what is the matter?

"Hopelessly broken down," is the gloomy answer.

"Can you get a few turns more of the screw out of her?"

The officer, after a careful examination, replies,—

"We may just manage to keep her steering way on her for another quarter of an hour, that is all."

Darcy remained for a moment as if in doubt, then, as if having formed a resolution, he regains the deck, and, taking the helm himself, gives his orders.

"My lads, we have but one chance. We must take her by board. Arm, every one of you; and as we run

into her, throw yourselves on board, and fight like
devils !"

At the same time he had the helm hard a-lee.

The Spitfire, quickly answering to her helm, came
round, describing a wide semicircle, until she was bow
on to the Wabash. Then he steadied her, and steered
right for the frigate.

Not a shot had been fired from the Wabash, although
she lay broadside, and with ten guns run out.

All awaited the result in breathless suspense, expecting
each moment that the frigate would deliver her terrible
broadside. The Spitfire was now slowly steaming right
down on her, so as to take her amid-ships. Doubtless
the latter would deliver her broadside immediately before
the moment of contact, and Darcy shuddered as he
thought of the horrible carnage the raking discharge
would effect.

Nearer and nearer they approach the sloop, steaming
down at the rate of about four miles an hour. Darcy
hopes by the shock to disable and perhaps sink his
opponent, or, failing that, to take her by board. Surely
such an insane attempt was never made or thought of
before—a sloop with some hundred and fifty men, deliberately to attempt boarding a frigate with some four
hundred. And now a distance of only a hundred yards
separates the vessels. Onward goes the sloop slowly,
determinedly, while the frigate still remains as if all on
board were wrapt in slumber. Another half-minute, and
crash they must come together.

" Steady, boys, steady," cried Darcy from the helm, as
his men, urged to desperation, crowd on the forecastle
and in the fore-shrouds.

The next moment a shout is heard from the Wabash,
as if hailing them ; but Darcy cannot distinguish what
is said, for his own men are yelling forth cries of defiance
and fury.

Instantaneously those scattered cries are hushed, and
for a moment there is a dead silence. The next, and a
tremendous roar of triumph broke forth from the crew
of the Spitfire—a prolonged shout of exultation and
victory.

What means it?

Darcy Leigh, whose eyes have been for a moment re-moved from the enemy, again glances towards her. He can scarcely believe his eyes. Can it indeed be true? Yes, by Heavens! the Yankee flag is being slowly hauled down.

THE WABASH HAS STRUCK HER COLOURS TO THE SPITFIRE!

CHAPTER XXXV.

TARGET PRACTICE.

FOR a moment or so Darcy Leigh remained in utter and blank astonishment. He could scarcely believe in his good fortune. It is true he hoped ultimately to escape, because he was one of those spirits who might justly use the motto, "*Dum spiro spero;*" but assuredly he never thought for a moment that the frigate would strike her colours without firing a shot. At first, when he realized the fact that she had really done so, he suspected that some treachery was intended, but they were soon so close to the frigate that he could perceive there were very few men on her decks. The guns even were not manned, nor were there any men prepared to resist his boarders. As soon as he perceived all this he shouted,—

"Stop her!" and almost instantly the engines were stopped, and the Spitfire bore onwards merely from the former impetus. Still this was so great as to carry her on with considerable speed, and although by his orders the engines were reversed, the next moment the sloop ran into the Wabash.

The shock was terrible, throwing nearly all off their feet The rebels, however, with loud shouts threw themselves on the deck of the enemy, of which they soon had undis-puted possession.

They found on board only some twenty or thirty men, who at once threw down their arms, while the officers, who were assembled on the quarterdeck, offered no resistance.

All this was incomprehensible to Darcy. As soon as grappling irons were fixed, he left the Spitfire, and leaping on board the frigate hastened to the quarter-deck.

"Who is in command of this vessel?"

"I, Captain Seth Peabody," said an officer coming forward.

"Surrender your sword, sir."

Captain Peabody drew it, and, handing it to Darcy, said,—

"Resistance is useless, I am aware; we are in your power now, but the day will come when you will pay dearly for the treason and outrage.

Darcy took the sword somewhat contemptuously, and, turning to the other officers, he also demanded theirs, which they gave up without hesitation.

"Captain Peabody and gentlemen," said Darcy, "if you choose to give your parole of honour not to attempt to escape, or recapture the ship, under any circumstances whatever, I shall not put you under any restraint."

"May I be eternally confounded if I do anything of the kind, Mr. Rebel," said Captain Seth; "and if I had had only but a hundred of my brave crew, I would have captured you and hung every one of you to the yard-arm."

Darcy gazed in surprise at the speaker.

"Your crew—where, then, are they? I thought that when you intended to surrender you had ordered them below."

"Ordered them below? No, sir," said the Yankee captain, bitterly. "A higher power than yours or mine has ordered them below. Know, sir rebel, under what circumstances Captain Seth Peabody surrendered his ship. Four hundred and fifty brave seamen perished in yesterday's storm. They have gone to their last account, and found a sailor's grave in the depths of the Atlantic Ocean. A part were lost when the masts went, as they were endeavouring to secure the sails; the remainder were swept overboard by a tremendous sea when she broached-to. I have not twenty uninjured men on board."

"This, then, accounts for the surrender of the

Wabash," said Darcy. "Sir, I beg your pardon, I confess, till this moment, I thought the Wabash was commanded by a coward!"

A crimson flush mounted to the cheek of the Yankee captain.

"No, sir," he said, bitterly, "this does not account for it. Had that been all, I and my officers would have ourselves assisted the poor remnant of my brave crew to man the guns. We would have done this, and fought you and your traitor men to the last. But there is another reason which made resistance impossible."

"And that is?"

"*The Wabash is sinking!*"

CHAPTER XXXVI.

A MAD VENTURE.

A GLANCE over the side convinced Darcy that the Yankee spoke the truth, for the muzzles of the guns were quite close to the water.

"Man the pumps!" he shouted; "all hands to the pumps!"

Roused by the loud and angry tones of his voice, the sailors crowded around and commenced to work at the pumps.

No water, however, followed their efforts.

"The pumps are choked," said the Yankee captain, gloomily; "we were engaged in cleaning them when we discovered you. We might even have succeeded in keeping her afloat, but the fire of your carronades killed and wounded a dozen of my poor fellows, who were saved from their comrades' fate, and broke the pump-chain, so we were left at your mercy. I congratulate you on your exploit, sir. You have fired into and captured a sinking ship, manned by some twenty men, worn out by continuous labour at the pumps."

So saying, the Yankee captain turned away, with an expression of bitter regret on his features, and, followed by his officers, descended to the cabin.

It was only by the most strenuous exertions that the pumps could be repaired in time to save the ship from sinking. Indeed, had not another party of sailors, under the command of Wharncliffe, proceeded to throw overboard some of the guns and stores, it is probable that the Wabash would have sunk under the feet of the captors. As it was, however, a couple of hours' hard work so much reduced the water in her hold, as to place them out of danger, unless they were overtaken by another storm. Fortunately, this was not the case, for the day turned out fine as could be wished, with a moderate breeze from the north-east.

Before even the frigate was quite clear of water, a jury foremast had been rigged. The engines were not out of order, and by nightfall the fires were lighted and steam got up.

Darcy determined himself to take charge of the Wabash, handing over the command of the Spitfire to Wharncliffe, giving him some fifty men.

The decks having been cleared, and the wounded cared for, the Wabash took the Spitfire in tow. The course was altered to west-south-west; and, with smooth water and fair wind, the two vessels proceeded on their way.

Darcy had determined to run right for Charleston harbour, and take his chance of getting safely in.

The night passed without further adventure. The morning broke on a calm sea and cloudless sky, and, as far as the elements were concerned, nothing could be more favourable. During the night the damaged engines of the Spitfire were repaired, and, steam being got up, the sloop was enabled to dispense with the tow-rope from the Wabash.

About noon, Darcy caused a boat to be lowered, and went on board the sloop with all the other officers, with the exception of one, whom he left in charge. He had no fear of treachery, for the remnant of the Wabash's crew were disarmed and outnumbered ten to one by his own men. Darcy's object in going on board the sloop was to explain his designs to his brother officers, who were at a loss to understand what was meant by their

R

present course, which would bring them right to Charleston harbour, off which cruised the United States' fleet.

The preceding events had occurred in rapid succession —danger had followed danger; and even when all seemed to have been surmounted, the fury of the storm was such as well nigh to bring the career of the mutineers to an abrupt close. Scarcely had they escaped from this last imminent peril, than once again they found themselves in the jaws of the enemy—in other words, right under the guns of the Wabash.

And now, owing to the crippled state of this latter, Darcy Leigh is once more enabled to congratulate his crew and officers in having brought the enterprise—mad, insane, as many at first deemed it—to the verge of a successful issue.

There remained but one more peril to be met and surmounted; this, though last, was by no means least. They had now either to elude or run the gauntlet through the blockading fleet, and make good their entry into Charleston harbour.

Since the first brief consultation in the cabin, the young rebel commander had not discussed probabilities or unfolded his plans to any of his brother officers. Many of them were now exceedingly anxious to know what course they were about to pursue; and several of those who remained on board the Wabash during the night, had sought to elicit from Darcy what was the nature of his plans, and how he hoped to escape the fleet off the harbour for which they were now running a direct course.

To all these Darcy had quietly replied that he had decided on a plan which he thought was sure to succeed, and which he would unfold to them all in a general council on the morrow.

Many were the surmises as to what was the nature of this unknown plan. Many thought that Darcy Leigh absolutely intended to give battle to the whole fleet, making a running fight of it until safe under the guns of the Charleston forts. Desperate as this attempt appeared, still such was the confidence of all in Darcy's skill—bravery, and, above all, in his good fortune, that not a man would have hung back or have refused to follow him.

But Darcy was fertile in expedients, and had devised a scheme by which he confidently expected to deceive the whole squadron, and anchor in Charleston harbour without the necessity of firing a gun. His plan was remarkable, as well for its audacity as the elements of success it possessed; and the more the young rebel thought on the point, the more confident he felt of its feasibility.

When all the rebel officers were assembled in the cabin, Darcy himself, who had remained on deck till last, went below. Every one rose on his entry, and way was made for him to reach the head of the table, where was placed a vacant chair. He nodded familiarly around, and at once took his place, with as much quiet ease as if he had been an admiral all his life, and accustomed to lead fleets into action.

He was still deadly pale, for he had lost a great quantity of blood from the wound in his head. The terrible excitement and fatigue of the last day or so might well cause exhaustion in the most robust, apart from a dangerous wound; and it is not to be wondered that Darcy Leigh, always pale-faced, should be deadly white, and that his bright, fresh eye should blaze with a feverish light.

Of all that assembly now grouped around the cabin table, Darcy Leigh was the youngest, except three midshipmen; but so great an ascendancy had his daring, courage, and skill gained him, that all looked up and awaited his words as though he had been an old commodore. It was a rare instance of the force of mind and character.

There was a plentiful supply of wine and spirits on the table; and Darcy, on taking his seat, immediately filled a tumbler with wine, and then rising to his feet, said,—

" Gentlemen, I drink to the future prosperity of the Confederate States of America."

Instantly each glass was filled, and the toast earnestly, though quietly, drunk.

All having taken their seats, Darcy was about to commence, when Wharncliffe, who was on his right hand, touched him on the shoulder.

"Half a minute, Darcy, please."

Then addressing the others, he said,—

"Gentlemen, we have just drunk success to the Confederate States. I have yet another toast to propose—a toast which if any man refuses, he is that moment my mortal enemy."

He filled his glass, and holding it aloft, said,—

"Here is success to as brave, gallant, and skilful an officer as ever buckled on a sword; whose head planned, and whose right arm has so far carried out, this enterprise. Without further words, I drink the health of our leader, Captain Darcy Leigh."

Instantly every man arose and pledged their captain, many crowding around him and pressing his hand.

When the excitement which this toast of Wharncliffe's produced had somewhat subsided, all again took their seats, and Darcy spoke in a low and somewhat tremulous voice, for he was faint, and his wound pained him much. Nothing, indeed, but his indomitable, unconquerable spirit could have sustained him.

"I thank you, gentlemen," he said, "for the honour you have done me, and, with your permission, we will at once proceed to business. Thus far our enterprise has been most successful. We started from New York Harbour with one ship, we have now two, and in the Wabash we have secured at once heavier guns than those we were compelled to throw overboard, an ample sufficiency of coal, besides abundance of ammunition. So far so good; but we must not forget that all this will be useless to us unless we succeed in taking both the Spitfire and our prize safe into port. In order safely to accomplish this, the following is the plan I propose to adopt. We are, as you are probably aware, steering straight for Charleston Harbour. I propose that we keep in that course and run straight in,"

" And fight the fleet cruising outside; or do you hope to elude their notice ?" asked Lieutenant Wilton.

" Neither," replied Darcy. " I propose to steam right through the middle of the squadron without firing a shot, and, I trust, without being fired at."

" Impossible !" cried a young officer at the other end of the table ; " they would blow us to eternity in no time !"

" No, sir, it is not impossible, not even improbable, and if you will listen to me I will explain how I hope to accomplish this."

All waited with breathless interest to hear the plan by which they were to pass with impunity through a hostile fleet.

" Of course, by this time the seizure and escape of the Spitfire is well known to the Charleston squadron."

" Undoubtedly."

" My plan, then, is very simple. Probably not only the Charleston fleet, but all the United States' cruisers, have by this time heard of the affair ; what more natural than that one of them should retake the sloop from the rebels ?"

Darcy paused and looked around the table. Doubt and uncertainty were on every face. He smiled, as if wondering at their dulness. Wharncliffe alone, who sat on his right hand, seemed to gather an inkling of what was coming.

" Go on, captain, go on—I think I understand."

" Well," said Darcy, " I propose that we steam right up to the fleet in the Wabash, with the Spitfire in tow, the United States' ensign floating from the peak, as if we had recaptured her from the rebels. The commodore and all the other officers will be completely thrown off their guard; for, not knowing the circumstances, they will never dream for a moment of such a frigate as the Wabash being captured by the Spitfire and a rebel crew. They will, of course, imagine that the Wabash fell in with the sloop, discovered her character, and, after a sharp engagement, captured her. Both the frigate and the sloop have suffered in the late gale, one having lost all three masts, the other two. This will appear as if the effects of the battle. To favour this idea, we will presently remove all hands on board the Wabash, and commence a little target practice at the sloop, knocking a few ugly holes in her, but being careful not to hit her below the water-line. Thus she will present the appearance of having been riddled by shot in the desperate engagement. We will sail boldly up to the flag-ship, with our supposed prize in tow, nearly all her crew being below, while those on deck shall be carefully dressed in the United States' uniform. A few marines on guard over the hatches, as if the rebel prisoners were confined below, will also favour the delusion. I propose to steam right by the flag-ship, and pass on up the harbour at full speed until we are enabled to anchor under the batteries; once within range of these latter, down come the Stars and Stripes and up go the Stars and Bars. Gentlemen, you hear my plan; what do you think of it?"

A murmur of surprise and admiration went round the assembly. The project was at once so simple and so feasible, that every one wondered he had not himself thought of it.

"Now, gentlemen," continued Darcy, "I am willing to listen to any suggestions, or answer any questions any of you wish to put. Although you have elected me your leader for the time, I am by no means so vain-glorious as to despise your advice."

The advantage of this course was soon apparent, for several suggestions were made and adopted. One young officer, addressing the meeting, said,—

"There is one thing which seems to have been overlooked. Some of the ships in the fleet will certainly hail us as we pass, and an answer must be returned. Now, in all probability, the officers of the Wabash, at least some of them, are well known, and if any of us, who are, of course, by this time all denounced by name as traitors, should answer, there would be great risk of a discovery."

"I had not forgotten that point," replied Darcy Leigh. "I thought over it, and it presented a serious difficulty. I came to the conclusion that the best mode to be adopted would be for he who answered to have his head and face bandaged, as if wounded ; then if asked as to any of the other officers of the Wabash, he could reply they were either killed or wounded in the engagement."

" Yes," was the reply, "the face might be concealed, but how about the voice ? There may be an intimate friend of the man you personate on board the flag-ship ; in such a case the deceit would be discovered at once."

" True," replied Darcy, gravely, "I had thought of that ; but unless you can suggest an alternative, we must, I fear, take our chance."

" Well, Captain Leigh," replied the young officer, whose name was Hamlin, "I think I can suggest a remedy. There are very few vessels in Uncle Sam's service who do not number some Southerners among their officers. The Wabash is not one of those few. I myself know several of the officers who are Southerners by birth, and one in particular I feel convinced will join us, and reply to the hail from the flag-ship."

" His name ?"

" George Merton."

" Good!—he must consent. If he chooses to join us, very good ; if not, he must perforce answer as he is ordered."

"But suppose he should take the opportunity to betray us ?"

" He will not do so," replied Darcy, quietly ; "I shall stand close beside him with a revolver; if he dares to say one word, I shall blow his brains out. Then we must do our best, and run the gauntlet as best we can. This is no time for half-measures. We are engaged in a desperate enterprise, and must at any sacrifice carry it through. But I have little fear of the result. I do not think there will be any difficulty in prevailing on this Mr. Merton to join us, if he be indeed a Southern gentleman."

Darcy Leigh now rose, and all following his example, the conference terminated.

In half-an-hour's time they were again all on board

the Wabash, even the crew of the sloop being ordered to
leave her, and come on board the frigate.

This measure created great astonishment and some
little dissatisfaction among the men, many of whom had,
sailor-like, formed quite an attachment for the vessel in
which they had served.

If their surprise was great, however, it was nothing to
that of Captain Seth Peabody and his officers, when, half
an hour later, the Wabash was hove to at about a couple
of hundred yards' distance from the sloop, and commenced
pounding away at her with her big guns.   The cannon-
balls smashed and crashed through the bulwarks and
rigging of the Spitfire, making the splinters fly in all
directions, till in a very short time she presented the
appearance of a vessel which had been engaged in a
desperate battle.

When this was accomplished, the gunners were ordered
to cease firing ; the crew were again sent on board ; and
Captain Seth Peabody, who, with his officers, was not
placed under any restraint, remarked to his first lieutenant,—

" Mad, sir, mad !—stark staring mad, these rebels !
First they mutiny and run away with the smartest sloop
in Uncle Sam's service, and then, by G—d, they make
target practice at her ! Mad, by thunder ! every mother's
son of them ; and that d——d young traitor Leigh, the
maddest of the lot."

Little did the Yankee imagine they had so much
method in their madness.

CHAPTER XXXVII.

CHARLESTON HARBOUR.

LEAVING the Wabash and the Spitfire steaming ahead
for Charleston Harbour, we will, with the reader's permission, anticipate them at that stronghold of secession.

Some three or four days after the events described
in our last chapter, the inhabitants, both military and
civilian, are thrown into a great state of excitement by

the news of the arrival of two steam vessels of war off the port, in addition to the United States' squadron permanently established there to watch the harbour. Of course the mutiny on board the Spitfire, the seizure and subsequent escape of the ship, are well known. Most of the officers, including Darcy Leigh, have friends in Charleston, and the anxiety as to their fate has been great; many were the conjectures as to the course the daring mutineers would pursue. Some thought that they would run the vessel ashore on some quiet part of the coast, while others thought Darcy Leigh would endeavour to take her into a neutral port; but none imagined that he would attempt to run her into Charleston, in face of the blockading squadron.

Great fears were entertained, from the fact of no news having been received, that the Spitfire had been recaptured by one of the Yankee cruisers sent in pursuit.

It was during this state of doubt as to the fate of the Spitfire and her rebel crew that, shortly after dawn one day, the signal went up from the flagstaff battery of "two steamers in the offing."

The vessels composing the United States' blockading squadron, which lay off the harbour just beyond range of the shore batteries, also perceived the approaching strangers, for signals were rapidly being exchanged between the flag-ship and the others.

The two steamers continued to approach, and by ten o'clock in the forenoon were only some four or five miles distant, and were steadily kept on a course which would lead right through the Yankee fleet.

Seeing this, the crowd of spectators, assembled on every point where a view could be commanded, at once came to the conclusion that the new arrivals were United States' vessels.

Such was the universal opinion among a group of young officers and others assembled on the flat roof of a large and handsome house, commanding a good view of the harbour and the sea beyond. Although all were not in a regular uniform, yet it was still apparent, by their carriage, manner, and the swords they wore, that they were rebel officers, who were to command those armies which a short time later did such desperate battle against the invaders of their country. Most of them were young —certainly under thirty—with two exceptions; one of these was a dark, handsome man, with beard and moustache, apparently about forty years of age; was in plain uniform, with coat buttoned close up to his throat, and Kossuth hat with a plume of feathers—the head-dress now universally adopted by the Confederates. He said little, but gazed dreamily out on the sea; in fact, he seemed to be buried in thought.

This was a man afterwards famous—no other than General Beauregard. The other was far more singular and striking in appearance—of the middle height, but gaunt and ungainly in build; he sat on the edge of the parapet, looking out with keen interest from beneath his shaggy eyebrows on the fleet and the two strange steamers in the offing. He was not in uniform, though he wore a sword; and from his stooping and awkward figure, a looker-on would never have imagined he was a soldier. His features were rugged and irregular, but the glance of his grey eye was keen and sharp as that of an eagle. But notwithstanding his uncouth, somewhat common appearance, it was evident, by the deference which some of the younger men paid him, that he was a man of some mark. Even at that date, though only a colonel, there were many who recognised in this rough, unpolished man the germs of future greatness. Nor were such disappointed, for this man was no other than he who was afterwards the terror and bugbear of the Northern armies and Northern generals. His name was a host in itself, and many a Yankee trembled in his shoes when the telegraph flashed the news that he was in the neighbourhood, or was advancing.

His name was Colonel Ruggles, and he had greatly distinguished himself in the Mexican war.

" What do you make of them, colonel ?" asked General Beauregard, his superior in rank.

" Yankees, I reckon, general," was the laconic reply.

At this moment all who were seated rose, and those

who were standing turned respectfully towards the staircase which led up to the roof.

" Be seated, gentlemen—pray do not let me disturb
you."

The voice was that of a female, exquisitely sweet and
clear, and with a slight foreign accent.

The next moment a tall and very beautiful girl stepped
among them in a manner perfectly unembarrassed, yet
without the least boldness or forwardness. Even the
rough and uncouth Colonel Ruggles could not help an
involuntary bow at sight of such all-powerful beauty as
that which now stood before him.

" Allow me to introduce my friend Colonel Ruggles to
you," said General Beauregard to the young lady.

She bowed acquiescence.

" Colonel Ruggles—Mademoiselle Coralie Andrée St.
Casse, whose guests we at present have the honour to
be."

The lady bowed gracefully and smiled sweetly, while
the colonel, who was no ladies' man, stammered out a
few words ; and she, seeing his embarrassment, moved
gracefully away, with another bow, intended to put the
general's friend at his ease. He remained for some moments gazing as if spell-bound at the beautiful form and
face before him. Nor, indeed, was it to be wondered at,
for Coralie St. Casse seemed sent to adorn and brighten
all around her.

She had a profusion of dark-brown hair, of a rather
brighter shade at the temples and near the neck ; black
eyes, large, clear, with dilated pupils, which gave them a
majestic look as that of an eagle. Notwithstanding this,
they were at the same time mild and soft as those of a
dove. Her small mouth, formed like Cupid's bow, was
brilliant as coral, and wreathed in smiles. Her tapering
hands were antique in form, as were her arms, and
dazzlingly fair. Her figure, flexible, graceful, and firm,
was like that of a statue of some goddess of old. Her
feet were small, and all her limbs exquisitely moulded,
while the pose of the head and neck on her rounded
shoulders was such as might drive a statuary mad with

vexation, for assuredly it could never be imitated. As for her face, it was perfection itself; in it were united all the beauties of womanhood, with the bright, graceful elegance of a girl. Her face was ravishingly beautiful; but, perhaps, if not the greatest charm, certainly that which had the greatest effect upon the beholder, was the complexion, which was brilliant in the extreme. It was not a wax doll-like complexion of pink and white, but a gloriously rich one of red and brown. Indeed, were it not for its great purity and transparency, it might have been considered even swarthy. As it was, however, all agreed, as they gazed on the rich brown pellucid skin, through which, at each varying emotion, the red blood mantled and flushed, that to alter or to make it brighter by even a single shade, would be to detract from its beauty, and spoil the effect of the whole. It was this complexion, at once dark and gloriously clear, which had procured for its beautiful owner a name by which, in her absence, she was always spoken of—a name by which all the young Southerners toasted her as the acknowledged beauty of the South—before whose splendour the feeble, pale charms of Northern belles paled as a star of the fifth magnitude in the brightness of the mid-day sun. That name was the *Black Angel*.

Such was Coralie Andrée St. Casse, and, having described imperfectly her person, we will devote a short space to her history.

CHAPTER XLII.

CORALIE ANDRÉE ST. CASSE.

THE father of Coralie was Colonel George St. Casse, who inherited from his father—one of the original French planters, an exile, who, driven from his country by the terrors of the revolution, had adopted America as his country—large estates and plantations in the State of Louisiana. Colonel St. Casse, on the death of his father, found himself in possession of ample wealth, surrounded by none of the cares which sometimes ac-

company it ; and he did not fail to take advantage of the
facilities it gave him to lead a life of reckless pleasure.
It was in the city of New Orleans that he made the
acquaintance of Coralie Crevasse, the mother of our
present heroine. She was the daughter of a wealthy
merchant of New Orleans, one Louis Crevasse. He was
himself a French creole, that is to say, descended from a
French stock, but born in Louisiana. The old gentleman
took a prodigious liking to the dashing young St. Casse,
and the latter, on his part, also took a prodigious liking
to the only daughter, Coralie. In due time he married
her. As for the mother of his bride, she had been dead
for nearly twenty years, and her name was scarcely ever
mentioned. On one occasion only the old merchant
stated that his dead wife was French by her father's side,
but her mother was a Spanish lady from Mexico.

Colonel St. Casse was not a man to trouble himself
about a mother-in-law who had been dead for twenty
years, but quite content with his beautiful bride, bore
her off to his own plantation in Virginia.

It was customary at that time for fathers to give
dowries with their daughters, proportionate with the
wealth of their husbands.

Now, the old merchant was also a planter and slave-
owner, being possessed of a valuable estate, well stocked
with slaves in Louisiana, about twelve miles from
New Orleans. This estate, called St. Hilaire, was, with
the slaves thereon and all slaves whatever owned by
Crevasse, made over to his daughter's husband immediately on their marriage.

Colonel St. Casse shortly afterwards sold the plantation, and removed the slaves to another plantation he
had purchased in Virginia. Two years after his marriage his young wife was attacked by yellow fever,
and notwithstanding all that care and skill could do, died
after a short illness, leaving the widower an only
daughter, the present Coralie St. Casse. The young
lady, as she grew up to girlhood, was furnished with the
best masters, and received the very highest education the
country could afford. Surrounded by every luxury—

every wish gratified by her fond father—it is not to be wondered at that Coralie grew up a wayward, high-spirited girl.

At an early age she gave promise of very great beauty, nor was the promise broken, for as the girl budded into the young woman, she seemed to grow each day more beautiful. Childish beauties and graces developed into woman's glorious beauty, and before she was fifteen Coralie St. Casse was considered on all hands as the handsomest girl in the Old Dominion.

From the age of fifteen to seventeen her life was one round of pleasure and excitement. Her father, who could refuse her nothing, and who was as proud as he was fond of his lovely daughter, took her everywhere with him; Charleston, New Orleans, New York, were all visited, and at each the glorious beauty of the young creole created a perfect *furore*.

It may be imagined that Coralie was beset on all sides by flatterers and admirers, but she paid but little heed to either, treating all alike with gay, sparkling good humour, and charming by her grace, innocence, and wit, while a certain in-born dignity effectually repelled all attempts at familiarity.

As for love and marriage, when young men talked of them to her, or endeavoured to lead the conversation in that direction, she laughed in their faces.

But, alas! at the end of two years a dreadful shock awaited Coralie St. Casse.

At a grand state ball in Washington, one night, she was so much annoyed by the persistent advances of a young man of whom she knew but little and disliked, that, to get rid of his importunities, she danced one dance with him. During the whole of the dance, the young fellow, who was the only son of an enormously rich Boston merchant, poured in her unwilling ear a long string of flatteries and fine speeches, some of which were so coarse as to bring the blood to her cheeks.

The dance happened to be the last before supper, and so, to her inexpressible annoyance, she was compelled to accept the distasteful escort of her partner.

She lingered in the ball-room till every other couple had left, in hopes that her father would appear, or some friend to whom, with some excuse, she might escape.

But it was not so to be, and she had to accept the arm of her partner, and they descended together.

Unfortunately the staircase was quite deserted, and on one of the landings the young man, rendered audacious by the wine he had been drinking, attempted to kiss the girl beside him, and next proceeded to take grosser liberties.

Imagine the indignation of Coralie, proud and pure as she was. She broke indignantly away, and with flashing eyes and flushing cheek, rushed with dishevelled hair to her father, and told him what had happened.

Great and ungovernable was the rage of the colonel. Pale as death, he immediately procured a cowhide, and sought out the insulter of his daughter.

Then he proceeded to inflict a terrible chastisement. He lashed him till his arm ached, and the blood ran in streams from his body. Then he changed the whip to his other hand, and again commenced the furious castigation, nor was it until his prisoner fainted away that he desisted. Then, throwing the inanimate body from him, and administering a parting kick, he turned away, and said in a loud, threatening voice,—

"Thus I punish any man who dares to insult my daughter."

He then strode from the room, and with Coralie, who was alarmed at his terrible violence, which she had been far from expecting, he returned to his hotel.

But, unfortunately, the affair did not end here. The fellow whom he had flogged had not the courage to seek redress. He had, however, a cousin, a captain in the militia. This cousin was poor, a bully, and a noted duellist. It was said, and universally believed, that this fire-eating captain had actually been hired, like the bravoes of old, to kill the colonel. Be that as it may, they met, and the duellist sought occasion to pick a quarrel with Colonel St. Casse. The colonel—hot tempered—

was not sparing in his language, and the result was an immediate challenge.

Colonel St. Casse was advised not to go out by all his friends, as it was thought on all hands to be a planned affair; but he would not listen to a word.

They met the next day; at the first fire Colonel St. Casse was shot through the head; and Coralie was an orphan.

He had made his will before he went out, bequeathing his whole fortune to his daughter, and thus at the age of seventeen Coralie found herself the richest young lady in the State.

Profound was her despair and grief at her father's untimely end; no wealth could atone to her for the loss of his loving care.

From that moment she conceived a bitter and intense hatred for the Yankees, as all Northern Americans are called. She would never even willingly meet one, much less allow one to set foot within her house.

It was about this time that the first notes of the coming terrific struggle were struck. Coralie went heart and soul for the cause of secession, and before she was eighteen years of age her house in Charleston, where she had resided since her father's death, was the resort of the most desperate, as well as the most gifted, of the intending rebels.

She herself possessed talents of no ordinary order, and was looked up to and worshiped by young men, while even greybeards and veterans could not help being infected with her enthusiasm for the Confederate cause, and admiring her manifold beauties both of person and mind.

Two years had elapsed since her father's death, and at the date of which we write Coralie was just nineteen years of age. The promises of her girlhood had been amply fulfilled; and at nineteen she was as perfect a specimen of female loveliness as was ever imagined in painter's, sculptor's, or poet's dreams.

Even before secession was an accomplished fact, and while yet the Union hung in the balance, the house of

Coralie St. Casse was much frequented by such Southerners as had determined to throw off the Northern yoke. Her great wealth as sole heiress of the late Colonel St. Casse, her enthusiasm for the rebel cause, and, above all, her peerless beauty, caused her acquaintance to be much sought after.

Many were the balls and parties which took place in her spacious saloons, and many and vain were the attempts by young officers of birth, wealth, and position, to gain the heart of the wealthy girl. All these attempts had been in vain, for she, although receiving with hospitality all such as were introduced to her, still showed no preference to any, and conducted herself with such dignity and propriety as to repel all attempts or advances from such of the young officers who were smitten with her beauty.

And notwithstanding her position as an orphan, without near relations, and residing alone, still no envious voice even of a female rival had yet been raised against her character, for, like Cæsar's wife, she was above suspicion. No better evidence of this could be found than in the continual presence at her house of the best and most respected men of the South—not gay, dashing young officers only, but senators, generals, and such stern, rugged, plain men, full of earnest purpose, as Colonel Ruggles.

This was the first visit of the latter to the hospitable mansion of the young beauty, whither he had been brought by his friend General Beauregard, and such being the case, Coralie thought it incumbent on her to pay some little attention to the rugged soldier; so passing through the group of young men, who fell back respectfully before her, she made her way to the future hero. He was seated on a corner of the parapet, at a little distance from the others, and appeared to be intently watching the approaching vessels.

" Well, Colonel Ruggles," said Coralie, laying her hand lightly on his shoulder, " what do you make of them?"

The old man started as the sound of her gentle accents fell on his ear, and absolutely blushed.

Yes, the stern soldier, the future conqueror in many battles, was completely abashed before this dark beauty. Quickly recovering himself, however, he handed her the telescope he held, and replied,—

"Indeed, I am at a loss to make them out; there is no flag flying on either—one seems to be towing the other, which appears terribly disabled and shattered."

Coralie took the glass, and after looking through it stedfastly for some time, said,—

"Does not the smaller vessel—the one being towed—resemble the Spitfire, that was seized and run away with by Lieutenant Leigh and some other Southern officers?"

Her voice was faltering, and handing back the glass, she looked anxiously in the other's face for an answer to her question.

The colonel took it somewhat hastily from her hand, and again levelled it towards the two vessels.

Scarcely had he done so, than a puff of smoke came from the flag-ship of the squadron, which was followed by the report of a cannon.

"We shall know directly," said the colonel; "the gun was a signal for the strangers to hoist their colours."

Still the two vessels kept on, as if determined to take no notice of the signal gun. Suddenly, however, flags were run up to the peak of each.

There is a moment's suspense, as all endeavour to make them out; then the colonel, shutting up his glass violently, exclaims,—

"You are right—it is the Spitfire, and she has been recaptured by the other vessel."

"And what of Lieutenant Darcy Leigh and his brother officers?" asked the young girl by his side.

"What of them?—why, they are doubtless prisoners."

"Prisoners!—great Heavens! and is there no help for them?—can we not give them aid—rescue them?" she asked, distractedly.

"Impossible; it was an insane attempt, and must have ended disastrously. I foresaw this."

The old colonel spoke gloomily and bitterly enough.

"Hand me the glass a moment, colonel," said a young

officer, approaching them. "I can soon tell you whether that sloop in tow is the Spitfire; for I have sailed in her."

So saying, he took the glass from the hands of the colonel, and looked attentively towards the two vessels.

The blockading squadron lay, as we have said, just beyond the range of the shore batteries; and the two steamers, which the reader doubtless recognises as the Wabash and Spitfire, were now within hailing distance.

"Yes, that is the Spitfire, sure enough," said the young man who held the glass; "I know every plank of her—terribly knocked about, too, she seems to be."

"Can you make out the other vessel?" asked Colonel Ruggles.

The young man turned his glass towards the Wabash. Suddenly he gave an exclamation of astonishment.

"What is it, sir?" asked Coralie St. Casse. "What do you see?"

"Darcy Leigh, by Jove! and on the deck of the frigate."

"Darcy Leigh!" exclaimed the young lady, in breathless excitement; "but if that is the Spitfire, he must be a prisoner."

"By Heavens! it is though," continued the young man, "and there is Wharncliffe by his side. I could swear to both of them. Darcy has his head bound up as if wounded."

"Wounded," said Coralie, mournfully, "and a prisoner!"

"Wounded, yes—but a prisoner, no—for, by thunder, he is giving orders!"

"Giving orders? impossible!" said Colonel Ruggles. "If that is the Spitfire, she must have been captured by the other; then, of course, Lieutenant Leigh is a prisoner."

"That is the Spitfire, and Lieutenant Leigh is not a prisoner nevertheless. Take the glass, colonel, and look for yourself. That officer whose head and shoulders you can just see over the bulwarks is Darcy Leigh, and he at the foot of the mizzen-mast is Lieutenant Wharncliffe. Both are friends of mine, and I could swear to them were they double the distance,"

The colonel took the glass, and directing it on the Wabash, looked intently through it.

"Are you quite sure of what you say, sir?"

"If you mean am I quite sure that I recognise Lieutenant Leigh and Wharncliffe—yes."

"And he standing by the companion-way is Darcy Leigh?" continued the colonel, still with his glass to his eye.

"Yes."

"And the other, by the mizzen-mast, Wharncliffe?"

"Yes."

"Then they are no more prisoners than I am. I now see by their actions that they are giving orders and being obeyed."

The two vessels were now right abreast of the foremost one of the blockading squadron, and even without the aid of the telescope the numberless spectators could see all that passed. Indeed, the decks of the vessels were visible to those who were on lofty situations in the town, while of course they were hid by the bulwarks from the view of those on board the Yankee vessels.

The deck of the Wabash, which had the Spitfire in tow, was crowded with men, but they were all lying down at their guns, or otherwise concealed. The decks of the Spitfire, on the contrary, were almost deserted. There was a man at the wheel, two or three on the main deck, and one officer in the United States' uniform,— that was all.

As the two vessels passed the first of the squadron, an officer of the last was observed to hail the strangers. The hail was answered by an officer on board the Wabash, and appeared satisfactory, for she steamed on without further challenge.

Now the two vessels pass slowly and majestically through the squadron, seemingly steering right for the flag-ship, which lay nearest the harbour. A thousand eyes are on them, but few suspect their true character.

As for the group on the housetop, they are in a state of utter confusion and uncertainty, for the news has flown like lightning that Darcy Leigh, Lieutenant

Wharncliffe, and some other of the officers who seized the Spitfire, have been recognised on the deck of the Wabash, and not as prisoners.

Many conjectures are hazarded as to the meaning of this, but none guess at the solution.

"They must have thought better of it, and taken the sloop back," said one.

"Or surrendered her without firing a shot. This Lieutenant Leigh and Wharncliffe, perhaps, going over to the enemy, and by betraying their friends, purchasing immunity from punishment."

"Never!" exclaimed Coralie St. Casse, passionately. "You, sir, who thus speak, do not know Darcy Leigh. He is incapable of such conduct."

The officer who had spoken fell back abashed.

The next instant a singular commotion was observed on board the Wabash. She had just steamed up abreast of the flag-ship of the squadron, and the commodore, as they judged, as well as they could tell at the distance, had hailed the frigate and received the reply.

Then the commodore appeared again to hail, as if giving orders to the captain of the frigate, which latter immediately altered her course, as if to cross the bows of the former, and anchor just inside her.

At this moment a figure was seen to run up from the cabin of the Wabash, and jumping on the bulwarks, hail the flag-ship. Darcy Leigh was seen to throw himself in the way, but so sudden was the rush of the other that he was not able to stop him.

Scarcely, however, had the latter jumped on the bulwarks and hailed the commodore's ship, than a general rush was made towards him from all sides. At least a dozen men threw themselves upon him and dragged him down.

All this was utterly incomprehensible to the spectators on the housetop, until one of the officers, who had served on board the Wabash, exclaimed, as he who hailed the flag-ship was dragged away,—

"Why, may I be —— if that wasn't Captain Seth Peabody, the captain of the Wabash."

Meanwhile the hail of Captain Peabody seemed to have produced a prodigious effect on board the flag-ship.

Officers could be seen running hither and thither, signals were run up, and the roll of the drums beating to quarters might plainly be heard.

Soon the deck was covered with the crew assembling to quarters, and the guns were rapidly run in and loaded. And if the change from repose to action was great and sudden on board the commodore's ship, it was much more so on board the Wabash.

A minute back, and but two or three men could be seen on her deck; now, as if by magic, her crew swarmed around her guns, the forecastle was crowded with small-arms men, and the big guns were run out. Loud shouts and cheers might be heard even at this distance.

"What, in the name of all that's holy, is the meaning of this?" asked some one.

"The meaning, sir, is this," replied Coralie St. Casse, slowly and deliberately: "instead of the Wabash having captured Darcy Leigh and the Spitfire, the Spitfire, under the command of Darcy Leigh and his gallant officers, has captured the Wabash, and they sought, by hoisting the Yankee flag, to deceive the squadron and pass safely through their midst into the harbour. The man whom we saw jump on the bulwarks and hail the flag-ship was doubtless the captain of the Wabash, who, watching his time, escaped from custody and gave the alarm. Now all is known, and God send them safe into harbour."

"You're right, miss, you're right, as sure as my name is Ruggles," shouted the colonel, jumping to his feet. Then hurrying up to General Beauregard, who still appeared lost in astonishment, he spoke a few words to him. At first these were received with incredulity.

"Yes, general, I tell you it is so; send the order to the batteries."

General Beauregard nodded in token of assent.

The colonel hastily wrote a note on a slip of paper, and handing it to one of the junior officers, said—

"Take this first to the flagstaff battery, next by boat to Fort Sumter—lose not a moment. Now, gentlemen all, to your posts. Haste, quick to the batteries. Those two steamers coming in are our friends, and the Yankees may seek to follow them; if they do we will give them a hot reception."

Scarcely were the words out of his mouth than the roar of cannon was heard from the bay, and the excited spectators beheld the whole squadron enveloped in fire and smoke.

CHAPTER XLIII.

A TERRIBLE BATTLE OFF CHARLESTON BAY.

FLASH! roar! the great guns thundered, as ship after ship, slipping her cable (for since the affair of the Spitfire in New York harbour this precaution had been invariably taken at anchor), brought her broadside to bear on the frigate and sloop.

These had now thrown off all disguise, and at the first broadside had hoisted the rebel flag, steaming at the same time towards the harbour. The nature of the channel necessitated both vessels to present nearly their broadside to the fleet, thus rendering their escape more slow, and keeping them longer within range, as they were compelled to advance in a diagonal direction.

But this also enabled them—at least the Wabash—to pour most destructive broadsides into the nearest of the squadron; indeed, at one time so close and well directed was her fire, that the crew of the flag-ship were thrown into some confusion, and for a few minutes fled from her guns. This was fortunate, or otherwise both vessels must have been soon sunk by the heavy guns at so short a range. In the course of a few minutes, the Spitfire and frigate—the former having passed ahead from her superior speed—had approached the narrowest part of the channel. Once through this, they alter their course, and run right in. This narrow passage, however, was commanded by the fire of the fleet, every vessel of which had now got into

position, and was thundering away, might and main, at
the audacious rebels. Some were steaming in pursuit,
and should any accident happen to the engines, the fugitives would be overhauled and brought to bay before
they could get well under shelter of the shore batteries.

And now the roar of battle is terrific along the whole
line. The round shot howls and crashes through the air,
dashing into the water and throwing up the foam in all
directions—ahead, astern, on all sides, nothing can be
seen but the splashing of the cannon balls as they bound
and ricochet along the surface of the waves. It seems
miraculous that the two vessels are not utterly destroyed
amid the iron storm so constantly poured forth. Shot
after shot comes roaring through the air, smashing into
them, splintering the timbers and killing the men at
their quarters.

The damage done to the Wabash is in a few minutes
so terrible that the rebel officers almost despair of carrying
her through the tempest of shot. She is especially sin-
gled out by the enemy, both as being the larger and
slower of the two vessels, and also because her decks are
more crowded with men. After the first few minutes of
the running fight she ceases to return the fire, so terrible
and fierce is it. Her decks are strewn with killed and
wounded men, while the air around is alive with the terrible rushing cannon balls and splinters of timber. In
face of the terrible and imminent danger, Darcy Leigh
stands on the quarter-deck, surrounded by a few officers,
giving his orders as calmly as if at a naval review, instead
of in the midst of as terrible a fire of shot and shell as
ever was opened on a vessel.

He looks anxiously at the Yankee war steamers, then
at the harbour and batteries, as if measuring the distance.

"Oh, for ten minutes' time, and we should be safe!"
he exclaims.

By this time nearly the whole squadron is in motion,
following the same diagonal course in the pursuit as the
two rebel vessels had taken. Several of the ships are
gaining on them, still keeping up a most destructive fire.
In order to do this, the foremost vessel yaws round, and

when broadside on, delivers her fire; immediately afterwards resuming her course, another vessel having, in the meantime, taken her place, executing the same manœuvre, and in turn falling back.

Thus the Wabash and Spitfire sustain a constant fire; while the Wabash is alone able to reply, and that, as may be imagined, but imperfectly.

An officer hurries up to Darcy Leigh.

"Captain," he says, in a hurried whisper, "the ship is hit in several places between wind and water, and is filling fast. In twenty minutes the fires will be put out."

"Get all the boats ready for launching," was the prompt and undaunted reply, "and have a tow rope ready to carry to the Spitfire. When our fires are out the sloop must tow us."

"What! under this fearful fire?"

At that instant a shot struck the mizzen-mast, and a splinter knocked down both the speaker and Darcy Leigh. Instantly, however, he was on his feet, only bruised by the shock.

"Aye," he said to the officer, who also gathered himself up slowly and painfully, "were the fire ten times as terrible, I am determined to take both ships in, or die in the attempt."

"Very good, sir," said the young officer, with prompt naval obedience, moving off slowly and limpingly.

"Are you hurt, Osborne?" said Darcy, kindly.

"Not much, I hope; it was a hard knock, however."

The young man was deadly pale, and staggering to the bulwarks, was obliged to hold on for support. Darcy hastened to assist him, and perceived that his left arm was broken.

"Come below—you are not fit to remain on deck," he said, endeavouring to lead the young man below.

"No, no—this is no time for skulking. Every man must die at his post. I for one am ready, for I ——"

Scarcely were these gallant words out of Osborne's mouth, and before he had concluded his speech, than the brave fellow's career was cut short for ever. The loud howl of a second shot was heard, then a dull sound, a crash, and the next moment the brave fellow was lying on the deck a horribly disfigured corpse.

A round shot had struck him on the shoulder, tearing off the limb, and of course causing instant death. Darcy gazed for a second on the mutilated remains. He was a dear friend, and as he looked a tear stood in his eye.

Hastily he brushed it away.

" Starboard—starboard—hard !" he cried to the helms-man. " Mr. Wharncliffe, get the boats ready to launch —we are sinking !"

This order was quickly carried out, and the wounded men, who each moment increased in number, were placed in them. The decks were now in a fearful state —torn, splintered, and running with blood. Still, how-ever, the frigate kept on her course, slowly, painfully, like a wounded stag pursued by the hounds. ·

The Spitfire, those in charge having perceived the sinking state of the Wabash, had slackened speed, and was now only about one hundred yards ahead. Both vessels were well within range of the shore batteries— in fact, between them on one side and Fort Sumter, with its hundred guns, on the other.

Darcy Leigh calculated that if they could only keep on for ten minutes more, they would be safe, for the Yankees would be well within range of the batteries, if indeed they were not so already. Anxiously the young commander watched these, hoping and hoping in vain to see the flash and smoke of their guns.

They were now nearer to the shore than the fort, and it was from the batteries of the former he hoped for assistance, when suddenly a loud hissing and sputtering is heard in the engine-room, succeeded by dense volumes of steam.

It needs not the words of the officer in charge of the engine-room, who hurries up, to inform Darcy that the fires are out, the water having flowed into the furnaces.

" Out with the boats ; quick, as you value your lives. The launch first, with a hawser for the Spitfire."

This is quickly done, and the boat's crew of the launch, giving way, row with might and main for the sloop.

Their progress is necessarily slow, having to drag the hawser, but half the distance is accomplished in safety.

On board the Spitfire all wait and watch the progress of the boat and her gallant crew with breathless suspense. The Wabash is still steaming slowly ahead, for although the fires are out there is still sufficient steam to work the engines for some minutes.

As soon as the boat is perceived by the pursuing vessels, a perfect storm of shot is rained around her. This, for the moment, is advantageous, for the terrible iron hail which had been flying incessantly on the Wabash ceases for a moment, giving time for her officers and men to launch the other boats without danger. The boat, too, in comparison, was but a speck on the waves, and hitherto, although the shot flew around her in all directions, she had escaped being hit.

She is within a dozen yards of the sloop, and all on board both congratulate themselves on her having passed unscathed through the ordeal, when a huge shell from one of those terrible engines of warfare, a Dahlgren gun, comes, roaring, tearing, splashing over the waves, now leaping high in the air, now, as it were, burying in the sea. Onwards came the dreadful missile, and plunged into the water about a hundred yards from the boat. All on board the frigate breathed more freely, for they thought the danger over. Alas! it was not so, for the enormous shell again ricocheted from the sea and dashed, with a terrible crash, full on the boat; and the next moment all that could be seen of her was a few struggling men and shattered planks.

For a moment or two there was a dead silence on board the Wabash; even the noise of the engines had ceased, for they had stopped from want of steam.

Then followed the roar of guns from their pursuers, and shot and shell once more rushed and howled in the air, splashed in the water, and crashed among the woodwork of the Wabash. The work of death had recommenced.

Darcy Leigh jumped into one of the quarter boats.

"Who volunteers to come with me and take a hawser to the Spitfire?"

A dozen voices answered his appeal, and the boat was soon crowded.

"Lower away," cried Darcy.

Scarcely, however, was the boat lowered a foot from the deck, and long before she touched the water, than she was struck by a cannon ball, one side being torn to pieces.

Darcy quite coolly stepped back on the deck and went over to the boat on the other side.

"Better luck next time," he said, with grim fun; "since the enemy won't let us have the larboard boat we'll try the starboard."

Then he stepped into the boat, and the volunteer crew having followed him, he seated himself in the stern sheets and again gave the order to "lower away" as coolly as if nothing had happened. This time the boat reached the water in safety, and the end of the hawser having been handed in, the seamen gave way with a will, and they started on their short but terribly dangerous cruise to the Spitfire.

Once again the shot and shell splashed in the water around them, and roared in the air overhead.

Those in charge of the sloop, seeing the disabled state of the Wabash, and also the attempt to send a hawser on board, slackened speed so as to allow the latter to come up with them. It thus happened that in this second attempt the boat would only have to row a distance of some hundred yards or so. Still, from the fact of the enemy having obtained the exact range, their danger was imminent.

Before they had rowed a dozen yards two of the oars were broken by a shot, the men holding them seriously bruised, and all in the boat splashed with the water thrown on board. While this constant and terrible fire is kept up on the boat by a part of the squadron, others are still pounding away mercilessly at the Wabash; and the shot every now and then plumping into her, bid fair soon to reduce her to a perfect wreck—if, indeed, the waters do not swallow her up, which the alarming nature of the damage she has received, and her rapid settling down, render only too probable.

Notwithstanding the state of wreck, confusion, and bloodshed in which her decks are, prompt measures are taken by Lieutenant Wharncliffe to get everything ready for a start in the boats, for all on board knew well enough that she could not float much longer, and would probably sink long before they could get her safely into the harbour.

Of course their object, and the intention of Darcy Leigh, was to take her in and run her aground, so that she could not sink; but if, in spite of all they could do, she went down under their feet before that time, they would abandon her and make for the Spitfire. Everything, then, was got in perfect readiness, officers and men working rapidly, but quietly, notwithstanding the storm of shot flying about them. By the time the boat had arrived within a few yards of the sloop, the Wabash was completely riddled with shot; her decks were torn, and splintered in all directions; while as for bulwarks, she might as well have been without any, so completely were they knocked away. Of the officers on board her, seven were severely wounded, eight others slightly, and one, poor Osborne, killed outright.

With breathless anxiety all on board the unfortunate frigate watch the boat as she rows up to the Spitfire.

Now she is quite close, and a rope is thrown from the sloop to the boat, in order to bend on the hawser. Unfortunately it falls short and the suspense is prolonged, though for but a little time, for the next instant another is heaved, which reaches its mark. In an amazingly short space of time the hawser is bent on and cast adrift from the boat, which latter instantly returns to the Wabash, the men at the oars making her fly through the waters at a terrible pace, now they are no longer encumbered by the weight of the hawser.

CHAPTER XLIV.

DARBY KELLY'S OPINIONS OF THINGS IN GENERAL.— THE BATTLE CONTINUED.

A LOUD shout of triumph breaks from the crew of the Wabash as they see this result successfully achieved, and with a very few strokes of the oars the boat is again alongside, and Darcy Leigh jumps on the deck, amid the congratulations of all who witnessed the daring feat.

The cheer from the frigate was echoed by another from the shore batteries, for they were now sufficiently near to hear, and on looking closely, the gunners could be seen at the cannon waiting to open their fire on the Yankee fleet.

"Confound them! why don't they fire on these fellows behind us? surely they are in range," muttered Darcy. "Do they mean to let them chase us right into the harbour?"

It really seemed almost as if such were the intention, for both the Spitfire and Wabash had long passed the narrow passage, and were now steering a course which took them every moment further from the batteries, and nearer to the guns of Fort Sumter. This latter, however, was far out of range, and they could expect but little assistance from that quarter. Neither Darcy nor any of his officers at that time had any idea of the designs of the Confederate officers, and both naturally chafed at being thus made targets of within range of the guns of their friends on shore.

These designs aimed at no little matter, and there was every probability of their being carried out to the tremendous discomfiture of the enemy.

"Now then, my lads!" shouted the young commander, "out with the boats, and, at the word of command, pull like demons for the sloop."

This order was promptly carried into effect, and soon the boats were all safely launched and towing alongside. The Spitfire having her in tow, they were once again progressing slowly. Darcy himself, who was well acquainted with the channel, directing the helmsman **of** the Wabash, and signalling to the Spitfire.

Their progress, however, **was** necessarily **slow,** for the frigate was rapidly sinking in the water; **in fact,** was almost water-logged.

" Go and find **out** how high the water is in her, and how much longer **she** will keep afloat," said the young captain **to his** lieutenant.

Wharncliffe **left,** and soon returned **with** the answer.

" The water is up to her lower deck; she may float **a** quarter of an hour, **but** she may **sink in** ten minutes **or** even less."

" We will hang on to the last moment," said Darcy.

" Are we not incurring **a great** risk ?" asked Wharn-cliffe. " She may heel over and go down at any moment."

Darcy walked **to the** side, and looked over **to** observe how near they were to the water. It was almost level with the **guns** of the main-deck.

" Yes, yes," he said, hurriedly, and anxiously glancing again first at the land batteries, and then at the **gunners.** " I know we **run a great** risk, **but I** think **we avoid** a greater. **Do you** notice **the course we** are steering, and that steered **by the Yankees ?"**

" Yes—nearly at right angles."

" Exactly. They have not yet rounded the shoal at the narrows, and though they are going two feet to our one at present, we are getting further from them every minute. Don't you notice that within the last few minutes, since they have **been** obliged **to** haul up to the southward, that most of their shot have fallen rather short ?"

" Yes, true, but that **is** more the result **of** bad aim than distance, for were we twice as far we **should be in** easy range."

" Yes, so we should, **but** observe, **now—while we** are every moment increasing our distance **we** are continually altering the range, **and** at present they seem to have lost it. Besides, **we are not in such** danger here as in the boats, for a **few** shot **in the** Wabash more or less will soon make little difference, while even one striking **a** boat would be very disastrous. All the boats must necessarily be very crowded, and if the pinnace or long boat should be sunk, it is doubtful whether we could pick up the men without so overcrowding the others as to sink them. For this reason, then, I intend to stick to the ship, if she will float so long, until these cursed Yankees astern round the shoal, and again steer straight for us."

"Darcy, old fellow, you ought to be Commodore of the Confederate navy. By Jove! I never knew a fellow with such a head."

"Commodore of the Confederate navy!" said Darcy, unable to restrain a smile, "truly the post would be almost a sinecure, for as far as I know, the Confederate navy at present consists of this battered wreck and our poor old Spitfire there, with all her teeth drawn—her guns overboard."

"Ah! but we will have a navy and an army too."

"Yes," replied Darcy, seriously, almost solemnly, " the accursed Yankees may despise and talk of crushing us Southerners. Europe and the world may be incredulous; but as surely as the sun now shines, *we, the people of the Confederate States of America, will make an army, a navy, and what is more, we will make a nation !*"

The words and manner of Darcy Leigh seemed almost prophetic. His cheek flushed as he confidently propounded as a certainty that which all, or nearly all, but the determined and desperate Southerners deemed impossible.

After a moment's silence, Wharncliffe was about to speak again, when the sound of a big gun from the battery on shore diverted their attention.

Darcy and the lieutenant jumped on the bulwarks to watch the effect of the shot.

To their great surprise, it fell far wide of the pursuing ships. It struck and threw up a column of water some hundred yards astern of the last of the Yankee vessels; and what surprised Darcy Leigh still more, it was far short of the mark.

He knew that they must be in easy range, and was at a loss how to account for such bad practice, for of course the engineers were, or ought to be, aware of the exact distance of so important a point as a narrow passage leading to the harbour. Still more to his surprise, the shot was not followed up—the artillery officers seemed to think that the enemy were out of range.

Darcy jumped down from the bulwarks and stamped his foot with rage.

"This is too bad," he cried; "the passage is in easy range, and so it would be were it half a mile further; and they to let them pass safely in!"

"I beg yer honour's pardon," said the big Irish fireman, "for spaking, or for being on deck at all at all; but ye see, yer honour, that, do all I could, I couldn't fire up no ways; for, by gory, what's the good of shovelling coals in when we're all under water, furnaces and all?"

"Well, my man, what is it you have to say?" said Darcy, smiling.

At this moment there was a comparative lull in the firing from the pursuing vessels, and the Wabash went ahead steadily enough, giving none of those heels and lurches which invariably presage the foundering of a ship, so that Darcy was not indisposed to listen to what he might have to say.

"Well, my lad, speak on."

"Well, sir, once again entreating your honour's pardon, I heard what yer said just now about the shore batteries and the inimy. I paid particular notice to it, for I meself was just thinking the very same thing as yer honour. Says I to meself—why, the blue blaze, don't them spalpeens on shore as is our friends shoot at the inimy, seeing as they are close enough; hit them and hurt them too, be jabers! for if them big cannon balls that I've seen many a time in the flagstaff gun-battery yonder wouldn't hurt 'em, I'd like to know what would. Well, says I to meself, 'Why don't they shoot?' So I thinks and thinks on, at last I has it—I found 'em out, yer honour."

"Found 'em out—found who out, the enemy?"

"No, no, yer honour, not the inimy, but them

T

chaps ashore with the big popguns—the friends I may zay. Well, as I was saying, yer honour, I found 'em out."

"Well, go on, make haste and tell us what you found out. Wharncliffe, keep an eye on the ship."

At this time all was going on comparatively smoothly, for the Yankee ships were just rounding the shoal, where the navigation is very difficult, and the firing was by no means so heavy.

"Well," continued Darby Kelly, "yer honour knows that the channel's mortal narrow where the inimy is now."

"Yes."

"Well, there's another narrow place, a little further on."

"Yes, quite right; you ought to be a pilot, Darby."

"True for you, yer honour, and I don't know but what I may take to it some day. I ain't 'xactly made up my mind yet, but I mean to be either a pilot or kernel."

"A what?" said Darcy.

"A kernel, yer honour, a soger kernel.

Neither Darcy nor Wharncliffe could refrain from laughter at hearing the great Irishman, rough, shaggy, and black with smoke and coal dust, declare his intention of being a "soger kernel."

"Ah, well, yer honour, ye may laugh, but it's thrue as gospel; it is, be jabers! Well, I'll go on wi' my story, for time's short, I guess. I suppose yer honour's heard of the Duke?"

"What duke?"

"An' would ye ask me what duke?—sure the great Duke—the Irish Duke I mane."

"The Irish Duke?" said Darcy, in amazement.

"Av course, the Irish Duke—the great Irish Duke— the Duke of Wellington, as was, and as ought to have been the Duke of Ireland, which is his country."

"What on earth has the Duke of Wellington got to do with Charleston harbour?"

"Hist a bit, an' I'll tell ye. Did yer honour ever hear

tell of the ——th regiment, the Fighting ——th, they called 'em. They fought in the Peninsula and in ivery battle as ever was in any part of the world since iver they was a regiment."

"The devil they did!" said Darcy, again laughing; "they must have been worthy of their name then. But what on earth has the Irish regiment got to do with us and the Yankees?"

"Iverything; ye jist hould on a bit and I'll tell ye."

"It seems, then, that the Irish have a good deal to do with Charleston—first, the Irish Duke, as you call him, and then the Fighting ——th."

"In course they have, yer honour—why shouldn't they? Sure yer honour knows that *the country belongs to the Irish and Gineral Jackson*."*

"The deuce it does!" said Darcy; "I thought we had something to do with it."

"Say, Massa Darby, if de country belong to Gineral Hickory Jackson and de Irish, who does we niggers belong to?"

This came from Jupiter, the black fireman, who, seeing his friend in conversation with the officers, crept up behind to hear what was going on.

"Is that you, ye black spalpeen?" said Darby, rolling his eyes round; "come out of that wid ye. What do you mane by listening when a gentleman's a talking to his honour here?"

"I's a-going, Massa Darby," said Jupiter, grinning, "but jist tell a coon who we niggers belong to if all de country belongs to de General and de Irish."

"Who do ye belong to, ye black varmint? why ye belongs to the divil, and he's lint you to the Yankees."

"O my lor' a gor' A'mighty!" said Jupiter, rolling his eyes and showing his white teeth.

"Come out, will ye? or I'll shoot ye," said Darby, taking up a cannon ball which lay on the deck.

* This curious assertion is frequently to be heard in the progress of street squabbles, &c., between the Irish and native Americans.

Jupiter, not fancying the idea of being shot in so strange a fashion, promptly vanished.

"Well, well, get on with what you have to say," said Darcy, impatiently. "We have no time to stand here all day gossiping, with death all round us."

"Well, yer honour, I'll be quick. I was spaking of the Fighting ——th; my father was a soger in it, an' at the battle of Talavera, after fighting like divils all day, and losing half their men, towards evening the regiment drawn up in square was charged by the French cavalry, and some of the dragoons broke the square and got inside. Well, yer honour, after the fight was over, the Duke—he wasn't duke then, but only gineral or lord, or something—sez to the kernel (he was an Irishman, and his name was O'Brien) the Duke sez, sez he, 'Well, colonel, so the inimy got into your square to-day.'

"'Yes, gineral,' says the colonel,' some of the vagabonds did get in, but, be Jasus, they niver got out agin.' Nor more they did, yer honour, for I mind my father tellin me he stabbed four of 'em himself with his bayonet."

Darcy was silent for a moment or so.

"Does yer honour see my maning?"

"Yes, Darby, I do, and, by thunder, you're right, I do believe. Wharncliffe, I think I see now why the batteries have not yet opened fire. This brave fellow is right in his conjecture, although he has a most tedious way of telling it. They mean to let them pass the second shoal, and then, like Colonel O'Brien, they will never let them out again."

At this moment the Wabash gave a long and heavy roll to starboard—so heavy indeed that she was almost on her beam-ends, and thus remained for some time.

"Quick, Wharncliffe, quick," said Darcy; "man the boats, and pull away from the ship for your lives; she'll be down in five minutes more."

The ship righted herself, but so slowly, and, as it were, wearily, that all well knew the end was very close.

"All hands to the boats," shouted Darcy, in a loud, clear voice,—"quickly and quietly—no rush, no hurry, but let every man take his place in the boat he is told off to."

The deck sounded with the tramp of many feet as the crew hastened to obey this order,—without confusion, however, and with admirable discipline.

Every boat was now manned, and awaiting the word, with the exception of the gig, which Darcy had reserved for himself and ten men, determined to be last to leave the ship.

The deck was now quite clear; the ten whom Darcy had told off for the gig jumping into it at a signal given; the young captain standing alone at the helm.

The ship was deserted, and he who had planned and so successfully carried out this desperate venture, stood calmly surveying the scene.

He gazed around him, first at the town of Charleston: every housetop—every balcony—every available place, in fact, was crowded with eager spectators; then at the frowning batteries on shore, and then at the Yankee steamers in pursuit, who still kept up an incessant fire. He had seen so much of this, however, during the last half-hour, that he no longer heeded the howl of the round shot overhead, or the more terrible crashing of timber which showed the ship was struck.

CHAPTER XLV.

THE WABASH, A SHOT-TORN HULK, IS ABANDONED.— THE BLACK ANGEL FIRES THE FIRST SHOT FROM THE BATTERY.

DARCY LEIGH, alone at the helm, gazed around him, and for the first time an expression of triumph and pride came over his pale, handsome features. The pallor made them appear almost feminine, while the light flush which for a moment illumined them quickly faded away, and he stood calm and pale as a marble statue.

The Wabash gave another terrible lurch to starboard, this time going even further over than before, and being even longer in recovering herself.

" The next lurch will be her last," muttered Darcy ;
" she will go down."

Then he left the helm, and ran to the side.

" Cast off and pull away," he shouted. " Give way
with a will, men, and in a minute you will be on board
the Spitfire."

Then all the boats, with the exception of the gig,
cast off, and with a parting cheer, pulled for the sloop.

Darcy Leigh coolly went up to the flag locker, and
bending a flag on to the signal halyards, proceeded
deliberately to hoist it to the jury-mast, so that it
might be the last thing visible when the frigate went
down.

When it reached the mast-head, the roll in which it
was made up burst, and the rebel flag—the Stars and
Bars—floated in the breeze.

Another cheer broke from the boats' crews, which was
answered from the Spitfire ; and all along the shore that
cheer was taken up. From batteries, forts, windows,
balconies, and housetops, the thousands of spectators at
once saluted their flag, and yelled forth their defiance to
the hated Yankees.

For some time back the fire of the vessels giving chase
had been less heavy, for the navigation of the channel was
very difficult, and to bring their broadsides to bear they
would have to change their course, which, for a minute
even, would expose them to the dangers of running on to
the rocks and shoals on either side ; but now the winding
course of the channel again enabled the foremost vessels
to open fire with all their guns ; and the instant the boats
appeared in sight, a perfect storm of shot hailed around
them, also the Wabash and Spitfire.

Fortunately the distance to be pulled was short ; and
the Spitfire at the same time slackening her speed, the
boats all arrived without any damage of consequence.

It was not till he saw them actually alongside that
Darcy Leigh jumped into his boat, which was towing at
the gangway. Then, with a last look around the shattered, blood-stained decks, which he had so well defended,
he leaped into the boat and gave the word to pull off.

At this time the air seemed perfectly alive with shot; nearly all the vessels of the squadron were blazing away with their whole broadsides; and the rushing in the air, combined with the splashing in the water all around, and the roar of a hundred guns, made up a fearful scene.

It really seemed miraculous that any floating thing could live a moment in such a storm of shot and shell.

The Spitfire was now suffering terribly, shot after shot striking her now in the rigging, now in the hull. A quarter of an hour's practice such as that would sink the finest ship afloat.

The gig in which Darcy Leigh was seated, urging the men to their utmost, had barely moved half the distance, than a shot struck her on the bow, killing the bow oarsman, and wounding two others. The next instant, and she sank beneath them, and all were struggling in the water. The man who was killed by the shot, and one of the two wounded, sank immediately, and were seen no more. Most of the others could swim, and such as could not seized an oar or a plank, and all struck out for the sloop.

And now the enemy, in a most dastardly manner, ignoring all the laws of civilized warfare, commenced firing with grape and canister at the struggling men who were swimming for their lives.

During the battle of Trafalgar, and ere yet victory had declared for the English fleet, boats were sent from an English ship to pick up the drowning men of a sunk Frenchman; but the Yankees were as incapable of the generosity of an Englishman as they were of the daring courage of Nelson, and wreaked their spite and hate by firing at men swimming for their lives.

Fortunately, notwithstanding the deadly intent, not a man was hurt, and a boat sent from the Spitfire picked them up without being struck by a shot.

And now the whole fury of the Yankee fire is turned on the sloop, and she soon bids fair to be as completely a shot-torn wreck as the Wabash. Two large Dahlgren shells struck her, one immediately following the other, and she also received a shot under water. Both the shells exploded on her lower deck, and the water rushed in through the hole made in her side at a fearful pace.

Fire quickly followed the shell, and dense volumes of smoke ascended from her hatches, while, to make matters worse, another shot plunged into the machinery, rendering one engine completely useless, and damaging the other.

Darcy at once saw the imminence of the danger.

The instant, all wet and dripping, he leaped on deck, he said,—

"Hoist a flag with the stars downwards, and commence firing blank guns towards the batteries as a signal of distress."

This was instantly done, and a gun which had been saved when all the others had been thrown overboard was loaded with powder and fired several times.

For a few moments Darcy gazed at the batteries in suspense—then the smoke of a heavy gun belched forth from an embrasure. The shot hurtled through the air, and without once ricocheting, it smashed right into the foremost of the pursuing ships.

All who saw hailed the shot with a shout of joy, not so much for its sake alone, but because it demonstrated the fact that the Yankees were in range of the shore batteries with their terrible great guns, to which the ship guns were but playthings; and that the *Spitfire* was safe.

Almost immediately after they saw the shot take effect; it was followed by an explosion, flames, and a dense body of smoke.

The shot, or rather shell, had done good service. The ship it struck was on fire like the sloop, and Darcy threw up his hat with delight.

It was a good and true shot.

General Beauregard himself pointed the gun, and the Black Angel fired it.

CHAPTER XLVI.

THE FIRST GUN FROM THE BATTERY

INTENSE was the excitement among the numerous spectators on shore of this running fight of the Wabash and Spitfire. Fervent were the prayers breathed by many a fair maid and mother for the safety of the daring crew who were attempting to make the harbour.

The details of the seizure and escape of the Spitfire from New York harbour had long since arrived, and it had been subject of serious fear lest she should have been captured at sea by one of the cruisers sent in pursuit.

No wonder, then, that the excitement was tremendous when the news rang through Charleston that the little Spitfire had actually captured the United States' frigate Wabash, and was endeavouring to run into harbour with her prize. Most were disposed at first to disbelieve the news, but the thunder of the cannon soon convinced them of its truth.

At first shouts of joy and exultation rent the air, as the sloop and Wabash were seen to have passed through the squadron in safety. These shouts of triumph, however, were soon hushed, when it was seen that the two vessels were being closely pursued, and also that both were being fearfully knocked about by the enemy's fire.

Now all eyes are anxiously turned towards the batteries of the harbour, for the squadron apparently intend to pursue their prey within their range.

We have said that every eminence, every housetop, is crowded with eager and anxious spectators. Flags are displayed, and handkerchiefs waved from many different places in encouragement of the rebels, while the hoarse roar of the dense crowd on the quays bears witness to the intensity of the excitement.

Immediately after the commencement of the fight, the party who were assembled on the housetop of Coralie St. Casse left—officers, civilians, and the young lady herself, all going to the flagstaff battery, which was at once the

most heavily mounted of the harbour defences, and commanded the channel most completely.

Coralie was in a great state of excitement; her black
eyes flashed and glittered, while a crimson flush mounted
to her cheek as the loud boom of the cannon told how
fierce was the conflict.

The whole Yankee fleet was now blazing away at the
two vessels, and the effect of this fire they could perceive
even from the battery, to be fearful.

"Are they in range, sir?" asked Coralie of the artillery officer in command of the battery.

He measured the distance with his eye and paused
before he replied. Coralie waited in breathless suspense.

"Scarcely," said the officer; "in three minutes more,
however, if they keep on their course, they will be so."

The battery had that morning received an accession of
the very heaviest guns in use. These had just been
mounted, and the gunners proceeded to load and train
them.

All was ready, and after carefully sighting each piece,
the officer mounted on the parapet and gazed forth on
the enemy.

An artilleryman stood with the string in his hand,
which, at the appointed word, would discharge the tremendous ordnance.

The big guns protruded from the embrasures and
seemed to glare threateningly on the Yankees; but as
yet their iron throats were silent. Minute by minute
rolled by, and still the cannonade from the Yankees continued. They could see from the battery the water torn
up in all directions by round shot, while occasionally a
cloud of splinters and smoke would show where one of
the apparently doomed vessels was hit.

These hits were now very frequent, and the Wabash
soon began to look a perfect wreck. Large rents were
torn in her bulwarks, and in one place two port-holes
were knocked into one.

General Beauregard and Colonel Ruggles stood aloof
from the others, and occasionally muttered together as
they watched the unequal combat.

" They'll sink them both," said the former to the old colonel.

" I reckon they will," was the calm reply.

Next moment a large Dahlgren shell struck the Wabash between wind and water. This was instantly followed by smoke and fire; it had exploded on her decks.

Even at this distance the confusion it created could be observed.

The crew could be seen hurrying backwards and forwards, as they endeavoured to put out the fire. Scarcely, however, was this accomplished, than several other shot struck the unfortunate frigate, and it was soon apparent, from the slow pace at which she crawled along, that she was almost completely water-logged. Next there was a dense volume of steam issuing from her engine-room hatch.

" The water has risen in her hold, and put the fires out," said a naval officer present.

When the steam cleared away the Wabash was almost motionless on the waves, her fires were out, and her engines stopped.

" She is sinking," said General Beauregard, mournfully, to his friend.

" Not a doubt," was the quiet reply.

" The Yankees are within range, general," said the artillery officer in command, addressing General Beauregard, whose rank was highest; " shall I open fire ?"

The general consulted for a moment with the colonel, and then replied quietly,—

" No, sir, not yet."

" Not yet!" exclaimed the Black Angel, passionately. " They are within range, and yet we do not offer our friends aid. Surely, general, you are not about to let them perish at the hands of the Yankees without firing a shot ? Let our guns open fire ; then the enemy will be obliged to relinquish the pursuit."

General Beauregard glanced at the Colonel, and the artillery officer anxiously watched his eye for the word to fire.

But the word came not.

"Not yet, young lady," was the reply.

Now a boat is seen putting off from the Wabash, having the end of a hawser.

"They are going to take her in tow of the sloop," said the same naval officer.

This was the fact, and intense was the excitement as the little boat proceeded on its mission. The sea all around was in a perfect foam from the hail of shot poured forth by the pursuing vessels.

"She will never reach the sloop," said some one, sadly.

The next moment this gloomy prognostication was confirmed, for a round shot struck her amidships, and all that could be seen of her or crew was a few floating bits of wood and struggling forms.

The Yankees still kept up their fire as the poor fellows struggled with the waves. General Beauregard's eyes glittered with anger, as did those of most others, who saw and understood.

"The dastards, the ruffians! to fire on drowning men," he said.

"General! Colonel!" said the Black Angel, hastening up to them, with flashing eyes; "do you really mean to let our friends perish before our eyes without firing a shot?"

Some one standing by exclaimed suddenly,—

"Another boat, by Jove! and Darcy Leigh himself in it."

It was true enough, for the second boat was launched; and in the stern-sheets could be seen the form of the young commander. At this sight Coralie could no longer restrain herself. Tears of anger and grief started to her beautiful eyes.

"In the name of Heaven, General Beauregard, do you intend them all to be murdered? See poor Darcy Leigh, he is looking here as if demanding aid. See, too, yonder goes a signal of distress from the ship. Brave, noble fellow! the danger must indeed be imminent when he asks for aid."

" Do you know this Lieutenant Leigh ?" asked Colonel Ruggles.

" Do I know him ?   Yes, I know him well—and know him to be as gallant an officer and as honourable a gentleman as ever buckled on a sword."

Then tears of vexation and grief coursed down the cheeks of the beautiful Coralie.   This melted the rough heart of the old colonel.

" Look here, young lady," he said, in a somewhat softer tone than was usual with him, " they tell me you are heart and soul for our common country, the Confederate States, for which and our new flag we are about to do battle."

" Those who know me know it is so," she said proudly.

" As such, then, you must see the justice of any measures which conduce to our success."

" Undoubtedly."

" Do you think that the capture or destruction of the whole fleet off Charleston would be a great success to us, and a great blow to the enemy ?"

" Certainly ; but why ask such a question ?   A fleet is not to be destroyed by refusing to fire at it," replied Coralie, impatiently.

" A fleet, in this case, is to be destroyed or captured by withholding our fire until the proper moment."

" And that is when——"

" When they shall have pursued those two vessels so far that they cannot get back.   They do not know, I imagine, what heavy guns we have mounted, or they would not venture.   Were we to open fire, it would undeceive them, and they would steam back in time.   If we allow them to go on till past yon shoal, marked by the red buoy"—and the colonel pointed with his finger— " they cannot get back in safety, for the channel is narrow, and two vessels can hardly thread it at one time. They will be fully within our range, and it will take at least half an hour for them to get out again.   In the meantime we shall have knocked every ship to pieces, or compelled them to strike their colours.   Now you see why we reserve our fire.

"Alas! and the price must be the sacrifice of Darcy Leigh and his brave crew?"

"Perhaps."

"No—their fate is certain; already one vessel is sinking, and the other fearfully injured."

"Let us hope. See—the boat has safely taken the hawser on board and returned!"

In tow of the Spitfire, the Wabash once again made some little progress through the water; but it was very slow, and her frequent heels and lurches gave evidence of her desperate state. They saw the boats launched, and the whole crew safely conveyed on board the Spitfire, while Darcy Leigh stood alone and undaunted on the deck of the sinking ship. They could see his face turned towards the battery as if looking for aid, and wondering why he did not receive it. Then the Wabash gave a terrible lurch, and Darcy entered the boat, and with shot and shell flying around, was rowed to the Spitfire.

And now the whole fire of the pursuing squadron is concentrated on this latter. The round shot and shell crash through her timbers, howl through the air, and dash into the sea around, throwing columns of water high aloft.

A signal of distress is run up.

"Lost—lost!" cried the Black Angel, despairingly; "General, give the order to fire, and save them from this terrible cannonade."

Beauregard looked at the colonel, on whose opinion he appeared to set great store. The colonel looked doubtful.

"Colonel," said Coralie, imploringly, "save them!"

"And lose the fleet," was the gloomy reply; "no!"

"General Beauregard!" she cried, clasping her hands, "in Darcy Leigh and his brave crew the Confederate States will lose what is more valuable than any fleet. Ships can be built, but such brave, daring spirits as that of yon boy hero are few and far between."

Both Beauregard and the old colonel looked doubtful.

"Are the guns trained on the Yankees?" asked the former.

"Yes, sir," replied the artillery officer.

Beauregard himself approached one of the great guns, and looking along the sight, slightly depressed the muzzle. Then he returned to his post by the side of the colonel.

"The guns command the fleet easily," he said, "what do you say?"

Coralie St. Casse, the Black Angel, still stood before them with clasped hands, in all the radiance of her young beauty.

Hard indeed must have been the heart which could have resisted such an appeal.

"Let us leave it to this young lady," said Ruggles, with a smile.

Beauregard nodded good-humouredly, and the next moment said to the artillery officer,—

"Open fire and blaze away, sir! Shot and shell—let them have it!"

The gunners crowded around their cannon, and all was bustle and hurry at the welcome order.

Coralie, with a cry of joy, darted away, and running up to the gun which Beauregard had trained, snatched the string from the gunner's hand, and, with a jerk, pulled the trigger, and fired the piece.

The roar of the cannon was succeeded by the rush of the shot through the air as it sped on its errand of death.

All jumped on the ramparts to watch the effect.

Onwards sped the huge mass of iron till it crashed full into the flag-ship.

A loud shout of joy broke forth from all. The shell exploded, setting the Yankee on fire, and the next moment the iron throats of twenty great cannon belched forth their fire, smoke, and shot. hurling death and destruction to the pursuing fleet.

CHAPTER XLVII.

THE ships of the pursuing squadron now found themselves in "considerable difficulties," as the Yankees say. The guns of all the batteries commanding the approaches to the harbour opened on them, and they, in turn, were exposed to as terrible a fire as that which the Spitfire and Wabash experienced.

The commodore ran up the signal to retreat, and instantly all the engines were reversed, and the vessels made the best haste to veer round, and retrace their path. Not a ship of the squadron escaped the effects of the fire opened on them from the batteries—a fire which was the more terrible from the fact of its being from fixed batteries —while theirs in return was not nearly so effective, from the greater difficulty of aim.

Not a shot was now directed towards the Spitfire or Wabash, but all their efforts turned to replying to the batteries and making good their escape.

This at last they effected and got safely out of range, but with so great a slaughter and damage as to give them little cause to congratulate themselves upon their abortive pursuit.

Great was the chagrin of General Beauregard and Colonel Ruggles at the escape of the fleet, for they felt sure, had the fire been delayed, they would have passed so far up the channel as to render return impossible.

It was in vain that Coralie St. Casse was begged to retire from the battery, which is now a mark for the enemy's shot and shell; she refused, and expressed her determination to remain, encouraging the gunners and fearlessly exposing herself.

After half-an-hour's fierce cannonading the fire ceased on both sides, for the fleet, terribly crippled and knocked about, was now out of range. The order was given to cease firing, and the thunder of the guns is hushed.

"There, young lady," said Colonel Ruggles, gazing

spitefully after the fleet, "see what we have done by listening to you. Those cursed ships have escaped."

"True, colonel; in losing them we have saved what is of more value, the lives of loyal and brave men."

"We shall never have such another chance; they will never venture within range of our batteries again."

"They're fools if they do," said Beauregard, good humouredly, "after the lesson we have given them."

"Got off scot free," muttered Ruggles.

"No, not scot free, certainly," said the artillery officer; "my children here," pointing to the great black guns, "have knocked a few holes in them."

"And, besides, we have saved Darcy Leigh, his brave brother officers, and crew," said Coralie.

"Young lady, you seem to take deep interest in this Lieutenant Leigh," said Ruggles, glancing at her from beneath his grey eyebrows; "I am sure the young man ought to thank you, and so ought the Yankees. I don't know which should be the more grateful, for, by thunder, it was you who saved both!"

Coralie coloured up under the colonel's searching glance, and replied,—

"Well, colonel, I am content. Come, gentlemen, who will accompany me home? I shall be happy of the company of all to lunch; I hope also to be joined by those gallant officers who have carried to a successful conclusion this desperate enterprise, and will beg you, general, to send one of your orderlies to await their landing on the quay, and invite them to join us."

General Beauregard bowed and at once gave the necessary order, while Colonel Ruggles said, slily,—

"Not forgetting Lieutenant Darcy Leigh."

He glanced towards Coralie, but if he hoped to detect any sign of confusion he was disappointed. She met his look unflinchingly, and replied, proudly,—

"No, Colonel Ruggles, not forgetting Darcy Leigh, for he is more welcome to me than any."

The old colonel turned away somewhat suddenly.

"A noble girl, a splendid girl, beautiful as Venus, haughty as Juno."

U

Whatever else were his thoughts he did not suffer his face further to express them, but rousing himself up he took the arm of General Beauregard and strolled off from the battery in the direction of Coralie's house. His talk was of military matters, of the approaching campaigns, and sieges; but who can say that the thought of the bright beauty who but now stood before him did not obtrude and somewhat derange his mental plans of campaign?

As they left the bastions in a group, almost with one impulse they turned at an angle which would have hid the bay from their view, and looked back. The Spitfire, was still steaming slowly ahead, having cast off the Wabash, now rapidly settling down in the water. At last, with a heavy lurch, she lay on her beam ends, and with her torn and blood-stained deck turned towards them. Thus she remained for a brief space, slowly settling down, till suddenly she pitched heavily forward and plunged beneath the waves head first.

The waters eddied and foamed about the place where she had been, but the jury-mast which had been rigged after the storm was still visible above the surface. She had gone down in shallow water, and still from the mast might be seen floating defiantly in the breeze the rebel flag—the Stars and Bars.

The Yankees had sunk the ship, but they had not sunk the flag. All gazed in silence at the scene for a minute or so. Then Coralie St. Casse, who had lingered behind, said gravely and seriously,—

"So shall it be throughout this approaching war; our armies may be destroyed, they cannot be defeated; they may shoot us down, but they cannot make us strike our flag. What say you, gentlemen?"

At the same moment the rattling of the Spitfire's chain is heard over the windlass as she is brought to anchor in Charleston harbour.

In reply to the words of the Black Angel, one of the younger officers present, taking off his cap, waves it above his head and cries, "Three cheers for the Stars and Bars."

The cheer is led by the group around Coralie, taken up by the soldiers and artillerymen, then again by the crowd in the streets, on the quays, till the loud shout of many thousand voices swells forth to welcome Darcy Leigh and his gallant crew.

CHAPTER XLVIII.

RECEPTION OF DARCY LEIGH IN CHARLESTON.

As soon as the Spitfire was brought to anchor, Darcy ordered all the boats to be lowered, and the prisoners to be brought on deck. These, to the number of some thirty, were ordered into the launch, while Darcy himself, accompanied by Wharncliffe and six other officers, stepped into the gig and pulled off from the sloop, leaving the other officers and crew in charge. His object was to report himself to the officers in command of the town, and also to procure surgical aid for his numerous wounded.

They arrived at the quay amid the deafening cheers of the crowd assembled to receive them. First, Darcy himself and officers leaped on shore, and awaited the arrival of the launch with the prisoners under guard.

Captain Seth Peabody, of the Wabash, was the first of those who landed. Poor man! he looked gloomy and crestfallen enough. His attempt to attract the attention of the squadron, and so save his ship, had only ended in her being sunk—and that, too, under the rebel flag.

Behind the prisoners came Darby Kelly, who had begged for permission to accompany Darcy. He carried in his hands all the swords which the Yankee officers had surrendered, and wore on his head one of their cocked hats, which he had appropriated as a trophy of war.

His appearance was both grotesque and terrible.

Imagine, good reader, an enormous figure, naked to the waist, black with coal-dust and smoke, and in places splashed with blood, which during the terrible ordeal the Spitfire had gone through, had been plentifully sprinkled about.

The cocked hat on his head, and the bundle of swords which he carried on his shoulder, completed his costume, with the addition of a pair of canvas trousers.

Loud and deafening were the cheers, not unmingled with laughter, which greeted the extraordinary figure of Darby Kelly.

" Bravo, cocked hat !" shouted some one in the crowd ; " you're the boy for blood and thunder !"

" By jabers, you're right there, honey. It's meself can do a bit of foighting."

Then to himself he muttered, complacently,—

" By the powers ! now I believe they take me for the captain. What a thing it is to have a commanding extarior !"

If such, however, was the opinion of any among the mob, they were soon undeceived, for a mounted orderly rode up—

" Make way, there ! make way !" And the crowd gave way on all sides before the clattering hoofs of the horse.

" Which is Lieutenant Darcy Leigh ?" said the horseman, gazing around him.

Darcy Leigh stepped forward.

" That is my name."

A murmur of surprise and admiration ran round the crowd, in which even the mounted messenger shared.

That slight, pale boy, Darcy Leigh, who had planned and carried out such a daring enterprise ! (for the whole history of the affair from beginning to end was, by this time, well known all over Charleston).

" My name is Darcy Leigh," again repeated our hero.

" General Beauregard desires me to say that he will be glad to see you at the house of Mademoiselle St. Casse."

A flush of pleasure illumined the face of Darcy.

" Coralie St. Casse—she then is in Charleston ?"

" Yes, sir ; she was on the flagstaff battery all the while the action lasted."

" Good—I will attend. I presume my officers are to accompany me ?"

" Undoubtedly."

" And the prisoners ?"

" I had no orders respecting them. I think you cannot do better than march them up to the barracks
under guard. You are wounded, I see ; if you will permit me, I will see to that, while you proceed at once to
the town and have your hurts dressed. You will find a
surgeon in the first street—afterwards, General Beauregard and the officers in command of the town await
you."

" Thanks, sir. And now one thing more—will you
see that surgeons are at once sent on to aid the sloop,
for many of my poor fellows are desperately wounded ?"

" I will see to it, sir."

Then the officer rode off, and in a few minutes a file of
soldiers appeared, who marched the prisoners up to the
barracks, while Darcy and his friends proceeded on their
way to the house of the Black Angel.

A gentleman among the crowd, who had his carriage
at hand, now stepped forward, and insisted on Darcy and
his comrades using it. He would take no denial, so they
accepted his offer, and all seated themselves, Darby Kelly
mounting the top by the coachman.

Then they commenced their progress through the town.
It was, indeed, a triumphal march; the bells of the
churches rang forth a joyous peal; flags were displayed
from every window, while cheers and shouts of welcome
pealed forth on all sides.

It was a proud moment for Darcy and his friends. As
they were drawn through the thronged streets, a thousand fair faces appeared at windows, on balconies, and
on housetops; handkerchiefs were waved, and many a
bright glance was thrown towards the carriage which
conveyed them. The crowd which accompanied them
was so dense, that to approach the carriage was impossible; but even now, one or other of the Spitfire's officers
was recognised and called by name from houses as they
passed.

Darcy Leigh's name was frequently heard above the
din of the crowd, for he was well known and liked in
Charleston; besides, the fame of the *regime* of the Spit-

fire had long preceded him, and he was known **as the**
leader and originator of the attempt.

" Darcy—Darcy Leigh !" shouted a voice from **a balcony.**

Darcy rose, **and,** looking in **the** direction whence it
came, perceived **a** young man, an intimate friend of himself and brother.

He waved **his** hand towards our hero, who, standing
up, returned **the** salute.

" Hurrah **for** Captain Darcy Leigh !" shouted a voice
in the crowd; " three cheers for Darcy Leigh !—that's
he standing in the carriage."

Then **a** cheer pealed forth, which made the very walls
of the houses tremble.

" **That Darcy Leigh !**" said a man **in** the crowd, in
surprise; " that the man who seized one ship, ran away
with her; then captured a frigate sent in pursuit, and
ran the gauntlet through the squadron ?   Why, man,
you **must** be dreaming !   That pale boy can't be the
captain—more likely one of the midshipmen."

But **at** that **instant** Darcy again arose in answer to
loud and repeated calls, and bowed to the crowd on all
sides in acknowledgment of the **honour** they did him. It
was **not** only the last speaker who **could** scarcely believe
that **the** slight **form** and pale face before them were
those of Darcy **Leigh,** the audacious **rebel,** who had accomplished this most daring **seizure, capture,** and ultimately escaped.

Those **who were not formerly acquainted** with him
pictured to themselves a dashing looking officer, with
commanding **appearance** and **stentorian** voice, and gazed
with a feeling akin to disappointment on the slender
figure and face of almost girlish beauty before them.

CHAPTER XLIX.

DARCY LEIGH AND THE BLACK ANGEL.

AND so, amidst the shouts of the crowd, the waving of
flags, and the fluttering of handkerchiefs, bells ringing,

and bands playing, Darcy Leigh and his officers were drawn to the house of Coralie St. Casse.

At the moment when the carriage drew up at the door, the hostess and her guests were in the dining saloon. A sumptuous lunch was spread on the long table, and all only awaited the arrival of Darcy and his brother officers to commence the repast.

When, therefore, a negro announced to his mistress that a carriage with sailor officers in it was at the door, Coralie, followed by several of her guests, hastened out to receive them.

General Beauregard and old Colonel Ruggles, as be-fitted their rank and dignity, remained behind.

Darcy Leigh had just alighted from the carriage and was then thanking the owner, when Coralie came forth from the house. His words of thanks were cut short, a hand is laid lightly on his shoulder, and a voice – a sweet tremulous voice, whose every accent he knows well, says, —

" Darcy."

He turned, and stood face to face with the Black Angel. His pale face was lit by a momentary flush, his eyes glittered, and a glad smile came over him as he replied, taking the lady's hand,—

" Coralie, is it indeed you ? "

Still holding her hand, he gazed long and earnestly in her face, until, unable to bear it any longer, Coralie dropped her beautiful eyes to the ground, and blushed. When she again raised them, Darcy was still regarding her with the same fond look of admiration.

" Well, sir," said the young girl, laughing through her blushes, "you are having a good look at me ; pray what is your opinion ? do you think I am altered since last you saw me ? "

" Altered ?   No ; except in this, that you are hand-somer than ever."

" A compliment! and from Darcy Leigh ; wonders will never cease," cried Coralie. " However, a truce to your soft speeches. Come in with your friends, and let me introduce you to mine."

So saying, Coralie turned, and leading Darcy by the hand, conducted him up the portico steps into the house.

"Gentlemen," she said, to most of her guests, who had accompanied her to the door, "allow me to present to you my very good friend, Darcy Leigh, late of the United States' Navy, but now and ever, let us hope, a soldier or sailor, as duty may require, of our common country, the Confederate States."

Some among them were acquainted with Darcy Leigh, but all, strangers or not, hastened to grasp the hand of the young hero, and bid him welcome to Charleston. These greetings and congratulations over, Coralie again took his hand.

"Come," she said, at the same time making a motion to the others to follow, "come with me; I have yet other friends to introduce you to, and you need refreshment."

Thus she led him across the hall into the saloon, where Beauregard, Ruggles, and one or two old officers had remained. Many of the assembled guests gazed enviously on Darcy Leigh, and thought how gladly would they accept his lot—bandaged head, wounds and all, to be thus led by the hand of Coralie.

She, however, not heeding the glances of admiration cast upon herself—of envy and surprise on her charge, passed right on into the saloon and up to General Beauregard.

"General Beauregard," she said, proudly, while a bright flush came to her cheek, "allow me to introduce to you my friend Darcy Leigh."

General Beauregard at once stepped forward and grasped his hand.

"Sir," said he, "I am proud to know so brave and skilful a man. Accept my congratulations in the name of the Government for the eminent services you have rendered. It shall be my task to see they are duly acknowledged and rewarded."

Darcy bowed in silence, and Colonel Ruggles advanced. He gazed curiously, almost rudely, on Darcy Leigh, as he stood before him.

His looks seemed to say,—"Can this effeminate-looking, pale boy be indeed he who has done this deed?—a deed with the renown of which the whole country, North and South, now rings."

Then the old warrior, removing his piercing glance from Darcy, fixed it on Coralie, who stood beside him. He seemed by his keen look to be desirous of reading the inward thoughts of both.

"And you, sir, are Darcy Leigh?" he said at last, bluntly.

"I am Darcy Leigh," replied our hero, smiling.

"Then, Darcy Leigh, here is my hand; it is a rough one, but it is the hand of an honest old soldier, who will strike, please God, many a hard blow for the Stars and Bars."

Darcy gave his hand, whilst a flush of pleasure came over his face. The simple, blunt words of the old colonel gave him greater pleasure than a star from an emperor's hand would have done.

He had never known Colonel Ruggles personally, but had heard much of the fine old soldier.

Colonel Ruggles retained the young man's hand in his for a short space. He turned it over curiously as if it were a toy or a plaything.

"Young man," he said, "your hand is as soft and white as a school-girl's."

"Strange that such a delicate affair as this can give such hard knocks, eh, colonel?"

"No matter, it ain't the hand, my lad, it's the heart; and where that's in the right place a silken glove may do as desperate deeds as a mailed hand. You're a brave lad, and if I'm not mistaken, will be heard of yet."

"I mean to be, colonel."

"You have been heard of, Darcy," said Coralie, proudly; "already your name rings forth North and South."

"Aye, aye, it has rung forth so loud that more than one fair lady has heard it, and thought not unkindly of its owner, I'll be bound."

Colonel Ruggles glanced keenly at Coralie, who dropped her eyes in confusion.

But only for a moment.

"I for one have heard it," she said, proudly, "and am only too glad that Darcy Leigh is my friend. Now, Darcy, see and get your wounded head attended to, then let us to lunch. Your companions, too, will doubtless be glad to wash and make themselves presentable, for at present you are all terribly begrimed with dirt and smoke."

A surgeon who was among the company now stepped forward, and volunteered to attend to Darcy and those of his friends who were hurt; and they were all shown to the upper part of the house, where every convenience awaited them. Some of the gentlemen present sent for changes of clothes and linen, Darcy and his friends having come quite unprovided for in that respect.

In half-an-hour they all re-appeared, looking wonderfully improved by the processes they had undergone, and the repast commenced. Coralie took the head of the table, while General Beauregard, at her request, seated himself opposite. She, by a look, brought Colonel Ruggles to the seat on her left hand.

The old soldier took his seat by the left of his beautiful hostess with awkward pride, and noticed that there was a vacant place on her right hand.

"Who the d——l is she going to put there?" thought the old lion.

He thought he knew, and yet almost hoped he might be wrong.

Coralie gazed down the table till her eye rested on Darcy, who had taken his seat unobtrusively some distance down.

She caught his eye, and with a sweet smile, but imperious look, she signified to him her command to take the post of honour.

Darcy rose and seated himself by her side.

Colonel Ruggles, whose keen observation nothing escaped, saw this, and for an instant, he felt, he knew not why, angry and vexed. But he drove away the feeling.

"Pshaw!" he said; "what an old fool I am; I ought

to be ashamed of myself. He deserves all the bright glances and loving looks he gets, for his was a perilous venture, and its success glorious; besides, is he not young and handsome?"

"And I—" he glanced down at his great rough hands and somewhat ungainly limbs, and continued,—

"And I, a rough old log—a regular old alligator—and a d——d old fool to boot."

It was a merry time, indeed, that lunch; wine in profusion flashed and bubbled, and soon the talkative and the high-spirited got more talkative—the taciturn and the quiet brightened up, and even rugged old Ruggles warmed up with the occasion. Indeed, so noisy and uproarious did the party become, that their lovely young hostess, not wishing on such an occasion to be a damper to their mirth, thought it best to withdraw. Accordingly she watched her opportunity, and bending low, whispered to her right hand neighbour,—

"Darcy, I am about to leave the table; will you follow me in about half an hour? I will wait in the drawing-room. I do so long to hear the history of your adventures."

Darcy coloured with pleasure, and bowed assent.

Then Coralie rose, and with a gesture requested silence.

As soon as the company saw their hostess on her feet, every voice was hushed, and each also respectfully rose.

"Gentlemen," said Coralie, "pray do not let me disturb you; I hope you will none of you think of leaving—to do so would be a poor compliment to those gentlemen whom we are assembled to welcome. I will see that you are supplied with abundance of wine. If you require anything else you have but to order, and my servants will obey. Pray keep your seats."

Then, with a parting bow and a bright smile, Coralie St. Casse swept from the room, a murmur of admiration following her.

No sooner was she gone than a perfect Babel of noise arose. Every one spoke at the same time, and on the same subject.

"By Jove! Leigh, you are a lucky fellow," said a young man down the table; "I really believe that our beautiful hostess is struck by your good looks and daring deeds."

This and a dozen other remarks to the same purport followed.

Darcy felt angry and annoyed. He rose and said, when silence was somewhat restored,—

"Gentlemen, I must request and insist on one thing, that during her absence the name of our hostess be not thus lightly mentioned."

"Well spoken, young man," said Colonel Ruggles; "and, gentlemen, I agree with what Mr. Darcy Leigh says, and must add the weight of my voice to his."

This well-deserved rebuke had the desired result of silencing the somewhat inconsiderate tongues of the young men.

The subject was dropped, and the conversation turned on the seizure and escape of the Spitfire.

Darcy was requested to give the whole history of the affair, from the mutiny in New York harbour to the running into Charleston.

When he came to that part of his narrative where he described how he had deceived the Wabash on first falling in with her, and continued also to get rid of the Yankee prisoners, Colonel Ruggles exclaimed,—

"By Jupiter! young man, that was a stroke of genius —that was worthy of a Napoleon. The rest was sheer hard fighting and pluck; but the way you fooled the Yankees, that was 'a caution to snakes.'"

The next point which elicited the admiration of the colonel, was the *ruse* by which the Spitfire was towed through the fleet by the Wabash, as if she had been captured by the latter.

Darcy explained, how, but for the sudden escape of Captain Seth Peabody from the cabin where he was confined, the two vessels would have steamed right under the guns of the batteries before the Yankees could have discovered their true character. Unfortunately, however, Captain Peabody succeeded in jumping on the bulwarks and giving the alarm. This caused a terrible effusion of blood on both sides, and the Yankee captain himself was so desperately wounded, that it was not thought he would survive.

"Well," said Ruggles, "he's a Yankee, but he's a brave fellow, and ought not to be blamed for trying to save his ship."

"Assuredly not," said Darcy, "and none regretted the fact of his being hurt more than myself; but in the struggle to secure him, he was struck in the chest by a cutlass, which passed right out at his back. He has had, however, every possible attention, and I gave especial directions that when the surgeons came on board to attend the wounded, he should be at once seen to."

Darcy's narrative over, the conversation again turned on general subjects, and General Beauregard approached the end of the table at which he was.

"Well, colonel," said the general, "the question now is what are we to do for this young man and his brave companions? They are naval officers, and unfortunately, with the exception of the Wabash sunk, and the Spitfire, with difficulty kept from sinking, we have no navy. It would be a poor compliment to make our friend here captain of a sinking hulk, or commodore of a navy which does not exist. It is a pity you have no knowledge of military matters, sir."

"Pardon me for my presumption, general," said Darcy, "but I think I may claim a fair knowledge of drill and military manœuvres. The drill I learned when in command of marines ashore, to which, at my own request, I was temporarily consigned. And as to military manœuvres, I have made them my study. I am well up in fortification and field evolutions in all but one respect, and that is practice."

"I am glad to hear you say so, young man. What do you say, colonel? I think we can manage to find something for Mr. Leigh."

"What do I say!" replied the colonel, "why I say that this lad's word may be taken—I would take it. If he said he was able to command a division in the field, I would believe him."

Darcy felt a glow of pleasure at these words.

" I am far from being capable of commanding a division, or even a regiment," he replied, " but I think a company."

" Aye, a company ; there's the rub ! It is easy enough to make you a captain, but to give you a company is quite a different affair. We have very few troops in the field, and certainly we have not a regiment near Charleston which is not fully officered. However, we will consider about it, and, in the meantime, I will at once confer on you the rank of captain, and place you on my staff."

Then General Beauregard called his *aide-de-camp*, who was present, and ordered him to have prepared the necessary papers which should give Darcy Leigh the rank of captain in the Confederate army.

He announced the fact to the officers present,—

" Gentlemen, I have to inform you that I have conferred the rank of captain on Mr. Darcy Leigh, and he will henceforth rank as such."

The General and Colonel then left, and Darcy duly received the congratulations of all, on his receiving his first commission in the service of the Confederate Government.

It was some time ere he could tear himself away from the friends who surrounded him, but on the first opportunity he slipped out of the room, in order to join Coralie St. Casse, according to promise.

When Darcy Leigh reached the drawing-room, he found that General Beauregard and his friend had preceded him.

" What, young gentleman ! " said the former, " tired already of the mirth and jollity of those hare-brained young men down stairs ?"

" No, general ; but to tell the truth, my head is rather painful, and I thought a cup of tea would be more likely to cool it than the wine, so plentifully provided below, and which I could not avoid drinking, for not a moment passed but one or another insisted on my pledging them."

" See what it is to be a hero," said Beauregard.

" Poor fellow," said Coralie, " come to the sofa, and I will make you a cup of tea. I do hope the wound in your head is not serious."

" See what it is to be young and good-looking," said Colonel Ruggles. " Now, I'll be sworn if my ugly old head was knocked into a cocked hat, I shouldn't find fair lips to say poor fellow, nor fair hands to make me a cup of tea."

" Then you would be sworn to what is false, Colonel," said Coralie, warmly. " I do not know whether you speak seriously or in jest; if the former, you are greatly mistaken, as you can prove, should you ever be wounded, or in want of a woman's aid. If you spoke in jest, you were wrong to jest on such a subject; it is disagreeable to me."

Poor Colonel Ruggles subsided instantly at this rebuke, and looked terribly chapfallen.

Beauregard laughed at his friend's discomfiture.

" Well, well," said the latter, " I didn't mean any offence, young lady; it's only my cursed bearish way. I can't help it. I'm a rough old log, and not fit for ladies' company. I'll go back to my regiment, and when the hour of battle comes, Colonel Ruggles, rough and coarse as he may be, shall not be found wanting."

There was a tear in the old man's eye as he spoke.

He had not meant any offence, but he had acquired a habit of speaking cynically and bitterly at all times; and though possessed of a rare generous heart, frequently gave offence where he least intended so to do.

Coralie was instantly sorry for her words, provoked though they had been.

She darted to the colonel's side, and seizing his rugged hand, said imploringly,—

" A thousand pardons, colonel. I am sorry I offended you. I am but a girl, and you must pardon me this time."

He merely bowed, and turning away, muttered,—

" Only a girl, only a girl ; it's all very well to say only a girl, but may I be hanged, only a girl as she is, if she don't make an old fool of me."

General Beauregard now mentioned the fact of Darcy being a captain.

" Unfortunately, Miss St. Casse," he said, " there is one difficulty we are in, with regard to your young friend. We can't find him a regiment at present, so that he is a captain without a company."

" General," said Coralie, eagerly, " will you leave that to me ?"

" Leave what to you—Captain Leigh ? Of course I 'll leave him to you if you wish it," he replied, smiling.

" No, no, don't tease me ; you are as bad as Colonel Ruggles. I mean leave the difficulty to me."

" Assuredly, if you wish it. I hardly see how you can help us in this case."

" Never mind, leave it to me. When may I see you again—to-morrow ?"

" No, not to-morrow, but the day after if you wish."

" Very good ; by that time I shall be able to make a suggestion, which will, I think, solve the difficulty."

" Let it be as you say, young lady. Now, Colonel, I think it is time we left. Miss St. Casse and Captain Leigh are old friends, and doubtless have much to say. Doubtless, Othello-like, he has many a tale of daring and adventure for her ear."

" I hope, Othello-like, he will not smother me with a pillow," said Coralie, smiling.

" And may no Iago, with accursed plots, step in," said Colonel Ruggles, who was now himself again.

" Come, colonel, you are making the lady blush. Good day, Miss St. Casse. Good day, Captain Leigh."

Then, of course, Darcy Leigh was obliged to repeat the history of his adventures since he left New York ; nor was he allowed to miss any particular, so close did the lady question him, and so deep an interest did she manifest.

Having disposed of the past, they commenced to talk of the future, which looked black and gloomy enough.

Coralie, however, was full of enthusiasm and courage, and declared that she did not for one moment doubt the issue of the coming struggle, unequal as it appeared.

" And what of your brother Gerald, your father, and your sister Laura ? " she asked.

" I have not heard from Gerald for a long time. My father and sister are, I believe, at Richmond, or the Virginia plantation. When last I heard of Gerald he was in Baltimore with his regiment, but I do not doubt for a moment, that if he has not already resigned, he is only waiting for a fitting opportunity to do so and join us."

" You are quite certain, then, that he will not remain in the Yankee service ? "

" Quite; but tell me, fair Coralie, if you please, how you design to solve this difficulty of which the general spoke. At present there are more colonels than regiments, captains than companies. Do you know of any fresh regiments about to arrive, or do you expect that some officer will resign in my favour ? "

" Neither, sir ; but do not be curious—I will tell you the day after to-morrow."

" Such being the case, I suppose I must wait patiently till then. And now I will take my leave, for I am quite tired out, and shall be glad of some rest."

" Will you not take up your quarters here ? "

" Why, what on earth are you thinking of, Coralie ?— what would people say ? No, believe me, I have too much regard for your fair fame to give a handle for the malicious."

" *Honi soit qui mal y pense,*" said Coralie; "there can be no harm or discredit to my sheltering a brave officer and old friend."

" No matter: I thank you deeply for your kindness · but in this case I think it best, even at the risk of being thought churlish, to decline. And now, for the present, adieu. I shall go to the nearest hotel."

But Coralie would not permit him to leave thus ; she insisted on accompanying him to the hotel in question.

Many were the glances of envy and admiration cast on the pair, as they walked together from the house of the

x

heiress to the hotel. The bandaged head, somewhat unsteady gait, and deadly paleness of Darcy (for fatigue, pain, and loss of blood had done their work), would alone have attracted attention; but the presence of the Black Angel, on whose arm he leaned, made them the observed of all observers.

She bade him adieu at the hotel door, exacting from him a promise to visit her again on the day but one after. As for Darcy, he was only too glad to retire to rest, although it was yet early in the evening. A long and refreshing sleep went far to renovate exhausted nature, and when he awoke on the following day he felt greatly refreshed and invigorated.

CHAPTER L.

HOW CORALIE OVERCAME THE DIFFICULTY.

THE reader already knows that the Wabash went down in the very hour of victory, although in shoal water. Considering her terribly crippled state, it was hardly thought worth while to raise her, which, however, was done more for the sake of the guns and stores, than for the ship herself.

The Spitfire was also terribly knocked about, and leaked so badly that a gang of men had to be sent from the shore to keep her from sinking.

After some hours' unceasing pumping, she was freed from water, and hauled into dock to undergo repairs.

Darcy Leigh was consulted as to what should be done with her, and he at once gave it as his opinion that she should be cut down and cased with iron, as completely as circumstances would permit. He argued justly that to attempt to put to sea with a small wooden sloop, where the ocean swarmed with the enemy's cruisers, would be madness; while, by casing her with iron, she might be made available for many purposes. For instance, where no other iron vessel was present, she might defy and destroy a whole fleet of wooden ships with impunity. It was true that this iron casing must of necessity be very imperfect, but it would be incomparably more shot-proof than wood; and in time, as the resources and skill of the Confederates were developed, he doubted not that a regular iron-clad navy might be formed.

The authorities not only took the advice of Darcy Leigh as to casing the Spitfire with iron, but also confided to him the direction of the processes and the mode of armament.

Darcy at once entered heart and soul into the affair. He resolved, as soon as the Spitfire was transformed into an iron-clad gunboat, to ask for the command of her. He had little fear of being refused this, and imagined he saw before him a great career.

Visions of numberless Yankee merchantmen, captured and burned, floated before him; and he pictured to himself the Spitfire under another name scouring the seas, and proving a perfect scourge to the Yankee commerce.

The necessary alterations, however, would take at the very shortest computation four months, and even then she would not be ready to put to sea.

Darcy, accordingly, resolved in the interval to devote his whole time to military matters, and to accept the first command offered him in the field. The whole of this, his first day, was passed in superintending the docking of the Spitfire, and giving the necessary orders for the work of cutting down to be at once commenced.

All her stores, crew, wounded men, and prisoners had been landed, so that in the evening the sloop was hauled into dry dock; and urged on by Darcy Leigh, vigorous preparations were made for commencing the work on the following morning.

Darcy was so busy, that he absolutely had forgotten he had promised to visit the Black Angel, and it was not till near evening that he left the ship-yard and made his way in the direction of her house. He found a considerable company there, as usual, among whom was General Beauregard.

x 2

Coralie warmly greeted him, and drawing him on one side, said,—

"Now, sir, I will tell you what I promised you the day before yesterday."

Darcy's head had been all day so full of the Spitfire, and the great deeds he meant to accomplish with her, that he had forgotten all about the promise.

"What was that?" he asked, absently.

"You ask me what?" said Coralie, reproachfully gazing full in his face with her large beautiful dark eyes. "Is it possible that you have forgotten? Do you, then, treat me as a child—a foolish girl, whose words are as light as her heart? Darcy Leigh, you wrong me!"

"A thousand pardons, lady," he said; "I really was so buried in thought, that I did not at first hear what you said. Of course I had not forgotten your promise. You said you would this day solve the difficulty of my being a captain without a company."

"And I will keep my word. I want your assistance, however. Do you promise it me beforehand?"

"Willingly."

"Very well, then—the rest is easy."

She motioned to General Beauregard, who quickly joined her.

"General," she said, "when you spoke the other day of the difficulty you were placed in of finding a command for our new captain here, I said I could solve it. I am now prepared to do so."

General Beauregard smiled, and bowed for her to proceed.

"A regiment is the thing wanted, I believe. There are, I understand, officers enough for several; it is men you want."

"Exactly—soldiers."

"Well, general, you know I am wealthy. I do not see how I can better employ that wealth than in the service of the Confederate States. I will, at my own expense, raise, equip, and arm a regiment of at least eight hundred men. Thus, you see, I shall be able to provide companies for ten captains, besides a colonel, major, lieutenants, and subalterns. Now is not the difficulty surmounted?" asked the Black Angel, triumphantly.

Both General Beauregard and Darcy Leigh were taken by surprise at this munificent offer.

"Lady," said the former, "the noble offer you have just now made is worthy of you. I should be no true soldier of my country were I to refuse it. Surely where our very women show such devotion, our cause must succeed."

Darcy Leigh was profuse in his expressions of gratitude; but Coralie stopped him, saying,—

"A truce to your compliments and fine speeches. Let us consult how we may best carry out my plans."

"In the first place," said Darcy, "we must open an office and procure the men."

"Will you undertake that?" she asked.

"Willingly."

"Next," said the general, "I suppose your men must be armed."

"I will do that at my own expense," she said, hastily.

"Nevertheless you must procure the arms from government, for all private stores have long been bought up. However, I will see to that for you, also that you have the necessary authority from government."

"A thousand thanks. All then is easy, and within a week or so, I hope to have a regiment of my own in the field. May they do good service."

"They must indeed be cravens if they will not fight for such a mistress. What say you, Captain Leigh?"

"For myself I answer that I will lay down my life but too willingly, if only to show my devotion to the fair Coralie, of whom our country may justly be proud."

"Thanks, Darcy Leigh," she replied, "a compliment from your lips is all the more welcome from its scarcity. And now haste and see what is to be done."

General Beauregard took his leave, and after a few minutes' private consultation with Coralie, Darcy followed. He looked strangely flushed and excited as

he strode down the street. He must indeed have been
more than human had he been insensible to the glorious
beauty and flattering preference bestowed on him by
Coralie St. Casse.

He proceeded to search out his friends, Lieutenant
Wharncliffe and the officers of marines who had served
with him on board the Spitfire. Then they went into
the principal street of the town and hired an office in a
good situation. Their next errand was to a printing-
office, and in the course of an hour a printed bill was
affixed above the office door. It ran thus,—

"VOLUNTEERS FOR A NEW REGIMENT.

" NONE BUT THE BRAVE DESERVE THE FAIR.

" MADEMOISELLE CORALIE ANDREE ST. CASSE having
patriotically and liberally offered to raise and equip a
regiment at her own expense, the general commanding at
Charleston has been pleased to accept the offer.

"Authorized recruiting agent, CAPTAIN DARCY LEIGH.
Men of the Confederate States who wish to join are invited
to present themselves for approval at once.

"Drill and organization will at once commence, and the
regiment will take the field as soon as equipped."

It was not long before a crowd collected round the
office, and before it was closed for the night, the parch-
ment muster roll of the new regiment bore the signatures
of a hundred men.

"Not so bad, old fellow," said Darcy to Wharncliffe,
as they left the office together; "a hundred in half
a day. We shall soon have our complement; then
hurrah for the Stars and Bars!"

They were strolling leisurely towards their hotel,
when they heard a voice behind them.

"Mister Darcy"—

Turning, they perceived the big Irishman, Darby
Kelly, with the nigger, Jupiter.

"Well, Darby, what is it? do you want to be made
colonel of the new regiment?"

"Ah, now, yer honour, it was a bit of a mistake, I
was after making. Sure it wasn't kernel I meant, at

all—at all—but corporal. I knew it begun with a K— and it's to ask yer honour to make me a corporal that I spake now. Sure Jupiter and me, as soon as we heard the talk, comes down to the office to list, but the office was shut; so sez I to the nigger, here, I'll just make so bould as to ask his honour to make me a corporal."

Darcy smiled, but hesitated to reply.

" Do you know your drill?"

" Devil a bit; but I can shoot like blazes!"

" That's hardly sufficient qualification, I fear. How- ever, just cruise about the town to-night, and pick up as many of your countrymen as you can. Bring them with you to the office to-morrow, and then when you have learned your drill, we'll see what can be done for you."

With this Darby Kelly went off in high glee, in all the pride of being appointed recruiting officer. Soon both he and Jupiter had adorned their heads with large streamers of ribbon, and, procuring a fiddler, they pro- ceeded on their mission, and in the course of the night, succeeded in hunting up and rallying to their standard half the Irish in the town, and getting themselves gloriously drunk.

Darcy Leigh found the task of raising a regiment under the auspices of the Black Angel and himself an easy one. Coralie St. Casse was famous for her beauty, wealth, and devotion to the cause, and many young Southerners of good birth actually volunteered as privates in her regiment.

The name of Darcy Leigh, too, was a tower of strength. His daring exploit with the Spitfire was the theme of every tongue, and his popularity in Charleston was immense.

Darby Kelly had succeeded in rallying around his standard some thirty Irishmen, who came in a body one morning and registered their names. By the end of a week, over five hundred men were enrolled. Officers and non-commissioned officers were appointed, and they were being rapidly drilled and organised into a serviceable force.

The full number of men required might have been

long since made up; but a strict selection was made, only picked men being allowed to join.

Darcy and his brother officers justly considered that in the course of a few weeks, they would be able to offer to the Government a regiment of picked men, which, for discipline, drill, and in *physique*, would be unapproachable in the service.

The lowest standard of height was five feet ten inches, except in the light company, which was judiciously composed of small and active men.

As for the First or Grenadier Company, every man was above six feet in height, and with great muscular strength.

The task of officering the regiment was an easy one, as there were many officers of merit and experience only too glad to take service. Indeed this abundance of skilled officers on the Confederate side was one of the most remarkable features in the war.

As a rule, the cadets at West Point Academy, and most of the officers in the United States' army and navy, were of Southern birth, extraction, and sympathies, and as a consequence, on the breaking out of the rebellion, they deserted the Stars and Stripes and flocked around the Confederate standard.

CHAPTER LI.

THE BARRACK-ROOM, AND HOW DARBY FURNISHED IT.

DAY by day new regiments increased both in numbers and efficiency.

Darby Kelly had attained the object of his ambition, and having sufficiently learned his drill was made corporal. His application, however, to Darcy Leigh to be made a colonel had got wind, and he was now universally called Colonel Kelly. Sooth to say, Darby, so far from being annoyed at it, seemed as pleased with his title as though he were indeed a colonel.

" What a foine thing intellect is, captain," he said one

day to Darcy; "ye see thim spalpeens call me colonel; an' for why?"

" Why, indeed?"

" Shure it's intellect—it's the power of a suparior mind."

" Well, just exercise your superior mind in cleaning my scabbard and sword-belt for evening parade, and don't bother me, for I'm busy."

"Shure an' I will, captain, an' just ask one more question—don't I always clean yer honner's 'coutrements well? don't they always glitter like gould, silver, and mountain-dew, wid a sparkle or two of starlight, to say nothing of diamonds?"

" Well—yes, if you like," replied Darcy, abstractedly.

" Thin, it proves what I said—it's the power of intellect."

Then, as Darcy made no answer, Darby Kelly set to work, and was soon deep in the mysteries of pipe-clay and polishing powder.

The honest Irishman had taken an immense liking to Darcy Leigh, and had appointed himself as orderly and servant. He had taken especial pride in arranging the furniture and fittings of the barrack-room, to which Darcy had removed from the hotel.

As a military man, Darby thought that his master's quarters should present a military appearance.

Imagine, then, Darcy's astonishment on moving into his new quarters, which, after four days' hard labour, Darby had at last declared ready. But we will briefly describe them as arranged by Darby.

The whole of the furniture proper, consisted of a table and four chairs; but the lack of this was made up abundantly in other ways. The first thing which struck the beholder's eye was an enormous cartoon, painted on coarse paper in all the glories of red, white, blue, green, and yellow. It had been executed by one of Darby's companions, whose " intellect " had a turn that way.

It professed to represent the " Irish Duke" at Waterloo.

About seven hundred horrible caricatures of soldiers

in red coats and white trousers were running after an
immense number of other soldiers in blue coats and red
trousers. These latter, of course, were the French, and
as nearly as could be guessed, they numbered several
hundred thousand.

Strange to say, although the red-coated soldiers
were pursuing the flying enemy, they all had their heads
twisted round over their shoulders, and were looking
back either at the Duke or the spectators. Every one
of these Darby declared was a portrait and a speaking
likeness of all the soldiers in his father's regiment, the
fighting ——th.

The accuracy, however, of the portraits may well be
doubted when it is known they were all painted not
even from memory, but as the painter asserted, from an
accurate description given him by his father, who, like
Darby Kelly's, had served in the regiment.

However, that is immaterial. The great feature in the
portrait was the Duke himself, who was seated on an
enormous piebald war horse. The hero was of course
gorgeously attired, with pistols both in his belt and
holsters. He held a drawn sword in one hand and a
trumpet in the other, which he was vigorously blowing.
He wore a cocked hat with a large white feather, which
stuck straight up in the air. His features were very
terrible, ferocious, but did not at all correspond with the
conventional idea of the "Iron Duke." He had in the
painting a snub nose, an enormous grey moustache, and
bushy red hair. Such was the Duke according to Darby
Kelly's friend. The cavalry in the battle was repre-
sented by four horsemen several miles away, and right
in the midst of the enemy.

As for artillery, there was only one piece. This was
posted immediately behind the Duke, and kept up apparently a terrific fire between the legs of the piebald horse.

The fury of this cannonade may be imagined when we
state that no less than six enormous cannon-balls may be
discerned in the air at the same time, all having issued
from the same piece.

The foremost of these is several miles away apparently, and the enemy can be seen even at that distance scattering in all directions to avoid the terrible missile. The last is just passing between the legs of the piebald horse, and is of such an enormous size, that it never could have come from the small field-piece, or, indeed, any other cannon that was ever cast.

All the rest of the picture is filled with fire and smoke, and a lurid glare in the sky over some mountains in the background Darby stated to be caused by the burning of Paris.

When this latter fact was disputed on historical grounds, and especially because Wellington could not have been at Waterloo and setting fire to Paris at the same time, he got out of the difficulty by asserting that "Blooker" did it.

Such was the Battle of Waterloo according to Darby Kelly.

This splendid cartoon took up the whole of one side of the room. Immediately opposite it, on the other wall, was a military trophy composed of seven rifles and bayonets, with a dragoon's helmet for the centre-piece.

Another of the walls was covered with swords, cutlasses, pistols, and boarding pikes. There were about twenty swords of all sorts and sizes, from the fencing-foil to the dragoon's sabre.

On the last of the four walls Darby had hung up two saddles, also bridles, spurs, curry-combs, and halters. Then, surrounding these, which formed the centre-piece, he had suspended all the uniform coats, trousers, accoutrements, &c., and even all the private clothes Darcy possessed, the whole being surmounted by a Kossuth hat with an enormous ostrich plume.

We have said that there were but four chairs in the rooms; but to atone for this scant allowance Darby had prepared a seat of honour at the head of the table. This appeared at first to be a sofa or couch covered with a large flag.

"There, yer honner," he said, when, with great pride, he conducted Darcy to the room, "there's a seat for a soldier."

So saying he lifted the flag, and discovered a broad slab of wood supported by two barrels.

Darcy and Wharncliffe, who accompanied him, burst into a loud fit of laughter.

"Ah! ye may laugh, yer honner," said Darby, in high glee, "but jist look in the barrels, an' under the table."

They did so, and discovered first under the table a small field cannon loaded to the muzzle, and uncovering the barrels, found one full of bullets, the other of powder.

"Well, I'm ——!" said Wharncliffe; "why it's enough to make one's blood run cold!"

Darcy first looked grave, then angry, and finally burst out laughing at the utter absurdity of the whole scene.

"Come, Darby," he said, "I can stand a good deal, but there is a limit to human endurance. Take that powder away and the bullets. Where on earth did you get them from?"

"From the quarter-master."

"Did he give them to you?"

"Av coorse he did. I made a requisition for two barrels of powder, two kegs of bullets, two cannons, and a thousand cartridges, for Captain Leigh, an' I got them like a shot."

"Two kegs of powder, two cannons, two kegs of bullets, and a thousand cartridges. Why where are they all—they're not all here?"

"No, yer honner, there wasn't room for them, so I put 'em under the bed in the other room."

"Angels and ministers of grace defend us!" cried Darcy; "you don't think I'm going to sleep there, do you? Do you imagine I want to be blown up?"

"Av coorse not, yer honner. I argufied that point over to meself. Sez I to meself, Darby, sez I, there's a deal of blow up in bullets and gunpowder—specially gunpowder. 'Spose the captain was to be blowed up? Then sez I, in the first place, it's not likely he'll be blowed up; and, in the second, it's the duty of soldiers, officers, as well as privates, to be blowed up."

"The devil it is!"

" Then, sez I, it ain't likely as he'll be blowed up,
'cause tho' powder and bullets is very combustious,
specially powder, yet they won't blow up if no one don't
set light to them.   So I sez to myself, if they won't blow
up without some one doing it, it ain't likely they'll blow
up at all, because it ain't likely any one would set light
to them ; for if they did, don't you see, your honner, it's
most likely they'd be blowed up too."

" Confound your likelys and not likelys ! just set to
work now, and clear all this ammunition out and return
it to the quarter-master, for it isn't likely I am going to
sleep in a powder magazine,—and look here, I shall be
back in half-an-hour, and if by that time you have not
taken it all away, it's extremely likely that I shall kick
you down stairs."

So saying, Darcy and his friend left, leaving Darby
gazing with rueful face on his ammunition and arrangements in general.

Scarcely had they left than a thought struck him ; he
put his head out of the window, and shouted to Darcy
and Wharncliffe, who were crossing the barrack yard—

" Captain ! by your leave, a minute."

" Well, what is it ? "

" It's all about the cannon ; may we keep the two
beautiful little cannon—bekase, if we don't, I must ax
yer honners to come up and help me down with them.
It took six of us to get them up."

" Confound you ; keep them if you like."

" I thought that would do it," muttered Darby to
himself ; " his honner's in a hurry, and I knew he
wouldn't come back."

Somewhat consoled at being allowed to keep the
cannon, Darby set to work to clear away the kegs of
powder and bullets.   He could not, however, make up
his mind to part with them altogether, so he took them
down to the coal-cellar, and carefully covering them over
with coal, there left them.

CHAPTER LII.

NEWS FROM WASHINGTON.

It was, in this martially-decorated barrack-room that, on the occasion of which we speak, Darby was exercising his "intellect" in polishing up his master's accoutrements; while the latter was busily employed writing.

The sharp words of command of the sergeant drilling the recruits in the barrack-yard, and the distant boom of artillery practising on the plain beyond the town, were the only sounds which fell on the ear. Darby was just giving the finishing touches to his work, and Darcy Leigh had folded up his papers, and was about rising, when a sharp knock was heard at the door.

"Get up, Darby, and see who is there."

Darby arose and opened the large oak door.

"Is Lieutenant Leigh in?"

"Captain Leigh, by your lave, sir."

"Ah, to be sure; I had forgotten. Is Captain Leigh in?"

Darby, in reply, stood on one side, and motioned the new-comer to enter; at the same time saying to his master,—

"A gentleman, sir."

The next moment a young man, in undress cavalry uniform, stood before him.

Darcy at once recognised the uniform of his brother Gerald's regiment of horse, and after gazing in doubt for a moment, also remembered the wearer to be a brother officer of Gerald's, whom he had once or twice met.

He rose, and perceiving that his visitor's dress was travel-stained, and that he seemed greatly fatigued, he politely motioned him to be seated; and said,—

"I think I remember you as being in the Second Cavalry with my brother. Have you any news of him?"

"It is on his account that I have now come, having travelled night and day from the Potomac, as soon as I escaped from the custody of the Yankees, by whom I was captured."

"My brother Gerald!—what of him?" asked Darcy, anxiously; for he observed a deep and mournful shade on his visitor's face. "Is he well, or has anything happened to him?"

"Sir, you are a man," was the reply, "and I may at once be frank with you."

"Speak--let me know the worst."

"The worst that could possibly have happened to your brother, short of death, has happened. He was captured by the Yankees while endeavouring to join a party of horse he had raised, and which had preceded him. They were bound across the Potomac at Harper's Ferry, and intended to join the Confederate army."

"Captured! and he is still a prisoner?"

"He is still a prisoner, and with a friend, who was taken with him—a young fellow known as Captain George, an Englishman—is sentenced——"

He hesitated, and his voice faltered.

"Go on," said Darcy, in a husky voice.

"Is sentenced to be shot!"

There was a deep and solemn silence for some time.

Then Darcy, who had leant his head on his hand, covering his eyes, as if in prayer or deep thought, said,—

"And when was the sentence to be carried into effect?"

"I left the Potomac more than a week back. Then a fortnight's delay had been granted, because the English minister had desired a full investigation before a British subject was executed. After the fortnight another short delay may be granted; but that the sentence will be ultimately carried out on both there is not the slightest doubt."

"You left Washington, or rather its neighbourhood, a week back, you say?"

"Yes, but I was delayed on the road."

"I can reach there in three days."

This was said in a musing, reflective tone, and again there was a long silence.

Darcy, by his troubled countenance, seemed to be re-

solving on a course of action.   At last he seemed **to**
have decided.

"Yes," he said, rising, "**it** must be done ; he must **be**
rescued **at** all hazards.   Do **you** know where he is confined ?   Not **in one** of the **forts, I trust ? "**

"No, not in one of the forts, but where, I know not.
It is known, however, that he **is in** the custody of the
Provost Marshal."

"Then he would be in the quarters **or barracks** of some
of the troops—probably in one of the guard-rooms.
Darby, pack up my valise—I shall leave this in an
hour."

"**Surely you are** not so mad as to go to **Washington ?**
You will but involve yourself in his fate, without saving
him."

"**Sir,**" said Darcy, **with calm** determination, "I have
already succeeded in one desperate venture, as, perhaps,
you may have heard.   I will now save my brother or
perish **in the attempt.**"

"Madness !"

"So **be it ; were I to** suffer him to perish **it would be**
cowardice.   I leave this in an hour's time.   I shall **re-**
turn with **my** brother, or share his **fate.** Now, sir, **if**
you will relate to me something of this affair, I shall feel
obliged."

Then he listened patiently, **while the** other circum-
stantially related all he knew of the attempt which ended
so **disastrously in the** capture of Gerald Leigh and Captain **George.**

"And you **say that when last you** saw him you left
him going **to bid farewell to** Webster Gayle's daughters
at Holkar Hall ?"

"Yes."

"And you think that by the treachery of some **one** who
was in your secrets he was betrayed, **and the** party of
dragoons sent on to capture him ?   Have **you** any idea
any suspicion, as to who was the traitor ? "

The young officer hesitatingly replied,—

"Well, there was a rumour going about among us—
indeed, we had actual **and** distinct warning that treachery

was intended by a person who had obtained information of all our movements."

"And who might that person be?" asked Darcy, while, for a moment, a fierce light blazed in his eyes.

"I scarcely like to run the chance of accusing an innocent man; but as it was such common talk, I may as well say that the cousin of the Misses Gayle was and is suspected."

"Lupus Rock! But he has promised to join our cause. It was but yesterday that one of our generals received important information of the enemy's plans from him."

"Perhaps," was the reply, "he is a double traitor—a traitor to both. Who can say?—for my part, I distrust him."

"And so do I; and if my suspicions are ever confirmed, God have mercy on him, for I will have none."

Again there was a silence, which Darcy broke by exclaiming,—

"Darby, confound you, haven't you packed that valise yet?"

"All right, yer honner."

"Go saddle my horse, and bring him round."

"Is yer honner going?"

"Yes."

"Might I be so bould as to ask where to?"

"Washington."

"And would yer honner be afther lavin' me behind yer?"

"You could do no good, Darby, and would only risk your life," said Darcy, kindly.

"As to risking my life, yer honner, it's yerself that knows I don't care a jiffy for that. Maybe what yer honner says about my doing no good is true enough. I know I'm but a poor ignorant haythen, an' I beg yer honner's pardon for makin' so bould as to think I could be of any sarvice to gintlemen like yerself."

Darcy saw that the honest fellow's eyes were full of tears, and taking his hand, said,—

Y

"Darby, my boy, I beg your pardon for speaking unkindly. If you wish it, you can accompany me."

Darby's delight at this was unbounded, and he disappeared after the horse.

"You, sir," said Darcy to the cavalry officer, "do you remain in Charleston?"

"I shall remain for a month, and then join one of the Confederate cavalry regiments."

"Even in this town of Charleston I fear there are some traitors, and were it known I had gone to Washington I might be betrayed. I can depend on you not to mention to any person whatever where I have gone."

"You have my word, sir."

Darcy pressed him to stay and partake of some refreshment, but he declined and took his leave.

Our hero then seated himself, and wrote two letters.

One was to Wharncliffe, and ran as follows:—

"Wharncliffe.—My dear fellow,—I dare say you will be surprised at my sudden disappearance; but take my word for it, that it is an errand which, although fraught with danger, I cannot delay. If you do not hear from me or see me in a month's time, you may conclude that I have failed, and that our enemies have sent me to 'that bourne from which no traveller returns.'

"Your Friend,
"Darcy Leigh."

This was the other letter:—

"Ungrateful, unkind, and mysterious as my disappearance may seem to my friends, and to you especially, yet believe me when I say, on the word of a gentleman, that I cannot act otherwise; and that if you knew my reasons and my object, you would hardly dissuade me, dangerous and even desperate as is my errand. You have ever been to me the kindest of friends; no sister could have been more to me than your own fair self. Believe me that I shall never forget, but shall always treasure up your memory in my heart. Now, dear Coralie, farewell—perhaps for ever. If in one month you do not hear from me, you may conclude that all is over with

"Darcy Leigh."

This letter he addressed to **Coralie St.** Casse, and laid it with the other on the table.

Scarcely had he done this, locked up all his private papers, loaded his revolvers, buckled on his sword, supplied himself with money from his desk, and put on a large military cloak and foraging cap, when Darby **Kelly** reappeared, accompanied by his friend Jupiter.

" Plase yer honner, here's the nigger, an' he wants **to** come too."

Jupiter, rolling his eyes and blubbering, here spoke.

" O my lor a' mussy, Massa Darcy, let dis chile como too."

" **Oh, confound it!**" said **Darcy**, impatiently; " what on earth's the good of your coming? What earthly good can you be to me?"

" I'se very strong, massa," said Jupiter, pointing to his big arm.

" Strong! that may be, but strength is not what **I** want."

" An' I'se orful cunning, massa."

" The deuce you are!" replied **Darcy**, laughing. " Why what on earth could you do?"

" Work de oracle, massa."

" Work the oracle! but I don't want the oracle worked, nor the telegraph either."

" I can play 'possum, Massa **Darcy**—do de contraband."

" Do the contraband! what do you mean?"

" Why, massa, you's agoing to Washington, dis Irisher say."

" Who the blazes do you call a Irisher, you black scaramouch? I'll thump the sowl out of ye if ye call me a Irisher."

" By golly!" replied Jupiter, with a great grin; " I thought you was a Irisher, Massa Kernel Kelly; but dis chile don't care—Englisher, Yankee, nigger, all de same to me—which you like to be, if you ain't a Irisher?"

" By Jabers! if you call me any of thim names, I'll give ye kibosh; when a nigger like you spakes o' the likes o' me, I'll thank ye to say an Irish gintleman."

" Come, stop your wrangling," said Darcy, impatiently.
" What do you mean by doing the contraband ? "

" Why, massa, you know that all slaves that escape
from rebel masters is took in at the North."

" Yes."

" Wall, den, by golly, I go in de lines and say I'se
escaped from a orful rebel. Den, perhaps, dey put me
to work all day ; anyhow, I go where I please at night—
all round de houses—picks up all de knowledge I
can, den slips down to the river, swims across, lets
dis Irisher (Irish gintleman, I mane) know all about
what 's goin' on—dat 's what I call doin' de contraband."

" Doing the contraband, you call it. I expect tho
Yankees would call it doing the spy."

" I specs they would," said Jupiter, with a grin.

" And do you know what would be the fate of a spy?"

" No."

" They 'd hang you."

" By golly ! would they though ?—an' me wid my free
papers and certificates ?"

Jupiter stood somewhat aghast at this idea ; but
seeing that Darcy was about leaving with Darby Kelly,
he suddenly made up his mind.

" I say, massa, dat dere's orful, ain't it ?"

" Very."

" Nebber mind !—who's afraid ?—by golly, I'll chance
it."

And so it was settled that Jupiter should go along with
them.

Darcy then locked up the barrack-room, sent Darby
Kelly to Wharncliffe with all his keys and a message,
saying a letter was on the table for him.

In half-an-hour more Darcy Leigh, the Irishman, and
the nigger, were leaving Charleston behind them on their
way to the North.

Wharncliffe received the message and the keys sent
him by Darcy with some surprise. Not being able to
extract any information from Darby Kelly beyond the
fact that a letter was awaiting him on the table, he

hastened from his quarters to those of his friend, and, unlocking the door, opened and read the letter.

His astonishment and dismay were very great.

"What mad scheme is he now engaged on?" he muttered; "it must indeed be desperate when he thinks fit to conceal it even from me, his most intimate friend."

His eye fell on the other letter left on the table, and he saw that it was addressed to Mademoiselle St. Casse.

"This, perhaps, may clear up the mystery," he said, taking it. "I will go now and give it to her."

Accordingly he went out, relocked the door, and made the best of his way to the house of Coralie St. Casse.

"A letter—for me, and from Darcy Leigh?" said the young lady, in some surprise. "Surely he might have taken the trouble to have come in person if he had anything so important as not to keep till to-morrow, when I have an appointment with him."

However, as the best means of arriving at the truth, Coralie broke the seal and commenced reading the letter.

Wharncliffe watched her countenance as she did so, and was struck by the agitation it exhibited.

Surprise—sorrow—anger—succeeded each other on her handsome and expressive features.

"Does he tell you in the note whither and why he has gone?" asked Wharncliffe.

"He tells me nothing but that he is compelled to leave," replied Coralie, with ill-concealed bitterness.

She did not press Wharncliffe to stay, so he took his leave.

The Black Angel remained standing with the letter in her hand. Her large dark eyes gazed vacantly straight before her, her bosom rose and fell rapidly, her lip quivered, and a tear trickled slowly down her cheek. It was evident that she was deeply hurt by Darcy's sudden departure, and the scanty information he thought proper to give her.

Quickly recovering herself, however, she hastily brushed away the tear, as if ashamed of her weakness. Then she tore the letter up in small pieces and scattered them angrily around.

"Why should I be angry?" she said to herself—
"What right have I to feel aggrieved? None. And
yet, were I indeed, as he says in his brief note, a
sister"—she laid a mournful emphasis on the word—
"he would hardly leave me without so much as coming
to bid me adieu. It is not thus that I would leave any
friend, least of all Darcy Leigh."

It was a bitter struggle, and pride had well nigh
gained the day, but, just at the critical moment, some
broken memories of old days flashed across her mind,
and, sinking into a chair, she buried her face in her
hands, and wept bitterly.

Darcy Leigh, could you have seen her then, and known
that those tears were caused by your unkindness, surely
you would have knelt at her feet and sought permission
to kiss them away.

CHAPTER LIII.

ACROSS THE POTOMAC.

It is night—dark night—the wind moans and soughs
among the trees—the dark waters of the Potomac flow
silently down to the sea, and, except the occasional challenge of a distant sentinel, or the boom of a signal gun,
all is still as death. Two figures are crouching down
beside the stream, and appear to be anxiously watching
the opposite bank.

The forms are those of Darcy Leigh and Darby Kelly,
the Irishman.

The latter appears much the same as when we last saw
him in Charleston; but the former—can it, indeed, be
Darcy Leigh? He is no longer attired in the undress
uniform of the Confederate States, which he had donned
on receiving his rank as captain in the service. It is replaced by a suit of striped cotton, such as worn by slaves
on the plantations—a battered straw hat is on his head,
the hair of which is cut quite close, and a gaudy-coloured
handkerchief is loosely knotted round his neck, and another round his waist, by way of scarf. In this latter is

stuck a small revolver, his only weapon. But, if changed in dress, how much more so in person! Darcy Leigh was always rather pale than dark in complexion, but now his skin is of a deep tawny brown, too deep for that of a quadroon, almost dark enough for that of a negro.

Indeed, many negroes might be found with a fairer skin; as for mulattoes, few could boast of so dusky a hue.

Darcy Leigh had stained himself a deep brown, and might now well pass for a mulatto slave.

His object in doing so was twofold—first, to disguise himself, and render it almost impossible for him to be recognised in case of capture—and secondly, that he might the more easily penetrate the enemy's lines in the character of a fugitive slave.

Moored close to the bank, beneath the shadow of over-hanging brushwood, was a small boat, just capable of carrying two persons.

Suddenly a bright streak of light is seen in the sky on the other side of the river—it is a rocket.

Darcy Leigh, who had been anxiously watching, as if in expectation of this, made a sign to Darby Kelly, who placed himself in the canoe, followed by the young officer.

Taking up a paddle, Darcy lost no time, but com-menced impelling the boat across the stream by long, slow, and silent strokes.

As they emerged from the shade of the high bank and approached the centre of the river, they could dis-tinguish the distant lights of Washington, the watch-fires of the pickets, and even the dark forms of the Yankee sentries as they patrolled the bank of the river.

Slowly, silently, Darcy paddled on, both he and Darby crouching low in the boat to escape the vigilant eyes of the enemy.

They were being all the time carried rapidly down the stream, while their progress across was very slow, for often, when abreast of a sentry, whose form could be seen standing out against the sky, Darcy would cease paddling and allow the boat to drift further down.

Then, when he judged they were at a safe distance, a

few vigorous strokes with the paddle would send the light boat many yards nearer the shore.

The sky was clouded, and there being no moon it was very dark. Still, however, they could just distinguish the forms of the sentries on the high banks.

Not a word, not a sound, not a breath, disturbed the utter stillness, broken only by the rippling of the stream and the gentle splash of the paddle.

Suddenly the silence is broken by a dull crash—the canoe just impelled onwards by a few vigorous strokes of the paddle, has run stern on to a "snag" or floating log.

They are within twenty yards of the shore, and in ear-shot of the sentries.

Darcy and Darby crouch down in breathless suspense, and hope that the alarm may not be given.

"Who goes there ?"

It is the challenge of the sentry.

No answer.

Darcy takes his revolver from his belt, and prepares to place it between his teeth.

"Be ready, Darby," he says, in a low whisper; "we may have to swim for it."

"Who goes there?" again cried the sentry, peering out on the river, and endeavouring to discern the cause of the sound he had heard.

The situation was critical in the extreme, for lately a great many spies from the Confederates were known to have crossed over, and therefore the strictest watch was kept on the bank of the river.

"Who goes there ?" again challenged the soldier; "answer ! or I fire."

As before, all is silent.

Then is heard the sharp click of the rifle, followed by the flash and report, as it is fired in the direction from which the sound came.

The flash of the piece is but momentary, but that moment is sufficient to reveal the little boat with its two occupants.

"A boat ! a boat !" shouts the sentry, hastily reloading his piece.

Now is heard the tramp of feet and the rattling of arms as the pickets hurry up to the soldier who has given the alarm.

The loud voice of the officer in command is heard.

" What is it, my lad ?"

" A boat, sir, making for the shore. I challenged twice, and received no reply ; then I fired, and saw it by the flash."

" Fire again."

Flash—bang !

A shout broke from the soldiers as the boat was again seen for an instant.

" Fire !" shouted the officer in command.

Instantly the flash and rattle of twenty rifles light up the river bank and awake the echoes. The bullets hiss through the air and sputter in the water.

CHAPTER LIV.

" WHO GOES THERE?"

" Now for it, Darby," muttered Darcy.

He then placed his revolver between his teeth, and lowered himself quietly into the water. Darby Kelly followed his example, the constant rattle of musketry covering the noise they made. Darcy gave the boat a violent shove, which sent it shooting down the stream, and struck out in an opposite direction.

Darby Kelly followed him, and in a very brief space of time the boat was borne out of sight by the current. The alarm was now general along the whole line of sentries ; torches and fireballs were lit, and the boat was soon riddled with bullets. Fortunately, it was not discovered that it was empty, the soldiers imagining that its inmates were lying down to escape observation, or were wounded.

Thus it happened that while the boat was being followed down the bank, and constantly fired at, Darcy and Darby, who were swimming vigorously against the stream, escaped observation. The current was so rapid, that it was with great difficulty they could make head against it; still, however, they did make some progress, and in about ten minutes the shouts and cries of the enemy, mingled with the irregular fire still kept up, were at such a distance as to promise safety.

Accordingly, Darcy Leigh, who was much exhausted from the violent exertion, and the fact of being obliged to keep his revolver dry, which he could only do by holding it in his mouth, struck out for the shore, which was only some thirty yards distant. The place he had selected for landing was well suited; the banks were precipitous, and an abundant growth of brushwood right down to the brink rendered the darkness more intense.

Darcy Leigh, on reaching the bank, crawled up and threw himself at full length on the ground to recover breath. Darby Kelly also scrambled ashore, and though not so much exhausted, was glad of a few minutes' rest.

"Now, Darby, we must push on," said Darcy, when somewhat recovered; "it will never do to remain here. It wants but a couple of hours of daylight, and before then we must be far from this."

He then carefully examined his revolver, and satisfied himself that it was not rendered unserviceable.

To make assurance doubly sure, he placed a fresh cap on each nipple, and primed it with dry powder from his waterproof flask.

"Have you got your knife?" he said, in a whisper, to the Irishman.

Darby produced a large sheath-knife, which he wore in a belt round his waist.

"Go and cut two big sticks; the report of my revolver may be fatal, and if attacked, I will only use it at the last extremity."

"Is it a shillelagh you want?"

"Call it what you will, only make haste."

While Darby was gone on his errand, Darcy went cautiously a little further down the stream to reconnoitre. He could discover, by the light of torches, that the boat from which they had escaped was on the point of being drifted ashore. Of course, when it fell into the enemy's hands, they would perceive that its inmates had escaped, and would proceed to search the banks of the stream.

A loud shout apprised him of the fact that the boat had drifted to land. He could see the forms of the soldiers as they crowded down to the bank.

The sputtering fire which had been kept up was silenced, as also were the shouts and cries. Next he saw the dark group disperse, and then he knew that they would spread themselves in all directions in search of the escaped spies.

No time was to be lost; should they be discovered, he knew full well that their fate would be sealed. It would only be a drum-head court-martial—a file of soldiers, and the death of a spy.

It was now evident, by the flashing of torches and the voices of the enemy, that they were spreading both up and down the river in search of the fugitives from the boat.

Darcy hastily retraced his steps and rejoined Darby Kelly, who had cut two big cudgels, and was now awaiting him.

The bank of the river was lined with thick brushwood, with here and there a small tree; but at a distance of about a hundred yards there was a wood of large old trees.

Followed by Darby Kelly, Darcy Leigh advanced cautiously in this direction. At every few paces he paused, and both listened intently, and gazed earnestly forth into the darkness to see that all was quiet, and that no enemy or sentry was before them.

Once in the deep shadow of the wood, he trusted to be able to conceal themselves till such time as it would be safe, in his assumed character of a runaway slave, to venture into Washington.

Before them, at a distance of only some twenty yards, stood a large and wide-spreading oak tree. The sounds from the river bank betokened the rapid approach of the pickets, so accordingly Darcy quickened his pace.

"Come on, Darby," he said, in a low tone, "we must make haste to conceal ourselves, for the blood-hounds are on our track"

They now saw that the large tree in front of them was dead and withered, and that in one side there was a large hollow.

The soldiers' voices could now be heard on the river bank immediately behind them, and they appeared to be about penetrating the brushwood.

" Get into the hollow of the tree, Darby—I will mount into the branches—quick ! "

This was said in a rapid whisper, for sounds issued from the brushwood behind them as if a considerable body of men were advancing. Darby Kelly advanced in front, and was just about to ensconce himself in the hollow, when suddenly there appeared a form from the other side of the tree.

Darby stopped as if shot.

" Who goes there ? "

It was the hoarse challenge of a sentry who had been posted behind the tree.

For a moment the heart of Darcy Leigh stood still. The suddenness of the shock might well for a moment paralyze the bravest. Darby Kelly, who also stood transfixed with astonishment at the sudden apparition of the soldier, was roused by the sharp clang of the rifle, as the sentry brought it to the " charge."

" Who are you ? " again asked the sentry, at the same time cocking his piece. " Speak, or I'll blow you to eternity."

Darby and the soldier were scarcely a yard apart, so that it would be easy to carry out the threat.

" Arrah, honey ! " said Darby, in his richest brogue, " sure an' I's only an Irish gintleman out for a stroll ; so plaze to let me pass on."

" Irish or no Irish, you don't pass here ! " was the gruff reply. " Just stand where you are while I call the guard. If you attempt to advance or retreat, I'll fire."

During this time Darcy Leigh, who was fully alive to the imminence of the danger, had stolen cautiously round to the right of and behind the soldier.

Darcy well knew that an alarm would be fatal ; therefore, at the very moment the man was about to shout for the guard, or perhaps attract notice by firing his rifle, he sprang forward, and with one desperate bound threw himself on the sentry, and before he could fire his piece or give the alarm, had him by the throat. Had it not been for the tree he would have been dashed to the ground—as it was, this saved him, for he was thrown forcibly against it and managed to keep his feet. He was a powerful man, and struggled desperately.

Taken aback by the suddenness and fury of the assault, he was at first at a disadvantage. Darcy still held him by the throat with so firm a grasp that he could not cry out, but as the struggle proceeded he was enabled partly to free himself.

The two forms swayed backwards and forwards, heaved and writhed in the fierce struggle for some time in almost perfect silence.

Darby Kelly stood looking on, club in hand, afraid to strike lest he should injure Darcy, so closely were the two entwined. At last, with a tremendous effort, the soldier released his throat, and at the same time managed to draw a dagger he had at his belt. Darcy had no weapon but his revolver, which he dared not use even if he could.

A slight cry of pain, followed by a quick gasp, and an oath from the soldier.

" Darby, I am wounded—he has stabbed me ! "

"Thunder and blazes ! " muttered the Irishman, in a tone so loud as to be hardly safe ; "look out for yourself, Master Darcy—keep your head on one side for jist half a minute, an' I'll scatter the vagabond's brains about."

Another cry of pain was again followed by a fierce oath from the sentry, who had again succeeded in wounding his antagonist with his knife.

It was the last he ever uttered.

For a brief space of time the two struggling forms were slightly separated. Darcy had shrunk back involuntarily from the sharp pain of the wound. It was the opportunity for which Darby Kelly had been watching, and he did not fail to profit by it.

The great club with which he had provided himself

swung in the air for a second; then, wielded by his brawny arm, it descended full on the head of the sentry with the force of a sledge-hammer. In the struggle his hat had fallen off, so that the terrible blow took full effect on his bare head.

There was a dull crash, and then the body of the soldier slipped from the arms of Darcy, and lay huddled up at his feet.

" By jabers !" said Darby, with a snort of relief.

" By Heavens! you have killed the man," said Darcy, looking on the prostrate body before him.

" Killed him!—I rayther guess I have; an' if it had been six heads all made of cast-iron instead of one, such a bang as I gave him would have smashed 'em."

Darcy Leigh stooped and examined the lifeless body. Darby's words were but too true, for the whole front of the skull was completely smashed in. The head and face presented a horrible spectacle, and Darcy at once knew that the man had been killed instantly.

" Dead !" said Darcy, rising from his examination; " I am sorry you hit so hard as to kill him, Darby."

" An' what did the vagabone mean by knifing yer honner ? See, now, how the blood's running from your shoulder. Besides, suppose I had only hurt him, an' he'd been able to call out, why we'd have had the whole brood of them on us."

" True," said Darcy, staunching the wound in his shoulder as well as he could with a handkerchief.

Fortunately, neither of the two stabs were deep or dangerous, and, with Darby's assistance, they were soon bound up.

It now became a question as to what was to be done with the dead body, and next what course they themselves should adopt. They had not an instant to lose, for at any moment a picket or guard might appear, and discover them.

Now is heard from the brushwood the regular tramp of a body of men approaching.

" Quick, Darby, place the body in the hollow tree, and clamber up."

Darby dragged the corpse, and huddled it into the hollow space as best he could, but when he came to examine the tree he found that for ten feet or so it was quite smooth, so that he could not climb it.

"Up on my shoulder, Mister Darcy; you can reach a branch."

"But what will you do? Can you climb up?"

"Not I, by jabers!" was the cool reply; "does yer honour think I'm a monkey?"

"What will you do?" asked Darcy, still hesitating.

"Do? stay down."

"But you will be discovered."

"Well, if I am, I am, and it can't be helped. I know well, it's life and death. Quick, yer honour, jump up— here they come—I've got a skame in my head to fool them."

Somewhat reluctantly Darcy mounted on Darby's shoulders and swung himself up into the tree.

"I wonder what his scheme is," he thought.

He gained a secure footing on a branch, with another to lean his arms on, and so placed as to command a view around.

He carefully examined the nipples of his revolver, cocked it, and leaning it on the branch of a tree which formed a rest, he muttered,—

"One, two, three, four, five, six barrels. With so good an opportunity for aim as this, I can guarantee that each shall take effect. Before I am taken, if I am to be taken, six Yankees at least shall bite the dust."

CHAPTER LV.

AN INQUISITIVE CORPSE—THE "ROUNDS."

DARBY KELLY, immediately that Darcy had mounted the tree, commenced to put his "skame" in operation. He stripped off the cross belt, ammunition pouch, and tunic of the dead soldier, and quickly put them on himself. Then he searched for, and found his uniform cap. Next he dragged the dead body into an upright position

in the trunk of the tree, for as it lay at present it was in
the way, and more easily discovered.

Having propped the dead soldier up, he possessed himself of his rifle, which lay on the ground at a little distance,
and took up his post at the hollow tree, with his back
against the dead body, so as effectually to conceal it from
view.

The situation was horrible in the extreme, and no one,
without great nerve, could have gone through the ordeal.

As Darby stood, rifle in hand, personating the sentry,
the corpse was standing stiff, and stark behind him,
absolutely touching him, with its ghastly and horrible
face leaning over his left shoulder.

Darcy, who had watched all his proceedings with
breathless interest, now spoke in a low voice.

"You are going to personate the sentry, Darby."

"Yes, plaze goodness."

"It's desperately dangerous."

"Sogering generally is dangerous—at any rate, so I
am tould."

It was evident Darby wished to make light of the desperate nature of his enterprise.

"Suppose some of the enemy come up——"

"I'll challenge them, and *get the countersign*."

Darcy was not generally slow, but on this occasion the
incalculable advantage of getting the countersign had not
struck him, until Darby mentioned it; indeed, if the
thought had ever entered his head, he certainly never
dreamed of obtaining it in such a fashion.

But could Darby obtain it?   The risk was fearful!

He might challenge a guard or picket, and demand the
countersign; but would they give it? would they not
probably at once detect the fact that it was a false sentry
who challenged? and then, what would be their fate with
the dead body of the real sentry concealed in the trunk
of the tree?   This by no means pleasant train of thought
was abruptly brought to a conclusion.

The tramp of armed men, advancing rapidly through the
brushwood, warned them to be prepared for the worst.

Darcy again carefully examined his pistol, and leaning

over the branch, placed himself in such a position as command a view of the ground immediately around the tree

Tramp, tramp, tramp—on came the troops, with slow and measured steps.

"It's the relief," muttered Darcy; "all is lost! They are coming to relieve the man whom Darby killed. Darby, my boy," he said, in a loud whisper, "be prepared for the worst; it's the relief—let's sell our lives dearly, and die like men."

Darby made no reply, but the sharp click of the rifle as he full-cocked it, and his hard breathing, showed that he was prepared to do his part. Onwards they came, and now the dark column may be discerned issuing from the brushwood and advancing across the open space.

Darcy muttered a short prayer, then a long breath, set his teeth, and nervously clutching his revolver, made ready for what he felt was a desperate and hopeless conflict. Suddenly, when the agonizing suspense is wound up to the greatest pitch, the voice of the officer is heard,—

"Halt!" Then, after a moment's consultation,—

"Left wheel—quick—march!"

They are saved, at all events for a time, and can again breathe freely. The picket or relief-guard, whichever it might be, had gone off in another direction.

Now almost the only chance they had was that some straggler would pass, of whom Darby, personating a sentry, would demand and obtain the countersign. Once furnished with this, they would at once boldly make their way through the lines, and trust to fortune for the rest. Minute after minute passed on while they waited in suspense for the expected straggler.

"Hope deferred maketh the heart sick!" and assuredly the hearts of both Darcy and Darby Kelly began to faint within them at the dismal prospect. It wanted but an hour or so of daylight; and then, beyond all doubt, the sentries would be relieved.

Darcy turned over all imaginable projects, and once the idea flashed across his mind of creeping down to the bank and swimming back across the river; but it was instantly dismissed.

Z

"No," said Darcy, "I will accomplish my errand, or perish. To-morrow, Gerald Leigh is to be shot! I will save him, and take him back with me, or I will never return at all."

Now, once again, is heard the tramp of troops, but this time from a different direction.

In the course of a couple of minutes they can distinguish a light advancing towards them from the direction of Washington. As they approach yet nearer, they can make out that the light is borne in front by a boy, and that about half a company of soldiers, formed four deep, are marching behind.

"It is the 'rounds,'" Darcy called to Darby from up the tree; "I can see the drummer-boy with the lantern. Challenge them before they get close; you will have a better chance."

"All right, yer honner."

Darcy shifted his position and peered through the branches at Darby, to see if there was anything about him that would betray his real character.

A shudder passed through his frame. "Ah," he cried, sharply, "Darby, look out for the dead body, its head is hanging over your shoulder and may be seen."

This was the fact; for the pale, ghastly head of the dead man was lying forward over the Irishman's left shoulder, and might possibly be seen by the enemy.

"Stand straight, ye spalpeen," growled Darby, irreverently, thus addressing the dead; "what the blazes are ye so inquisitive about, peering over my shoulder wid yer white banshee face? Sure an' ain't I relieved ye of your sintry duty, and can't ye just keep quiet and mind yer own business?"

But when Darby shifted the dead body from his left shoulder, instead of remaining erect, it dropped over on his right, the glassy eyes staring vacantly out into the night, and the jaw working hideously at every movement, as if it were gibbering and mocking.

"Bad luck to ye, ye inquisitive haythen; can't ye keep yer head straight? sure ye know ye're kilt, and why can't ye keep quiet, and not interfere with gintlemen's amusements and bizness ?"

But do all he could, Darby could not succeed in making the corpse keep its head straight.

First over the right shoulder, then over the left, it glared with its ghastly eyes, and gibbered with its horrible mouth, with dropped jaw and glistening teeth.

Darby Kelly, in spite of his hardihood, could not but feel the horror of the situation. A horrible supernatural fancy possessed him, that when the party now approaching were challenged, the corpse would also speak out and betray his slayer.

The perspiration streams down his face, a deadly icy terror is fast creeping over him, till no longer able to to bear it, he challenges.

" Who goes there ?"

" Rounds."

" What rounds ?"

" Grand rounds."

" Halt, rounds, and give the countersign."

Will they give it ? Will he be discovered, or will the dreadful corpse, still glaring over his shoulder, proclaim in hollow, dreadful tones the deceit ?

Such were Darby Kelly's thoughts as he waited in an agony of suspense for the reply.

CHAPTER LVI.

UP A TREE.

By the dim light of the solitary lantern borne by the boy, Darcy, from his perch in the tree, and Darby, from his post, could plainly see the soldiers standing to their arms, and a group of some four or five officers at their head, who appeared to be consulting together. One of these latter they at once recognised by the uniform as a general officer. No reply was given to Darby's challenge, and the suspense became fearful.

Were they discovered, or was there only a doubt in the minds of the officers ?

Darby Kelly was deadly pale—as pale almost as the ghastly face which peered over his shoulder. He was no coward, but now so horrible was the suspense that he felt his strength rapidly deserting him. His hair and beard were wet with a cold perspiration, and his knees trembled under him.

Unable longer to bear this terrible uncertainty, he collected himself, and challenged as firmly as he could again.

"Who goes there? Give the countersign."

There was a moment's silence, and a deep voice answered—"Baltimore!"

"Pass on, Baltimore—all's well."

They had got the countersign.

Darcy Leigh, in his perch in the tree, felt a thrill of joy, and imagined that all was well, and that the rounds would pass on.

But he was grievously mistaken.

After the countersign was given, the officers at the head of the party again consulted together.

Then one, who, by his uniform, Darcy at once knew to be of superior rank, advanced straight towards the tree.

Darby Kelly, who had congratulated himself on being out of danger, saw with dismay the officer striding towards him.

He grasped his rifle tightly, and, with finger on the trigger, muttered—

"May the Lord help you, my fine fellow, if you find me out!"

Darcy, too, up the tree, again took deliberate aim with his revolver at the breast of the officer.

"A field officer—a general," he said to himself, as he noticed the uniform; "good. If I am taken, the Confederate army will lose a captain, but the Federals a general; for if we are discovered, that fellow is a dead man!"

He was now within a dozen yards of the tree.

"Do you know the orders of the night?" he said, in a severe voice, to the supposed sentry.

It was a terrible moment for Darby Kelly.

"It's myself that does," was the bold reply.

"Give them."

This was a poser, but Darby, who knew something of military service, resolved to make a shot.

"To keep a bright look out, and let no one pass without the countersign."

"Come, sir, that is not all," said the officer, angrily.

"By jabers, yer honour, that's thrue for you ;—but I niver had no mim'ry. I mind now, when I was a spalpeen at school, the thumpings I'd get bekase I niver could remimber."

"Silence, sir ! What regiment do you belong to ?"

"Ah, now, yer honour's afther poking fun at me. Shure yer honour knows what rijiment—ain't it yer honour's own rijiment ? "

"I am a general, and not a regimental officer," was the angry reply ; then to himself he muttered, "I suppose this fellow is one of Colonel Quin's raw recruits— fellows who don't know one end of a rifle from the other, their front from their rear, and will take six months to lick into shape. You are of Colonel Quin's regiment, I suppose ? "

"Faith, an' I am, gineral."

"Very well, sir. I shall have you put on the list for extra drill and fatigue duty. Now listen to the orders of the night :—To let no one pass without the countersign, and at the sound of any one approaching, to challenge. If one man only endeavours to pass without the word, you are to fire, then charge with the bayonet, and make prisoner, if not killed ; if a party, you are to fire, then retreat to join supports, loading and firing as you do so. Keep a bright look out, and remember that the punishment for sleeping at your post is death."

With these words, the officer turned on his heel, and strode back to the others. They heard the sharp words of command, "Quick—march," and then the soldiers marched rapidly off, and for the time Darby Kelly and Darcy were safe.

It was extremely fortunate for them that it was a

general officer who was not personally acquainted with the men in Colonel Quin's regiment. Had a captain or subaltern advanced, he could not have failed to discover that the supposed sentry did not belong to his regiment at all.

The armed party were soon out of sight, and at a distance of a quarter of a mile or thereabouts the challenge of another sentry might be heard as they went on their round along the chain.

Darcy, when satisfied that all was safe, slipped down the tree, and Darby Kelly only too gladly shifted himself from the unpleasant neighbourhood of the dead sentry, who fell forward on his face, and there lay.

"Ugh!" said the Irishman, wiping his streaming face, and drawing a long breath; "by jabers, captain, I thought it was all up that time, and that we should have a short passage to kingdom come. What with the inimy in front and the corpus behind me, I niver felt in such a flurry since I was born. Bad luck to ye, ye haythen"—apostrophizing the dead man—"what do ye mane by frightening the sowl out of a gintleman's body?"

"Come, stop your noise—this is no time for talk."

Darcy considered for a moment as to how he should dispose of the dead body.

"Darby, drag the body down to the river."

"An' throw him in?"

"Yes, throw him in; but first see that you secure its sinking by placing stones within its clothing. It's a sorry burial for a soldier," he added, mournfully, "but necessity has no law. Our very lives are at stake; and were that dead body to be found at his post, the deceit would be discovered, and it would be known that spies had done it, and, having got the word, penetrated the lines. So, Darby, drag him down, and give him a watery grave in the river."

"Aye, aye, yer honour; but as for dragging, I think I can carry him easier and quicker — anyhow here goes."

So saying, Darby exerted his great strength, and

hoisteu the dead man on his back; he tnen marched off
to the river bank, leaving Darcy standing beneath the
tree.

Darby was not gone more than ten minutes, but when
he returned a faint light in the east proclaimed the
approach of day. During his absence, Darcy had been
considering on their course of action, and decided to
hasten on and rejoin Jupiter; and then to lie concealed
the whole day, while the negro went into the town and
gathered all the information he could.

Although possessed of the countersign, he knew it
would be madness to attempt to penetrate the lines
during the day, and resolved to wait for the night.

On the next night, then, he fully resolved to make the
attempt which would decide the fate both of himself and
his brother Gerald.

Should he fail and be captured, he did not doubt for
a moment the fate that would await him. That he might
be shot like a soldier, and not hung like a criminal, would
in that case be the only favour he could ask or expect.

And as for Gerald, he, Darcy, had already learned that
he was to be shot on the very next day, with the other
prisoner, Captain George, whose nationality would not
save him.

"Come on, Darby, let us haste; the day is breaking,
and before it is light we must be in a place of concealment."

Then he strode rapidly on, followed by Darby. He
made direct for a small hill with a clump of trees at
the top.

In a very few minutes they gained the summit, where
they found Jupiter the negro, asleep at the foot of a
tree.

Darcy woke him, and he started to his feet.

"Hi, ullo! what de debbil's the matter? Oh, it's you,
massa Darcy—all right—bin asleep, I reckon."

"I reckon you have. Well, what news?"

"I went in, and guv myself up as a slave nigger run
away from the rebel plantation; den dey guv me something to eat, which wor all right; den dey put me to

work at de batteries, which wor all wrong—leastwise in
dis chile's estimation, which orter go for some. Well
den, when night comes, dis nigger jist takes a cruise
round the houses, and picks up what he can."

"Well, what did you learn?" asked Darcy impatiently.

"Well, in de fust place, de information about massa
Gerald is 'orl korrect;' dey's gwine to give him goss
to-morrow morning at eight o'clock—him and t'other
gentleman, Massa Captain George dey call him."

"They are to be shot to-morrow, then?"

"'Xactly—leastwise if notbing don't interfere."

Darcy was silent for a moment or so on receiving this
fatal confirmation of his worst fears.

"Where are they confined?"

"Somewhere in de lines, but where I couldn't find
out," replied Jupiter, shaking his head.

"And what about Webster Gayle, his daughters, and
Lupus Rock? Have you inquired, as I told you?"

"Yes, massa."

"Well—the news."

"Lupus Rock and de Misses Gayles are at Holkar Hall;
Massa Webster Gayle, no one know where he is."

"And that is all, then, you could discover?"

"Dat is all, massa."

Darcy sighed. It was but meagre information on
which to act, and yet act he must, and that promptly, or
otherwise the day now breaking would be the last he
would ever see.

He promptly determined that while Jupiter again
endeavoured to discover something of the whereabouts
of the prisoners in the city, he would in the ensuing
night make his way to Holkar Hall.

He felt convinced that, could he succeed in seeing
either Stella or Angela Gayle, they would give him all
the information they could as to his brother Gerald. He
knew, or thought he knew, the girls well enough to
make certain of their sympathy and aid to rescue an old
and dear friend like Gerald from so terrible a fate,
albeit he were a rebel and they Unionists.

" Well, Jupiter," he said, after a long pause, "make your way back to the town; and during the day, and also the fore part of the night, discover all you can concerning my brother Gerald. Meet me here at midnight to-morrow, or rather to-day, for it is fast becoming daylight."

"All right, massa."

" By the way, have you brought any provisions with you ?"

" Oh, my Lor A'mighty, if I hadn't near forgotten; ain't it orful ?"

Darcy smiled faintly, for although he had not tasted food for nearly twenty-four hours, he felt no appetite, and only asked because he knew that in the perilous enterprise of the following night he would require all his strength.

Jupiter produced from a bundle, biscuits, cheese, and two bottles of wine.

" Thanks, good Jupiter ; and now off on your errand, and do not fail to be here to-morrow night."

" All right, massa—I'll be here, as sure as God made little apples."

Then Jupiter went off in the direction of Washington, and Darcy, looking around him, selected a favourable tree.

"Come, Darby," he said, " let us climb up here ; we must be squirrels till night, and live among the boughs."

The tree was an easy one to climb, and they were soon among the topmost branches.

Darcy selected a good resting-place, and motioning Darby to do the same, he brought out the biscuits, cheese, and wine, and partook of them, though sparingly. Then, having lashed themselves securely by pieces of cord they had with them, both officer and private—master and man — sank to sleep in this strange resting-place.

Hoping that after the perils and fatigues of the night they may enjoy sound sleep and refreshing dreams, we will for the present leave them.

CHAPTER LVII.

CONDEMNED TO DEATH.

THE condemnation of Gerald Leigh and Captain George followed quickly on their capture by the United States' dragoons. Desperately wounded as they were, they were brought and tried a week after the night of their desperate attempt, and, as a matter of course, the verdict was *guilty*, and the sentence death.

Gerald Leigh, having belonged to the United States' army, was, in the formal wording of the indictment, cited as guilty of treason, mutiny, and rebellion, while Captain George was simply accused of *murder*, from the fact of having killed one of the Federal soldiers.

His nationality procured him a brief respite from the execution of the terrible sentence—had it been otherwise both would have expiated their rashness long ere Darcy Leigh could have known of it.

Gerald, be it remembered, thought his brother Darcy had been killed in the attempt to run the Spitfire out of New York harbour; so that he could hope for no aid from him, even if it were possible he could effectually render it.

The fact of Captain George being an Englishman delayed the execution of the sentence for three weeks, during which time every possible influence was used by the friends of Gerald to obtain a remission, or at all events a modification of the sentence. The prisoners were allowed no intercourse with any one whatsoever, and the most urgent entreaties of Stella and Angela Gayle could not obtain them leave to see the condemned men. The utmost their efforts could obtain was permission to communicate in writing, and one interview.

Angela Gayle gave way to utter and blank despair at the fearful prospect before her friend Gerald; but Stella, true to her nature, never slackened in her efforts to save the condemned men. Even Lupus Rock, much as she hated and despised him, knowing also that he was the cause of the arrest—she bent to her purpose, and compelled to use unremitting endeavours to procure a reprieve.

Lupus, who was now thoroughly cowed and afraid of the fierce spirit he had raised in his cousin, consented, with as good a grace as possible, himself to head a petition in favour of the prisoners. But though compelled thus to act, he felt all but certain that it would be in vain, and that the authorities had determined to carry out the sentence.

Thus the nearer the fatal day approached, and the further the hopes of mercy being extended, the more vigorously did Lupus strive, or appear to strive, to obtain a reprieve.

Stella Gayle, although she suspected her cousin of the original treachery, had no positive proof, and so well did Lupus play his part that at times she almost doubted whether it were not possible she might have wronged him.

Lupus had discovered the false step he had made by allowing Stella to think or imagine that he triumphed over the downfall of Gerald Leigh, and now did all in his power to correct the impression and reinstate himself in her good graces.

His skill and address, when he chose to curb his passions, were consummate. He also contrived that Webster Gayle in his letters to his daughters should always speak of him in the most affectionate manner, and should inculcate implicit obedience to and confidence in him.

And now the fatal day is at hand. The last sun has risen which the condemned men will ever see set.

During the whole of that day Stella Gayle exerted herself unceasingly to procure at least a respite—in vain. Lupus Rock now felt certain that nothing could save the prisoners, and accordingly appeared almost beside himself with anxiety. Stella exhausted all her arts, even calling in the aid of her great beauty, to soften the hearts of rugged and vulgar officials—but in vain—in vain the proud Northern belle bestowed her sweetest smiles, which anon changed to tears, on men whom in her heart she loathed. Night closed on the scene of her labour of love, and the only answer she could get was the stern words, "*They must die!*"

With the setting of the sun all hope faded out in the bosoms of the two girls—with the setting of the sun, which they also witnessed, all hope died out in the breasts of the condemned, and they prepared to meet their fate like men.

Angela Gayle, giving way to the intensity of her despair, locked herself in her own room, while Stella, whose grief and terror were no less than her sister's, had her feelings more under command—she even partook of supper alone with her cousin Lupus—and but for the deadly pallor of her face, and a certain wildness in the large dark eyes, it would have been hard to tell what a storm of passion reigned within that fair breast. The meal passed in almost complete silence, no word being spoken of the forthcoming terrible event which was uppermost in the mind of each.

Stella arose, and bowing coldly to her cousin, for whom her old antipathy seemed suddenly to have revived, she went out on the balcony of the first floor.

The night was dark and sultry, while but a light breath of air bore onwards the heavy masses of clouds that arose in the west and passed over Washington.

The calm was deadly and oppressive, the darkness gloomy, and the air sultry and close. It was the calm which so often precedes a storm. Stella seated herself in a chair by the side of a small table, and bending forward her head she hid her face in her hands, and prayed long and fervently for aid from on high for the condemned men.

When her prayer was concluded she yet remained in the same attitude, and thought of the happy past. The form of Gerald Leigh, as she had seen him but a short time previously, rose in fancy before her eyes. She remembered him in all the pride of youth, hope, and high aspirations, and thought of him now—a prisoner condemned to be shot. Then yet another image obtruded itself—that of another and once well-loved friend, whom she believed to have gone to his last account. Her thoughts were of Darcy Leigh. She remembered with bitter self-reproach, that the last words she had ever addressed to him were those of insult and scorn.

Hot tears forced themselves through her fair fingers as she murmured, utterly spirit-broken,—

"Oh, Darcy Leigh—Darcy Leigh! could I but bring you back to life, how gladly would I sue for pardon! Darcy, if you can hear my prayer in another and a better world, I know I may count on your forgiveness!"

She was still murmuring to herself in an incoherent manner, when a slight rustling among the creepers trained around the balcony caught her ears.

This was followed by a well-known voice, which, welcome under other circumstances, sent the warm blood back to her heart, leaving her face, to the very lips, of an ashy paleness.

"Stella!"

It was the voice of Darcy Leigh, and raising her eyes, his apparition stood before her on the balcony. He was dressed somewhat as when she had last seen him—that is to say, was stripped to the shirt and trousers. The face appeared to her to be of a dreadful leaden hue, while from a wound in the forehead blood trickled slowly down.

Stella gazed but for a second, and then, with a choking gasp, exclaimed, "*The spirit of Darcy Leigh!*" and fainted.

When Stella recovered from her deep swoon, she found herself reclining in the arms of the supposed spirit—which said spirit, in a most unspiritual manner had more than once pressed his lips to hers. It was this latter fact which fully brought the young lady to, and caused her to open her eyes.

Her first thought as her eyes fell on Darcy was as before, that it was indeed a phantom, but by a process of reasoning of which none but a strong-minded young lady would have been capable, she decided that it was no spirit in whose arms she lay, but Darcy Leigh himself, who therefore was not dead.

Terror being banished from her mind, pride and anger succeeded, and forcing herself from his grasp, she started to her feet and confronted him with flashing eyes and the old haughty look.

"How now, sir! how dare you thus intrude yourself on me?"

"I ask your pardon," replied Darcy, whom Stella's words and look had recalled to himself, and the object with which alone he had sought her, "for intruding myself, but the business on which I have come is that of life and death—my brother Gerald."

Stella eagerly interrupted him—

"Gerald! Can you, then, hope to aid him—can you procure his pardon?"

"His pardon, no; nevertheless, I hope to aid him; in short, to procure his escape."

"His escape—ah! but you yourself, how is it I see you here? Are you not dead?"

"Scarcely," replied Darcy, with a smile; "did you then think me so?"

"Did I think you so?" replied Stella, "assuredly I did, and so did all. Did I not see you shot down on the deck of the Spitfire, in New York harbour?"

"Shot down, yes; but the wound was only slight, and in a few minutes after being carried below, I returned to the deck."

"How then did you escape? Where is the ship, and whence did you come?"

"I will answer your last question first. I came from Charleston."

"You succeeded in escaping with the vessel you stole?"

"I succeeded in escaping with the vessel I stole, as you are pleased to express it. Have you further questions to ask, or, as I am a thief, do you intend to give the alarm and have me apprehended? Perhaps you might be soon enough to cause my execution with my brother to-morrow morning—who knows? There would be a triumphant spectacle for your loyal eyes—Gerald and Darcy Leigh, whom you once called friends, shot side by side—the one betrayed by your cousin, the other by yourself"

The colour had returned to Stella's face, but at these bitter words, which her own had provoked, she again grew deadly white.

" Darcy Leigh," she exclaimed passionately, her dark eyes flashing, and her voice trembling with passion, " you are a rebel, a traitor—and I hate you—and hate you all the more for your audacity a while back."

" Pardon—I will not repeat the offence," replied Darcy, with a smile, which seemed still further to exasperate Stella.

" You dare not, sir, you dare not," and she stamped her small foot on the ground ; " but listen, and do not interrupt me—I repeat that I hate you—nevertheless in supposing that I could betray you, you wrong me bitterly."

" And you once wronged me."

" When—how ? " she asked, though she foresaw the answer.

" You called me coward. I have proved I am not such. Confess it."

" You have proved yourself a traitor ? "

" No."

" A rebel ? "

" Yes, and as such I am prepared to die. Our fathers of old, Stella, were rebels when they fought the great fight of Independence. Washington himself was a rebel ; yet none have dared to throw dirt upon his memory. I also am a rebel, and dare both own it and risk all consequences. But enough of this. I perceive my mission here is vain. I was about to have asked you for information respecting——no matter. Adieu."

So saying, he sprang lightly over the balcony, and was about clambering down by the same way he had ascended, when she spoke.

" Darcy Leigh, stay."

He paused and turned fronting her, holding by the iron rail.

" What is it you were about to ask ? "

" What matters ? You and yours would not assist me."

" Was it concerning Gerald ? "

" It was."

"Then I will tell all and everything I know, and God grant it may be of some assistance to him in this hour of terrible adversity."

"But is not he also a rebel, a traitor—perhaps, also, in your estimation, a thief ? "

" Why seek to provoke me ? " she answered; "let it suffice that I will answer you."

"I wish to know where he is confined, and under what guard; do you know ? "

"I do, and will tell you."

Then, in a very few words, she proceeded to inform him with great exactness the building in the guard-room of which he was imprisoned. She described the situation and the approaches to it with great minuteness.

"And the guard—under what guard are they ? "

" I do not know the number of the soldiers, but there is an officer in attendance night and day."

"Good. Now listen to me. Gerald Leigh shall be freed from his bonds and safe across the Potomac before the sun rises, or——"

"Or what ? "

"Or Darcy Leigh will share the fate in store for him."

"You are then about to attempt a rescue ? "

"I am, and shall succeed. You see yon dark clump of trees on the other side of the river, or at least, if you cannot distinguish them in the gloom, you know their position."

" Yes."

"When you see a rocket sent up from there, know that is a signal that Gerald Leigh is safe and across the river."

" I shall look in vain for it."

"You will not. Now adieu."

Without another word he turned, and leaped lightly to the ground.

Stella remained motionless, almost as pale as a statue.

"Gone ! gone ! and with nought but the memory of bitter words to cheer him in his desperate undertaking.

For the memory of old and happy times, for his brother's, his sister's sake, I might at least have pressed his hand, given one kind word, and let him know I am neither so cold nor so cruel as he deems me, and as I appear. Now it is too late. Assuredly he will perish in this mad endeavour to save Gerald, and his last thoughts of me will be as of an enemy."

Her thoughts were interrupted by the sudden entrance of Lupus Rock, who rushed in white and scared.

" A ghost! a ghost! I have seen a ghost, Stella."

" What ghost? "

" The ghost of Darcy Leigh. He passed me just now in the road, pale, horribly pale, with the blood still streaming from the wound in the shoulder."

Lupus glanced around the room, and peered into the dark corners in ill-disguised alarm.

Stella knew not how or whence it came, but all at once a thought took full possession of her mind. She would use the terror of Lupus Rock to aid the escape of the prisoners. She had no definite plan, but it seemed to her that even to see them and inform them a rescue was about to be attempted, might do good. Accordingly addressing Lupus, she said,—

" I also have seen it, and have spoken to it."

" What does it want? " asked Lupus, eagerly; " we will do anything—anything to prevent it again."

" Do not interrupt me," said Stella, without appearing to listen to him. " You must find means to communicate to Gerald Leigh this night—at once—in an hour's time."

" Impossible."

" Then on your head be it." Stella at this glanced over her shoulder towards the balcony, and purposely gave a slight start or shudder.

The face of Lupus Rock instantly again assumed its former look of abject terror, and he stammered out,—

" What is it, Stella? What do you see? "

" Nothing, no matter," she replied, at the same time removing nervously as far as possible from that end of the room. " Only I am rather alarmed—I cannot help it, Heaven knows I would if I could, but if it cannot be

A A

done, it seems dreadful that the innocent should suffer these terrible visitations with the guilty."

Her voice was apparently choked by sobs, and she stood with clasped hands glancing now and again timidly over her shoulder. Stella was an excellent actress, and her alarm seemed so genuine that it could not fail to add to the guilty terrors of Lupus Rock.

" Good Heavens! Stella, do not talk in that dreadful way," he faltered, following the glances of sham terror, which she ever and anon threw towards the balcony. " I will do everything."

" I must see Gerald Leigh."

" Impossible; nothing but a written order from the Commander-in-chief could procure permission."

"They are still confined in the same place?"

" Still in the guard-room of the 24th New York Regiment, whence, to-morrow, they will be marched out on the plain and shot."

Stella shuddered at the word, and asked hurriedly—

" Who are the officers in command of the guard to-night?"

" I do not know."

" You can find out. Go, and return in half an hour with the news."

" I think it is young Vavasour and Captain James."

" Captain James, who has so often called here, and whom we met last spring at Saratoga?"

" The same."

" Go at once, make certain that it is indeed he, and the affair is easy," said Stella, eagerly.

" Why so? Do you think that because he is an admirer of yours, that he dare so far break the rules of military obedience, as deliberately to disobey an order so positive as that which forbids all intercourse with the prisoners?"

" No matter, ascertain the fact—leave the rest to me. Come, sir, do not stand there, but do my bidding."

Lupus, the effects of his fright having now somewhat worn off, regarded his cousin with some surprise. Strange to say, her terror, but a moment before so great, had also fled, and he was somewhat puzzled to account for the change in her manner.

However she looked so beautiful as she impatiently stamped her foot for him to be gone, that he felt constrained to obey. Indeed, he was not sorry to make his peace with her by any means in his power, for it was fatal to his plans to be at open enmity with her. However base and dastardly his ultimate designs might be, he well knew that at present he was powerless against her.

Casting one glance of irrepressible admiration on her queen-like form, and meeting for a moment those flashing eyes, which seemed to burn into his brain, Lupus went out on his errand.

"By Heavens!" he muttered, "that girl's beauty is enough to drive one crazy. I must, indeed, beware lest, intending to be absolute master, and have her destiny in my hand, her fascinations do not overpower my reason, and bring me to her feet. No, no, fair Stella, I must guard against that. At present the day is yours; yours is the triumph—mine the humiliation! But my time will come—the time when, if you spurn my addresses, I will command that which I failed to obtain by soliciting; and you, in your turn, shall kneel to me and beg for mercy!"

Thus musing and muttering, Lupus strode on towards the city.

Stella Gayle well knew that there was no hope of obtaining an interview with the condemned men; nor, indeed, did she wish one. Her designs lay in quite a different direction.

She knew that Darcy Leigh would certainly attempt to rescue his brother, and she judged that he would make the attempt by stratagem, and not by force.

A fierce, wild desire had taken possession of her from the moment he uttered those words of bitter reproach, to show him how far her thoughts were of betraying him by actually aiding him.

There was a slight struggle in her mind for a short time between patriotism and friendship, aided by wounded pride, and a feeling that she had been wronged in thought.

True—she had bitterly wronged Darcy Leigh, but it was in word only. When she used the word "coward" coupled with his name, she well knew how utterly false it was—that though a rebel, he was true and brave as steel.

But his words to her were very different.

She saw that he believed, or, at least, thought it possible, that she would betray him into the hands of his enemies, and however much this might have been owing to herself, the thought was unbearable. That Darcy Leigh should think her capable of betraying him and Gerald to an ignominious death!

'What have I done,' she thought, the bitter tears of anger and vexation rising to her eyes, 'that he should think me thus base? It is true I insulted him, but I meant not my words; and even had I been mistaken in him, surely he never could have been mistaken in me. Surely he never could have thought that *I*—from very childhood the friend of himself, brother, and sister— could have betrayed him? He never could have done so!'

But, alas! the conviction forced itself on her mind that he *did*, and she instantly resolved to prove to him how unjust were his suspicions by, at least, *endeavouring* to aid him in this his desperate attempt.

But how was it to be done? How could she, a girl, give him the slightest help? How, indeed?—that was the question, and Stella, who was by nature somewhat logical, commenced to reason.

First she asked herself how would the attempt be made? It appeared certain to her that whatever means Darcy possessed, stratagem would be used. She felt certain of the impossibility of any considerable number of men crossing over with him from the rebel side, and penetrating the camp.

Therefore, she argued, he has probably only two or three with him. She knew also that, as the attempt must be made on the guard-room, where he was confined, the principal danger and obstacle would be the vigilance of the soldiers and officers on guard, and especially the officers.

If, then, that vigilance could be impaired or caused to slacken, how much more hopeful would the venture be? She arrived thus far by a clear process of reasoning, and now the real difficulty presented itself. How could she cause the guardians of the doomed men to relax in their vigilance?

Suddenly a thought strikes her, and she is at once certain she has hit on the only plan which could be of service. It came by no process of reasoning, by no chain of ideas, but presented itself unexpectedly to her as by inspiration.

No sooner had Lupus left, than she hastened to put her design into execution. She hurried up stairs to her own room, and unlocking a cabinet, she took from it a small object and then made her way to the underground ice-house, or cellar, where the wine, and, during the hot weather, provisions also were kept.

In the course of ten minutes she issued from the cellar, carrying a small oil-lamp in her hand. Having replaced what she took from the cabinet, she again went out on the balcony to await the coming of Lupus Rock. Now, however, instead of leaning as before with her head on her hand in listless apathy—almost despair— she passed up and down impatiently, muttering to herself every now and again, her dark eyes flashing, her cheek glowing, and her whole frame in a fever.

CHAPTER LVIII.

THE SCHEME MATURED.

Lupus Rock was barely gone half-an-hour, and yet to her excited mind it seemed as if half the night had passed.

" Well?" she asked, eagerly, as he entered the room.

" It is as I thought," he replied; " Vavasour and James."

" Then Vavasour or James must be bent to my purpose."

" I fear it is hopeless—Vavasour is but a subaltern, and has no authority, and James, I know, dislikes me."

" Does he dislike me ?"

" You! no, certainly not ; but surely, Stella, you would not wish to solicit from him ?"

" This must be managed, Lupus, in some way, no matter what the sacrifice." She fixed her eyes on him, and after a moment's pause continued,—

" If you do not succeed in this, Lupus, I return to New York to-morrow."

These words filled Lupus Rock with the utmost alarm, as the return of Stella to New York—of course accompanied by her sister—would be fatal to his plans. It had only been by procuring a constant succession of letters from Webster Gayle, urgently pressing them to remain, and to put themselves entirely under the guidance of their cousin, that he had been enabled to prevent the return of the girls to their father. Such a result would have been fatal to all his hopes and schemes, and Lupus had spared no trouble to guard against it.

He well knew that if Stella once declared her determination to return, nothing short of actual force could stop her, and unfortunately for Lupus, *that* at present was out of the question.

" I do not see how it can be managed, Stella," he said gloomily, " unless you choose, *yourself*, to make it a personal favour with Captain James."

" That I could not do ; but could you not, without exactly committing me, lead him to suppose such was the case ? Suppose you were to go round to the guard-room as the bearer of an invitation here. Supposing, also, you were to take with you a few flasks of that splendid old Burgundy my father prizes so much."

" The Burgundy he had presented to him by the French ambassador. Why there are not a dozen left, and it is worth twenty dollars a bottle."

" No matter if a thousand."

" I might do so certainly. You know my uncle and

your father as well as I, and you also know that he
would be more furious at missing two bottles of this his
favourite wine, than if he lost a ship load of mer-
chandise."

"No matter. I will undertake the responsibility.
Here is the key. Get the wine, remain for half-an-hour
and partake of one bottle; then return here and I will
give you a note, requesting a last interview with the
prisoners."

Lupus Rock hesitated.

The terror of the ghost had almost worn off, and the
determination and energy of his cousin aroused his
suspicions.

"What was the meaning of this?" he asked himself,
and was unable to answer the question.

"As you please, Lupus," said Stella, angrily. "If you
don't choose to go I will go myself, and to-morrow sees
me on the road to New York."

"As you please, Stella," said Lupus, moodily, after
a pause; "I will go—give me the key."

She gave it him and he left the room—but as he
turned away from her there was a smile of triumphant
cunning on his face.

'I know not what is the reason of this deep anxiety on
Stella's part to see the prisoners, nor what scheme she
may have in her head, for if I am not greatly mistaken
all this solicitude does not proceed from fear of the
phantom—if phantom it were. Ha! what if it should
not have been a spirit at all—but Darcy Leigh in person—not dead but alive—that would account for all her
anxiety to see them, doubtless to aid the cursed young
rebel in effecting their escape, for if it were he in person that is undoubtedly his object. Could it be—who can
say—but then that ghastly livid face, with the blood
streaming down from the bullet-wound in the forehead
No—that could have been no deception.'

He shuddered, and at the thought the old terror came
over him.

'No matter, ghost or no ghost, I will do as she wishes
me, as far as her wishes do not absolutely clash with my

plans. I will take the invitation and the wine. I will stay for half-an-hour and help to drink it, then will return and get the note, but I will never deliver it. Then if she has any plan in her head for the relief of the prisoners it will be utterly frustrated.'

Lupus in his cunning, overreached himself. It never struck him for a moment that Stella Gayle did not wish the letter delivered, and, indeed, would never give it to him to deliver. He little thought that the first part— the delivery of the wine,—was all she wanted.

Wrapping himself in a large cloak, he procured the wine, and placing a bottle in each pocket, started on his errand. He did not go alone, however; his superstitious fears after his fright would not allow him to do that, but took with him one of the negroes from the house.

By this time it was near midnight, and by the time Lupus reached the guard-room, another day had commenced—the last, in all probability, that Captain George and Gerald Leigh would ever see.

CHAPTER LIX.

THE GAME AT CARDS—WIN OR DIE.

THE guard-room in which the condemned men were confined was situated in the quarters of the —th New York Regiment. These consisted of a block of rough wooden buildings, forming three sides of a square. These confined a large open space, used as a drill and parade ground. On the fourth side of the square was the entrance. This, by day, was through large wooden gates, capable, when open, of admitting waggons and artillery; but, by night, these were closed, and a small wicket, constantly guarded by a sentry, alone gave ingress and egress.

On the right of the gate was a dead wall: on the left the guard-room, at the back of which were the prisoners. They had been removed here as soon as their wounds were sufficiently healed for them to leave the hospital, and had remained ever since, awaiting the execution of the sentence which the court-martial had pronounced.

This would long since have been carried into effect, had it not have been for the fact of Captain George being an Englishman, and the questions it raised. He himself, on his trial, had not raised the point, but boldly acknowledged that he was about to join the Confederates when arrested, and asserted his right to do so.

He declared that he had as much right to carry his sword to the Confederates in the approaching struggle, as the Federals had to accept the services of Irish, Germans, and other aliens. This plea availed him not; it was treated with contempt, and, as the reader knows, he was found guilty of the charge against him, and condemned to death.

Gerald Leigh, in his defence, declared that he was not a Northerner, but a Southerner, a citizen of a State which had seceded from the Union, and so no longer held any allegiance to the Federal Government. He was not a deserter or a traitor, because he had resigned his commission in the Federal army, and was making his way south to his friends and countrymen, when attacked and cut down by the United States' dragoons. For these reasons he demanded to be treated as a prisoner of war.

This defence fared no better than that of Captain George, and was scarcely listened to. The court deliberated only five minutes, and then found both guilty; and, as a consequence, both were sentenced to be shot.

Strenuous exertions were made to save them, at least from the punishment of death, but in vain.

Gerald Leigh had many and powerful friends, but although they exerted all their influence, they were unable to obtain even a commutation of the sentence; and on the previous day, it was known in Washington that the last appeal had been rejected—that the dread fiat had gone forth, and that Gerald Leigh and his friend were to die.

They, themselves, had been prepared for the worst from the very day of their capture. Gerald had repeatedly cautioned his friend not to build any hopes on the fact of his being an Englishman, for that would not save him. Captain George, however, took it very coolly, and repeatedly declared his firm conviction that he was not to die this bout—that something would turn up at the last.

Let us visit them in their gloomy prison-room.

This was situated at the back of the guard-room, and was entered by a strong wooden door from the latter. There were neither windows nor chimney, and a small oil lamp was all the light they had night and day. Each had a mattress on the floor, and this, with a couple of horse-cloths and a campaign-blanket, was all they had in the way of bedding. They were, however, allowed all their private clothing, and as both were well supplied, they did not suffer in that respect.

A table, two chairs, and a wash-stand completed the furniture of their prison.

The outer room was occupied by the two officers, who were ordered to be constantly with the guard over them.

By day the drill-ground was constantly filled by soldiers passing and repassing, so that, with the exception of the two officers and the sentry at the gate, there was no special guard over them.

Gerald Leigh is seated at the table, leaning his head on his hand, and looking gloomily straight before him, evidently buried in thoughts of no pleasant nature.

Captain George, the Englishman, is pacing up and down the narrow space with impatient steps, casting an eye every now and again on his companion sunk in lethargy.

After one of his short turns up and down, he suddenly halts at the table, and slapping Gerald on the back, addressed him in a voice which, even under these desperate circumstances, still has something cheerful, almost defiant, in its tones.

" Come Gerald, old boy, cheer up—all is not over yet, and even if it were, we can only die once ! "

" Death ! " replied Gerald, moodily ; and raising his head, "it is not death I fear—it is the manner, the circumstances attending it—to be led forth like a criminal, and shot down like a dog. Amid the hurling of shot, the

hissing of bullets, the thunder of artillery, and the wild
shouts of the combatants, it is easy, even glorious, to
die; but in the cold, grey, silent morning, to be led
forth to die a disgraceful death, that is a very different
matter!"

"Bah!" replied the other; "if we must die, what
gnifies the manner of our death? For my part, I shall
equest the firing party to aim at my head—there will be
flash—I shall feel a sudden shock, a blaze of light—then
utter darkness, and all will be over. Do you know,
Gerald, I think there is little or no pain accompanying
a sudden death. I once received a blow on the head
from a slung shot. I felt nothing—absolutely nothing
—not even the blow. It was as if I had been for a time
utterly and painlessly annihilated. Doubtless it will be
the same to-morrow, if we are to undergo the experi-
ment. Ready! Present! Fire! and before we hear the
report, we shall both be in kingdom come."

"Don't speak of it in that light, careless manner,
George. It jars on my feelings. I am no coward; had I
have been so I might have ridden off and left you when you
so insanely turned and rode after that man in the brush.
By the way, you never explained the meaning of that
insane escapade which has consigned us both to this fate.
I think you said you would."

A shade came over the features of the other. He was
silent for some time, and took a turn or so up the room
before he answered.

"Gerald," he said, stopping again before his chair,
"it is a long story—too long to relate now. This much
I will tell you, however: the man whom I rode after, and
whom I should have cut down had not my horse fallen,
is my most deadly enemy. I have sworn to take his
life."

"Then I fear much you are in danger of breaking
your oath," replied Gerald with a bitter laugh.

"Gerald," said Captain George, laying his hand on
his shoulder, "I shall not break my oath. Do you believe
in presentiments?"

"No, I don't," replied Gerald, bluntly. "I believe

we shall both be shot an hour or so after daylight."

" Do you think, Gerald," continued the other, "that
on our road to the place of execution I could possibly
have an opportunity of seizing a weapon and killing any
one ? "

Gerald looked in surprise at his friend; he almost
thought he was taking leave of his senses.

" Certainly not," he replied.

" Ah, then, that is all right. We shall not die to-
morrow, at all events."

" How do you mean ?—how is it all right ?—and what
has the fact of your not being able to seize a weapon on
the road got to do with our dying ? "

" Everything. If it is impossible for me to possess
myself of a weapon, it is impossible for me to kill any one,
and I shall not die until I have slain the man you saw me
ride after the other night. I have a presentiment—you
do not believe in it—very good—let the event prove."

Captain George went to his valise and brought forth
a small flask of Schiedam, also a pack of cards. Glasses
were on the table, and after pouring out some for Gerald
and himself, he took a chair.

" Come," he said, " let us have a game at *eukre*."

" And you mean to say you are going to play *eukre* an
hour or two before you are to be shot ? "

" My dear fellow, I don't believe I am going to be
shot; besides, I am a philosopher—what must be must
be, and my playing *eukre* will make no difference one way
or the other. Come, cut for deal."

" I don't like *eukre*," replied Gerald, wearily ; " it was
always my abomination."

" Well, *écarté ?* "

Gerald shook his head.

" Cribbage ? "

" As you please," he replied ; and taking up the pack,
he wearily, absently shuffled them, and handed them
back.

" Cut for deal."

They did so, and Gerald won. The first deal Gerald

held twelve in hand, gained four by play, and held fifteen in crib.

Captain George only held five.

It was now his deal.

" Gerald," he said, looking up smilingly, " I have confidence in myself and in my star. I will bet you five hundred dollars I win the game."

Gerald laughed aloud, not a mirthful, but a bitter laugh.

" Five hundred dollars! What on earth should I do with them if I won?—and how will you get them? Am I to take them with me to 'kingdom come,' as you call it?"

" Not a bit of it—take them down south with you, and spend them in Richmond or Charleston."

" What nonsense you talk, man, as if we should ever see Richmond or Charleston. Do you forget this is our last night on earth?"

" I don't forget that we are sentenced to be shot, but I do not believe that the sentence will ever be carried into effect—no! I would not believe it even were we on the fatal ground with the firing party drawn up in front."

" George, you are mad; the fever which followed your wounds cannot have left you yet."

" I am not mad; I know what I am saying, and I feel an inward conviction that we shall not be shot to-morrow. Let this game decide. See, you are twenty-six ahead. If I win we shall live. If I lose we shall die."

" I accept the omen," replied Gerald, with a faint smile.

George dealt the cards to himself and opponent.

The latter scored between fifteen and twenty. George only eight in both hand and crib.

" What do you say now, George? The game is as hopeless as our own chance of life."

" *Nil desperandum!* It is my deal, I think."

George dealt the cards.

This time Gerald held nothing and made nothing by play.

Captain George held eight in hand, twelve in crib, and played four.

Soon Gerald Leigh was within seven of the winning point, while the other still wanted twenty-six.

Gerald played a six. George played another, two holes; Gerald a third, six holes; and his opponent a fourth, twelve holes—in all fourteen. This, with the last card and ten in hand, brought George within one hole of winning.

Gerald held nothing in hand but the six he had made by play, which also brought him to the last hole but one.

The situation was certainly exciting. Gerald, in spite of his incredulity, could not help being, in a measure, infected by what he considered the fatalism and superstition of his friend.

Captain George had declared his firm conviction that they should not die, and both had accepted this game as the gauge of the truth or falseness of his presentiment, if such it could be called.

It was the Englishman's deal. Each wanted but a single point of the game.

Captain George dealt the cards, and then cut for crib. Gerald did likewise.

"Cut me a card," said the former.

Gerald was about to do so.

"Stay, Gerald. I will tell you the card you will cut me. It will win me the game. You will cut me a knave."

"Pshaw! nonsense!" replied Gerald, reaching his hand over to the pack.

Notwithstanding his incredulity, his hand trembled slightly, and he could not resist a feeling of mingled hope and anxiety which possessed him that the words of his friend might prove true.

"What nonsense," he muttered, "to pay a moment's attention to such old women's tales. Here goes."

He cut the cards.

George turned up the top one.

It was a knave, and he won.

At the same instant voices were heard in the next room, where the two officers were.

Gerald, in spite of himself, almost trembled with excitement at this strange fulfilment of the prophecy, and a thrill of hope passed through his frame.

" Perhaps, after all, there is something in this fellow's presentiments," he thought.

" Hush!" he exclaimed in a low tone, and grasping Captain George by the arm, " that is the voice of Lupus Rock."

" Yes—and it is the beginning of the end!"

CHAPTER LIX.

ANXIOUS MOMENTS.

BOTH Gerald Leigh and the Englishman were silent, and listened intently to what was passing in the next room.

" Any news, Mr. Rock—anything fresh?" they heard Captain James say.

" No—nothing. I heard at the Fremont, in Pennsylvania Avenue, that you and Vavasour were on guard, so I thought I would look round to hear what news you had. There has been a council of generals, has there not, this afternoon, Captain James, in which your uncle took part?"

" Yes; and a stormy debate the old general tells me it was."

" By the way," interrupted Lupus, " I thought, as I was coming to visit soldiers on guard, I could not do better than bring something with me."

Lupus produced the two bottles of wine.

" Here are two bottles of the very finest Senator Gayle has in his cellar. In his eyes the few dozen left are beyond price, and I had the greatest difficulty in prevailing on my cousin Stella to let me have them."

" Oh, your cousins! I forgot to ask for them. Are they well?"

" Quite, thank you. As I was saying, I had some

difficulty in prevailing on my fair cousin to give me the wine, knowing how the senator prized it. Have you a corkscrew?"

The corkscrew was produced, and the prisoners next heard the cork of the bottle drawn.

This done, glasses were brought out, and Lupus seated himself at the table with the two officers.

" Your cousin, Miss Stella, then, knew you were coming here to-night?"

" Oh, yes—I told her so."

Captain James looked proud and pleased, and raising the glass before him, said,—

" Well, sir, I drink to the health of your charming cousins."

He drained the glass, and continued,—

" Perhaps it was her own fair hands which brought up these bottles of rare wine? if so we are doubly honoured."

" No," replied Lupus carelessly; " I asked her for the key and fetched them myself. But I was going to ask you the result of the council to-day. On what have the President and General decided? Are our forces to advance at once into Virginia, and give battle to the enemy or——Stay, can we be heard in the next room?"

" By the prisoners? Yes; but what matter? Poor devils, in a few hours they will be shot."

" Is there no hope of their lives being spared, of a reprieve, at the last moment?" asked Lupus.

" Not the least; the subject was incidentally mentioned at the council, and the idea of pardon or commutation of sentence was utterly scouted. It is now midnight; in eight hours they will go forth to their execution."

A gleam of savage joy shot across the features of Lupus Rock, as he heard these words.

Gerald Leigh and Captain George also heard, and although they needed not this confirmation, for they had long given up all hopes of clemency on the part of the authorities, still it sent a chill through them, in spite of their fortitude.

Gerald Leigh was seated at the table, briefly employed

in writing. He had **written** and addressed a letter to his father, containing **his** last wishes and requests. Letters also to friends and **relations** he had written and sealed, **and he was** now engaged **in** writing one to his brother Darcy.

Captain George had ceased pacing up and **down the** room, and was leaning with folded arms against the door, so as to hear all the conversation in the next room. He was naturally **pale**, but now, what **from** weakness caused by his wounds—the subsequent **fever**, and his desperate situation—a pallor as of death was on his handsome features. It **was** not, however, the pallor of fear, for the lips were tightly compressed, and his heart beat as calmly and regularly as if in sleep.

A clock in the barrack-yard pealed forth the midnight hour.

Immediately the clang of arms and the tramp of feet are heard outside.

" Sergeant of the guard!" Captain James calls out.

The sergeant entered.

At the same moment the voice of the sentry at the gate is heard challenging.

" Who goes there ?"

" Jupiter, by Jingo ! "

The men composing the sergeant's guard laughed at this reply to the challenge.

" Halt ! and give the word "——

" Baltimore ! "

On this word being given, the sentry lowered his rifle, which he had brought to the charge, and permitted the stranger to approach.

" Well, nigger, what do you want ? "

" De officer of de guard."

" In the guard-room to the left," said the sentry, allowing him to pass through the wicket.

Jupiter marched boldly in, and stood in the presence of the two officers, Lupus Rock, and the sergeant, who was just receiving his orders from Captain James.

" How far do the pickets of your regiment extend ? "

" Our furthest commands a view of the river and the rebel forces on the other side."

" Let the sentries be doubled everywhere in view of the river.   There was an alarm last night—a spy attempted to cross in a boat."

The sergeant saluted, and was turning away, when Captain James stopped him.

" Sergeant, you have not got the new word for the night. It is past twelve."

" I beg pardon, sir. I thought, perhaps, it was not to be changed."

" The word is changed every twenty-four hours.   For to-day, it is ' Bunker's Hill.' "

The man again saluted and went out.

" Fours, left, quick, march."

Then the sergeant's guard tramped off on their rounds, Jupiter remaining standing before the two.

CHAPTER LX.

CROSS-EXAMINED.

" WELL, nigger," said Captain James, " what do you want? who sent you here? the devil, eh? "

" No, massa, de debil no send me.   When de debil want you, massa, he come hisself an' fetch you."

James laughed at this retort, and Jupiter grinned from ear to ear.

" Well, who sent you, and what do you want? "

" General—general ——— Oh, my lud a Gor a mighty, massa, I forget de name, but it was some general told me to come here."

" What for?"

" To gib myself up."

" To give yourself up? "

" Yes, massa, I's a contraband escaped from the house of bondage, and from the hands of the wicked."

" Oh, you 're a runaway slave?"

" Dat's it, 'xactly, massa ; my boss, he's a orful rebel, so dis childe bein' a Unioner—a reg'lar screaming Star and Stripe coon—makes tracks for de glorious Union army; and here he is, and now de question comes, what de debil you's guine to do with him, eh, massa?"

Jupiter acted his part admirably, so that neither Captain James nor Vavasour for a moment doubted him.

"Well, what did the general, whoever he was, send you here for? How do you know he was a general?"

"Because he told me so, massa; he sey, ' Jist you go to the nearest guard-room, nigger, and report yourself—say I sent you, General ——' (I forget de name—' de password 's Baltimore,') and wid dat he rides off, an' I come straight here."

"Where did you meet this general?"

"Out on de road, about a mile towards the ferry."

"Oh, it's all right, one of the generals going to ride round the outposts to satisfy himself that a good look-out is kept—let the beggar go," said Vavasour.

"Wait a minute, let us see if we can get any information from him."

"You have just come from the rebel lines. Where did you cross the river?"

"At de ferry."

"Harper's Ferry?"

"Yes, massa."

"Are there any rebel troops near there?"

"Dere's a regiment of cavalry twelve miles off, an' dey reconnoitres down by the ferry every day."

"Is that all?" asked Captain James, in surprise, "I thought they had a large force a short distance from the river."

"Dere's only two regiments of infantry and four of cavalry on dis side of Fredericksburg, except at Manassas, where dere's a horse artillery regiment, and two Carolina volunteer regiments."

"Is that all? I thought they had at least forty thousand men near the river."

Had Captain James said twice forty thousand, he would have been nearer the mark.

"Forty thousand, massa," said Jupiter, rolling his eyes in affected astonishment; "why, I don't believe as dere's forty thousand in de ole army of de South, and what dere is, is all a lot of ragged skunks as would rather run a mile than fight a minit."

"A hopeful chance for the rebellion, Vavasour," said Captain James, with a smile.

"Bah!" said Vavasour, contemptuously; "if ever they stand up before our troops they will go down like chaff before the wind."

"Not much doubt of that, I think," replied the other, in a half-satisfied tone. "What men they have are all rowdies, and as for their officers, the Southern planters, the climate has rendered them effete, and made them, physically and morally, of a lower type than a hardy Northern gentleman."

How utterly absurd and unfounded their opinions were, the desperate resolve with which Southern soldiers, led by Southern officers, have fought against the vast hordes of the North, has sufficiently shown.

At this time, however, such opinions were in vogue, and it was confidently predicted that the rebellion would be crushed out in three months at the latest, and the ringleaders hanged.

It now became a question with Captain James what to do with the negro. He did not for a moment doubt the truth of the latter's story, but was at a loss to understand with what object the general, whoever he might be, had given him the pass-word and sent him in.

While the officer was thus deliberating with himself, Jupiter was carefully scanning the guard-room, and noticing the position of doors and windows.

The door which opened into the prison room was an object of close scrutiny. His eye rested for a moment on the iron bolts, then on the massive padlock which secured the door, and then wandering round the room, on a large key hanging above Captain James's head. This he conjectured was the key of the padlock.

Gerald Leigh was still busily employed in writing, when Jupiter appeared before the two officers, while Captain George still stood with folded arms leaning against the door.

At the first sound of Jupiter's voice Gerald paused in his writing, and the next instant started to his feet, and reaching the door stood listening and almost trembling with excitement.

Captain George, surprised at this sudden change from apathy to interest, even excitement, was about to speak, when Gerald grasped his arm and signified him to be silent.

Gerald at once knew the voice of the negro, who had at one time been a slave on his father's plantation, having been presented with his freedom for eminent services rendered. He was well aware of the gratitude and affection Jupiter bore the family, and on hearing his voice a wild hope possessed him that the presence of tho coloured man was in some way connected with himself.

He listened intently to the whole conversation, and when Jupiter's examination was finished, and he was about being dismissed, he resolved to speak, in order to let him know, if he were not already aware of the fact, that he was there confined.

Accordingly he knocked loudly at the door to call attention.

Captain James rose, and coming to the door, asked—

" What is it you want ? "

" We have no water—I am thirsty," replied Gerald.

The latter listened intently to catch any exclamation of surprise which might escape the negro at the well-known voice.

But none came.

'Ah !' thought Gerald, ' he is not surprised—he knows I am here. There must be something in this. Surely he would not come with such a tale, every word of which I know to be false, without some object ? Perhaps a rescue is contemplated ? A rescue ?—impossible ! Nothing less than an army could rescue us by force from the midst of the Federal lines ! '

And the hopes which began to rise in the doomed man's mind were dashed aside when he thought of the many brigades and regiments around the outposts, the pickets, and the double chain of sentries.

"You shall have water immediately the guard returns," Captain James said, "they have gone round on relief duty."

Gerald did not reply, and Captain James, turning to Jupiter, said,—

"Well, you fellow, I have not the least idea why you have been sent here ; but as you have the word, you can pass on into Washington, and report yourself again in the morning."

Berry good, massa."

So saying, Jupiter turned, and was about leaving, when Lupus Rock addressed him.

"Look here, nigger, I've seen you before, have I not?"

"Lor-a-mussy only knows, massa," replied Jupiter, gazing innocently in the speaker's face ; "dis chile don't remember."

Lupus was silent, and seemed trying to recollect. He had a confused memory of the negro in connection with a fiddle, but could not sufficiently arrange his thoughts to say when or where they had met. In good truth, he had seen Jupiter dozens of times in attendance on Darcy Leigh in New York, before the seizure of the Spitfire ; and the last he had seen of him was when he sat on the capstan of the sloop, and played defiantly and mockingly "Yankee Doodle" as she steamed past the admiral's ship.

It was well for Jupiter that the memory of Lupus for this once failed him. Again and again he racked his brains to recall the circumstance to his mind, but in vain.

"Look here, sir," he said, after puzzling himself for a minute or so, during which time the negro stood innocently and humbly before him, "you can play the violin, can't you? Where did I hear you last?"

"No, massa," replied Jupiter, with well-feigned sorrow, "I ain't a musicianer—leastways, not on no musical implements ; but dis chile can sing. Would massa like a little melody?"

"No, no!" said Captain James impatiently ; "we don't want your melody. Be off!"

Jupiter, nothing loth departed.

"I would give something to remember where I have seen that fellow's face before," said Lupus Rock, suspiciously; "for that I have seen him somewhere I am certain."

"Oh, nonsense! these niggers have all the same features and voices. I have often been deceived, myself. I suspect the fellow has never been north of the Potomac."

"I doubt it much."

Jupiter on getting outside the wicket, instead of making for Washington, walked quickly in the opposite direction, and when out of sight of the sentry, turned off from the road, and started off at a run.

The two officers and Lupus Rock were now again alone; and broaching the remaining bottle of Webster Gayle's choice old wine, resumed the conversation which the sergeant of the guard and Jupiter had interrupted.

"What, then, was definitely decided at the council to-day?" asked Lupus.

"All the members were in favour of energetic action; for fighting a great battle, and decisively defeating the rebels, driving them out of Virginia."

"When is it proposed to march against them?"

"Some of the generals were for immediate action; but the commander-in-chief, General Scott, pronounced emphatically against it. Ultimately, it was decided that in about a month's time the whole army should leisurely cross the Potomac at Harper's Ferry; and about the middle of June—that is to say, in about six weeks' time—advance into Virginia, viâ Manassas Gap, defeating the rebels if they oppose, which is in itself an absurdity; and driving them before them if they think discretion the better part of valour, which, doubtless, they will do."

Captain George and Gerald Leigh, in the next room, heard every word of this conversation, and much which subsequently followed. The Federal officer went on to relate to Lupus Rock all that he had gathered as to the result of the council of war, and Gerald and Captain George in the course of half-an-hour were thoroughly conversant with the projected movements of the army of the Potomac.

After partaking of one glass from the second bottle of wine, Lupus Rock rose, and wishing the officers good night, left the guard-room.

James and Vavasour continued talking and laughing for some minutes after his departure, and then there ensued a long silence.

For a time Gerald and the Englishman believed that the two officers had left shortly after Lupus, but they were soon disabused of that idea. The silence was quickly succeeded by long slow breathing, which convinced the prisoners that their guardians slept. They could hear the measured tramp of the sentinel outside the gate, and the occasional rattle of his rifle as he halted in his patrol and grounded it.

Half an hour passed and the guards returned from their rounds. The sergeant entered the guard-room with the intention of reporting "all well," but finding his officers both asleep, retired without attempting to awake them.

At two o'clock, according to orders, they were again to go on their rounds. At a few minutes before the time, the sergeant having marshalled his men in the yard, again entered the guard-room, and found the two officers still asleep.

"Humph!" he muttered, "asleep; the wine seems to have told a tale. Shall I wake them?"

He appeared to deliberate for a minute, and then, having apparently made up his mind, marched his men off.

Scarcely had he passed them through the gate, than the clock in the barrack yard pealed two.

Then the footsteps of the soldiers faded away in the distance, and all was still.

The deep breathing of the two officers in the guard-room alone broke the deadly silence.

Suddenly the sentry at the gate challenged,—

"Who goes there?"

"A friend!"

" Halt ! and give the word———"

" Bunker's Hill."

Gerald, who had again seated himself at the table, started to his feet, and gave vent to an exclamation of astonishment and bewilderment.

" What is it ? " asked Captain George.

"That voice—my brother, Darcy Leigh!—by Heavens!"

CHAPTER LXI.

A CRITICAL SITUATION.

No sooner had the sergeant's party disappeared in the distance, than three figures, who had been attentively watching them, advanced boldly towards the sentry at the gate. They did not come from the road, but from the direction of a clump of trees, a few hundred yards to the left.

These three figures were, as the reader has doubtless guessed, those of Darcy Leigh, Darby Kelly, and the negro Jupiter.

Darcy at once replied to the sentry's challenge, and advanced boldly up to him, followed by the others.

" What is it?—what do you want ? " asked the sentinel, on receiving the password.

" The officer of the guard," replied Darcy, approaching the soldier.

" Pass on into the guard-room on the left," he replied, standing on one side so as to let them by.

Darcy Leigh, having placed himself on the threshold of the wicket, stopped and turned round to the sentry.

" Lend me your rifle," he said, quite coolly, reaching forth and laying his hand on the stock of the weapon, which the sentry had now shouldered.

" Hands off ! " said the astonished sentry, retreating a pace, and bringing it to the charge.

Darby Kelly was close behind him, and seeing the time for action had come, threw himself upon him, and before he could utter a cry had dashed him to the earth. His iron hand was in a second on the sentry's throat, which he compressed so tightly as nearly to choke him.

They were quite close to the wicket leading to the barrack yard, and although the unfortunate sentry had no opportunity of giving an alarm, still the struggle, brief as it was, was not entirely unaccompanied by noise.

Darcy and Jupiter stood for a moment, and listened in breathless anxiety.

But all within was quiet.

The sentry, on whose throat Darby still kept his iron grip, struggled once or twice to release himself, and then, with a choking gasp, lay still.

Darcy Leigh deliberately produced and opened a clasp-knife, and kneeling down, felt for the man's throat, and pressed the sharp point against it.

The man, who was not quite utterly insensible, gave vent to a gurgling groan as he felt the cold, sharp point of the knife.

Horrible must have been his sensation for those few moments.

"Now listen, my man," said Darcy, pushing the knife so as to break the skin, and inflict a slight wound.

The man, thinking his last hour had come, gave a desperate struggle.

"Another motion and you are a dead man!" said Darcy, in a deep whisper. "Your life is in your own hands. If you attempt to resist or raise any outcry, I cut your throat. Lie still, and you shall not be harmed. Darby, remove your hands."

Darby hesitated for a moment before he complied with this order.

"Take your hands away, Darby," repeated the other, "he will not resist."

The Irishman did so, and though free from his grip, the sentry lay perfectly motionless. He still felt the cold sharp point of the knife, and knew that the moment in which he struggled would be his last. He was utterly ignorant of the cause or meaning of this attack, but fully realized the fact that the aggressors were terribly in earnest.

"Jupiter, the gag! Quick!"

The negro produced a piece of wood about six inches long, and forced it between the man's teeth, who suffered him to do so passively. He then bound a handkerchief around it so as to completely cover the mouth, and tied it tightly on by a piece of string around the back of his head. This done, Darcy rose from his knees, and removed the threatening knife from the prisoner's throat.

"Jupiter, remain here and watch this fellow; if he attempts to move kill him."

"All right, massa."

"Darby, come, follow me; no time is to be lost. The guard will be back in a few minutes."

Then Darcy passed quickly through the wicket and towards the guard-room, followed by Darby Kelly.

He fully expected a desperate struggle, for of course he knew from Jupiter that the two officers were there.

Judge, then, of his astonishment when he dashed in, a knife in one hand, and a revolver in the other, when he found that the place was only tenanted by two sleeping men.

Their flushed faces and heavy breathing at once caused him to surmise that they were intoxicated.

He cast a rapid glance around the room, until it rested upon the key hanging on the wall, as Jupiter had described to him. The Irishman stood sentry over the sleepers, while Darcy cautiously reached down the key.

Darby Kelly had brought with him the rifle taken from the sentinel, and now stood over the two sleepers, prepared to dash out the brains of the first who should be unfortunate enough to awake.

Not a word was spoken, and not a sound to be heard, but the regular breathing of the two officers.

Darcy having possessed himself of the key, advanced cautiously to the door and placed it in the padlock. It was impossible to turn it without making a slight noise, which, of course, was heard by the prisoners confined in the inner room.

Darcy feared that, not knowing who was thus tampering with the lock, one or other of them would call out to demand who was there.

His fears were well founded, for the next instant he heard the deep voice of his brother Gerald,—

"Who is there? It is not yet daylight. Surely, what few hours we have to live, may be left to us in peace——"

Gerald spoke loudly and angrily, for he had relinquished the idea that it was his brother's voice which had challenged the sentry as too improbable—almost impossible; for, in the first place, was not his brother dead? had he not had convincing and reliable testimony to that effect? He heard nothing of the struggle with the sentry, and as the two officers still gave evidence by their deep breathing that they slept, he imagined that all was well.

As soon as Darcy heard the voice of his brother angrily demanding who was there, he gave up all hopes of being able peaceably to effect their escape. The voice was both loud and deep, and he doubted not that it would certainly awaken the sleepers. Convinced of this, he withdrew the key from the padlock, and drawing his revolver, which he had again placed in his breast, he turned savagely round, prepared for a death-struggle.

To his astonishment, however, the two officers still slept as calmly as if the enemy were not in their camp.

"They must indeed have been drunk!" he muttered, "and yet I see but two bottles of wine, one half full. Surely it cannot be raw spirits they have been drinking?"

He raised one of the bottles, and placing it to his lips, just tasted it.

"Burgundy, by Jove! good wine, but not sufficient.y strong to account for this. A half-dozen bottles would scarcely suffice to make two men so helplessly drunk as these."

All this passed through his mind in less than a tenth of the time it has occupied in relating. Seeing that they still slept, he judged it advisable to bind and gag them at once.

They are too drunk to resist now, but if they should suddenly wake, it might undoubtedly give the alarm and bring others to their assistance.

The operation of binding and gagging was finally performed. To the utter bewilderment of Darcy Leigh, even this operation did not rouse them. An inarticulate grunt or so was the only result. Both were bound, gagged, and secured to the chairs on which they sat.

Then Darcy quickly unlocked the padlock, removed it, threw open the door, and stood in the presence of his brother Gerald and Captain George.

Gerald gazed for a moment in utter bewilderment. Could he believe his eyes? was it indeed his brother Darcy who stood before him? His features certainly, but the complexion was that of a mulatto. The next moment Darcy spoke, and the voice dissipated any doubts he had in his mind.

"Come," he said, "this is no time for explanations or questions. Escape—the way is open; and in an hour's time you may both be safely across the Potomac."

CHAPTER LXII.

ESCAPE AND RECAPTURE.

GERALD LEIGH, when really convinced that it was his brother, wasted no time in talk, but passed into the other room and gazed around it. The two officers were still sound asleep, bound and gagged. With but one glance of surprise at the tableau, he passed out, followed by Captain George, Darcy, and Darby Kelly.

Suddenly he paused at the wicket before passing through, and whispered in a low tone to his brother—

"The sentry—what about him?—must we kill him?"

"He is safe," was the reply; "come, let us haste."

And the next moment Gerald nearly fell over the prostrate body of the unfortunate soldier. Once clear of the barracks, they all started off at a good pace, Darby leading the way. He led them straight to the shelter of the clump of trees.

Scarcely had they reached there, and the tramp of a considerable body of men was heard approaching. Darcy knew that it was the sergeant's guard returning from the rounds.

"Quick—let us be on. The escape will be discovered in a few minutes."

All started off again with the exception of Darby, who remained behind. Darcy Leigh did not immediately miss him; when he did so, however, he halted.

"Where is the Irishman?" he asked in surprise of his brother, who was nearest to him.

But he was not to be seen, and Darcy hurried back to the clump of trees where they had rested for a few seconds. He met the faithful fellow, to whose devotion and courage he owed the success of the escape, just about to follow them. He held in his hand a bottle, from which he was drinking as he walked.

"Come on—are you mad?" said Darcy, grasping his arm.

"All right, yer honour; I thought it would have been a murthering shame entirely to lave the wine, so I made so bowld as to bring it with me. And, be jabers, I have just finished the last gulp."

With these words he threw the bottle away, and hurried on with Darcy. They had but just rejoined the other two, when they heard a loud outcry at the gate of the barracks. The sentry had been discovered bound and gagged, as also the two officers in the guard-room. They heard the shouts of the sergeant, the rattle of arms, and the discharge of several rifles at random.

"Bugler, blow the assembly—turn out the guard! Scour the woods!—the prisoners have escaped!"

Then the bugle pealed forth a loud blast—the assembly—and in half a minute the barrack-yard, before deserted, swarmed with some hundreds of soldiers, some in their shirts, others hastily arming, and getting their uniforms on.

Darcy and his companions did not wait to listen to the confusion, but started off at a run in the direction of the river, which was about a mile ahead at the nearest point.

The darkness of the night favoured them, and soon the sound of the shouts, cries, and words of command died away, and they halted, thoroughly out of breath, by the side of the road leading from Harper's Ferry to Washington—the same road on which Captain George and Gerald had been captured, weeks previously, in their attempt to cross the river.

By common consent they halted by the side of the road, and threw themselves flat on the ground with the double object of concealment and rest.

After a repose of a couple of minutes Darcy rose.

"Come," he said to the others, "let us get across the river—we are now close to it. All can swim, and in a few minutes more we shall be in safety."

Gerald, Captain George, and Jupiter followed his example, and prepared again to start.

But Darby Kelly remained on the ground, and gave no signs of moving.

"Come on," said Darcy, touching him with his foot.

This produced no effect.

"What is the meaning of this?" muttered Darcy; "poor fellow! he must have been wounded in the struggle with the sentry, and has fainted. We can't leave him. What must be done?"

At that moment the sound of horses' hoofs was heard in the distance, coming from the direction of Harper's Ferry.

"Hark!—the mounted patrol!" cried Darcy. "Quick, Darby, my brave fellow, rouse yourself, or we shall be discovered."

At that instant the moon burst through a cloud and bathed the whole scene with light.

They could see coming down the road a body of cavalry; they were cantering on in loose order, some in the road, others among the trees on each side. In another moment the horsemen would be upon them, and they would be inevitably discovered.

Darcy stooped, and beckoning Gerald to assist him,

frantically endeavoured to raise the prostrate form of
Darby Kelly, but was unable to succeed, for the Irishman was fully sixteen stone, and lay helpless and inert
as a log.

Then, to his utter disgust and despair, he discovered
that he was not wounded—not dead—but asleep, fast as
a rock.

"All is lost!" exclaimed Darcy; "let us resist to the
last, and die fighting."

The next moment a shout from the foremost of the
horsemen apprised them they were discovered, and the
next they were upon them.

"Cut them down if they do not surrender!" they
heard the voice of an officer say.

Darcy fired his revolver at the foremost; it missed,
and with another shout to surrender, which passed
unheeded, they were ridden down, and a dozen troopers,
leaping from their saddles, hastened to secure them.

So sudden and vigorous was the onslaught, that effec-
tual resistance was out of the question; and, to the
bitter mortification of the four, they were secured without having been able to unhorse a man, and without
themselves receiving a wound. And this on the very
verge of success.

Bound and guarded closely, they were compelled to
march each between two troopers on the road towards
Washington.

Darcy, till this, had been hopeful and sanguine of
success. Now, however, despair took possession of his
soul.

"It is our fate," he muttered to himself; "we must
die!"

Even Captain George now gave way to deep gloom.

"My presentiment, then, was false," he thought; "we
must die!"

As for Gerald Leigh, he resigned himself calmly to
his fate; and, without a word, they were marched on to
their doom.

CHAPTER LXIII.

A TERRIBLE FATE.

In the sudden confusion of the attack, and the darkness combined, the moon being again overclouded, Darby Kelly, who lay on the ground asleep, and on whom the noise and shouts produced no more effect than the previous efforts of Darcy Leigh, remained unnoticed, and the other prisoners were marched off without him. Nor did any of the four miss him, each thinking that he too had been captured, and was being carried prisoner to Washington.

They walked on in silence for some distance, until, at a word of command, the troopers halted, when, after a moment's consultation between the officers, the word was given "left wheel," and they struck off from the road and in a direction away from the river, not towards Washington or the camp, but as if about to make a circuit so as to avoid both.

Darcy Leigh, who knew more of the state of affairs in general than the other two, was somewhat surprised at this.

'Where can they be taking us?' he thought; 'strange that they should not at once conduct us to head-quarters in the camp.'

As for Gerald and Captain George, they knew nothing of the Federal movements or position of the troops, and thought, naturally, that they were proceeding straight to a detachment of troops, or perhaps to the head-quarters of the army, which, for all they knew to the contrary, might be at Baltimore, in place of Washington.

They had progressed but about a hundred yards from the road when once again the word "Halt" was suddenly and sharply given. On both these occasions both Gerald and Darcy Leigh fancied they had before heard the voice.

"Bind each of your prisoners to a tree," the same officer said, sternly; "quick, we have no time to lose."

In an instant Gerald, Captain George, Darcy, and

C C

Jupiter were dragged to four trees close together, and securely bound.

'Great God!' thought Darcy Leigh, 'they are going to shoot us in cold blood in the dark, and without even the pretence of a trial.'

"Cowards! murderers! ruffians!" shouted Captain George, who also interpreted this movement in the same manner, "do your worst, I defy you. Shoot us—I don't fear death. I will show you bastard Yankees how an Englishman can die."

The officer deigned no reply to this, but gave the terrible order to his troopers,—

"Load your carbines, my men."

The prisoners heard in the ring of the ramrods their death-knell, and resolved to meet death as brave men should.

"George, my boy," said Gerald calmly, to his friend, who was nearest to him, "how much now for your presentiment?"

"I was a fool. I do not fear death, but it is a bitter thought that I must die while my mortal enemy, whom I have sworn to slay, still walks the earth."

"Gerald, brother, adieu, our hour is come," said Darcy; "I have done my best to save you, and in these, my last moments, am comforted by the thought that we die together."

"Darcy, farewell. I could die happier were it not that you have lost your life through attempting to save mine."

"Good by, Jupiter, my brave fellow," said Darcy, "these brutes will not spare you."

"Oh, my Lor a God a'mussy, massa Darcy, I isn't afraid if you isn't. I know I'se goin' to glory. It won't take long, will it, massa Darcy?"

"What, going to glory, as you call it? I hope not."

At this moment a trooper advanced to each, carbine in hand.

No help was near; there was no hope; they knew they must die.

"Farewell, brother, once more farewell," replied Darcy.

"Farewell, gentlemen both," said Captain George. "I only know one of you, but I take the liberty of offering both a piece of advice. Ask these murderers to shoot you through the head. I have never tried it, but I am convinced it's the easiest way."

"Shoot me through the head, if you please," he added to the trooper in front of him, "I hate to have bullet holes bored in my clothes."

The officer in command gave a signal of impatience, and the four troopers advanced each close to his victim, and presented their carbines.

But we are bound, in gallantry, after so long an absence, to return to the sisters, Stella and Angela Gayle.

CHAPTER LXIV.

LOVE, DEATH, AND HOPE.

WHILE the events related in our last were in progress, Stella Gayle remained on the balcony, wrapped only in a shawl to protect her from the cold night air.

She watched Lupus Rock go forth on his errand, accompanied by a negro, his fears of the ghost not allowing him to go alone.

She saw the latter return in about half an hour, and sending for him, learned that her cousin had so far complied with her commands, and had entered the guard-room where the man had left him.

A timepiece in the room chimed the midnight hour, and soon afterwards her sister Angela came out on to the balcony.

"Stella, are you not going to retire?" she asked.

"And why?" asked Stella, bitterly—"to sleep? Do you think I can sleep, when to-morrow morn the earthly career of our friend, Gerald Leigh, is to be brought to a close?"

"Stella, it is the will of God—willingly would I lay down my life to save his."

The voice of Angela trembled; she hesitated for a

moment, then threw herself on her knees, and buried her head in her sister's lap.

"Oh, Stella, you know not, you never could know how deeply, passionately I have loved him—my brave, my noble Gerald—God give me strength to bear this trial."

"My poor child," said Stella, raising Angela's head, and kissing her forehead with all an elder sister's motherly fondness, "is it indeed so? But I perceived it long since."

"Oh, Stella, forgive me. I could not help it. He is so brave, so kind; and then do you know, I have thought sometimes that he loved me."

"He did—he did—I am sure he did," said Stella. "I have seen it in his looks, his actions, a hundred times."

Under any other circumstances how proudly happy would these words have made the gentle Angela; but now they only made the bitterness of the eternal parting the more bitter.

"And he must die to-morrow," she cried with a burst of uncontrollable anguish; "die, die! Oh, God of Heaven! God of the good! Great God of battles! wilt thou suffer this?"

Her voice rose almost to a shriek of agony as she gave vent to this appeal.

Her sister, fearing from her sister's intense and unusual excitement, that her mind would give way, sought to soothe her.

"Angela, do not give way thus. Listen to me. *There is yet hope.*"

Angela gazed wildly, incredulously in her face.

"Hope! hope! it cannot be, Stella; you are seeking to deceive me."

"No—no; I repeat there is hope."

"What hope? are they not both to be shot to-morrow, he and the brave Englishman? What hope can there be? who can save them now?"

"There is no certainty," replied Stella; "but there is a hope. They may be saved yet. There is one who is about to make an attempt, and who may save them."

"Who? who?"

"Darcy Leigh."

"Darcy Leigh—Stella, you are seeking to deceive me, or are mad. Darcy Leigh is dead."

"Darcy Leigh is not dead."

"Not dead! Did we not see him shot down on the deck of the Spitfire?"

"Darcy Leigh is alive. I saw him this very night—not two hours since."

Angela started to her feet and gazed in her sister's face. Had she taken leave of her senses? Seen Darcy Leigh that night? It was impossible, for Angela knew her sister had not left the house that day.

"I saw him to-night," continued Stella, calmly and deliberately; "he climbed up the balcony, and suddenly stood before me. At first I thought it was a spirit, and I believe I fainted, or nearly so. But it was no spirit—it was Darcy Leigh himself—disguised, and with his face stained like that of a mulatto. He came to endeavour to save his brother Gerald, and his object in climbing the balcony was to see you or me, and get all possible information as to where he was confined, the guard over him, and all other particulars."

"And you told him all, Stella; you received him with kindness, with joy? I need not ask—I know you did. Ah! there is, indeed, then, some hope. Darcy Leigh is a brave, noble fellow. Next to his brother, I like and admire him more than any man on earth. There is hope—more than hope. Darcy Leigh will succeed—I feel, I know he will. And Stella," she suddenly said, fixing her eyes on her sister, "you once called him coward!"

Stella coloured with confusion and shame at her sister's words. She remembered how harshly she had spoken and acted to Darcy, impelled by her pride, and her heart smote her.

"Yes, Angela, there is hope. Darcy promised a signal if he succeeded. That signal was to be a rocket, sent up from yonder clump of trees, on the other side of the river."

"Where? Point it out to me, Stella."

She did so, and continued,—

"If we do not see that rocket shoot up to heaven before daybreak, then, indeed, all is lost."

"Let us remain here and watch for it, Stella."

Stella proceeded to do so.

"Come, let us arrange ourselves, so that we can watch the little hill from which the signal of Gerald's safety is to ascend."

Accordingly they placed a chair in the corner of the balcony, facing the Virginian hills, on the other side of the Potomac.

Stella seated herself in the chair, and Angela at her feet.

"We will take turns in watching, Stella," she said; "you shall have the first half-hour."

Stella consented, and wrapping a part of her shawl around her sister's head and shoulders, silently watched for the hoped-for rocket.

She fixed her eyes on the little hill in the distance, as though momentarily expecting to see the fiery messenger shoot up in the sky, although it was impossible that, even if Darcy Leigh succeeded in his desperate attempt, he could reach there for several hours at least.

Angela, in whose gentle heart the fire of hope again burned, wearied out with grief and fatigue, soon sank into a gentle slumber—the sweet, calm sleep of innocence.

CHAPTER LXV.

"TAKE THIS HOUND TO HIS KENNEL."

At the close of the first half-hour Lupus Rock returned. Stella heard his footsteps pass through the courtyard and into the house, and heard him ascend the stairs into the room where a light burned. She heard him throw himself on a couch, and in less than a minute his deep, heavy breathing proclaimed that he slept.

Stella aroused her sister.

"Angela, awake! My half-hour's watch has long expired."

Angela gladly undertook her vigil, and Stella, rising, went into the room where lay her sleeping cousin, snoring like a pig.

She gazed at him contemptuously, and said to herself,—

" Good!—so far the scheme works well. He has drank of the wine, as have also the two officers on guard, Vavasour and James. They, by this time, are as sound asleep as he."

Then she touched a small hand-bell, and a negro servant answered the summons—for, of course, the household had not retired so long as their mistresses were up.

" Go call Pompey," she said to the man, who quickly reappeared with that sable personage.

" Remove that hound to his kennel," she said, pointing to Lupus Rock on the couch.

The negroes proceeded to obey their mistress's command, and raised the sleeping form of Lupus.

They carried him down stairs, and, arrived at the bottom, paused with their burden, who still slept deeply.

" I say, nigger," said Pompey, " dis here's a rum start; let's put him down an' consultate."

They did so.

" Drunk, by golly ! " said Pompey.

" Drunk, by golly ! " said the other.

" What did Missa Stella say, nigger ? " asked Pompey.

" Take dis hound to his kennel."

" Whar is de kennel ? "

" At de back, whar de dogs lib, ob course."

" An' what is we to do, eh ?   Answer me dat, nigger," asked Pompey, severely.

" Why take dis hound to de kennel."

And then both niggers set up a loud chuckle, and raising their burden, bore him off to the dog-kennel.

" By golly, ain't he heavy ! " said nigger number one.

" By golly, ain't he drunk ! " said nigger number two.

Lupus Rock was duly deposited in the kennel, and the

two negroes returned to the house, delighted at having thus literally carried out their mistress's order.

As for Lupus he slept there as soundly as he would have done in his own bed.

First one hound, then another, came up and sniffed inquiringly around him, and then, apparently satisfied, went off and left him.

It was fortunate that Gerald Leigh's big dog Lion was not of their number, or probably all that would have been found of Lupus in the morning would have been his boots and buttons.

CHAPTER LXVI.

WATCHING FOR THE ROCKET.

STELLA GAYLE, after giving the order respecting her sleeping cousin, which the negroes so willingly and literally executed, again joined her sister on the balcony, who had taken her place and was gazing fixedly out towards the little hill in the distance, whence they both hoped to see shoot up to the sky the signal rocket.

The wind howled and moaned among the trees, and whistled around the house, causing the sisters to draw their cachmere shawl yet closer around them. Yet still they kept to their posts.

The only sounds borne on the breeze were the distant challenge of the watchful sentinels, and occasionally the voice of drunken revellers in the city, who even at that hour still strolled the streets or crowded the bar-rooms.

The dreary ticking of the timepiece in the room and the beating of their own hearts were the only other sounds to break the deadly silence of the night.

One o'clock—half-past—two—the clock kept ticking —the wind kept moanfully sighing—the sisters wearily watching.

And all was still.

No rocket shot up from that hill on which such anxious eyes are bent.

The clock chimed two.

Shortly afterwards Angela, who was watching as only a man whose life, or a woman whose love depends on it, can watch; and Stella, kneeling at her feet, gazing out on to the Virginian hills, were startled by a sudden alarm. They could plainly hear shouts, the report of firearms, and bugle calls.

The sisters clung tightly to each other and listened. Stella gazing earnestly out in the direction of the alarm; while Angela, true to her vigil, kept her eyes fixed on the little hill.

The alarm they heard was that following the discovery of the escape of the prisoners.

Presently all again was still.

They waited, watched, and listened, little knowing that those on whom their thoughts were fixed were free and flying for their lives towards the river.

Another half-hour.

The wind still howled and moaned among the trees, the clock still ticked dismally in the room, and the sisters still patiently watched.

But they little knew that those on whom their thoughts were fixed had been free, had well-nigh made good their escape, and in the very height of their best hopes had been again captured, and were at that very moment being marched, gloomy and spirit-broken, back to their prisons—back to their doom.

Another hour passed. Still no meteor light dashed up into the sky from that Virginian hill.

A dismal howling was then heard from the yard at the back of the house.

A prolonged howl, half mournful, half savage.

"Heavens! Stella, what is that?"

"Gerald's dog Lion, whom I have kept, in spite of his having bitten our worthy cousin Lupus."

"Is it an omen, Stella? You have heard the Irish legend of the Banshee's shriek,—is the faithful dog of our doomed friend the Banshee?"

" Hush, Angela, there is yet hope."

She spoke of hope—she knew not that Gerald, Darcy, and Captain George were at that moment in the hands of the troopers—bound, unarmed, helpless, escape impossible.

Another hour. No light shot up into the sky from that dark clump across the river. Still the wind howled and moaned among the trees—the clouds flew in dense dark masses overhead, scarcely suffering the moon to show her cold face for a second—the timepiece ticked monotonously in the room; while, ever and anon, Gerald's great dog in the yard set up its dismal howl.

At that very moment the four prisoners were bound to trees, with a dragoon with loaded carbine in front of each, awaiting their fate. Suddenly the sharp report of fire-arms broke on the stillness of the night—a report as of several pieces discharged in rapid succession.

Then, again, all was quiet, save the moaning of the wind, the ticking of the clock, and the howling of the dog.

A shiver stole over Stella's whole frame—she knew not why.

That single sharp discharge, followed by silence, jarred painfully on her feelings. Angela clung yet closer to her, and they waited, watched, and listened.

But no other sound broke the quiet of the night. Even the wind, which had previously been high, now sank; and whereas it howled and whistled before, now only moaned feebly.

The dog, too, after one prolonged howl, was silent. The ticking clock, alone, and the beating of their own hearts, were the only sounds to break the dreadful calm.

Half an hour passed, and Angela, raising her fair young face, looked sadly, beseechingly in the pale one of her sister, and asked,—

" Stella, is there hope ? "

" Hope on, and pray."

Then all again was silent, Angela, as before, burying her face in her sister's lap.

Another half-hour, unbroken by a sound.

Stella Gayle, with compressed lips and fixed glassy stare, gazes forth to that Virginian hill in the distance.

Alas! all there is dark as the tomb. No light shoots up to the heavens, and as minute after minute passes on, the blackness of despair begins to creep over her soul.

"Stella, is there hope?" again Angela asks, again looking distractedly in her face.

But Stella has no hope to give, nor can Angela see any, even the slightest gleam in those pale, calm, lovely features.

Once again the younger sister buries her head in Stella's lap, who still watches on with desperate tenacity, even though the last spark be all but extinguished.

When next Angela raises her head she does not speak, but only looks in the pale face of her sister. Then she hurriedly, shudderingly casts a glance around her—first to that Virginian hill whence they have so long looked in vain for comfort, then her eyes sweep the horizon round by the west, to the north, to the east.

The blood freezes in her veins as she perceives a faint light in the clouds.

The day is about to break, the last sun which the prisoners will ever see, she thinks, is about to rise.

Alas! she saw them not, bound to trees more than two hours back, with those stern troopers facing them, loaded carbines in hand.

Nor can she see them now.

Again the gentle head is bowed down, and still Stella gazes fixedly out across the river.

For two hours she has never once removed her eyes from that little hill with the dark clump of trees at the top.

Minutes flit by, the solitary cock crows out its challenge to the orb of day to appear ; soon others follow.

Then is heard a distant bugle blast, then another, and another, as they sound the *reveillé.*

The faint gleam of light in the east deepens, lengthens, widens.

The pale, feeble grey brightens, and soon red hues mingle with it.

And now, not only in the east, but all around, the grey light of dawn steals on. The distant city of Washington, which was but a few minutes before but a dark mass, now gradually emerges from the gloom. First the whitest and most prominent houses appear, then the whole city, with its noble buildings, and wide, regular streets.

A mist hangs over the river and a heavy morning dew is falling, which wets the thin dresses of the sisters, and spangles the rich luxuriant hair of Stella, falling dishevelled over her head and shoulders.

What a study for a painter! Stella divested of her shawl, which she has wrapped closely round the head and shoulders of Angela, who kneels at her feet, clinging passionately, desperately to her, afraid to raise her face and learn that the last, the very last ray of hope has gone.

Stella, in her close-fitting evening dress, bare-headed, bare-shouldered, yet feeling neither the cold dew nor the colder morning blast. Though a hurricane tore over her head, what matter? Though the wind should blow, and the clouds pour down rain, sleet, hail, or snow, what matter to that fair girl with the large dark eyes, gazing fixedly, with desperate tenacity on that little Virginian hill?

She keeps her vigil bravely; nor till the sun shall have risen above the sky, driving before him the shadows of the night and the mists of the morning, will she relinquish her post and her watch.

Save for the rising and falling of her bosom, motionless as a statue, she might well serve as the model for one.

Observe the sloping fall of the shoulders, the graceful neck poising the small, antique head, with the true Grecian features and low forehead—in woman, so great a beauty.

Look at the faultlessly moulded arms, hands, and bust, and then at the rich dark hair, falling loose around her, all spangled with the morning dew; note the fixed, wrapt gaze of the large dark eye, and say, might she not be taken for the type of all that is lovely embodied in woman's form, and turned into marble?

Once again Angela raises her head, and with a feeling of desperate and utter despair, knows that all is lost—all hope gone.

When last she hid her face it was night, black, gloomy, dark.

Now it is almost day, and in a few more minutes the sun will be above the horizon.

One more long, last, lingering look towards that dark clump, which the dawning day reveals to be a number of tall pine trees, and Stella sadly, painfully, and with desperate unwillingness turns away her eyes and bends them on her sister.

For a moment they gaze in each other's faces.

"Angela, all hope is gone; let us pray to God to give rest to their souls."

Then she rose and knelt by the side of her sister.

"Great God of Heaven! have mercy on the souls of those for whom we have watched, and hoped, and prayed in vain. Pardon their sins towards Thee, their fellow-men, and their treason to their country."

Angela's lips moved, but no sound came from them, as she repeated the short, simple prayer after her sister.

For a few moments afterwards they remained, each putting up some little prayer, not even to be shared by a sister's confidence.

Angela rose first—Stella followed her; and they walked together towards the window, which opened on to the balcony, the scene of their sad and lonely vigil.

Angela passed on with slow steps, almost in a dream. Stella turns on the threshold, and gazes once more around.

Suddenly a shriek—a shriek torn from the very heart by desperate emotion—breaks from her.

She throws herself upon her knees, and, with clasped hands, gazes madly, with starting eyes, out across the Potomac.

Angela, ghastly pale with terror, rushes out again on to the balcony, and falls on her knees by her sister's side.

"Angela! Angela!" gasps Stella, "saved! saved!—look! look! Can it be true—or is it a dream?"

It was no dream. *From the dark clump of fir trees on that Virginian hill a rocket had shot aloft. High up above the trees it soared away into the sky*—dark from the background of black clouds.

Up, up it went, like a stream of fire, till it arrived at its extreme elevation.

Then it burst, and myriads of little stars scattered in all directions, and slowly fell to earth.

*   *   *   *   *

The bright sun rose in all his glory. He shone on that balcony, and on the inanimate forms of two young fair girls.

Weak nature had given way, and, locked in each other's arms, Stella and Angela lay in a deadly swoon.

CHAPTER LXVII.

A SLIGHT MISTAKE.

WHEN the dismounted troopers approached carbine in hand, each of the four prisoners made up their minds that the moment for their death had come. Jupiter, the nigger, dried his eyes and mumbled a prayer such as his limited education could at the moment command. Gerald, George, and Darcy, however, calmly and defiantly looked the men in the face.

One of the troopers then spoke:—

"Our orders are to shoot you instantly should you attempt to give the alarm or raise an outcry."

They were not, then, to be shot at once—each thought and wondered.

And then what was the meaning of the words about giving an alarm? What matter if they made the woods ring out with their shouts? It would be utterly futile.

Totally unable to understand this, they waited calmly in expectation of whatever fate might have in store for them.

And now is heard the distant rumbling of wheels, and, after a little time, the regular tramp of infantry.

At a word given in a low voice by the officer in command, all the troopers silently mounted and drew up in line.

Each man examined his carbine and the pistols in his holsters, and drew his sabre.

" Let not a man fire a shot without orders," said the deep voice of the officer, " let the cold steel do the work."

Again both Darcy and Gerald started. Both could have sworn they knew the tones of that rich, clear voice. And now in the direction of Washington could be perceived a dark mass moving along the road towards them.

The dragoons were at a distance from this road of some hundred yards or so, and now, at a word, advanced closer, and again halting, drew up in line, as if preparing to charge. The momentary gleams of moonshine from between the clouds shone on the bright blades as each man held his sabre drawn in his hand.

The dark mass in the distance approaches, the rumble of wheels grows more distinct, and the tramp of troops more marked.

The prisoners can now perceive that the approaching force consists of about a company of infantry, convoying two field guns, two waggons, and two ammunition tumbrils. The waggons, the guns, and the tumbrils were allowed to pass unchallenged, but no sooner had the first of the small column of infantry arrived opposite the concealed dragoons, than a shout rent the air, and the thunder of horses' hoofs burst on the ears of the astonished soldiers.

" Charge them, cut them down—Hurrah ! my brave boys !" cried the dragoon officer, raising his sword aloft.

The soldiers had not time to form square. They had but just time to give one irregular discharge, when the terrible cavalry were upon them—among them, cutting, slashing, shouting, and trampling them under their

horses' feet. The soldiers threw down their arms and
scattered in every direction to escape those gleaming
sabres. Some few, scarcely a fourth their number, got
away; the rest, in the space of a minute, were stretched
on the ground, killed or wounded.

The drivers of the waggons and the artillerymen,
seeing it was hopeless, made no resistance, and in the
course of a couple of minutes the combat, fierce and
short, was over.

Captain George, Gerald, and Darcy heard and saw
all this with utter amazement. What could it mean?

Scarcely are they captured themselves than their
captors frantically attack their own troops. Is it a
troop of madmen into whose hands they have fallen?

Suddenly, as a flash of lightning illumines the darkness
of the night, there shot over the mind of Darcy Leigh a
solution of this mystery.

Once, twice, three times he had fancied he recognised
the voice of the officer in command.

Yes, it must be so—it was so; and they had been
captured by a body of rebel cavalry, or one of those
daring night reconnaissances or raids which have made
that branch of the Confederate forces so famous.

*They had been captured by their friends, and of course
so near Washington, had been taken for Yankees.*

No sooner had this conviction forced itself on his
mind, than an exclamation of delight broke from Darcy
Leigh.

"My man," he said to the soldier on guard, "there is
some mistake here; you are Confederates."

"I rather reckon we air, so jist hold your d——d
Yankee tongue."

"But we also are Confederates, your friends."

"Bunkum," said the soldier, incredulously, "that
won't do with this coon."

"Call your officer; this mistake will soon be cleared
up."

"Hyar he comes, so you can jist pitch him what tale
you like; but if he's such a darned fool as to believe it,
may I be ——"

Gerald and Captain George had heard the words of Darcy, and the soldier's reply, and at once knew they were safe.

Captain George, whose eye had never quailed, could hardly realize the fact; while Jupiter, who, notwithstanding his assertion that he was "going to glory," did not at all like the prospect of the journey.

The next moment the officer in command rode up, his drawn sabre dripping with blood.

"Unbind the prisoners and place them on the captured waggons, under secure guard, and prepare to march."

"Sir," said Darcy Leigh, acting as spokesman, "there is some mistake here; when you rode us down and captured us, we thought you Yankees, and it appears you also thought us to be so. We are Southerners, at least two of us, and this negro, and the other an Englishman, a friend. My brother and he have just escaped from the Yankees, having been condemned to be shot for attempting to join our forces. I am Captain Darcy Leigh—General Beauregard himself conferred that rank on me; and this is my brother, a loyal Southerner like myself."

"What is all this I hear?—Southerners!—Captain Darcy Leigh, whose daring exploit with the Spitfire has made such a noise—can this be true?"

"Quite true; you can satisfy yourself. If I mistake not, your name is Irvin. I have met you in Richmond. I thought at first I recognised your voice, but could not remember where I had heard it."

This carried conviction to the officer's mind. He sheathed his sabre, and leaping from his horse cried to the troopers, "Release these gentlemen; it is a mistake, they are our friends. Captain Darcy Leigh, I ask your pardon for the rough treatment to which you have been subjected."

The next moment the prisoners were free, and Captain Irvin hastened to shake hands with them.

"You will come with us across the river, I suppose? We received intelligence from some of our spies of this baggage, ammunition, and artillery, and dashed across the river by one of the fords to cut it off. Seeing you

D D

in the road before us, it became necessary, supposing
you to be Northerners, that we should capture you;
hence the mistake. You come with us?"

"Certainly," said Darcy, laughing. "We have passed
through too many perils within the last few hours not
to be glad to join so gallant a force as yours."

"Three of the best mounted of you fellows give up
your horses to these gentlemen, and ride on the waggons
or walk as you choose. Now, gentlemen, to horse; we
have no time to lose. Some of those who escaped have
by this time, doubtless, given an alarm, and if we are not
quick, we shall have a brigade of cavalry about our ears."

Gerald, Darcy, and Captain George were quickly in
the saddle; Captain Irvin requesting them to ride at the
head of the troop with him. The waggons and guns were
driven off at a rapid pace, the troops following close
behind. They had not gone many yards when Darcy
suddenly remembered the faithful Irishman.

"Stay, sir, one moment," he said to the officer, "you
know the spot where you captured us?"

"Yes."

"There were five of us."

"Five?"

"Yes, and in the confusion you passed over one who
was lying on the ground."

"Confusion! then if you had indeed been Yankees, he
could have started off and given the alarm."

"Scarcely, for he was and I believe is still fast asleep."

"Asleep! what, all through the confusion and noise
of your capture?"

"Yes; I myself for some time could not understand
it; but I now remember he partook of some wine, and
from other circumstances I conclude it was drugged."

"Ah! well, we have no time to waste now in talk, but
we will not leave your friend. Sergeant Kennedy, take
four men and ride back to where we captured these
gentlemen. If you see any one there asleep or awake
hoist him up on one of your horses and hasten after us."

The sergeant hurried off with the four soldiers, while
the others proceeded on their way. They reached the

river bank in safety, and were there joined by the sergeant's party, one of whom had the still sleeping body of Darby Kelly slung over the saddle bow.

When Stella Gayle descended into the cellar it was for a good purpose. We have seen the effect of the wine on Lupus, on the officers in the guard-room, and on Darby Kelly. It must have been very strong, or *drugged*.

The operation of crossing the river was tedious, but it was safely accomplished. The guns, waggons, and ammunition were dragged up the steep bank on the other side; and now, after all their perils and their imminent danger, Captain George's presentiment was right, and our adventurers are safe on the shores of Old Virginia. The dawn was yet breaking as they accomplished the passage of the river.

Darcy asked for a couple of troopers to ride to a hill which he pointed out, about a mile distant. Captain Irvin readily granted them to him, and Darcy dashed off at a gallop for that little Virginian hill on which the eyes of Stella are so earnestly bent.

A few minutes' ride brought him to the summit, and dismounting, he proceeded to search among the brushwood. He quickly found what he looked for, having left it there before he crossed the Potomac on his perilous enterprise. It was a small valise, which he opened, and took therefrom a signal rocket. Having strapped the valise to his horse's saddle bow, he struck the fuse of the rocket, and instantly it shot high up in the air.

He watched its blazing course, and then slowly remounted his horse. It was now dawn.

'They will surely see it,' he thought; 'the light is not yet strong enough to prevent that. At all events, I have performed my promise; though a couple of hours ago I little thought that my hands would have ever sent it up.'

"Now, lads, let's on."

He struck spurs into his horse's flank, and in a few minutes had rejoined the troop of Confederate cavalry.

Shortly after the events just narrated, five travellers,

weary, dusty, and dirty, entered the city of Charleston, over which the "bonnie blue flag" triumphantly waved.

These travellers were our old friends Gerald Leigh, Darcy Leigh, and Captain George, the negro, and Darby Kelly.

And now north and south is heard the tramp of armed legions, the rumble of artillery, the clatter of horses' hoofs, as each prepare to plunge into the dreadful struggle about to desolate the land.

An army is being assembled at and around Washington, the famous Army of the Potomac, which is to overrun and conquer back the South; while another army, less numerous and worse armed, is mustering in Northern Virginia, to do battle with the invaders for the soil of the "Old Dominion." As yet there have been only a few unimportant skirmishes; the rival hosts have not met in the shock of battle. But this gloomy calm, presaging the coming storm, is doomed to be of short duration; the sky will soon be lurid with fire and smoke and the light of burning towns; the soil will be wet, and the rivers of this hitherto favoured land red with blood.

THE END.

Printed by W. H. Smith & Son, 186, Strand, London.